Maximilian Schele De Vere

Glimpses of the Inner Life of our Language

Maximilian Schele De Vere

Glimpses of the Inner Life of our Language

ISBN/EAN: 9783741186127

Manufactured in Europe, USA, Canada, Australia, Japa

Cover: Foto ©Andreas Hilbeck / pixelio.de

Manufactured and distributed by brebook publishing software
(www.brebook.com)

Maximilian Schele De Vere

Glimpses of the Inner Life of our Language

STUDIES IN ENGLISH;

OR,

GLIMPSES OF THE INNER LIFE OF OUR LANGUAGE.

BY

M. SCHELE DE VERE, LL. D.

PROFESSOR OF MODERN LANGUAGES IN THE UNIVERSITY OF VIRGINIA.

NEW YORK:
CHARLES SCRIBNER AND COMPANY.
1867.

Entered according to Act of Congress, in the year 1866, by

CHARLES SCRIBNER AND COMPANY,

in the Clerk's Office of the District Court of the United States for the Southern
District of New York.

PREFACE.

THE illustrious founder of the University of Virginia, Thomas Jefferson, appreciating with rare foresight, nearly fifty years ago, the importance of a scientific study of the English Language, inserted Anglo-Saxon among the subjects on which a course of lectures was to be delivered by the incumbent of the chair of Modern Languages. The author, whose good fortune it has been to fill that chair for many years, has been led to think that the increasing interest in the study of our mother tongue called for some aid and systematic guidance, and he has therefore endeavored in the following pages to point out those topics which deserve most attention, and those methods which lead to a profitable study on a historic basis. He hopes that his suggestions will call more general attention to the growing importance of a new science, which can already boast of a Müller in England and a Marsh in our own country, and to the charms of the inner life of a noble old tongue, which, through the nations who speak it, now rules the world in undisputed supremacy.

UNIVERSITY OF VIRGINIA,
November, 1866.

CONTENTS.

CHAPTER I.

CHAPTER II.

CHAPTER III.

CHAPTER IV.

CHAPTER V.

CHAPTER VI.

CHAPTER VII.

CHAPTER VIII.

CHAPTER IX.

CHAPTER X.

CHAPTER XI.

CHAPTER XII.

CHAPTER XIII.

CHAPTER XIV.

CHAPTER XV.

CHAPTER XVI.

CHAPTER XVII.

CHAPTER XVIII.

STUDIES IN ENGLISH.

CHAPTER I.

INTRODUCTORY REMARKS.

"'Ἀνδρός χαρακτὴρ ἐκ λόγου γνωρίζεται."—*Old Comedy.*

THE youngest of all European idioms, our great and noble language has yet spread farthest over the globe and now rules the world without a rival. More than fifty millions of men, forming the most enterprisiug race upon earth, speak it as their native and only tongue. The elder cousin, staid, precise, and settled, uses it at home in his counting-room ; the younger, bold and adventurous, carries it with him as he roves through the wide world. It has long since become the great instrument of European culture, superseding the Latin, which was once as general, though used mainly by the scholar and the churchman, and the French, the language of courts and the higher circles of the Continent. Even in the early days of Queen Elizabeth, the gentle Daniel, the Atticus of his age, foresaw its future greatness and sang : —

> " Who knows whither we may vent
> The treasure of our tongue ? To what strange shores
> This gain of our best glory may be sent
> T' enrich unknowing nations with our stores ?
> What worlds in the yet unformed Occident
> May come refined with accents that are ours ? "

The prophecy has come true, and wherever on this wide earth men may meet, in the merchant's busy marts or on the prairies and pampas of America, amid the nomadic tribes of Asia, or in the mysterious heart of the land of Ham, ice-bound in polar regions or becalmed under the tropics, — everywhere they may hear words familiar to their ear and dear to their heart. For our good English has become the language of the world ; and strong with the colonist, cunning with the merchant, and bringing the blessings of the gospel with the missionary, it promises soon to spread the benefits of civilization, and the glory of God over the whole earth.

Surely, then, such a language deserves to be well studied, to be thoroughly known by those whose precious birth-right it is, and by all who agree with old Roger Ascham that, " even as a hawke fleeth not hie with one wing, even so a man reacheth not to excellency with one tongue." Modern science has done much to acquaint us with the form and the nature of our fellow-men. It goes and counts their inches, it weighs them by the pound, it meas-ures their skulls and examines their bumps, it counts the years of their life and the hours of sickness, it knows how many cubic feet of air they breathe and what are their chances of marriage or suicide — and should it not inquire what they tell each other and how they say it ? Is not language, daguerreotyped thought as we may well call it, more expressive than manners and customs, law and con-stitution, history and literature ? As there is no race among men that possesses a character so sharply defined as the English, so there is no tongue upon earth more clearly expressive of the nation's mind. Boldly and freely the Englishman uses his mother tongue, boldly and freely it proclaims him abroad, by its simple forms, its nervous power, its deep meaning. It never forgets its own dig-nity, its noble descent. For the English has an ancestry unparalleled in the history of languages. It is heir to all the greatness and all the power of the two idioms that represent the two ruling races of Christendom, — the Romance and the Germanic. Here alone they are fused

together to form a harmonious whole of unsurpassed effi-
cacy, in striking contrast with the Roman French and
the Gothic German. Flowing from a bold mixture of such
elements, freeing itself by the power of its own mighty
current of all incumbrance and superfluity, adopting with
wise discrimination whatever it finds good and useful in
other idioms, as historic events bring it in contact with
foreign nations, it has become well-nigh incomparable, the
simplest of all languages in form, the most spiritual in its
mode of expression.

With a just pride, therefore, based on a legitimate ap-
preciation of its great beauty and powers, Englishmen
and all their descendants have ever loved it dearly and
used it freely. It was their affection for it that made
them, centuries ago, scorn to pray and to worship their
Maker in a foreign tongue when the whole of Europe, under the sway of Rome, yet held Latin sacred. They used
their vernacular before all their kindred races for prose
writing, and thus showed their early mental maturity, since
prose requires knowledge and deep thought, whilst poetry
may at least and often does content itself with the expression of feelings. Never did foreign idioms play the master in England, as they did on the Continent; never did
her great writers disgrace their names by a subservient
preference for foreign languages. How different is this
from the German, which was despised by the great Fred-
erick, held in contempt by Leibnitz, the most renowned
philosopher of Germany, and, to some extent at least, laid
aside even in our day, by the master of modern writers,
Alexander von Humboldt, avowedly for the purpose of
making his works, written in French, accessible to scholars
of all countries. Men who have thus abandoned the tongue
of their fathers may have gained individually, but they
have lost the pleasure of writing in their mother tongue,
inseparable as it needs must be of greater force and
stronger individuality; they have abandoned at once all

hope of the eternal renown of having created a language like the immortal Dante.

The same love and pride, whioh Englishmen thus showed in their strong attachment to their language, and their stubborn resistance to all influence from abroad, has ever protected them against tyranny at home, and they alone of all nations have always enjoyed unrestrained freedom of the press. Already Hermes notices with natural satisfaction, that England never knew an Index Expurgatorius, nor has its genius ever been shackled by an Inquisition. On the contrary, this freedom of speech called forth and fostered a corresponding spirit of free inquiry and led the way to that prudent enjoyment of liberty, of which the British people have just cause to be proud, amid fallen thrones and shattered democracies.

With all these attractions, however, and in spite of the rich reward held out to the diligent student, little has as yet been done for the proper study of English. Much time and labor are bestowed in schools and at home on Greek and Latin; French and Italian, Spanish and German, receive their share of attention, but everybody is apparently expected to know English by instinct. Where efforts have been made in the right direction, they have been thwarted by the old scholastic method, which fills our grammars with Latin terms and contents itself with long-winded definitions. We seem to forget entirely that language consists of two parts, like man himself — of the outward form, the word corresponding to our earth-born body, and of the inner meaning, which represents the immortal soul. The knowledge of words themselves is worth little. It was this view which led the great Polyglot-cardinal to reply peevishly to an indiscreet flatterer: "What am I but an ill-bound dictionary?" To attain a thorough knowledge of the meaning of words and of the manner in which at different times and under changing influences they may be made to succeed in expressing it in their outward form, this is the true object of the study of language. We must never lose sight of the fact that words are the only medium of the inner life between man and man, and that, as Montaigne already expressed it, "Nous ne sommes hommes et nous ne tenons les uns aux autres que par la parole."

Nor must it be forgotten that, interesting as the history of words is — and Dean Trench surely has convinced his many readers of this fact — there is also a history of languages, which may be studied with profit and pleasure. Their pedigree is as complete and as full of adventure as that of the Rohans, though it may not lead us with them to the door of Noah's Ark. Few subjects in the whole range of human knowledge are fuller of interest and richer in instruction than the gradual development of a national language, exhibiting as in a mirror the many changes going on in the nation's mind. We all have felt this more or less distinctly, when we have marked the difference between the *virtus* of the manly Roman, and the *vertù* of the degenerate but art-loving Italian of our day, or when the *knave* of our day recalls by chance to us those lines of the version of the great Wickliffe, in which St. Paul calls himself reverently "a knave of Jesus Christ." It is not accident nor arbitrary power that makes

> "——— words, whilom flourishing
> Pass now no more, but banished from the court,
> . Dwell with disgrace among the vulgar sort,
> And those, which eld's strict doom did disallow
> And damn for bullion, go for current now."

What is true of words, is equally true of the whole language; it ever bears on its surface the impress of the mind of the people by whom it is spoken, and he who studies it with History by his side and Philosophy coming to his aid, will soon find that it leads him directly to the most retired and inmost parts of the soul of a nation, the secrets of which no other key can unlock.

It is the purpose of this Essay to throw out some suggestions and to furnish some information that may aid in thus studying a language, of which the master of philology, Grimm, says that "in wealth, wisdom, and strict economy, none of the living languages can vie with it." The richer, the wiser, and the more perfect in its mechanism it is, the greater of course the difficulty of appreciating it fully and of entering deeply into its secret chambers. Noble efforts, however, have been made toward this end in England and abroad, and there is reason to hope that we shall soon be fully acquainted with the private as well as the public history of our language, and then agree with the sentiment of an enthusiastic admirer, who sings, that —

> "Stronger far than hosts that march
> With battle-flags unfurled,
> It goes with Freedom, Thought, and Truth,
> To rouse and rule the world."

CHAPTER II.

ENGLISH RELATIONS.

" Idioms have their kindred as well as men." — *Duponceau.*

WHEN a man rises to eminence in our midst, friend and foe become alike anxious to ascertain who his forefathers were and what relations he has now among men. To trace his pedigree back beyond a few generations is generally found a difficult task, which is finally, if not altogether abandoned, as is apt to be the case in this country, referred to the Herald's College, where fact and fancy are happily blended. There it is all well ascertained and duly attested, but in spite of shield and motto we do not believe the statement quite as readily and as fully as the ingenious officers would have us do. It is not otherwise with languages. Let one of them become great and powerful, and at once curiosity and genuine interest are eagerly at work, to ascertain the early history of the idiom. Here also easy and complete solutions are freely offered. Now the Sanscrit is declared to be the common ancestor of all languages, and now the Hebrew; some prefer the Celtic, and others again trace all words back to the famous nine syllables of the great Murray. In our day, even, champions take up arms in behalf of the Interjections, and proclaim them to have been the original words from which all others have been derived, somewhat after the manner of Darwin's great theory, and immediately they are met by the advocates of the famous Bow-wow theory, as Max Muller calls it, who believe in the cries of animals and the voices of Nature as having taught man his speech.

In spite of all these varied explanations, however, the first .origin of language is still, to this day, one of those mysteries which a wise Providence has, for some good purpose, concealed as yet from our eye, even as our great mother Nature hides the grain in her dark bosom, until it breaks as a tender blade through the clod to greet the light of day. Whether language be a gift granted to man, like all other faculties, at the time of his creation, or whether he be capable to produce and form it by means of his own unaided powers, is a much vexed question. Nor have the wisest among us yet agreed as to the unity of language, for while some admit without doubt or gainsay the simple statement of Holy Writ, from the first moment of man's existence to the confounding of lips at Babel, others insist · upon this view, that as races owe their origin to different pairs of first men, so languages also have arisen from as many different mother tongues. Fortunately, it is not impossible to understand English well without tracing it back to the creation of the world. We are quite sure that the poor Egyptian boy, who was sent, with a goat for his sole companion, into the Libyan desert to teach Psammitichus by the first words he would utter the original tongue of the earth, did not speak English; and as the Spanish have settled it to their own satisfaction that Castilian is the language which has ever been used in heaven, we dare not present an equal claim for our English.

This only we know, that it had its first origin, as far as is known to history and to tradition, in the Orient. *Ex Oriente lux*, seems to be true with regard to languages as well as with creeds. For our researches point all to the one great fact, that, if we set aside the comparatively unexplored territories of the American and African idioms, together with the Chinese, there are in the whole kingdom of speech but three grammatical families to which every known dialect can be referred with unerring certainty. Each of these families bears its own distinctive marks, so clearly defined that there is no mingling between them, no possibility of mistaking the allegiance of even the latest descendants. The white, the red, and the black races are not more strikingly different from each other in color and character than the Shemitic, the Aryan, and the nomadic Turanian families of languages. With the first and the last of these groups our English has nothing in common, though the Bible has made some Shemitic terms dear and sacred to us, and trade and commerce have familiarized us with a few Turanian words. But there is neither kindred nor sympathy between those languages and our own. For the English is a child of the great Aryan family, so called from its ancient homestead in Asia, now known as Iran. Thence all the descendants of that most noble family have spread westward, until Asia and Europe formed, as to language, but one great country, and their vast brotherhood became known as the Indo-European. All the members of this family trace back their origin to one great central language, and all of them abandoned their first home in times far earlier than those when Homer sang, when Zoroaster gave his laws, and the poets of the Vedas wrote their marvelous myths. All, moreover, from the oldest known, the Sanscrit, to the youngest born, our English, are but varied forms of the same type, — modifications of the same language as it was once spoken in Asia. When they dwelt there, and where they ruled, we cannot now ascertain, for their early history goes back far beyond historic chronology; and yet that they possess an existence and a reality is proved by inductive evidence beyond all cavil and doubt. But this is not all, for recent discoveries have taught us even more surprising facts regarding these mysterious ancestors of our English. The most careful researches, the most sifting investigations, have failed to bring to light a single new root that has been added to the first common inheritance of these dialects, or a single new element that has been created in the gradual formation of their grammar since their first separation! On the other hand, it has been discovered that many words, which witnessed that early breaking up of the family, are still living in India and Europe alike, and thus bear evidence, now, of the common first origin. The terms for God, house, father and mother, son and daughter, heart and tears, axe and tree, dog and cow, identical in all Indo-European families, have thus been well compared to watchwords of a great army on its solemn march around the globe. For many of these terms, which sprang up more than four thousand years ago at Agra, at Delhi, and Benares, have but quite lately scaled the Rocky Mountains of Western America, and are rapidly filling the forests on the shores of the Pacific.

Of the many members of this family, seven have risen to such distinction as to have become, in their turn, founders of great and powerful races. Two alone have maintained themselves at home:

1. The *Indic*, represented of old by the Sanscrit, which was spoken more than fifteen hundred years before Christ, and yet produced in that hoary antiquity already the far-famed Vedas. Its living forms are the Prâcrit and Tâli, and another strange, uncouth language, long considered a mere jargon, and then traced back to ancient Egypt or Palestine, but now re-established in its genuine birthright. This is the idiom spoken by the Gypsies, who have at last succeeded in proving their melancholy claim to be considered exiles from Hindostan, their native land. It is they alone who have brought the few strange forms of Sanscrit words we know to Western Europe, as parts of their quaint language, in which the oldest words of ancient idioms mingle with the latest offspring of modern tongues.

2. The *Iranic*, famous under the name of Zend, as the language of Zoroaster's great work, Zenda Vesta, and of late much endeared to us by the remarkable discoveries made in the wedge-shaped inscriptions of Cyrus, Darius, and Xerxes, which so strikingly illustrate and confirm

numerous, hitherto unexplained, statements of the Bible. Both languages, however, are like the pure Sanscrit, now dead languages, and survive only in the slightly altered form of Armenian and the national language of the Persian, who could boast already a thousand years before Christ, of an illustrious poet, Ferdusi. The other prominent members of this family have, with the races that spoke them, left the cradle of mankind in Central Asia, and, in successive waves, made their way westward. One after another the idioms of the ruling nations of the world, they have each been supreme for a time, and then given way to a successor. The oldest of all these is —

3. The *Celtic*, which Herodotus already knew as the language of a people that had passed even beyond the pillars of Hercules, and who are, therefore, commonly looked upon as the oldest settlers in Europe. At the very first dawn of history it is found as the idiom used by the masters of Europe. It was heard alike in England and in Ireland, in France and in Spain, in Switzerland and in the eastern regions as far back as Thracia. But its splendor has departed as the sceptre has been wrested from the Celtic race, and now it is spoken by little more than ten millions. But it still bears marks of a strange individuality; its double words are so loosely joined together that the original elements may be easily seen and severed, and its mode of inflection differs strangely from that of all other languages, inasmuch as it affects not, as usually, the final, but changes, instead, the initial letters.

In Great Britain it has, from of old, exhibited a strict line of division between the *Cymric* or Old British, and the *Gadhelic* or Irish. The former is now represented by the Welsh, which alone survives in full vigor. The Cornish can hardly be said to exist any longer except as a written language, for the last person who spoke it as her mother-tongue is reported to have died more than seventy years ago. The Armorican, introduced by fugitive Britons into that part of northern France which, from the new settlers, took its name of Little Britanny, resembles the Welsh so nearly that Count de la Villemarque, a native of Bretagne, who used it in addressing a literary club in Wales, was understood by all who were present.

The *Gadhelic* or Gaelic survives as Erse in Ireland, where it still claims to be considered a national tongue. The Gaelic proper, carried across the channel to Scotland, is now only heard in the remoter valleys of the Grampian Mountains and in some parishes of the country lying between Cairn and Caithness. The Isle of Man enjoys its own Celtic dialect, the Manx, which is, however, mixed with Danish and other Norse elements.

Between these dialects and our English there is no other relationship than that of common descent, obscured by an early separation, which dates back to very ancient times. The mechanical admixture of Celtic words and forms of expression is but small, as there seems to have existed a strong, reciprocal repulsion between the Celts and all other European families and their languages. Theirs was the fierce warfare between the Druid and the priest, the mistletoe and the palm, and the victorious cross in those days spared not the beaten foe. Even in those counties of Wales, which were last Anglicized, not a dozen words have been adopted by the Saxon from the Celt — his mouth abhors their fluent gutturals.

After the Celts came those mysterious wanderers, whose sea-faring life marked them early among the nations of the earth, and earned for them the name of Pelasgi. Their idioms now in turn ruled the world, as

4. *Hellenic* in fair Hellas, after the four dialects of earlier days, the Doric, Aeolic, Attic, and Ionic had formed the common language of ancient Greece, and as

5. *Italic*, which, in its new home of Latium, became known as Latin. Like the Greek it also arose from a mixture of early dialects: the Oscan, spoken by the Samnites,

and not unknown to Rome as late even as the days of the
Cæsars, the Umbrian, which could boast of the earliest
priestly literature and the renowned seven "Tables of Igu-
vium," and the Latin of Latium. In its turn it has, after
the fall of Rome and the advent of new races, divided into
numerous branches, and bequeathed to our day the beautiful dialects, which we know as Romance languages. Its
descendants now spoken are the Italian, the Wallachian, a
quaint form of Latin mixed with Turkish, Greek, and ancient Illyrian, the Spanish with its younger son the Portuguese, the French, and the Provençal.

Among these the English finds itself already more at
home, and a striking family-likeness may be discovered
here and there. The French enters actually into our vernacular, and claims, since the days of the Norman Conquest, a large share of our vocabulary. What makes it
more important to us, is the fact that the distribution does
not seem to have been left to chance only, and close obser-
vation will easily show the remarkable lines that divide the
two elements. Where the true Saxon words have to do
with the sensible world, the French words deal with the
spiritual; the former stand for things particular and concrete, the latter for things general and abstract. Still,
there ever remains something foreign and uncongenial in
the descendants of the Romance family, which shows
clearly that there is no near kinship between them and the
older, dearer part of our English. " English words," says
Hare, " sound best from English lips," and though there are
many French terms, which we could not well do without,
we still prefer, in familiar language and for ordinary purposes, the good old Saxon terms. Thus we say rather like
than similar, give than present, beg than solicit, kinsman
than relation, neighborhood than vicinity, and praise than
encomium.

We feel much more at home with the members of the
6. *Teutonic* family, in whose midst our English stands as

the fairest and strongest of all.   Here it meets above all the High German, the oldest in culture, the richest in pure vowels, euphony and vigor, the greatest in intellectual strength for nearly ten centuries.   Inferior by far is the elder brother, who sold his birthright long ago, the Low German, although its oldest branch, the Gothic, was spoken by the conquerors of Imperial Rome, the followers of Alaric, Theodoric, and Attila, and grand old Ulfilas himself, who used it, not four hundred years after Christ, to render the word of God for the first time into a modern tongue.   A lowly branch of this family, the Anglo-Saxon, found its way from the Continent and Southern Denmark to the distant shores of England, and there rose slowly and painfully, to become in our day the language of the world.   The Old Dutch, which has gained its independence and a literature of its own only since the thirteenth century, is its nearest relation, and together with the old Frisic on the northern coast of Germany, which is unfortunately dying out since the Frisians have been held in subjection by foreign rulers, furnishes the best illustrations and exhibits the most striking resemblance to our Old English.

Of scarcely inferior rank and antiquity with the High and the Low German are the members of the Scandinavian family.   The Swedish preserves its oldest spoken forms in a few remote valleys of the interior, whilst the Icelandic, brought from Sweden to the Ultima Thule, can boast of the oldest written forms of these idioms.   The Danish and the Norwegian are comparatively modern, and can hardly lay claims to be considered truly national tongues, though the former has a literature worthy of the highly cultivated people by whom it is spoken.

These, then, are the nearest relations our English has among the many idioms spoken in Europe.   The languages of the first wave of immigration have receded to the far West of the Continent, and barely survive there in daily declining vigor and in wholly changed forms.   Those of the second wave, the Germanic, rule now in the centre of Europe, and between them and English the feeling of kindred is strong and the facility of interchange most abundant. The last-comer in Europe,

7. The *Sclavonic* family has not yet penetrated to the centre, though it is firmly and indefatigably pushing its outposts farther and farther westward. It holds supreme but somewhat barbarous sway over the gigantic East, and in the form of powerful Russian claims the assistance of its kinsmen, the Polish, Bohemian, and others, to aid in establishing a vast Panslavism. With them our English has nothing in common ; there may even be said to exist a feeling of antagonism, as if the languages, like the races, foresaw that the day cannot be far, when they will have to struggle, as their predecessors have done before them, for the sceptre of the world.

CHAPTER III.

ENGLISH ELEMENTS.

"The English, thanks to its varied elements, is a vehicle of marvelous power and beauty for the expression of thought."

A scion of the great Germanic family, our English is the direct and legitimate descendant of the Anglo-Saxon, but in the course of its long and prosperous career it has entered into many an alliance with other idioms and taken at least one other language, the French, to its heart and home, fairly dividing with it the rule of Great Britain. It may well be said that in English all the existing nationalities of Europe — the Sclavonic alone excepted — meet and mingle together. The Celtic race, the oldest of them all, has nowhere preserved itself so long and so nobly as here; the Germanic has here borne its earliest fruit, shown its greatest independence, and held its own bravely to this day against foe and rival; then the Northman vigorously entered upon the scene, and though possessing great power of his own blended willingly with the Saxon, and thus added the last elements wanting to national greatness. The Latin of ancient Rome, of the Church, and of Modern Science, brought each its fair offering; the Greek has supplied some recent wants, and hardly a race upon earth but has sent a tribute to the mighty idiom. The immense power of such a mingling of dialects, each endowed with its own peculiar strength, was early seen. The first result was not the adoption of any one prevailing speech, but the formation of a jargon, which not until the fourteenth century adopted a fixed, though degenerate form. And yet, but a few generations later this tongue possessed already the greatest poet the human race has ever known, and since then it has become the first of all languages spoken.

We would err grievously, however, if we were to conclude from this variety of elements, which constitute the idiom, that it is a mere farrago of discordant material, or even a mere continuation of one or more of the parent stocks. As a living organism English is an entirely new individual. It is neither Anglo-Saxon in a new garb, nor the offspring of a union between Saxon and Norman French. Both these languages were inflected, and had their rigidly fixed syntax dependent on inflections. In the continued struggle, however, during which the two tongues fought for supremacy, both lost all the looser forms and more changeable modes of expression, retaining little beyond the essentials of their substance. These the new idiom, English, freed from all inflections, and subjected to entirely new laws of syntax, which now make up its striking and exclusive character among the languages of Europe.

Nevertheless it is well worth while to inquire what were the different elements, the amalgamation of which could produce such remarkable results. The very heart of the language is, of course, Anglo-Saxon, but this was already not a simple idiom, but a mixture of various dialects, belonging to different races. The latter belonged, however, all to the one great German people, upon whose lands the increasing power of Imperial Rome encroached from year to year more forcibly. As her victorious legions pressed the unhappy tribes more closely, dislodging and expelling one after another from their native seats, they naturally retreated in the line which offered them the greatest advantages. This was marked out by the great rivers, the Rhine, the Elbe and their tributaries, all flowing in a north-westerly direction, and offering at the same time a ready means of protection in the rear, and an easy outlet in front toward not far distant lands.

Like all rude races, the Germans of those days suffered under the sad effects of jealousies of tribe, of family, and of class, losing thus in their earliest days, as in our own century, by the want of unity, the enjoyment of that vast power to which they are so well entitled by their numbers, their strength, and their intellectual superiority. Hence they did not migrate in large bodies, and when they came to England, they presented neither political nor linguistic unity, but they came in detached numbers, with varied peculiarities and distinct unwritten dialects.

When we speak of a conquest by Anglo-Saxons, therefore, we mean by it a gradual settlement of the British isles by a number of successive and totally distinct bodies of invaders from Germany, representing in unknown proportions all the races and tongues, which are found between the Elbe and the Eider, with contributions from other tribes dwelling on the Atlantic and the Baltic. At a time when history is still silent and tradition our only authority, it is difficult to speak with precision. So much only can be stated with certainty, that among these various elements three stood preëminent at the first invasion and have since left their impress unmistakably on the character and the language of the English people.

These are the Jutes from southern Denmark, who, pressed upon by their neighbors, the Danes, left their native land and settled in Kent, the Isle of Wight, and part of the opposite coast of Hampshire. Then there were the Saxons proper, from the modern Duchy of Holstein, between the Elbe and the Eider, a race of pirates and marauders, against whom Theodosius fought and triumphed under the Emperor Valentinian, and thus earned the name of Saxonicus. Their inroads became from year to year bolder and soon so frequent, that in the fourth century the sea-coast of England was known as Litus Saxonicum. At last they made themselves masters of all the lands south of the Thames. Extending their conquest east, west, and south, they founded the kingdoms of Essex, Wessex, and Sussex, and in the centre of all Middlesex. Great must have been their power and permanent their influence, for to this day the Welsh and the Gaels, following the example of their forefathers, call the English language Saesonaeg, and the Scotch Highlanders speak in like manner of their neighbors as Sassenachs. Finally, there came Angles from that part of Slesvic, which still bears their name, between the Eider and an arm of the Baltic. They took all the rest of the island, founding for their folk the two kingdoms of the north and the south, Norfolk and Suffolk, and extending in Northumberland northward to the Firth and the Clyde.

The Britons by no means succumbed at once. On the contrary, they fought a noble battle for their land, their liberty and their faith — a battle which lasted for nearly three centuries. Fate, however, was against them. They had fulfilled the purposes for which their race had been sent to these islands, and at last their Arthur lay buried at Glastonbury, and nothing was left them but the hope, that he will one day come back, rising once more in his might, and restore their former glory. When the struggle was over, the Saxons were masters of the land, but it was not on the battle-field that they had conquered the fierce Celt. Their victory was achieved, slowly and painfully, in the daily battle of life, in a silent but unceasing strife, not by the strong hand and the bloody sword, but by the power of a superior will and a better mind. Their energy and their stubbornness carried the day. The brilliant but unsteady and easily wearied Celt was no match for their unceasing perseverance. For a time, the two races lived apart and yet alongside of each other, the Briton under the shelter of his fortified towns, the legacy of his Roman masters, the Saxon in the open country, where "he loved to hear the lark sing." Scanty as their intercourse was, it led, in the order of nature, to a gradual mingling of races and exchange of words. Saxon princes appear under Celtic names, and Celtic tools became known by Saxon titles. After a while the weaker disappeared step by step, whilst the stronger, growing apace, not only spread from district to district, but also worked its way slowly to a common unity. By the time the miscalled Heptarchy came to an end, and the Saxon sovereignties were all united in the person of Egbert, the Saxons had conquered. Their enemies were driven to remote mountains and inaccessible morasses in the far off corners of the land, and with them their speech also disappeared. Even the few Celtic words, that had been temporarily grafted on the Saxon, withered again as they received no more nourishment from the parent stem, and soon Saxon stood alone as the national tongue of England.

But the rule of the Saxon, also, did not long remain undisturbed, for as the weak Britons had fallen an easy prey to the bold Saxons, so the disunited Saxons succumbed in their turn to the Normans. Those bold warriors and daring sailors, who according to the Chronicle of St. Gallen had already in the days of Charlemagne passed the Straits of Gibraltar, and whom Charles the Bald had sent out of France, not with steel, which might have kept them away, but with seven thousand pounds of silver, that but served to invite them again, subsequently crossed the channel and won all the fair lands of England in a single day. They triumphed at Hastings, and without mercy and without ceremony they made themselves masters of the land. The Domesday Book shows us now, how the broad acres, the lofty castles, and even the fair daughters of the Saxon nobles were given away with lavish liberality to Norman knight and Flemish weaver, to the brave in purple born and to the cunning adventurer from foreign lands. But there was that in the Saxon people which made them live even when almost crushed by their fierce masters; there was a spirit in their language which preserved it from destruction, when utter extinction seemed almost inevitable.

The nature of the conquest, moreover, aided the process of reconstruction. In the first invasion the Anglo-Saxons had thrown themselves upon the British isles as the object of their hostility, as well as of their cupidity. They had made them their own by the simple process of clearing the land of its occupants, killing those who resisted, and driving away those who preferred flight to destruction. This was the conquest of barbarism. Very different was that of the Normans. They knew too well the value of their colossal booty to expose it to ruin, and they appreciated fully the necessity of preserving the living intelligence and the matured skill which had produced its material wealth. Their conquest consisted simply in the subjugation of the people to a foreign government. There was no barbarism here. Both nations, the conquered and the conquering, were far advanced in civilization; the English boasting of a literature several centuries old and a church unsurpassed in splendor and in learning, the French, though of more recent date, already famous among the nations of the earth, for their skill in arms and in arts. Besides, the Conqueror had taken care to have his title well established in the minds of many Englishmen even, and to be sanctioned by the express approval of the Church. His friends in England were probably not less numerous or powerful than the Whigs who brought over his namesake six hundred years later. All these causes combined to rob the conquest of much of its ordinary destructiveness, and to prepare a speedy coalition between the two races thus brought in contact.

The only danger that threatened the English race and their language, was the necessity which forced the Conqueror to surrender his new subjects to more or less spolia-

tion for the sake of rewarding those who had aided him in his enterprise. Thus the balance of power was at once destroyed, and the small number of foreigners enabled to outweigh the vast majority of native English. The social system of the latter being utterly disorganized, their speech and their culture also went down, while French culture advanced and flourished. This was, however, the work of ages only. In the mean time, and before the combination of the two distinct forces could be brought about, the oft-repeated lesson was once more taught, that the strong arm. must bend before the strong mind. Triumphant Rome had sat at the feet of enslaved Greece, and the haughty conquerors of Spain had bowed low before the poets of Italy, when they held the land in chains. So here, also, the conqueror soon had to admit the supremacy of the con-quered native, and quietly, without war or rebellion, the parts were exchanged. "In the time of Richard I.," we are told by the greatest historian of our day, "the ordinary imprecation of a Norman gentleman was: May I become an Englishman! His ordinary form of indignant denial was: Do you take me for an Englishman? The descend-ant of such a gentleman, a hundred years later, was proud of the English name." The fact was that, for a time, there were three distinct languages spoken in England: Latin was the language of the Church, French that of the Court, and Saxon alone was used by the people. The latter never forsook their precious birthright; they cherished and guarded the tongue of their fathers like a sacred inheritance, and around the hearth not a word was heard, from the beginning, that could remind them of the hated Conqueror. Nunneries, also, were founded, like that of Tavistock, where it was appointed that some should be taught the knowledge of the Saxon tongue on purpose to preserve it and transmit it to posterity by communicating it, man to man and one generation to another. A few centuries passed away and, thanks to Saxon freedom and

Saxon vigor, the two races sat side by side in the House of Commons, and a new language had been formed, rude yet and unpolished, but already foreshadowing its approaching greatness.

These, then, are the two principal elements of our English, — the Saxon of our oldest forefathers and the French of our Norman conquerors. But there are other idioms, that have largely contributed to swell the number of our words and to fashion our grammar and syntax. We have already spoken of the Celtic, which has given us but few words, most of which are not found in Anglo-Saxon and must, therefore, have come in at a later period. They are now met with principally in the dialect of Lancashire, where a considerable population of Celts must have remained after the Saxon Conquest, and it is highly interesting to note, that where these terms are still in use, there also the excitable and mercurial temper of the Celt still contrasts with the stubborn perseverance and sturdy self-reliance of the German descendant. Sound and syntax were but little affected by the Celtic. It may have given to certain English words the exceptional pronunciation which we notice in *tough* and *enough*, and in the construction of our sentences it has probably bequeathed to us the power to omit the relative pronoun, as when we say, *The man I saw*, instead of, *The man whom I saw*, together with the great repugnance to use reflexive pronouns, which characterizes modern English.

The Danes, who for a time were masters of England and seated their kings upon the throne, were less civilized than their subjects, and adopted the language of the superior race, so that but few English words can really be traced to Danish influence. The relation between the two idioms was very different from what might have been expected under the circumstances. It showed, a second time in the history of our language, that the pen ever triumphs over the sword, the olive over the laurel, mental culture over barbarous violence, the written language over the spoken. The Danes had neither literature nor grammar. Hence their influence on English was only repressive and destructive. They abhorred difficult and subtle inflexions, and thus deprived the Anglo-Saxon of much lumber of that kind. So far from fashioning or affecting in any way the vernacular of their subjects, their own language at home declined from the day on which it came into contact with Saxon. Their court was often in England, their army lay there many years, and all laws and public acts, relating to England, were published in Anglo-Saxon. Thus even their chieftains and nobles could introduce but a single title into the conquered land, that of Earl, from the Danish Yarl, but that nobleman's wife resumed at once the Norman name of Countess. How little the Saxon nobles were willing to sub-mit to such a yoke, may be seen from the spirited resolutions they passed immediately after the death of Hardica-nute. No Dane, they agreed, should from that time be permitted to reign over England; all Danish soldiers in any city, town, or castle should be either killed or banished from the kingdom, and whoever should from that time dare to propose to the people a Danish sovereign should be deemed a traitor to government and an enemy to his country. A people that gave vent to such sentiments was not likely to adopt many words or to borrow many expressions from a hated master whom they no longer obeyed. A few, like *forse* in the sense of waterfall, and *gill* for a rocky ravine, have never been used in classical English until Wordsworth made them familiar words.

By the side of the unimportant contributions thus made by Celt and Northman, the additions we owe to Latin assume gigantic proportions and deserve separate treatment. Other idioms also came in to swell the mighty host. In the reign of Queen Elizabeth Italian phrases abounded, and old Fortunatus tells us that in 1624 —

> "Fantastic compliment stalks up and down
>   Trick'd in outlandish feathers, all his words,
>   Ilis looks, his oaths, are all ridiculous,
>   All apish, childish, and *Italianate*."

Under James and Charles it was the Spanish which framed the style of courtesy, and left us many allusions to grave dons and mighty grandees. In the days of Charles II. again, the nation and the language became equally Frenchified, and our own generation, led by great masters of wayward taste, borrows more largely from German than prudence and patriotism would seem to warrant.

On the whole it may be said, however, that every foreign element now has its own domain in English. Latin still furnishes us with theological technicalities, Greek with the majority of metaphysical terms; German is the language of mineralogy and of parts of geology; the fashions claim naturally French as their vehicle, and, oddly enough, share it with the science of war, whilst mathematics use Latin, Greek, French, and Arabic in fraternal union.

CHAPTER IV.

LATIN seems to have been determined, from early times, to obtain a footing in England and to lord it over her sons, as it had done triumphantly in France and in Spain, in Italy and in many an Eastern province. It never found a hearty welcome there, but no sooner was one attack successfully resisted by the sturdy islanders, than it returned to the charge. It came under all forms and at all times, now armed with the sword and escorted by the invincible legions of ancient Rome; then, bearing the cross aloft and swelling in anthem and hymn. A few generations later it followed the Conqueror in his victorious march, and for a time ruled supreme; later it reappeared in the train of fashion or claimed admittance under the guise of deep learning. Our English entered not into bitter warfare, nor did it churlishly close its door against the often unwelcome intruder. It did not submit, however, but quietly resumed its supremacy, admitting so much of the foreign element as was good and useful for its own great national purposes, and rejecting the surplus by the simple force of good taste and common sense. Thus it maintained its independence, gained largely in words and in terms, but never troubled itself to translate, — as the Germans do now with pedantic purism, by which after all but half of the sense is caught, — but rather preferred most sensibly to admit the foreigners and to naturalize them in accordance with their own native sound and use.

The first time that Latin touched the shores of the British isles, it entered probably under the auspices of the great Cæsar, when he appeared there for a month in the year 55. In the following year he landed once more and remained a longer time, forcing the British leaders to surrender, and carrying off several native princes as hostages. Still, throughout the Augustan era, Roman civilization and refinement were unknown to Britain, and no trace of their conquest remains visible. It was Claudius who first could glory in conquering the Britons, for " Julius Cæsar did no more than show them to the Romans." Even when this Emperor had received the honor of a triumph and the title of Britannicus for his success in the distant islands, the arms of the Romans had not yet penetrated beyond the southern parts of Britain. The subjugation was not completed until the age of Tacitus, when his distinguished father-in-law, Agricola, after having overrun the whole island far beyond the Firth, and after having sailed round it to reduce the Orkneys also, conquered it finally. Then followed the days of Roman rule, during which the country became studded with flourishing cities and with numerous towns and villas, in all of which Latin was spoken and Roman arts and civilization were known. Theatres and amphitheatres abounded, public baths were provided, and the gods of Rome as well as foreign deities had their temples in larger cities. The reaction, it is well known, came sooner than could well have been expected. The great empire was shaken in its foundations; fierce, mysterious barbarians came from the far East to claim the sceptre of the world for their race, province after province was lost, and the old, tried legions of Rome had to return to protect Italy itself from the invader. Thus Hadrian was already compelled to abandon all the land between the Solway and the Clyde, and between the Tyne and the Frith of Forth, and to build the great wall against the Picts. In 418, the Anglo-Saxon chronicle tells us, there was not a Roman left on the island.

Whatever may have been, in those days, the success of Latin on the Continent, it was comparatively powerless in England. There it drove out the Celtic, resisted successfully its great rival the German, and lived anew in French and Spanish. In England it never superseded the old Gaelic, and, in its turn, readily succumbed to the Saxon. Macaulay explains this striking difference by the opinion, that " it is not probable that the islanders were at any time generally familiar with the language of their Italian rulers." But there were other reasons, besides, which aided the Celtic in holding its own. The Romans lived almost exclusively in fortified towns, many of which bear, to this day, their Latin name; whilst in the country Celtic remained prevalent, and, after the withdrawal of the foreign legions, resumed its supremacy. Then it must not be forgotten, that whilst might and valor were on the side of the Romans, civilization and intelligence were with the Britons. The Irish Celts were not only superior to all others of their race, but actually sent out teachers and missionaries to the adjoining countries. In the beginning of the fifth century Christianity was already prevailing among them all, and had brought with it classic refinement and culture. Little Latin, therefore, in our English, can be traced directly to this first invasion; the essential and genuine contributions to our words are limited to three: *colonia*, which survives mainly in local names; *castrum*, in castle and Chester; and *stratum*, in those compounds in which it is not more clearly traceable to a similar word of the Anglo-Saxon.

Far more threatening in its aspect, and infinitely more permanent in its influence, was the introduction of Latin by means of the Church of Rome. The primitive British Church was a branch of the great Celtic Church which, planted as early as the first ages in the South of Gaul, extended rapidly into Ireland, and from there into Wales, the Western Isles, and many parts of Southern Britain. The zeal and the piety of this Celtic Church were so great as

to earn for Ireland the title of *Insula Sanctorum*, but their
learning was by no means in proportion, and hence priests
and officials generally came from the older churches in
Southern Europe. Thus already, in the sixth century, we
find Roman ecclesiastics formally installed in England; and
in the church and the convent, among priests and among
laymen, Latin had become the only language in which
matters of faith were transacted. Their prayers, their
chants, and their books, were, for a time, all in Latin. Unfortunately, the early Anglo-Saxon Church did not use a
Latin taken from the classic authors of Rome, but they
sought their words in the Origines of Isidore, and in other
writings of the same class. They affected, moreover, especially barbarous compounds from the Greek, like *elee-
mosynary*, which still survives with its seven syllables,
though the noun has shrunk, through the Anglo-Saxon
form *almesse*, into the monosyllabic *alms*. Nor was this un-
desirable form of Latin easily gotten rid of; we feel its
sad, demoralizing effects, even at this day. For through
the overwhelming influence of the Church, and its long,
undisputed sway, the whole system of theology in England
had become, as it were, incorporated in Latin, and this to
such an extent that even the English Reformers could
communicate by no other means than Latin with the fountain-head at Rome, or with their teachers and brethren on
the Continent. The vast mass of monkish literature, the
countless religious essays, the fabulous chronicles of those
days, and the few interspersed satires that have been
handed down to us, all are written in the barbarous Latin
found in the Fathers of the Church. This was the more
pernicious, as a large number of these so-called Latin
terms had themselves not long ago been derived from the
Greek, because of the great influence of the Greek
Church in the early days of Christianity. Some of these
are still in existence, and used in connection with the
Church, as —

Greek.	Latin.	Anglo-Saxon	English.
κλήρικος,	clericus,	cleric,	clerk.
ψάλλω,		psalm,	psalm.
ἐλεημοσύνη,		almesse,	alms.
κυριακή,		cyrice,	church.
πρεσβύτερος,			presbyter.
διαβάλλω,	diabolus,	deofol,	devil.
ἐπίσκοπος,	episcopus,	bisceop,	bishop.
μόνακος (?),	monacus,	munuc,	monk.

Many of these terms can be traced back to their early
introduction into English, none perhaps farther than the
last mentioned.　It occurs in the unique specimen of a
song composed by Canute the king, as he was one day
rowing on the Nen, when the holy music from the minster
of Ely came floating on the air and over the water.　It so
touched the hearts of the people, that ·the historian, to
whose care we owe the precious fragment, tells us that it
was "until to-day publicly sung in choirs and repeated in
proverbs."　It runs thus : —

> " Merie sungen the *muneches* binnen Ely
> Tha Cnut ching rew (rowed) there by :
> Roweth, cnihtes, noer the lant (land)
> And here (hear) we thes *muneches* saeng."

As will be seen from these examples, most of the Latin
words so formed and borrowed, were made anew for Church
purposes, and are, therefore, not to be found in classic
Latin.　They are almost all nouns; we find only a few
adjectives in English that can be traced back to this earliest source of Latin, and the still rarer verbs are generally
of doubtful origin.　Among those that were not derived
from the Greek we find again some that really existed in
the works of classic authors, and others which belonged
exclusively to the barbarous forms of later, corrupt Latin.
Some of the latter, almost offensive in their disguise, are
still to be found in the Parson's Tale of Chaucer as *ac-
cidīa, contimax, savacioun,* and *penitentia ;* others appear
slightly transformed, as *celestial, disordinate, elacioun,* and

pertinacie. A much larger number have adopted better forms, and are now fully naturalized. Such words, derived directly from Latin, without having first passed through the French, are, *e. g.:*

pundus, pound.	*præpositus,* provost.
moneta, mynet, mint.[1]	*missa (est congregatio),* mass.
ancora, anchor.	*corona,* crown.
petroselinum, parsley.	*ficus,* fig (tree).
febrifuga, feverfew.	*piper,* pepper.
pumex, pumice (stone).	*versus,* verse.
pallium, pall.	*prima,* prime (service in the
prædicare, preach.	morning).
candela, candle.	*regula,* rule.

To the same class belong also our *minster, porch, cloister, saint, parish,* the names of the *elephant,* the *lion,* and the *camel,* and of all our months.

When we consider the paramount power of the church in those days, the strong hold it had not only on the consciences but also on the minds of men, as the sole guardian of all learning and useful knowledge, and the wisdom with which such means were used for the purpose of controlling the people, the small number of Latin words which the English owes to this source appears quite surprising. We must not forget, however, that religion was with the Saxon race ever the bright reflection of patriotism. They were obedient children of the church, but they insisted, early and perseveringly, upon the right of worshiping God after their own manner, in their own tongue. Hence the sturdy independence of the nation even in matters of faith, and the early dissensions within the English church. Many of the most famous missionaries the world knows were expelled priests of England, men branded by the followers of Augustine, who went as true heralds of salvation abroad, and rooted Christianity in most parts of Europe. Hence

---

[1] The first silver money was coined at Rome 482 A. U. G.; the mint was in the Temple of Juno Moneta, and this circumstance occasioned the origin of our word "money."—*Hooke's Rome.*

also the preference the people early showed for priests of their own race, who knew no other law and no other tongue but that of their Saxon fathers. Roman law was almost unknown among the Saxons. Canon law, based upon the former, took root but slowly, and thus many of the most important.features of the Church of Rome were adopted but late in the distant island. Even spiritual weapons lose some of their force so far from the authority that wields them, and the wise moderation of Rome no doubt allowed her unruly sons much time to fall into the ranks. As a proof of this it may be mentioned that celibacy was unknown in England until a late period, and that during the whole time that Anglo-Saxons ruled over the island, the sacrament was administered in both forms. But what prevented Latin most from influencing our English more largely then, was the fact that for a long time the tongue of the church was the mother tongue. England produced the first Bible version in the vernacular; countless homilies and prayers, hymns and psalms were written in English, and the greater part of the ritual even was Saxon. Thus it is that the marriage service of the modern Episcopal church, with its hearty sound, and simple sterling substance, is almost identical yet with that used by the early church. Thus also was laid in darkest days the foundation for the sturdy Protestantism of the English people, and their independence of Rome; so that, when in later days the Reformers sought for weapons abroad and at home to fight the great battle of Liberty, they found in these Saxon writings almost all the theological views for which they contended, proving among other things that the Scriptures had, from the beginning, been read in the vulgar, and not in the Latin tongue, by a truly catholic people.

Nor ought it to be overlooked, that the Anglo-Saxons had terms for many of the doctrines and rites of Christianity long before the corresponding words of Latin origin, — a fact which is justly referred to as a proof of the early independence of the British church. Thus they used *full-ian*, from which our fuller, to wash white or to purify, for "baptize;" *aerist*, rising, for resurrection; *leorning-cniht*, a learning youth, for disciple; and *bispel*, a by-tale, the German Beispiel, for parable, — words which in simplicity and clearness far surpass the modern terms of foreign origin. Even as late as Wickliffe's Bible version, we find *unworschip* for dishonor, *provynge* for experience, *kyndli* for natural, *folkis* for nations, *forthenkynge* for repentance, *agenstendan* for resist, and *agenrysing* for resurrection, — all of them words which would answer their purpose almost as well in our day, and have the great advantage of being intelligible not to the educated only but to the masses alike.

It is to these characteristic features of our Saxon forefathers that we must mainly ascribe the comparative freedom of their and our language from a larger admixture of Latin. As neither clergy nor royalty disdained in England to use the vernacular, their example was soon followed by influential persons. Thus Anglo-Saxon was developed and protected against the baneful influence of dead languages, and grew rich even in prose-writings, at a time when in kindred Germany the mother tongue was despised or little esteemed, and when everywhere else Latin was considered the only language fit for subjects of graver import or of sacred nature.

A third time Latin came and claimed admittance into the English language, and now as at first by the brutal right of the stronger, though under a new disguise. The Norman-French, when they won the day at Hastings and awoke on the next morning masters of all England, brought with them their French, a bastard child of ancient Latin. They prescribed its use by stringent laws, they crammed it down the throats of their subjects with the point of the sword. For a time it seemed triumphant. The king and his followers, the courts of justice, the haughty barons and the insolent soldiers — they all spoke Latin-French, and would listen to no other tongue. The Saxons learned it from a sense of duty, from ambition, often even from hatred. Vanity also aided the new language, and this motive extended even to the lowliest peasants, of whom an ancient writer tells us that even the boors, in order to appear more respectable, used French terms by preference.[1]

With all the prestige of a conqueror's language, with all the immense pressure it must have exerted on the subjugated and ill-treated people, the Norman-French did not long maintain its power, nor even its independence. Once more the master had to learn from the servant, and ere three centuries had passed the relative position of French and of Saxon was reversed and the latter once more triumphant. Soon after the great plague in 1348, the fate of Norman-French as a national tongue was decided; from that year even the usual translations of Saxon into French were omitted by schoolmasters, and ere long a law forbade the granting of ecclesiastic preferments to any but English-born subjects. When Gower wrote his poor French verses, he had at least the grace to ask pardon.

> " Si jeo n'ai de françois la faconde
> Pardonetz moi que jeo de cco forsvoie
> Jeo suis Englois; si quiere par tele voie
> Estre excuse."

It is true that with the victories and conquests of Edward III. in France, the French element once more gained strength, and deriving fresh force from the fountain-head threatened, for a time, to become all powerful in England. It was then that French words were brought over by whole cargoes — *integra verborum plaustra* — and put up to public approbation by the great writers of the time. Courtly Chaucer showed the influence of this wholesale importation by his preponderance of French words, though he has, per-

---

[1] " Rurales homines — ut per hoc spectabiliores videantur, francigenari satagunt omni visu." — Higden, *Polychron*, p. 210, Ed. Gale.

haps unconsciously, his sly hit at those who spoke French
after home fashion, in the lines : —

> " Ther was also a nonne, a Prioresse,
> That of hire smiling was full simple and coy . . . .
> And frenche she spake ful fayre and fetisly,
> After the scole of Stratford atte Bowe,
> For frenche of Paris was to here unknown."
>
> *Canterbury Tales*, 118.

This new infusion came, however, too late to affect the
language in its essential features. The many new verbs
and nouns and adjectives made by the father of English
poetry did not, by any means, become permanently parts of
the language: some dwindled away and have long since
disappeared forever, whilst others took hold of the nation's
mind and preluded

> " Those melodious streams that fill
> The spacious times of great Elizabeth
> With sounds that echo still."

It is, therefore, not difficult to understand why this invasion should have been comparatively harmless, as far
as pure, classic Latin was concerned. The admixture of
modified Latin, in its Norman-French form, was of course
important alike in quantity and general influence. Thus
Sir John Mandeville, who to be sure " put his boke out
of Latyn into Frensche and translated it agen out of
Frensche into Englysche," uses, as Mr. Marsh informs us,
a larger proportion of Latin and French words than any
other poet of his country. From the careful and accurate
investigation of that eminent American scholar it appears
that a single work of this writer exhibits an addition of
about fourteen hundred words of Latin origin to the vocabulary of the previous century! The fact was, that the
Anglo-Saxon had lost its flexibility, and with it the power
to adapt itself to the new regime, and thus the common
necessities of the people called for the introduction of so
many Latin or Romance words into English. The blame for
this so-called corruption of the vernacular has often been

laid upon the poets of that age, but without justice. They only used the language as they found it.

All the more remarkable is it, that no Romance inflection penetrated into English. Except in a few words, it is even difficult in the extreme, from the form alone, to tell which words came directly from the Latin and which through the French. When Anglo-Saxon writers use *mint* from moneta, and Norman authors have *money* from the same source, the decision is easy enough. But in the majority of cases the history of the word cannot be so certainly traced, and then we must content ourselves with the mere fact, that the same word exists twice in English, once in its original Latin form, and again in a French-Latin form. Instances of such twin-forms are : —

factum, fact and feat.	*securus*, secure and sure.
factio, faction and fashion.	*quietus*, quiet and coy.
tractus, tract and treat.	*zelosus*, zealous and jealous.
balsamum, balm and balsam.	*gentilis*, genteel and gentle.
persona, person and parson.	*legalis*, loyal and legal.
captivus, captive and caitiff.	

Pure Latin was still spoken and written, but by so limited a class of men, that its influence on the national tongue was neither important at the time nor permanent in its effects. This want of direct power was partly due to the gradual but decided deterioration of Latin itself. From the beginning of the thirteenth century, the decline and fall of elegant literature is clearly perceptible, and with it the rapid disappearance of classic learning. The habit of speaking Latin correctly and elegantly, so common before among the scholars of all lands, was generally lost, and even at the universities the classic tongue degenerated into a mere jargon, without grammar or syntax. It was the era when a new learning seized hold of the minds of men, and when all studious aspirants for fame bowed to the absolute sway of scholastic logic and metaphysics. The same enthusiasm prevailed throughout Christendom; all the intellects of Europe were in a ferment. Oxford counted, a hundred years later, thirty thousand students in her University, and the number was probably even greater at Paris. Education and knowledge were diffused widely and liberally, but classic learning disappeared for a time, and with it the power and the happy influence of Latin.

A more distinct, and, to some extent, brilliantly successful attempt to introduce Latin, was made in the days of Queen Elizabeth. From the time of her accession to the Restoration, the study of Greek and Latin was once more quite general in England, and the majority of authors were thorough scholars in both languages; very naturally, therefore, a large number of Latin words then found their way into English. "The unlearned or foolish fantastical," says Thomas Wilson, in his "System of Rhetoric and Logic," published 1533, "that smells but of learning (such fellows as have seen learned men in their days), will so Latin their tongues that the simple cannot but wonder at their talk, and think surely they speak by some revelation." "If elegancy still proceedeth," says Sir Thomas Browne, himself one of the greatest speechmongers, "and English pens maintain that stream we have of late observed to flow from many, we shall, within a few years, be fain to learn Latin to understand English, and a work will prove of equal facility in either."

This was the age of adventure and experiment, not only on the high seas in search of new continents, or in the realms of science and faith, to discover new doctrines and creeds, but in language also. The whole world of antiquity, with its riches in words as well as in wisdom, was suddenly thrown open to all; no guide pointed out the way, no barriers limited the range of thought or taste, and the use to be made of these large treasures was left to the inexperienced direction of perplexed writers. A perfect flood of new words, mostly but half understood, inundated England, and formed with the good old Saxon words a jargon which, unhappily for the taste of those days, was hailed as a model of melody and refinement. Many writers of that time considered it a matter of national pride to imitate the scholars of the continent, who knew no other language but Latin for science and literature, and English was once more threatened with entire destruction.

The number of Inkhorn-Terms, as the words they manufactured were then called, was as great as their form was uncouth. We may well be grateful, that good taste and good sense have relieved us from words like the following, which were then in use among contemporary writers:— Subsanuation, ludibundness, septenfluous, disincorporation, discerptibility, septentrionality, incomprehensibility, and supervacuousness. The contrast of these magnificent and grandiloquent terms with the "native woodnotes wild" of simple Saxon, is generally rather a melancholy one, but it becomes at times quite ludicrous. Thus Jeremy Taylor, speaking of the bruising of the serpent's head, calls it, "the contrition of the serpent," and, as Bishop Heber notices, after having substituted excellent for surpassing, speaks consistently but absurdly, of a sinner as feeling "excellent pain."

This practice of using Latin, which had been brought in mainly since the reign of James I., was subsequently carried to still greater excess by the Puritans. It was this abuse which the keen satire of Butler ridiculed in the lines:

> " For when he pleased to show 't, his speech
> In loftiness of sound was rich,
> A Babylonish dialect,
> Which learned pedants much affect.
> 'T was English cut on Greek and Latin,
> Like fustian heretofore on satin."
>
> *Hudibras,* Pt. I. c. i. 91.

The words that the wise Bacon and the brave Raleigh spoke, are almost the only ones of those days that were free from such barbarism. Nobly and manfully struggling against the current, and despising an absurd fashion, they abstained from the formation of such Latinized words. But the most brilliant example of success in pure English,

under such trying circumstances, is found in the writings
of the bosom friend of Erasmus, Sir Thomas More, of
whom Ben Jonson says that, " his works were considered
as models of pure and elegant style;" whilst Hallam calls
them, "the first example of good English language; pure
and conspicuous, well chosen, without vulgarism or pedantry."   Many of his sentences, we are confident, would even
now be considered models of chaste and elegant English.
Other writers, however, resisted the current less successfully, and even the warmest admirers of Milton can hardly
venture to excuse his extravagant fondness for Latin, which
could lead him to write lines like these : —

> " With keen dispatch
> Of real hunger and concoctive heate
> To transubstantiate; what redounds transpires
> Through spirits with ease."
>
> *Paradise Lost*, v. 436.

We must bear in mind, however, that pedantry was all-
popular for the time, and that if divines and philosophers
could destroy a language it would certainly have been done
then.   The good sense of the people, and a returning consciousness of the superiority of the mother tongue, caused
them, fortunately, soon to drop words which could already
be found in English as brief and as forcible.   Such were,
for instance, Jeremy Taylor's coinings of funest (sad),
respersed (scattered), deturpated (deformed), clancularly
(stealthily), correption (rebuke), intenerate (soften), whilst
others which were used incorrectly, like the same writer's
immured for encompassed, extant for standing out, insolent for unusual, contrition for bruising, and irritation for
making void, were never allowed to pass current.

Besides, a large number of these words were torn up
from the Latin and transplanted into English, like flowers
and branches into children's gardens, without ever taking
root, and thus they soon disappeared.   Those only that
were really useful remained, and were duly naturalized in
the course of time, and the happy effect of the incorpora

tion of such terms into our English will be easily understood.

The Anglo-Saxon, mainly given to sensible objects, has from the beginning been sadly wanting in abstract terms. Philosophy and science were comparatively unknown to its exchequer of words, and the arts appeared almost exclusively under foreign names. These wants were now supplied, and this accession was all the more welcome as there was a full tide of knowledge rolling in upon the reawakening minds of those days, which soon overflowed the narrow channel of the language. But it was also then for the first time perceived what irreparable injury had been done to the mother tongue by its temporary subjugation. It had lost, whilst under the baneful control of the Norman-French, that plastic character, that power of adapting itself to new ideas and forming new words, which it originally possessed in common with all Teutonic languages, and which the German has successfully preserved to this time. In the new order of things, therefore, it could not keep pace; it had lost its pliancy, and with it the power to follow new modes of thought. In this necessity to create new terms in order to express new ideas, the Latin proved eminently useful, and readily supplied what was wanting in Saxon. Hence it is that, to this day, the Saxon words of our English have to do with the sensible world, foreign words with the spiritual; the former stand for things particular and concrete, the latter for things general and abstract. Where this does not seem to be the case, two terms are apt to present themselves for one and the same idea.

For the Latin of the Norman-French enriched our tongue, not only with new words, but also with many synonyms, both of which now express one and the same idea with apparently slight, but in reality quite important differences of meaning, once by an Anglo-Saxon term, and then again by a French word. Hence, our English is peculiarly rich in synonyms, and in them possesses a power unequaled in other idioms. This is one of its most striking features, and all the more important, as these synonyms are not double names of the same object, which is the case in a few instances only, as in ox and beef, calf and veal, pig and pork, but mostly express delicate shades of emotions or passions. Nor ought we to overlook, in this connection, the equally striking and suggestive fact that, whilst all the gentler emotions of love and kindly warmth are Saxon, the subtler and fiercer passions, jealousy and contempt, fervor and fury, bear French names. It is this that gives to our English such great moral expressiveness, and enabled Shakespeare to wield his marvelous power of clothing with living words so many of man's mysterious sympathies, and of showing us so much of his inner life.

The words thus introduced into English were generally pure Latin, and have changed, in the process of naturalization, nothing but their termination. All our nouns in *tion*, and *cion, tor* and *tory, ity, ance,* and *ure,* our adjectives in *ary* and *ory, ic* and *ive, ile* and *ible* or *able,* our verbs in *ate, act, ect, ict,* and *fy,* belong to this class. Many verbs of the same period were, however, introduced in the form of their supines, and some being afterwards verbalized anew, have produced rather awkward forms. Such are : —

abstraho,	*abstractum,*	adj. ábstract,	verb, to abstráct;
accipio,	*acceptum,*		accept;
acuo,	*acutum,*	acute.	
advoco,	*advocatum,*	subst. advocate,	advocate;
ago,	*actum,*	subst. act,	act;
exago,	*exactum,*	adj. exact,	exact;
transago,	*transactum,*		transact;

and a host of others, all formed in the same manner.

The influence of this Latin on the structure of our language is seen especially in the so-called periodic style, indulged in so largely by James Hooker, and, we must add, in connection with what has been said before of his poetry, by Milton in his prose. Dryden was certainly not unjust in accusing him of " Romanizing our tongue without complying with its idiom," when his imitation of Roman models could lead him to say, "The summer following, Titus then emperor, Agricola continually with inroads disquieted the enemy." — Hist. of England, Vol. II. This may be very good Latin, but it is most assuredly very bad English. Still, the periodic style, when not carried too far, does not want its admirers even among modern writers. Many applaud, and others try to imitate, the stately march and often majestic and organ-like harmony of Milton's prose. Coleridge spoke with rapture of its " difficult evolutions and solemn rhythm."

With the Restoration, however, a thorough change commenced; the periodic style gave way, and the simpler structure of our day took its place. At the same time, the great license of coining Latin derivatives also ceased, and English became substantially what it now is; asperities only have been filed away since, barbarisms refined, and redundancies thrown out. It is also to be borne in mind that whilst on one side this great fondness for Latin terms and Latin structure was carried too far, and therefore was censured with justice, it had, on the other hand, a most beneficial influence on the English of those days. For the intimate contact with the graces of diction and style, so prodigally displayed in the pages of the great writers of Greece and Rome, could not fail, gradually but certainly, to improve the taste and to refine the style of English authors. They only failed when they aspired to copy classical forms literally, and to transfer mechanically similar graces from one idiom into the other. Whenever they were content to imbibe the classic spirit of ancient writers and then to reproduce it, in conformity with the genius of the English language, they obtained great success. Even Milton occasionally uses Latin words with such tact and elegance as to show what great beauty may be found in them, and how much of the force of English must be attributed to them. Thus, in the beautiful lines —

> " So from the root
> Springs lighter the green stalk, from thence the leaves
> More aerie, last the bright, *consummate* floure."
>
> *Paradise Lost*, V. 478.

The question has often been asked : " What good has the Latin done to our English ? " The happy effect of its addition to the Saxon element is seen in two great advantages which English has gained over all the sister languages.

In the first place, English is the only one of all the European idioms which combines the two elements of the Classic and the Gothic, of ancient and of modern civilization, in such a manner that the Gothic forms the basis and the Latin the superstructure. In all other instances of a similar combination, as in the Romance languages, the Latin is invariably the principal and the governing element. By its own happy proportion, English can much more fully sympathize, through the overwhelming influence of its Gothic element, with modern thoughts and feelings, while it is perfectly familiar, through its treasures of classic origin, with the life of antiquity. In this connection it must not be overlooked, moreover, that whilst the Romance languages arose out of a struggle between classic Latin and a Gothic barbarism, which was at first utterly destructive, and produced its good results only after many centuries, the English arose out of an amalgamation of civilized Gothic with Norman French, which, so far from being barbarous, brought with it a culture in all the radiant bloom and buoyant pride of youth, and infused a new and higher life into native civilization.

The advantage thus obtained was not lost by any subsequent introduction of Latin, especially when such an addition was made by means of renewed efforts in science or art. As on the Continent, so also in England, the services of the Church, repeated in the same unchanging words since the first ages, kept up in the minds of the people even a dim, traditionary understanding of the classic language. We read of foreign ecclesiastics, who could not speak English, and preached in Latin — they could not be altogether unintelligible to their audiences. Men who could be moved to tears, and made to take the cross upon them by Latin sermons, may have been largely acted upon through their ears and their imaginations; still they must have caught, here and there, a word or a phrase which they could understand. Latin must have been heard, in those and long subsequent days, all over the land, and on a thousand occasions which now no longer exist. There were all the great teachers of universities, who lectured and taught in Latin, and all the students and scholars of monastic seminaries, who disputed and recited in Latin. Law and Physic in all their grades employed the same language, and countless hearers of these various teachers must have been found in every parish and in every village, from the parish priest to the wandering beggar, from the old man eloquent to the poor boy at his convent school.

This thorough leavening of the vernacular with a classic element could not fail to have the happiest effect, and thus to produce the second great advantage English owes to its Latin element. For the refining influence of classic studies contributed with silent but irresistible power to the formation of modern English. It was through this agency mainly, that the two great elements of our language, the Anglo-Saxon and the Norman French, were reduced to greater uniformity, and could thus as readily be fused into one idiom as the two races who spoke them amalgamated, under the influence of wise political institutions, first in the House of Commons and then throughout the land, into one great nation. Thus our tongue was molded, at the same time, into greater elegance and harmony ; its deformities of foreign, undigested importations were cut off, and its uncouthness diminished. Finally, it may be added, our English has derived from the Latin, as the language of the Church in olden times and of science in more recent days, a peculiar coloring, a faint but unmistakable perfume of classicity, which has never since been lost entirely, and is by no means one of its smallest charms.

The mania for Latin terms, displayed at a later period by Pope and Johnson, could not interrupt the even course of development for any length of time; the Essayists had too strong a hold on the mind of the people, and their style, always clear and elegant, rejected one after another the incongruous forms introduced from abroad.

Their influence on the public taste cannot be over estimated, and it is a matter of just congratulation that Addison should, to this day, be a model for eminent writers.

Strangely enough the only accusation of having introduced more Latin words into English, made since that time, has been directed against Americans. Among other charges, the Rev. Jonathan Boucher, the learned author of the well-known Glossary, rebukes them for nothing less than "making all the haste they conveniently can to rid themselves of the language" of England. He notices, as an evidence of this crime, certain innovations of this kind, collected from some recent publications, and mentions especially the words to *memorialize*, to *advocate*, to *progress*, the nouns a *mean* and *grade*, and the adjectives *inimical* and *influential*, as used in a moral sense. It need not be mentioned here, that all these terms are now in universal currency wherever English is spoken. But we cannot even claim to have originated them in our "heat of ignorance, presumption, and barbarism;" for most of them have been long in the language, and all the merit Americans can pretend to, is to have discovered valuable material that had been laid aside and was nearly forgotten. Thus to *advocate* is used by Milton, to *progress* occurs in Shakespeare, though as yet with the accent on the first syllable, and thus betraying its recent introduction, —

<blockquote>
" This honorable dew
That leisurely doth progress on thy cheeks,"
</blockquote>

and *inimical* is already inserted in Walker's Pronouncing Dictionary of 1772.

Even our own day is not free from the silent intrusion of new Latin terms, though it is but just to add, that the majority of recent importations come to us through the German. Thus we have but recently become accustomed to speak of *animus* as an inner and generally bad motive, of *cultus* as a system of worship, of *onus* as the special burden of an argument, of *status* as the visible, political or social, condition of states and individuals, of *curriculum* as the appointed course of studies, of *ultimatum* in diplomacy and general negotiations, of a *maximum* and a *minimum*, and even in agriculture of *humus* for mold.

Thanks to the general dissemination of education, and especially of a moderate but almost universal training in the classics, our own country is peculiarly active in naturalizing such Latin terms. Here even the masses have learned to understand, or at least instinctively to feel the meaning of words like *extempore, sine qua non, status in quo, vice versa, cui bono, quid pro quo, sub rosa,* and *bona fide.*

It may not be amiss, before leaving the subject of the true classic elements in our English, to refer at least in passing to the small admixture of genuine Greek terms which we use. Some of them still bear the impress of their foreign, pagan origin distinctly in their features ; others, however, have become so familiar even to the unlearned, that men would be not less surprised at hearing themselves accused of using Greek words, than Molière's hero was flattered by the discovery that he had been speaking prose all his life.

The paucity of pure Greek words of older date in English must be partly at least attributed to the fact that the first introduction of Greek was received with great distrust and much apprehension. Western Europe, it must be remembered, knew literally nothing of it until the fall of Constantinople; and as late as the sixteenth century the learned men of England were perfectly satisfied with Latin translations of Aristotle, made not from the original, but from Arabic versions! Greek quotations, which would occur now and then, were summarily dismissed with this marginal note: *Græcum est, legi non potest.* When the learned Grocyn first taught Greek at Oxford, under Henry VIII., his lectures, delivered with great pomp, were looked upon as a highly dangerous and alarming innovation. The very sound of Greek appeared to the fastidious ear of Englishmen abominable, and such as "no Christian could endure to hear." Oxford was divided into Greeks and Trojans, who waged a fierce warfare with each other, and even exposed the great Erasmus, who had been a pupil of Grocyn and taught Greek after him, to personal insult and gross misrepresentation.

Fashion, with its superior power, came soon afterwards to the aid of the dangerous language, and the reign of Elizabeth was the age of learned ladies, who read and wrote Greek with surprising facility. A whole host of noble ladies, with Lady Jane Gray to lead the erudite procession, vied with each other; some merely enjoying the study of Greek, others making their knowledge useful by valuable translations. Who does not recollect the two Margarets, the bright luminaries of the household of Sir Thomas More, and the four wonderful daughters of Sir Anthony Cook? "The maids of honor of Queen Elizabeth, for a time," says Warton, "indulged their ideas of sentimental affection in the sublime contemplation of Plato's Phædo, and the Queen, who understood Greek better than the Canons of Windsor, and was certainly a much greater pedant than her successor, James I., translated 'Isocrates.' But this passion for the Greek language soon ended where it began, nor do we find that it improved the national taste or influenced the writings of the age of Elizabeth." This was naturally to be expected from a zeal which was simply the offspring of fashion ; but the small effect, which this prodigious learning had on the national tongue, is easily explained by the profound ignorance which prevailed at that time among the lower and many even of the middle classes. While a few young ladies at court read Greek, Shakespeare's father, an alderman at Stratford, appears to have been unable to write his name, and under a king who boasted of his thorough mastery over numerous tongues nine men out of ten were content to make their marks for a signature.

The following words may, however, serve as examples of Greek terms, which have entered our language directly and without passing through the intermediate stage of a Latin translation : —

Χώλερα (disease),	Cholera, choler, choleric, &c.
Ὁρίζων (bounding sight),	Horizon, horizontal, &c.
Λίχεν (tree-moss),	Lichen.
Κατάρακτος (rushing down),[1]	Cataract.
Παράλυσις (loosening),	Paralysis, paralytic, &c.
Παραδόξη (outside of δόξη),	Paradox. So Orthodox, Heterodox, &c.
Κανώπη (tester against gnats),	Canopy.
Ξηρός (dry),	Sere.
Ἔκτασις (standing outside),	Extasy, extatic, &c.
Ἐνεργεία (in the work),	Energy.
Λιτουργεία (public work),	.Liturgy.
Χειρουργεία (hand-word),	Surgery *vice* Chirurgie.

Besides these, many others are of course used in works of scientific import, numbers having found a home in the nomenclature of Natural Science. Our own day, teeming with new discoveries and fertile additions to our knowledge, fabricates a vast number of technical terms from the Greek — with the exception of a few German words, the only manufacture of additions to our vocabulary now going on. The majority of these terms, however, do not belong to the flesh and blood of our language, and require, therefore, here, no farther explanation.

1 Used by Pliny X. 43, for two purposes: to denote a waterfall, and a seabird, rushing down upon his prey — probably the Solan Goose.

CHAPTER V.

ENGLISH SOUNDS.

" Words are the sounds of the heart." — Chinese Proverb.

No one who has traveled abroad, or listened with attentive ear to foreigners, can have failed to notice that every language has its favorite sounds, so that the careful observer may, from these alone, distinguish at once the nationality of any unknown tongue. The pure air and mild climate of Italy, the habit of her children to spend the largest portion of their lives in the open air, and their national endowment in point of music — all these are well represented in the abundance of vowels, which characterizes the favored child of ancient Latin. The Frenchman makes himself at once known, and by no means always most pleasantly, by his preference for nasal sounds — a taste which he is fond of ascribing to his descent from the old Romans, and which, it is true, was assiduously cultivated by the orators and elocutionists of Gaul. He is not a little proud of this gentle transition from consonant to vowel, which constitutes what he likes to call the musical element of his language. A French critic, Dupuis, went so far as to call these nasal sounds, from the analogy between the diatonic scale of vowels and the musical notes, the true bémols of the idiom. The German's "jaw-breaking" dentals are too often referred to, justly and unjustly, to require illustration. We know much less of the palate-sounds of the Slavonic idioms, which generally require such excessive pliancy in all the organs of speech as to make it a comparatively easy

4

task for the races who use them to learn foreign tongues.
This it is that enables the Russians in Paris to speak not
only good, but actually better, French than the Parisians
themselves.

Our English has the sad privilege of being well known
among the languages of the earth for the frequency of its
hissing sounds. It has not only the direct means of producing it in the letters *s, c, z,* and *th,* but, as if not satisfied
with these, it gives a kindred sound to numerous combinations of other letters. Thus Addison complains bitterly,
that in his day there has taken place " the abbreviation of
several words that are terminated in 'eth,' by substituting
an *s* in the room of the last syllable, as in 'drowns, walks,
arrives,' and innumerable other words, which, in the pronunciation of our forefathers were, 'drowneth, walketh,
arriveth.' This has wonderfully multiplied a letter which
was before too frequent in the English tongue, and added
to the hissing in our language." So grievous, indeed, is
this unmusical abundance of sibilants, that more than one
remedy has been suggested. But languages have a will
of their own, as well as men, and no power on earth can
mold them anew. Matters seem to have been worse yet,
in former days, when lisping was apparently considered an
accomplishment, for Chaucer tells us of his friar, that he

> " Somewhat lisped for his wantonness,
> To make his English sweet upon his tongue."

Not only every language, however, has its own peculiar
sounds, which constantly reappear and thus give a peculiar
and unmistakable character to its utterance, but every dialect is again apt to have its own exclusive sounds. So it
is in England, and even in the United States, — the leveling
process of universally diffused education and republican
intermingling of the masses has not prevented a marked
difference of utterance between the South and the North,
the East and the West. In England, the contrast is, of
course, more striking. For instance, the people of Devon-

shire are famous for their spluttering, turgid enunciation, which suggests to the ear a tongue too large for the palate. Far more pleasantly sounds the monotonous, but soft and soothing drawling of Durham. Norfolk and Suffolk have a peculiar, almost inimitable sound, which can only be described as an attenuated whine. It is found again, slightly increased, in the famous "New England drawl," carried to Yankee-land by the later colonists, who followed the first Puritans, from Norfolk and Suffolk. These peculiarities have, however, not remained stationary in their first home in the New World, but followed the sons of the Puritans to New York and some of the Western States, receiving in each a new, peculiar imprint. The speech of Northumberland is disfigured by a burr, and an exaggerated Scotch accent, for English becomes harsher and broader as it gradually moves farther northward, and even there the mountain regions have again still ruder and coarser sounds than the plains. Lancashire English sounds very much like Low-German, the broad Platt Deutsch of the plains of Mecklenburg and Oldenburg. A boy from that county sent to school in Hamburg, landed on a very hot day, and finding servants who drew water from a fountain, said to them : " Will you give me a drink of water ?" The reply was : " Was sagt er ? " (What says he ?) He repeated his request slowly, and separating the words. " Du kannst trinken " (Thou canst drink) was at once the ready answer, and Modern Lancashire and Old German were soon at home with each other.

The English of Northamptonshire, on the other hand, is singularly pure — an advantage the county probably owes to its central position. The best of all is said to be spoken between Huntington and Stamford. Already Fuller, the church historian, said of it: " The language of the common people is generally the best of any shire in England," because a hard-laboring man of that county, although he had to acknowledge that certain words in the psalms were

" above his comprehension," assured him that the last translation of the Bible agreed fully with the common speech of the country. It is certain that many words of the " well of English undefiled " are still lingering in the home of Shakespeare and Dryden, and even now the most uneducated part of the people there speak excellent English.

When the English traveler leaves his home to cross the ocean and comes to our shores, he is at once struck by peculiarities of utterance which give to his own tongue a somewhat foreign air. He is apt first of all to become acquainted with the nasal twang of the genuine Yankee in the New England States, which is likely to be familiar to his eye already through the amusing works of Judge Haliburton. There is no denying that it is exceedingly unpleasant to the ear of those who are not accustomed to it from early childhood. The South, on the contrary, is given to a slow, drawling utterance, thanks to a warm climate and indolent habits; the vowels especially become very indistinct and sound very differently from those of Northern men. The great West, again, has not only its own terms, but also a peculiar intonation, which may be the result of hard work, and of a life spent exclusively on the wide prairie or in the loud-echoing forest.

Intimately connected with this preference which every language has for certain sounds, is of course a corresponding preference for certain letters. In every idiom not only certain combinations occur more frequently than others, but the individual letters are used or neglected in so striking a manner that the type-setter can at once, and in fixed formulas, give the number of letters required to print in each language. Thus it is well known that the Latin had no aspirates, the Chinese has no *d* and *r;* hence Europe is there *Eulope, Ya-me-li-ka* is the name for America, and the name of Christ is disguised under the form of *Ki-li-yse-tec.* The Six Nations have no labials at all, so that they never articulate with their lips and cannot say Pa.

So averse, says Dr. Jonathan Edwards, are they to shutting their mouth, that they have even changed Amen into *Awen!* They share this peculiarity with several other Indian languages. The Society Islanders, on the other hand, have no gutturals, and Captain Cooke was to them *Tute.* Some native tribes of Brazil have neither *f* nor *l* nor *r* in their language, and hence the Portuguese accused them of being a barbarous people, without *fe, ley,* or *rey,* — that is, without faith, law, or king, in their language.

The final result of this frequency of sounds and preference for certain letters, peculiar to each language, is represented in its laws of euphony. These are as characteristic of each idiom as certain moral features are of each nation. Euphony, however, may be absolute, founded upon general and fundamental laws; and as such it is, of course, common to all nations. It may, however, also be relative, inasmuch as it depends upon the climate, the occupation, and the general habits of a nation. Euphony may, to a certain extent, even be personal; for many sounds appear harsh and unpleasant from some lips, and very different from others; as generally foreign languages sound more agreeable to the ear when spoken by natives. Nor must we forget the influence of individuality in cases similar to that of Mortimer's wife, to whom he said —

> " Thy tongue
> Makes Welsh as sweet as ditties highly penn'd,
> Sung by a fair queen in a summer's bower
> With ravishing division, to her lute." — *Henry IV.*, Part I. 1.

Applying the general laws of euphony to English, it cannot be denied that the language of our Anglo-Saxon forefathers was at first nothing better than the language of fierce, untamed barbarians, hemmed in by barbarians as savage as they were themselves, cut off from all intercourse with the rest of the world, and roving about as " sea-wolves " only to plunder and to destroy. Spending their lives in gloomy forests and on the fierce ocean, they were, like all northern nations under similar circumstances, given to stern, often morose, taciturnity. This disposition gave two peculiar features to their vernacular: it made it harsh and monosyllabic. Both these traits have been handed down to the English of our day. We cannot agree with Camden, who says, that " English possesses as much grandeur as Spanish, sweetness as Italian, delicacy as French, and energy as German." We may grant it energy, delicacy and grandeur, but it is not musical, it is not made for song like the Italian. What prevents this is that all its vowels are more or less dimmed, even when accented; for there are but few, if any, that are clearly and distinctly pronounced, as in Southern languages, whilst the skeleton of consonants stands out bolder and barer with us than anywhere else. We have a compensation for this want of beauty in the strong vigor of our stock, which, if it be harsh in itself, is peculiarly well adapted to bear grafts of a more sunny and softer climate. What is lost in beauty and softness of sound is gained in brevity and concise strength. A more serious reproach made to our English is, that its sounds are even now becoming daily dimmer, and its enunciation fainter. The change of the full $m\bar{y}$, as still pronounced by Americans, into the shortened sound of the same word in England, as in the orthodox " me lud," is a case in point. What exquisite delight we derive from a truly clear and accurate enunciation, and how rare an accomplishment it is in our day! We have heard of men who have gone home after one of the late Mr. Thackeray's lectures on the Georges, in which he quotes a poem by Bishop Heber, to read it over, and who have declared that, though familiar with every line, they had hardly known what it was until they heard it from the lips of the lecturer.

It is unfortunately but too true that English is becoming daily less euphonious. Even since the times of Elizabeth many " honeyed " words of Shakespeare have been lost, and this deterioration of sounds is progressing at a formidable rate. We must attribute the change mainly to the tendency to shorten all words by dropping even the few inflections that still remain, to the unsparing introduction of the hissing sounds and especially the letter *s*, and to other unmusical innovations. This is all the more to be deplored, as we ought to be, even in this respect, more careful in guarding words from corruption. We should not forget that, as Mrs. Jameson tells us well, we are obliged, for the purpose of circulation and intercommunication, to coin truth into words. It is important, therefore, to see to it that the coin is not adulterated, but kept pure and up to the original standard of signification and value, so that it may be reconvertible into the truth it represents. If language is really daguerreotyped truth, accuracy of language may well be considered as one of the bulwarks of truth. Is there not something inexpressibly shocking to English ears and English minds in the Italian idiom which gives to the guide for the sake of his glib tongue the name of the great orator *Cicerone*, which values proficiency in the fine arts as a virtue and calls the happy possessor a *virtuoso*, and makes him a brave man, a *bravo*, who murders in secret? The degeneracy of such words does not, however, depend on the meaning only; the sound is of great importance, and the violently curtailed slang word *hussy*, for instance, will never again rise to convey the charm and the dignity of its full and original form, the loving *house-wife*.

The tendency of our English to reduce words to their narrowest limits, which has led to its monosyllabic character, is in like manner daily growing stronger. It received its first impulse, no doubt, already in Anglo-Saxon times, from the causes indicated above, but its full development must be ascribed to French influence. It was the Normans who silenced the final *e* in a large number of words, and thus reduced them from two syllables to one. "*Les*

Anglais," said Voltaire sneeringly, "*gagnent sur nous deux heures par jour en parlant, parcequ'ils mangent la moitié de leurs mots*."　He little knew that his own countrymen were the authors of this change.　For in the French poetry of the twelfth and thirteenth century we find mute *e* already very generally substituted for the accented *e* of former years.　Chaucer sounds it only in verbs,—

> "The more quainte knackes that they make
> The more wol I stele when I take,"

but in other words it is mute,—

> "Ther was here hwete and eek here malt igrounde,
> Instede of melke, yet wol I gere hem bren," &c.

and in the popular verses of James Audeley, soon after 1400, the final *e* is invariably silent.　Almost the only protection against this shortening of words is found in German words, where the letters *g* or *v* preceded the final vowel, which have preserved and even developed their second syllable, as, *e. g.*: —

Anglo-Saxon.	*English.*	*German.*
fealve,	fallow,	falb.
gealga,	gallows,	Galgen.
geolve,	yellow,	gelb.
spearva,	sparrow,	Sper (ling).

This process was subsequently extended, by the force of analogy, to the letters *r* and *l* preceding *g* or *h*, *e. g.*: —

Anglo-Saxon.	*English.*	*German.*
burh,	borough,	Burg.
tealg,	tallow,	Talg.
bearh,	barrow,	Bahre.
baelg,	bellow,	Balg.
sorh,	sorrow,	Sorge.
mearg,	marrow,	Mark.

The result is that the number of monosyllables in English surpasses by far that of any other modern language, and this feature gives it a peculiarly direct and straightforward character, equally far from the courteously studied and indirect French and the lumbering, intricate German.　In

the following lines from Macbeth there are fifty-two words,
and of these fifty are monosyllables : —

> " That is a step
> On which I must fall down, or else *o'erleap*,
> For in my way it lies. Stars, hide your fires,
> Let no light see my black and deep *desires*.
> The eye winks at my hand. Yet let that be
> Which the eye fears, when it is done, to see."

There is in this inattention to mere sounds and this stripping of words of all so-called superfluities a great mechanical triumph, which reveals the eminently practical sense of
the people through the practical character of their language.
They evidently use such forms not in order to chat and to
amuse themselves by the mere utterance of words, but as
means toward action. They choose, moreover, for such
purposes, the shortest and simplest way, not only because
it suffices, but because they prefer it. There is even something poetical in this perfect mechanism, which thus produces the greatest end by the smallest means. In speaking
English the mind must ever be thoroughly active. There
is no abundance of words here, as in other languages, — no
fullness of forms, no minute details are given. On the contrary, the slightest and most delicate modifications of sound,
accent, and position must, unaided, convey to others the
subtlest and gravest shades of meaning. The ear must
not only hear, and hear most attentively, but the mind must
be hard at work, and the heart at the same time feel, in
order to understand. A mere hint suffices to replace all
the inflections of Latin and Greek, and the spiritual power
of the language is thus increased in proportion as the fullness of forms is diminished.

If we examine the letters and their sounds, individually,
we must not overlook the fact, that the Anglo-Saxon form
of our English lacked some of them altogether, which were
supplied only at the time of the Conquest. Such was the
modern *k* for which before that time *c* was used. The

Norman-French gave us the former, but the apparent gain was our loss, for at the same time we lost *ch* and *h* as gutturals, pronounced in the manner in which they now form so striking a feature of German. The combinations *sh* and *ch* were, on the other hand, introduced with their French sound, for they were as unknown to Saxon as they are still to German; and thus *sal* became *shall*; *cild*, *child*; and *kirk*, *church*. Even now the Scotch use *sal* for *shall*, as in the quotation "Listen or ye sal rue it," introduced in "Guy Mannering," ch. 46. Wickliffe has in St. Luke *shal* and elsewhere *schal*, but even Chaucer still says, " shal pay," 836. That the older Saxon, often called Semi-Saxon, did not give the modern sound to the letters *sch*, would appear from the fact that the hard sound of *k* is represented by the same letters. We find, therefore, in contemporaneous MSS

chirche,	schulde,	chestre,	riche,
worche,	thenche (think),	seche (sick),	liche (like).

It was this varying and undecided mode of spelling which led to the changes from French soft *ch* into hard English *c*, as from *chat* to *cat* and *chapon* to *capon*, words that are even now interchanged in Normandy and Picardy. *Chattle* and *cattle* are, in like manner, but different forms of one and the same word; and our modern word *cater* has hardly enough left to prove its derivation from the French *acheter*. Fortunately we find the gradual transformation represented in successive authors, for whilst Chaucer still says *achater* in his "Canterbury Tales," 570 and elsewhere, Ben Jonson in "The Devil an Ass," I. 3, shortens the word already to nearly its modern form, —

> "He is my wardrobe man, my *acater*, my cook,
> Butler and steward."

The letter *g* was anciently of a very peculiar nature as far as its sound was concerned, and this explains many strange anomalies in its modern pronunciation. It was certainly pronounced like our *y* in yes before the two vowels *e* and *i*. Thus the Anglo-Saxon *gealew* became yellow ; *gyrstawdaeg*, yesterday ; *geoglere, j*uggler ; *geong, y*oung ; *geoc, y*oke ; *geta, y*et ; *geolca, y*olk ; *gea, y*ea ; *gear, y*ear ; with its strong inflected plural of *gore*, our own *yore*. The old *geard* is now *yard*, though *garden* sounds differently now, whilst the Scotch insist upon pronouncing it *yard*, and Americans compromise by giving it an intermediate sound like *gyarden*. Its compound (*w*)*ort-geard* does not seem to have ever had a hard *g*, or it could not have become *orchard*, which was, curiously enough, once written *hortyard*, under the influence of a mistaken connection with the Latin *hortus*. Where the hard sound was really needed to preserve the true nature of the word, an *u* was inserted between *g* and *e* or *i*, and hence we write *guide, guilt* and *guise, guelders* and *guess*. The same sound seems to have been given to *g* at the end of words, for there it has almost invariably changed into *y*, as from *daeg* to *day, weeg* to *way, bælg* to *belly*, and from thence farther on into *bellow, belch, bulge, budget*, and *bully*. Here also an intervening *u* saves final *g* from deterioration, as in *plague, league* and *rogue*. When this change of *g* into *y* has taken place in the middle of a word, it leads to a further shortening into *i*, and then the word is apt to become monosyllabic. In wagon and (Charles') wain, the full and the shortened form both survive. Generally the contraction has taken place in German words, as in —

Anglo-Saxon.	*English.*	*German.*
haegel,	hail,	Hagel.
faeger,	fair,	
fugol,	fowl,	Vogel.
sugu,	sow,	Sau.
	nail,	Nagel.
	sail,	Segel.
	flail,	Flegel.
	lair,	Lager.
	maid,	Magd.

The tendency of changing final *g* into *w*, which is common to all Teutonic languages, prevails largely in English, and thus we obtain from —

Anglo-Saxon.	*English.*	
daeg,	day *and*	dawn.
drag,	dray,	draw.
lag,		law.
sagan,	say,	saw
maga		maw.

This change must, however, not be confounded with the constant interchange between the Saxon *w* and the French *g*, which likewise pervades the language, and gives us a number of valuable synonyms. Thus from the

French,	*We have English,*
garde,	guard *and* ward.
gardien,	guardian *and* warden.
guise,	guise *and* wise.
sergent,	sergeant *and* servant.

In other words but one form exists; thus *guichet* is *wicket*; *garenne, warren*; *gûter, waste*; *guerre, war*; *guèpe, wasp*; *gare,* (be) *ware*; *gages, wages*; *Galles, Wales*; *Guillaume, William*; and *Guelphs* only *Whelps*. How little the difference between *w* and *g* was observed of old, we see from the use made of the two letters in older poems. The Romaunt of the Rose has "In reward (regard) of my daughter's shame," and the Parson's Tale, "Take reward (regard) of thyn owne vallewe, that thou ne be to foule to thy selfe."

In the MSS. of the thirteenth and fourteenth century, *e. g.,* in Layamon's "Brut," Ernleye and others, a curious *g* is found, written differently from the ordinary *g*, and in English prints often rendered by a special *g* somewhat resembling *z*. It is evidently meant for the soft *g* of the Anglo-Saxon in its state of transition to *y* or *i*, as in *gif, gef,* if; *gea, geo, you*; *geong, gong,* young. It never can have had any resemblance in sound to *z*, although it was, no doubt from ignorance, often so written and even printed in Old English type, as when we find neighbor spelt *neizbour* in Chaucer, but it seems to survive with Scotchmen in the name of *Mackenzie*. In support of our theory, that it is but softened *g*, we may quote from the famous proclamation of Henry III. in 1258, " We senden *g*ew this writ open," and from a MS. in the Bodleyan Collection, 78, fol. 48, written by an author of the fourteenth century, who uses the peculiar form of *g* in all the following words : —

> " In Englis tonge y schal *g*ow telle,
>   *Gif ge* so long with me wyl dwelle,
>   Ne Latin will y speke, ne waste
>   Bot Englis that men uses maste,
>   For that ys *g*owre kynde langage
>   That *ge* hafe here most of usage."

The Anglo-Saxon combination of *cg* became in Old English *gg*, but changed its sound entirely, under French influence, into the modern pronunciation of *dg*, which it is not known to have had before the fifteenth century.

Anglo-Saxon.	*Old English.*	*Modern.*
ecg,	egg,	edge.
mycg,	mygg,	midge.
secg,	segg,	sedge.

In some words the sound of soft *ch* was merely inserted in order to preserve the soft sound of *g* which it had in French, without lengthening the preceding vowel. Thus the French *juge* became our ju*dg*e, and hence also our badge, ridge, hedge, and wedge.

Another letter, the sound of which presents some peculiarities in English in common with *g*, is *k*. Both were pronounced in Anglo-Saxon as they now are in German. That *k* was not silent, even as late as the fourteenth century, we can see from the quaint poem of " Pier's Ploughman," in which it must be sounded in order to produce the proper alliteration, *e. g.* : —

> " Thanne *k*am ther a *k*yng,
>   *K*nyghthood hym hadde,"

and

> " Yet I courbed my *k*nee
>   And cried."

"Letters," says Seneca (Epistle 114), "like soldiers, are apt to desert and drop off in a long march," and thus both these letters were silenced, mainly by French influence again, whenever they were initial and followed by *n*. The nasal sound of *gn* was, in the eleventh and twelfth century, already so rarely written, that we find in MS. of that period, alternately *montaigne* and *mountain*, *cocaygne* and *cocayne*, *soveraygne* and *soverayne*, *Alemaigne* and *Alemaine*, *Spagne* and *Spayne*. Whilst *k* and *g* became silent before the letter *n*, and thus gave us our *k*night, *k*nife, *k*now, *k*nave, reign, deign, *g*nome, *g*nostic, and phle*gm*, they were, by the same influence, at the end of words, changed into the true French sound of *ch*. Hence our bir*ch*, chur*ch*, star*ch*, ben*ch*, mu*ch*, ri*ch*, blea*ch*. The Scotch alone retained the original hard sound, and still uses *ilka* for each, *sick* for such, *whilk* for which, *kist* for chest, and *kern* for churn. Its conservative tendencies are not wholly to be ascribed to the character of the people, but largely also to the fact that Scotland was so much farther removed from the direct influence of Norman-French, and, when the latter threatened to change it, had still preserved much of its ancient Gaelic. Thus we find here also, alone in Great Britain, the original aspirate sound of *ch*, which was common to the Anglo-Saxon and to the Celtic of Scotland, and thus survived in its *Loch*, which the French could not pronounce.

Another letter which has lost its sound in many combinations, under the influence of French masters, is *l*; and what is most remarkable in this connection is, that our English has preserved it in many French words that have lost it in France. They were, it is true, generally imported from the Continent at a time when they still had a sound at home; but why we should have been more conservative than our neighbors is not quite so clearly perceived. Thus we have fault, false, veal, chisel, salmon, scaffold, pencil, vessel, culpable, vault, and fool, for the French *faute, faux*, *veau, ciseaux, saumon, échafaud, pinceau, vaisseau, coupable, voûte,* and *fou.* The explanation is found in the fact that the Romance languages have all, more or less, the same tendency to drop the sound of *l* after *a* and *o*, or other indistinctly pronounced vowels. This is not the case in English, and hence the preservation. Here, on the other hand, *l* is apt to become silent before *k, m, f,* even where it is still written, which is the reason why we do not hear it in ta*l*k, cha*l*k, fo*l*k, yo*l*k, ha*l*f, ca*l*f, pa*l*m, ba*l*m, and qua*l*m. It is only by the force of analogy that it has become silent in the words shou*l*d, wou*l*d, and cou*l*d. The Scotch here carry the matter farther than the English, for they pronounce gold as *gowd,* full as *fu',* call as *caw,* fall as *faw.* The liquid *l* of the French — their *l brouillé* — was lost in English apparently as early as the eleventh century, for we find there already William for *Guillaume,* travailer for *travailleur,* doel for *deuil,* perilous and marvellous.

The most remarkable of all old English letters, however, were the two signs which anciently represented *th,* of which one was used at the end or in the middle of a word and had a softer sound, whilst the other occurred only at the beginning and had a harsh, sharp sound. In modern English the two are used just the reverse; all pronouns beginning with *th* and their derivatives have a soft *th,* and the sharp sound is now almost exclusively found at the end, except in a few words like thin and thick, in beneath, smooth, with, and in verbs terminating in *the.* The reason of this strange confusion must be sought in the heathenish origin of the two letters. They existed already in the ancient Runic writing, and had been preserved even after St. Augustine had introduced, with Christianity, the Roman alphabet, because the latter had no equivalent for them. But as they belonged to a different era and a different faith, their precise force and meaning were soon lost, and hence, probably, the tendency to mistake one for another. They were, moreover, in their ancient form, unfortunately so much like the letter *y*, that to this resemblance we must ascribe the perplexing custom of older manuscripts, to write .continually *y* for *the*. Even printers, as late as the fourteenth and fifteenth century, continued the abuse, partly perhaps from the ignorance of transcribers, but partly also from pedantry, and Tyndale's Bible always has *ye* and *yt* for the and that, *ye*reof and *y'*of for thereof.

Whatever changes, however, these and other letters may have undergone in sound and form, enough is left of the ancient letters to bear witness to the remarkable conservatism of the English people. They have ever disliked revolutions, and prefer avoiding them even in the realm of letters; they have ever abhorred violent measures and a too ready abandonment of what is old and venerable. As in English law, therefore, a strange adherence to old usages and otherwise antiquated forms goes along with practical eminence, so in language also there is a remarkable contrast between antique orthography and modern pronunciation. This apparent inconsistency is but another proof of the great reluctance to change and thus to efface the traces of the past. It must not be overlooked, however, that in language such changes are next to impossible ; they can be brought about only by inner necessity ; external agencies are nearly powerless. Even the power of the Cæsars could not accomplish an innovation apparently so trifling as the introduction of a letter, for when Claudius desired to add an X to the Roman alphabet, he found all his power in vain, and Priscian tells us, in his great work on the Letters : "*Nulli ausi sunt antiquam scripturam mutare.*"

We Americans, on the contrary, love change, have no reverence for what is old merely because it is old, and reject indignantly the doctrine of the necessity of a " historic basis," for we live far more in the future than in the present, and have no past. With us alone, therefore, could radical changes of orthography ever obtain largely. Respectable and influential publishers, supported by an im-

mense capital and a large stock of energy and perseverance, could by means of popular dictionaries affect the
spelling of a nation, and induce even great authors, like
Washington Irving, to appear in their new and arbitrarily
imposed orthography. Their influence, however, can after
all be only temporary, as long as North America depends
exclusively on the mother country for its models of literature. Even on broader ground, we believe that these
attempts to change, by arbitrary decision, the manner of
writing a great national tongue, must necessarily fail for
two reasons. They are neither practicable nor desirable.
No combination of men, however powerful in themselves,
can permanently control a living organism, such as a language is, with its steady growth and self-wrought changes.
To make a change really useful, moreover, it would have to
be radical, and then we are reduced at once to phonography. It may look, at first sight, as if a large portion of
certain words, like the French *viennent* or *aôut*, the German
sieht or the English *though* and *pshaw*, could easily be
spared. But then we would at once lose the historic basis,
which is in Etymology as important as in the other sciences.
The letters in words of modern languages may not all be
pronounced now, but that is not their only purpose. They
give an essentially correct image of the pronunciation of
words as it was when the latter were first used. The
written word has remained, the spoken word has changed
continually. If the form were to follow the sound, there
would soon not a single trace be left of the language used
by our forefathers. This is the principal and all-powerful
argument against phonography, and the reason why the
French moralist called good spelling an infallible sign of
good breeding, " for," said he, " spelling is the rationale of
the written word, and only well-educated and refined people know that."

We should be extremely sorry to see the words of Voltaire, which he intended as a bitter sarcasm, now verified

in English : " *L'étymologie est une science où les voyelles ne font rien et les consonnes fort peu de chose.*" For languages change already rapidly enough, so that even our English has many words of the same origin which, in their present form, have not a single letter in common, and differ in meaning as far as in spelling. It requires all the resources of Comparative Etymology, and a thorough familiarity with the great laws according to which letters change in languages of a certain family, to detect the same roots under such varied forms. We may well ask, what would have become of English Etymology if the " Fonetic Nuz" had been started a thousand years ago? It is safe to assert that nobody would have had either the courage or the time to attempt mastering the history of our language.

CHAPTER VI.

ENGLISH ORTHOGRAPHY AND ENGLISH ACCENT.

BEFORE a strict judge our English would probably not be allowed to cavil at any attempts to improve its orthography, as long as it adheres so tenaciously to its almost vicious mode of spelling. It must be admitted, that in this respect we are yet in that happy age, of which Burns says : —

> "In days when mankind were but callans
> At grammar, logic and sic talents,
> They took nae pains their speech to balance
> Or rules to gie,
> But spak their thoughts in plain, braid lallans
> Like you or me."

Our orthography is the most anomalous on the face of the earth, and English makes of all languages the wildest and most extravagant use of letters in its written form. Nevertheless these very outrages upon principle and good taste have become so dear, so familiar, we might almost say so sacred to the mass of English speaking people, that the strongest objection to any reform in spelling is found in the grotesque effect, which any innovation produces. This impression has, as yet, proved too strong to be overcome. Thus we have to bear the evil as well as we may, and console ourselves with the undeniable fact, that the mere learning to spell is to the child a training as severe and as useful as any more generally respected branch of knowledge taught in common schools. For "to spell English," says

Mr. Ellis, " is the most difficult of human attainments," and this difficulty is probably the most serious if not the only impediment in the way of its ever becoming the language of the earth. Were it not obscured by its whimsically antiquated orthography, which disguises its words and requires long years to learn, it would certainly be the best fitted for universal adoption. From the highest to the lowest, all of us have at some time or other become familiar with the painful uncertainty of some word. Ingenuity has succeeded in devising the combination, "kaughy," which sounds like a familiar word and yet contains not a single letter of its proper form. Simple ignorance encouraged the indignant housemaid, whose letters were produced in court and excited great merriment, to repel an attack upon her way of spelling the odd looking word "yf," with the words: " What should wy eff spell, but wife ?"

The fault is an ancient one, and the sin has been handed down from our first fathers. The Anglo-Saxons wrote badly, the Norman-French wrote worse. The former, we ought to state in their behalf, had neither grammar nor criticism. Nor were they specially to be blamed for it, for it was no better with the oldest of all languages. Ancient Hebrew had to wait for the Rabbi Judah Ching to write its first grammar at Fez in Africa, in 1070. The Greeks knew no grammar at all prior to the Alexandrian age, because they ignored all other languages, and grammar cannot exist without comparison. Even the Romans were, if we may believe Suetonius, unacquainted with grammar until Crates Mellotes, the ambassador of king Attalus, brought one to Rome between the second and third Punic war. How then could our poor ignorant Saxons have one of their own? That much ignorance and much caprice prevailed among their writers, is true, but this also was more of a misfortune than a crime. They lived so far apart from each other, that they could not " compare notes." They were all monks, whose lives were passed in the quiet seclusion

of their cells, without intercommunication or exchange of
thoughts with others. Was not the venerable Bede, their
greatest Church historian, an inmate of the same convent,
from the seventh year of his life to the last, his sixty-second,
without ever having left its holy precincts ? We need not
wonder then, that each one of these pious men had his own
fancies and preferences for this or that mode of spelling,
to which he adhered in all innocence and with perfect
independence, and that thus no two versions of the same
work are ever found to agree. These writers were, moreover, not less distant from each other in time than in place.
They wrote at great intervals, and in the mean while
the language, never quite settled, much less uniform, had
changed much and often very seriously. How it must have
fared under such circumstances with a barbarous language,
still in process of formation, we may judge from the fate
of a well-formed idiom in times of peaceful development.
We are told by Pegge, that when Vaugelas in 1659, published his translation of Quintus Curtius, which had occu-
pied him for more than thirty years, he found that French
had changed so much in the mean time, that he was obliged
to correct the former part of his work in order to bring it
up to the standard of the latter part. This caused the wit
Voiture to apply to it the epigram of Martial on a barber,
who was so slow in his operations, that the hair began to
grow on one side of his face, before he had fully trimmed
the other side : —

> " Entrepelus tonsor dum circuit ora Luperci
> Expungitque genas, altera barba subit." — VII. 83.

Anglo-Saxon writers belonged, moreover, to different
races, each of which had its own dialect. England was
not yet one great kingdom, and it did not yet possess a
national tongue. Each learned monk naturally preferred
his own native idiom, even if he possessed the rare accomplishment of knowing another, and thus new forms and
new spellings were continually introduced. Besides, when

Christianity was first introduced, the difficulties it met with had been largely increased by the fact that its early messengers were foreigners, utterly ignorant of the language of the people to whom they were sent, and disposed to abuse their power and legitimate authority in point of language to the utmost. The priests, also, in later years, were not the most learned, and we may be induced to judge them less harshly, by remembering that even in the days of Queen Elizabeth, as Fuller tells us, " the clergy were ordered' to con over their lessons by themselves once or twice before' service, in order that they might be able to read them fluently to the congregation ! "

The influence of the Danish occupation on the orthography of English was grievous in the extreme. It did not change the words themselves, because Danish and Saxon were kindred, if not the same languages. For many of the Danes were no doubt Germans, who, rather than submit to the iron rule of Charlemagne, had taken refuge in Denmark. This very resemblance of the two languages, however, led to an almost boundless confusion between kindred words, which resulted finally in the breaking down of almost all inflections, and in a serious change of the pronunciation. This resemblance, so often denied, is still susceptible of easy proof. Already in that remarkable monument of distant Iceland, Snorre's " Edda," pages 275, 276, it is expressly stated of Englishmen and Icelanders, "*ver erum einnar tungu,*" — we are of one tongue, — and when Christianity was to be introduced among the followers of Odin in Sweden, Anglo-Saxon priests were sent from England to preach the Gospel, and found themselves, untaught, sufficiently familiar with Swedish for the purpose. A mixture of languages, so closely related and so similar to each other, is always accompanied by fatal results, and in this instance certainly did not fail to produce them at once. They showed themselves mainly in a largely increased irregularity of spelling, which is felt, if not always seen, to this day. The evil was still further aggravated by the fact, that both Danes and Anglo-Saxons were accustomed to great license in their earliest mode of writing, — the Runes, — for we find that, *e. g.*, the word *eftir* was found by the poet F. G. Bergman to have been spelt on runic stones in twenty-eight different ways, and even in monuments of the thirteenth and fourteenth century the same word still appears in seventeen varied forms.

In Anglo-Saxon we may safely say that the vowels were all interchanged one with another; and this freedom accounts mainly for the dimmed and obscure character of modern English vowels and their strange, ever varying pronunciation. The consonants were somewhat more faithfully preserved, but they also seem to have frequently interchanged, at least within the limits of their particular class. The transition becomes more evident if we compare the forms which the same word assumes in different languages. Thus in labials we find

Latin, nepos ;	*English*, nep*h*ew;	*French*, neveu;	*German*, Ne*ff*e;
volo ;	will ;	*Greek*, βούλομαι;	wollen ;
Anglo-Saxon, cnapa;	knave;		Knabe;

to which we may add as a familiar illustration, the oft-quoted inability to distinguish between the French words *boeuf* and *veuve*, ascribed to the Basques, of whom already Scaliger said sneeringly, —

> "Haud temere antiquas mutat Vasconia voces
> Cui nihil est aliud Vivere quam Bibere."

Thus, also, with sibilants, *e. g.* —

Latin.	*French.*	*English.*
plâceo,	plaisir,	pleasure.
licere,	loisir,	leisure.
securus,	sur,	sure.

With such a tendency to vary all letters, it is no longer a matter of astonishment, that English should exhibit more remarkable cases of mis-spelling than any other language. "Take a dozen MSS. of the ' Romaunt of the Rose,' " says

Pasquier in his learned " Recherches de la France," VIII. c. 3, "and you will find there as many different forms of old words as they were taken from different fountains." On the famous tapestry of Bayeux, which contains about the amount of a page of writing, six different ways of spelling the name of the Conqueror occur. They are: Wilielmi, Willelmi, Wilgelmum, Willielmus, Willem, Wilel. Of the great name of Shakespeare, Halliwell tells us, that there are not less than thirty-four ways in which the various members of the family wrote it; and in the Council-book of the Corporation of Stratford, where it is introduced one hundred and sixty-six times during the years that the poet's father was a member of the municipal body, there are fourteen different varieties. The modern "Shakespeare" is not among them. Well might already Chaucer say, therefore, in the last stanzas of his Troilus and Cressida, —

> " And for there is so greate diversite
> In Englyshe and in writynge of our tonge,
> So pray I to God that none miswrite the.''

Fuller mentions the name of Villers, spelt in fourteen different ways in the deeds of that illustrious family; these names seem to have been written down as they were seized by the ear; hence, for instance, Rawlie so often for Raleigh. Neither the Duke of Marlborough, nor his terrible Sarah, nor Queen Anne herself, could spell; but the worst of these short-comings is probably the young Pretender's blunder, who wrote his father's name " Gems," instead of James !

Matters improved but little even after the introduction of printing, since the first printers, and, in fact, almost all of them, down to the year 1531, were Dutchmen, who could neither speak nor write English. We find in Strype's " Memoirs of Cranmer," p. 60, that Grafton sustained his petition, in which he asked for a privilege of three years for his Bible, with the argument, that " for covetousness' sake these foreign printers would not employ learned Englishmen to oversee and correct their work," and yet they meant to pirate his work!

It must, unfortunately, be admitted, that even now our English has, as yet, no historical orthography, and that a universally acknowledged authority in matters of spelling and pronunciation, such as the French Academy claims to be, is still to be desired. As it is, the matter is left almost entirely in the hands of the popular writers of England, and great credit is due to their good sense and the innate conservatism of the nation, which have so far protected the language against hurtful neglect or violent innovations. The difficulty, however, is insuperable as long as we have forty-two distinct sounds in our language, and our defective alphabet provides us only with twenty-three letters. The sounds we obtained from the various sources which have contributed to form modern English; the signs we derive directly from classical sources only, without all the help that these sources might give us.

With all this, it must not be imagined that this question of spelling words in one way or in another is altogether indifferent. It may not be considered absolutely necessary for a language to indicate in every word its origin by its form, but in an idiom, consisting of such a number of heterogeneous elements as the English, it is, as we have already seen, an important object to show whence they come, and this, in many instances, helps the clearness and the force of their meaning. We do not like to lose the suggestion of *ph* pointing to a Greek origin of some words, or that of an inserted *b* in words like *debt* and *doubt*, which recalls to us their Latin origin.

Even more useful is that variety of spelling which indicates two different meanings of one and the same word, that may have come to us at two distinct epochs of our history, or in connection with two separate purposes. Thus we distinguish between *canon* and *cannon*, *cord* and *chord*, *dram* and *drachm*, *draft* and *draught*, *holy* and *wholly*, *steak* and *stake*, though all these double forms come from one root, — or between *bays* and *baize*, *sun* and *son*, *mote* and *moat*,-*mite* and *might*, *sent* and *scent*, *vail* and *vale*, which come from different roots. To abandon the twofold spelling for the sake of greater simplicity, would involve more or less loss of distinctness of meaning, and the sense would be very apt to suffer by the dimness of the form.

Besides the formal letters that constitute a word, and the conventional sound which we attribute to them, there is, however, a third element to be considered in all words, and one of hardly less importance and interest than the others. This is the Accent. It plays the same essential part in all languages, and exhibits its higher, spiritual nature by its very diversity. Almost everywhere we find it to have gradually changed from its earliest nature as a merely sensual accent, dependent on the tangible length of letters and sounds, to a second nature as a conventional, logical accent, determined by the mental power of the word. Thus, in Ancient Languages, quantity decided, in Modern Languages, quality; in the former the accent was uniform, because it was fixed by laws based upon tangible objects; in the latter it is varying. because it corresponds here with the different ways of thinking belonging to each people. Latin and Greek prosody were alike, but the name of Napoleon, familiar to all Europe, changes thus in our day: Poles and Bohemians, who always accent the penultima, without regard to length or position, say Napoléon; the French, Nápoleón; the Germans, Swedes, and English, Napóleon; and the Italians, Spaniards, and Portuguese, Napoleóne. We can now hardly understand the vast importance given to mere quantity in Latin; and the great and lasting effect which Cicero states to have been produced upon his audience by certain metres he employed at the close of an oration, is almost incomprehensible to modern assemblies. For, with us, tone alone decides, and in the composition of poetry it commonly suffices to make a syllable long if it but be accented, and short, if it be unaccented. In fact, the accent is in English as in Greek, entirely distinct from the quantity. Thus we can take the word *august*, with its two unmistakably long syllables, and accent either syllable, speaking of an *augúst* presence, or the month of *Aúgust*, without influencing the quantity of the vowel. Such at least, has been the established usage in English since the days of Latin church-hymns and the political songs of later centuries. For it was not always so. In Anglo-Saxon certainly prosody played a very important part, as we may readily see from a comparison of the words in a poem with its regular rhythm and classical metres. We learn then, that the same syllables were at one time long and at another time short, changing, however, their meaning with their quantity. Thus, *is*, with a long *i*, represented our modern *ice ;* with a short *ĭ* our *is ; god* was either *God* or *good ; ac* was *oak* or the obsolete form for *and ; hyrde* was *herd* or *heard ;* and *at* was *ate* or *at.*

Although, however, this distinction was clear to the ear and so important to the meaning, it was utterly neglected by transcribers, and is now most difficult to ascertain. Prosody, we may well say, is altogether lost in English. This is mainly owing to the influence of the Norman Conquest, and it took place during the time of the change from Anglo-Saxon through French into English. The difficulty arose from the fact that, as each language has its favorite letters and sounds, so it has also its decidedly marked and prevailing accent. Now the French accents by preference the last syllable, the English, on the contrary, the first. Hence the struggle, for when our English was formed the French words lost first their original accent, and then, with it, frequently their spelling, because those vowels which were now left unaccented, became short, and others which were accented, gained in length. It was thus that *partíe* became *párty ; ambassadéur, embássador ; chevaleríe, chívalry ; gouvernemént, góvernment ;* and *nécessaíre, nécessary.*

This process was of course not the work of one or two
generations; it continued during several hundred years,
and we can trace the gradual change, in almost unbroken
succession, from poet to poet. At first, we find naturally
the French accent all powerful, and it remained so even
as late as the times of Edward I. when poets still said:
*tresoún, baroún, batoún, miroúr, mayeúr, somnoúr, conséit,
battáille* and *beauté*. In the Romance of Athelstone, which
dates from the middle of the fourteenth century, the accent
is still on the last syllable, as in French : —

" An weten alle be comoún asént,
  In the pleyne parlemént."
" Both his castélles and his toures."

Reliquiæ Antiquæ, 85.

Chaucer presents us here, as in all great questions of
language, the turning-point in the history of this change.
He hesitates, because in reality the language itself thus
hesitated to abandon the French accent and to give to
foreign words its own Saxon tone. Thus we find in the
Canterbury Tales, " The Emperoúres daughter," "So prick-
eth him Natúre in his coráges," and "Of which Vertúe en-
gendred is the flour," " Then say they therein swich difficul-
tié," " And forth I led hire sayle in this manére." In other
portions again we find the modern English accent already
encroaching upon French words, as in the lines —

" And sicherly she was of grete disport,
And ful pleasánt and amiáble of port,
And peined hire to contreféten chere
Of court and ben estatelich of manére,
And to ben holden digne of reverence."

Whilst the metre makes it clear that at one time we are
required to read *servíce, solémpne, langáge, mariáge, pen-
ánce, vitaílle, scolére, honoúr, curát,* and *villáge*, we find in
other places the necessity of saying *trésour*, 7945, *cólour*
5068, *víage*, 4732, and *cónseil*, 4746. At times he seems
actually to affect the French accent for some purpose un-

known to us, and then he is apt to make two syllables out of one, for the occasion, contrary to the general tendency of our idiom, *e. g.*, —

> "A clerke there was of Oxenforde also,
> That unto Logicke *haddé* long ygo,
> And *lené* was his horse as is a rake,
> And he was not right fat, I undertake."
>
> *Canterbury Tales.*

This abuse of words, which have not of course maintained their lengthened form, can hardly arise from neglect, as has sometimes been claimed, because in that case contemporaries would hardly have praised his verses so much for their regularity and beauty of sound.

For some time after him the French accent probably maintained its supremacy, but ultimately almost all imported words adopted the English accent entirely, and they have ever since retained it unchanged. This change shows more clearly than any other modification in form or sound, because in a more spiritual manner, that the predominant genius of our language, in its music as well as in its grammar, was English still.

Spenser still says *forést, furioús, hideoús, dalliaúnce, merrimént,* and in his " Fairy Queen," VII. 7, we must read : —

> " In a fayre plain upon an equall hill
> She placed was in a pavillión,
> Not such as craftsmen by their idle skill
> Are wont for princes states to fashión,
> But the earth herself of her owne motión," &c.

In thus tracing the gradual rise and final triumph of the German accent in our English, we must not overlook the fact, that it probably prevailed among the mass of the people, who were so largely Saxon, long before authors, who wrote for the great, and consequently mainly for the French, dared adopt it in their writings. John Skelton occasionally uses the foreign form, perhaps principally for the sake of the metre, as when he says *queréle, counséle, mercý,* and *pleasúre ;*

but on the whole we must admit that he, as well as Thomas Wyatt and the Earl of Surry, shows but few deviations from the modern accent. The latter especially, so important in this aspect on account of the far-famed regularity and beauty of his verse, has almost invariably the German accent on French words, even where it appears to us objectionable, as in *cómmendable* and *írrefragable*. Other authors were, of course, not always as strict in observing, or as correct in determining, the proper accent. It is amusing to see some authors of those days writing not by the eye, but apparently by the ear only; they let us thus, unconsciously, into the secret of the true pronunciation of words in their days. Audeley, a good poet, but not a very learned man, of the beginning of the fifteenth century, thus writes naively, *correxeon, cruel, treusone, personache* and *knowlache.*

Amid this mass of words, carried along by the general current of the language, and representing the struggle between the French accent, which loves the end of words, and the English accent, which always seeks the beginning of words, we meet with numerous and instructive instances of the manner in which the accent will show the date of introduction of new words. Thus in 1684 coffee and tea had evidently not yet become familiar, for Locke writes them *caffé* and *thé*. Hence it is a sign of recent existence in English, when Chaucer writes *natúre*, Milton *prostráte*, Sylvester *theátre*, Cowley *académy*, Dryden *essáy*, and Pope *barriér* and *effórt*. This is not poetic license, as some have maintained, but simply an evidence that these and similar words were still French, and bore the French accent.

A somewhat analogous change of accent is even now going on in the transition of certain words from the Northern States of the Union to the Southern States. While the former adhere strictly to the tendency of the English accent toward the root and the beginning of words, the South not unfrequently carries it forward, as in the name of one of the States, which is thus sometimes called *Árkansas* (not from any supposed Indian analogy), and at other times *Arkánsas*.

Modern French words retain, of course, their own accent, as well as their own spelling, as long as they are not fully naturalized. We have not yet entirely Anglicised, although we cannot very well do without words like *protégé*, *prestige*, *menage*, *passée*, *ennui*, *outré*, *billet doux*, *amour*, and *connoisseur*. But we notice also that as soon as the sound is changed and made to agree with our English mode of pronunciation, the accent follows as a matter of course, and we say *búreau*, *pácket*, *óffice*, &c. Occasionally, it is true, the conflict has not yet been decided; for although our English has always achieved the naturalization of foreign words, and thus preserved its national integrity by insisting upon its own accentuation, as well as its own pronunciation, the process is necessarily not one of violent suddenness, and requires some time. Good authorities still hesitate between *rétinue* and *retínue*, *révenue* and *revénue*, *advértisement* and *advertísement*, *cómmittee* and *committée*. This applies not to French only, but to all foreign words. When we treat the lovely flower of the anemone as a Greek word, referring to Bion's account of the change of Adonis,

" Αἷμα ῥοδὸν τέκτεῖ, τὰ δὲ δάκρυα τὴν 'Ανεμώνον,"

we call it *anemóne*, but as soon as we speak of it as a true English flower, it changes into " our own *anémone*." Some French words have been twice or oftener incorporated into English at different periods, and few facts in connection with the history of our language are more instructive than the clear and precise manner in which the latter ever reflects the features of historical changes. Such double forms of the same word, differing only in accent, show at the same time the importance of what at first sight would appear a very trifling, and often hardly perceptible, variation, and that in these cases it is the accent alone which alters the whole nature and meaning of hundreds of our words. Thus it is with *antic* and *antique, human* and *humane, essay* and *assay, custom* and *costume, urban* and *urbane, gentle* and *genteel, property* and *propriety, désert* and *desért, íncense* and *incénse, gállant* and *gallánt, aúgust* and *augúst.*

Where there is a slight change of orthography connected with a change of accent, as in some of these examples, it is an evidence of the effect which the latter seldom fails to exercise on the form of the word. The accented syllable must needs be dwelt upon longer by the voice than the others, and hence will soon be represented in writing also as a long one. Hence we find that *e. g.,* the French *conseil, montagne,* and *fontaine* have lengthened their accented first syllable, and have thus become *council* [by the side of *consul*] *mountain,* and *fountain ;* whilst in *costume* and *genteel* it was the last syllable that underwent such a change, leaving again *custom* and *gentle* (with *Gentile*) by their side. Hence, also, *crevásse,* which still continues in use in the States adjoining the lower Mississippi, has become, by the effect of an altered accent, *crevice ; orison,* which was long pronounced with a long *i,* is now more commonly *órison,* and *bourgeois* has shortened into *burgess.* In words like *gouvernement, jugement,* and *capitaine,* the transfer of the accent has led to the loss of a syllable, for they are now only *government* (with a tendency to throw even the middle *n* out), *judgment* and *captain.* Others have their full form in writing yet, but are gradually losing a part of their substance in pronunciation, as in *medicine,* where the first *i* is generally silent.

Some accents are of quite modern origin, and not unfrequently even whimsical. The word *disciple* presents an almost unique example of advancing the accent, in direct violation of the general tendency of the language. It was anciently pronounced *dísciple,* and with such emphasis as to be often written *disple.* The word *balcony* has only so recently changed from its former accentuation as *balcóny,* that the poet Rogers complained of it bitterly, saying, "*Cóntemplate* is bad enough, *bálcony* makes me sick."

CHAPTER VII.

NAMES OF PLACES.

"Verba sunt rerum notæ." — *Cic. Top.* 8.

Names are the records of things, and especially so when
we examine the names of places, and read in them their
own history. It is but too little known, or at least too
rarely thought of, that names are in no language words
arbitrarily chosen, much less the product of chance, but
that they have all a meaning and a history. That we cannot always decipher the former and retrace the latter,
ought to be but an incentive to search more carefully for
those facts which are within our reach. The difficulty itself
was acknowledged by a great master of antiquity, for Plato
says already in his Cratylus, " O, Hermogenes, son of Hip-
ponicus, there is an old proverb, that beautiful things are
somehow difficult to learn. Now the learning relating to
names happens to be no small affair." So it is in our English, but great is also the reward. Nowhere are we made
more clearly to see and more fully to feel that words are
the most vital and most imperishable of man's creations,
than in the historical names of places. We find here
above all that, "as words are mysterious in their origin, so
have they something of an awful force and intensity of life,
which gives them a perpetuity beyond the decay of races,
and the revolutions of empires." To trace local names, it
is true, has, on account of its great difficulty, led to much
absurd guesswork, and confirmed the oft-repeated accusation, that etymology was but the *" scientia ad libitum."* We
ought not to forget, however, that as astronomy arose from

6

astrology, and chemistry from alchemy, so, generally, "truth cometh out of error." Besides, guesses in themselves are interesting, and in the majority of cases the only means of sifting out of much chaff the precious grain of truth. Inquiries into the meaning of the names of places form tributary streams of history, as that excellent journal, "Notes and Queries," has now for many a year proved most successfully. They serve to point out and to establish the changes of races who have inhabited the land; they remind us of extinct customs and superstitions; they augment our interest in our own and foreign countries by revealing the deep impress of our common humanity, even on what at first appears a set of purposeless sounds. Is there not a peculiar charm and a deep-felt interest in the fact that the name of Great Britain should be at the same time the oldest, lost in the remoteness of antiquity, and the most modern, by which the greatest kingdom of the earth is known to mankind? Does it not at once bring before the mind, and very forcibly, the singular union in England of the most ancient traditions with the most vigorous manifestations of modern life and civilization? Thus it is more or less with all local names, but especially so with English names, for nowhere can the fusion of races, by which the existing population of a country has been formed, be so clearly traced through the names of persons and places as in England. The more closely we investigate them, the more accurately do we learn to assign to each race its due share in the fusion, and as this connection with the races of our forefathers is by far the most interesting feature in their history, we propose to give a brief account of the various sources from which they were derived.

If we were to believe the first schoolmaster in England, who certainly was "most strangely abroad," — Eugene Aram, — we would have to look upon Celtic as the common parent of all languages, and especially as the one great source from which English is derived; for so he tells us in the manuscript of a Dictionary on the Principle of Comparative Philology, which he has left behind him. Modern science does not support his theory, but the large number of local names in England derived from the Celtic and still retaining their ancient form, might well have misled even a better scholar. We now know that some few words of daily use, some names of rivers and hills, many a surname of high and low, form the tiny rill, the bright, silvery thread of Celtic speech, that runs through our modern English. These words are generally of no great importance in the language ; the names belong largely to small and obscure places, but still they are extremely interesting in their relation to history and in themselves, because of the difference between their ancient form and the national language now spoken in the same localities.

There is, moreover, a peculiarly melancholy interest connected with them, which arises from the fact that our Celtic fathers have left here and there a ruined temple and a few popular superstitions behind them, sad relics of their pagan worship, but scarcely any clear and decided trace of their influence on the language or the institutions of England. It has been asserted by high authority that the Arabic words which are found in English are of more direct influence on the higher interests of man than all the Celtic words we have. And yet, no idiom shows more clearly than the Celtic the marvellous vitality of languages, how tenaciously they adhere to the soil, how they die only with the extinction of their race, and often survive it for ages. The Celtic had from of old apparently less vitality, less power of resistance, than any other language of Europe. In its whole known history, in England and on the Continent, it has never made a conquest; for the trifling inroad it is said to have made from Wales into the adjoining counties can hardly be counted as such. Ever feeble, ever waning, it has yet, to this day, never been entirely extinguished, and still survives, to a certain extent, in France and in England. A great many names still linger in these countries, which have evidently taken deep root in the soil and remain there long after the race that first bestowed them has given way to another and more vigorous stock. Ancient British names are still traceable in many towns and villages, and great natural landmarks, such as rivers and mountains, have retained until now their first names, surviving themselves in perpetual youth, unchanged amid the shock of revolutions and the press of invasions. Trod under foot by the stranger, they have, by some mysterious power, imposed upon the conqueror their own language untranslated and often unchanged, so that many names are found now in use, under Queen Victoria, which were already known and in use under Queen Boadicea. The only exception, perhaps, where the Anglo-Saxons gave entirely new names, even to great natural objects, are the mountains now called *Saddleback* and *Snowden*. But these isolated instances sink into insignificance by the side of a host of true Celtic names like *Thames* and *Tamar*, *Avon* and *Severn*, *Cam* and *Isis*, *Ouse* and *Derwent*, *Wye* or *Way*, *Medlock* and *Lune*, which have preserved their primeval forms.

It is peculiarly strange that here, as elsewhere, the names of rivers, and especially of more important rivers, should be memorials of the very earliest races. They seem to survive where all other names have changed; they seem to possess an almost indestructible vitality. Cities are seen to rise and to perish; the sites of human habitations are known to us no more; but the ancient river names are handed down from generation to generation, and from race to race. Even the names of the eternal hills are less permanent than those of the ever-changing waters. Over the whole of Europe we find towns known by Roman or Teutonic names standing on the banks of streams which still retain their ancient Celtic names.

Throughout the whole of England there is hardly a river name which is not Celtic.

With all other Celtic names they most abound, of course, where the Britons remained longest in power; but they furnish, with very few exceptions, altogether the oldest topographical nomenclature of England. Hence the old couplet relating to Cornwall, how, —

> " By tre, ros, pol, lan, caer, and pen,
> You know the most of Cornish men ; "

which Celtic words signify a town, a heath, a pool, a church, a rock, and a head or promontory. We have already alluded to the strange evidence of historical justice which has enabled the ill-treated Celt to give to the empire its final and grandest name of Great Britain. Of minor names we have the ancient *Pen*, which abounds in Cornwall and Wales. Thus we find *Pen Pont*, the head of the bridge, and *Pendennis* in Cornwall, the fortified headland. *Penrose* and *Penzance* both mean the end of the valley, and *Pen Mon* is the extreme end of the island of Mona. So in England proper, there is *Pen* and *Penard* in Somerset, Upper and Lower *Pen* in Staffordshire, and numerous other names of like origin in the midland counties. As we approach the north the Gaelic form *Ben* begins to prevail, as in *Ben Morris, Benlomond, Benledi*, and many others. *Cenn* is considered by some as another Gaelic form of the same root, and appears in *Kenmore, Cantire, Kinrose* and *Kenmare* in Ireland. But the original *Pen*, as a name for mountains, is by no means confined to Great Britain: it occurs widely diffused all over Europe, wherever Celtic races once ruled. Far in the southeast we find the *Pennine* chain of Alps, the *Apennines* in the west, and Mount *Pindus* in distant Greece.

In *Pen Hill* we have a remarkable name made up of two words belonging to different languages, but meaning almost the same thing,— a pleonasm arising from the ignorance of the people at large, to whom the word *Pen* no longer conveyed a clear and definite meaning. Similar repetitions occur elsewhere. Thus in the name of *Wansbeck-water*, *wane* is probably a corruption of Celtic *avon* (river), *beck* is Norse for water, and *water* itself a pure English addition. A similar instance occurs in Calabria, where the romantic *Mongibello* shows us a compound of the Norman *mont* with the Arabic *gebel*, which has the same meaning. There also the reign of the Arabs had been too short to leave in the mind of the people a recollection of the signification of the foreign word, and thus was produced the strange hybrid.

Besides *Pen* we have the two terms *Aber* and *Inver*, both meaning *mouth*, but the one Cymric, the other Gaelic. It is one of the rare instances of a clear line of division being maintained for centuries between two kindred races, that there is not a single name with *Aber* to be found in Ireland, in the Hebrides, or on the west coast of Scotland, marking thus the outposts of the Cymric settlements with unmistakable precision. Where they were permanently established, on the eastern coast, the *Aber* begins again to show itself frequently, but above all in Cumberland, to which they gave their name and where they left their mark long after their final expulsion into Wales. This *Wales*, however, is not, as is often imagined, a Celtic, but a Saxon name, for by the new invaders the Britons were looked upon as a race of *Weales* or strangers; as to their brethren at home the Italians were also Welshmen, and the Germans call Italy to this day Welshland. Thus the Anglo-Saxons called the first Britons also *Weales*, from whence our Wales, and those that were driven to the western extremity of the island, in order to distinguish them from the former, *Cornweales*; whence their land has obtained its still existing name of Cornwall.

This distribution of *Aber* and *Inver* is easily ascertained by a glance at the map; and the peculiar position of the localities that bear this name explains their meaning. Thus *Abernethy* and *Inverary* are identical; *Aberdeen* is at the mouth of the Den, and *Abergavenny* at the place where the Usk and the Gavenny meet. Berwick was anciently *Aberwick*, and Humber in like manner *Hum Aber*.

It is surmised, and not without good reason, that the word *Ebor* in *Eboricum*, our *York*, is a lost Celtic word, corresponding to *Aber*, if not in reality identical with it, and still surviving in the sadly mutilated form of the modern name. The name of the town of *Barmouth*, in Northern Wales, was formed of two Celtic words, *Aber* and *Man*, but as Celtic was gradually forgotten, and with it the meaning of the word *Aber*, the Man was changed into Mouth, to designate still the local position of the place.

Avon is the Celtic word for river, and remains unchanged in the case of many streams. The English Avon is immortal, its namesakes abound in England and in Scotland, and even in Ireland one, at least, has been rendered famous by Spenser, as

" Sweet Awniduff, which of the Englishmen
Is cal'de Blackwater."

The Celtic *Cam*, meaning crooked, has taken to itself a Saxon mate, and thus formed *Cambridge*, while the *Camel*, a crooked river of Cornwall, has entered into the name of the little village of *Camelford*. To this ancient derivation Dayton refers, in connection with its devious course, when he states that " she doth her proper course neglect, ever since

" the British Arthur's blood
By Modred's murd'rous hand was mingled with her flood."

The old *Ched-dar*, hill-stream, survives in like manner, in the name of the river itself, and in the more familiar town, in its Cheddar cliffs, and famous Cheddar cheese.

Strath meant a valley, and has given us *Strathclyde*; and *Ath*, a ford, survives in *Athlone*, properly *Ath-luain*, the ford of St. Lua ; and in *Athleague*, the ford of rocks. *Ard*, which means high, reappears in *Ardmore* and *Ardrussan*, and the old compound, *Ard-dene*, high wood, which has been preserved entire and unchanged in the town of *Arden*, in Warwickshire, which was first so called from an ancient forest, no doubt far more familiar to Shakespeare than the corresponding name of the Ardennes, in Belgium. *Bal*, a city, appears in numerous Welsh and Irish towns. *Den*, a sheltered region, has become a thorough English word, and hardly owes any longer allegiance to its own idiom. In *Bangor*, we read quite a historic lesson. It means Great Circle, and derives its name from the fact that at the first introduction of Christianity among the Britons, circles (*gor*) were formed for the purpose of better organization. When, subsequently, one of these circles became more numerous or powerful, it was called a Great Circle, (*Ban-Gor*,) and thus soon became the common designation of a superior monastery or congregation. Most of these names have long survived the language that gave them birth. Only in Cornwall the latter lingered longer. That province had its own dialect, long carefully preserved, and last used in divine service in Landewednach, the southernmost parish of England, about the year 1680. One or two generations later, it was still currently spoken in the region west of Penzance, and the last person who is known to have used it exclusively, was a woman called Polly Denreath, who died only toward the end of last century.

One of the most thoroughly Celtic parts of England is the ancient Móna of Cæsar, now the Isle of Man, where not only the local topography speaks of the Celts, but where, down to the present century, the local idiom, called Manx, a Celtic dialect, was generally understood, and even used in the church service of many remoter districts. A Manx sermon, we are told, is now but rarely heard, and though the language is still employed in some official formulas of the Tynewald or Ancient Court, like the " *La Reine le veult*" of Parliament, the old idiom of the island is very nearly extinct.

These local names are all the more important for our knowledge of Celts and Celtic, as there are but few other traces of their language left in modern English. The *yew*, anciently spelt *eugh* and *yugh*, is commonly considered as still bearing its Celtic name. *Ewhurst*, near Basingstroke, no doubt received its name from the number of yew-trees, of great antiquity, for which it is famous; and so did probably *Ewridge*, a hamlet in the parish of Colerne, in Wiltshire. With a few such exceptions, however, the number of Celtic words in English is very small, and of little importance. This must be mainly attributed to the fact, that there existed no Celtic MSS., because the people never wrote, and the Druids, as Cæsar tells us, thought it improper to commit their doctrines to writing. All their myths and songs were handed down orally, and by far the larger part of our knowledge of British Celts is derived exclusively from tradition. When the Romans subsequently conquered the island, they viewed the Druids as the props and supports of Celtic nationality, which must be destroyed to the very root. They took their measures accordingly, and their efforts were but too successful. Still, there are some Celtic words, which have remained in English mainly because they represent purely Celtic things, as *reel, kilt, clan, pibroch*, and *plaid. Coat, cart, prank, balderdash, hap* (ly), *pert*, and *sham*, have only lately established their claim to be true Celtic words.

Next came the Romans, and threw up their earthworks and roads and walled camps, which still, though long in ruin, tell the tale of the strong hands that raised them, and to which, here and there, a Latin name still clings. They came, they conquered, and left again, exercising, after all, but little influence on our language during their occupation of the British isles. Hence, we find that among local names, also, there are but few, which are with certainty both Old Latin and modern English. We know, in fact, but three : *castrum, stratum*, and *colonia*. The first survived, perhaps, in a few cases, without any change at all; it was, however, more frequently added by the Saxons to local names, in order to designate a Roman site, and these names are very numerous. It remained *caster* in the Anglican and Danish districts, whilst in the Saxon districts it changed into *cester*. The ancient *Durobrivae*, on the river New, thus survives as *Castor ; Ancaster* proves its origin by the many Roman coins found there, and *Tadcaster, Doncaster*, the ancient Danum, and *Lancaster*, on the river Lune, have the same origin. The Latin word was at an early period changed into *Cester*, as in *Cirencester* and *Gloucester*, the ancient *Glevae Castrum*, and in *Exeter*, the great city of Isca, which changed its Roman name into *Exan-ceastre*, from the river Exe. In Oxfordshire, *Bicester* and *Alcester* appear to be Roman sites, a presumption which, in the case of *Leicester*, has been amply proved by interesting remains of ancient mansions, and fine, tessellated pavements. *Manceter*, in Warwickshire, formerly Mandressedum, has lost an *s*, and *Wroxeter* is a violent contraction of *Wreaken Ceaster*, a name derived from the neighboring *Wrekin Hill.* A still later development of the Latin name is the softened *Chester*, repeated in *Chesterholm*, the old Vindolena, and *Great Chesters*, on the site of Æsica. It has given us, in like manner, *Chichester*, founded by Cissa, the son of Ella, and *Colchester*, the first Roman city, which was made a Colonia ; which, however, may have taken its name from the river Colne. *Rochester*, on the Medway, and great *Manchester, Silchester*, whose walls, still to be traced in the northern part of Hampshire, once included a circuit of three miles, and *Winchester* — all bear the impress of their antiquity. The latter corresponds, in quite a striking manner, to the French *Bicêtre ;* as in Germany the city of *Cassel*, in Hesse, represents the ancient *Castellum*, derived from the Latin *castrum*.

The second Latin word of great importance for our local

names is *stratum*, which recalls to us at once the magnificent roads that traversed the island in many directions, built, no doubt, partly, at least, by the manual labor of our British forefathers, but laid out by Roman engineers and finished under Roman direction and control. Each of the great lines of roads, constructed chiefly, if not exclusively, for the purpose of safe military occupation and control of the country, was called a *strata* by the Romans of the declining empire, and the Anglo-Saxon invaders of England adopted the word, which closely resembled a Gothic word of their own, as *straet*, adding it subsequently to many places situated on the old line of the Roman road. A village so situated became easily *Stratton* or *Stretham*, meaning Street Town, or Street Home, and if there was a ford near by, as readily *Stratford*, so that these and similar names often mark for long distances the course of former Roman roads, even where all other traces have disappeared. Ardwick *le Street* in Yorkshire, Chester *le Street* in Durham, *Stretton*, and others, thus tell us of their proximity to a Roman road. *Portway*, a name that belongs to several places, is in like manner connected with the military language of the Romans. *Cold Harbor* is said to occur as the name of seventy places in the neighborhood of the ancient lines of road, and seems to have signified a ruined house or station, where travellers could find shelter, but nothing else, after the manner of the German Kalte Herberge. It thus became a Saxon designation of a Roman locality, while often the idioms of the succeeding races mingle in the same name. Thus it is not a little curious that in Shakespeare's birthplace, *Stratford upon Avon*, we have the three successive masters of England represented jointly: the Celt, in the ancient name of the river, the Roman, in the first part of Stratford, and the Saxon, in the second half.

Colonia, the proud title of many a provincial town throughout the vast empire, survives here and there in local names, as in the above-mentioned *Colchester*, where the ponderous masonry of the walls of the ancient city of Camalodunum shows to this day how well the Romans guarded against the recurrence of such a calamity as was sustained there by the surprised and overpowered soldiers of the Ninth Legion, on the revolt under Boadicea. In the North we have *Lincoln*, once the noble city of Lindum, situated on a lofty hill, and commanding extensive views.

Besides these three great sources of modern names, we find not unfrequently other traces of Roman greatness, as in the case of the great wall of the Emperor Hadrian, which stretched from the Solway Firth to the mouth of the Tyne. Traces of the sites and names of Roman towns abound here, beginning with those of Segedunum, now *Wallsend*, near the eastern end of the gigantic work, now far more celebrated for its mineral treasures than the ancient Segedunum, the place of which it occupies. Among other local names, derived in like manner, may be mentioned Chester on the *Wale, Walltown, Wallwick* and *Thirl-wall*, where the river passes (drills) through the wall, a locality from which, in all probability, the name of the eminent scholar was originally derived.

The familiar name of Wattling Street, still surviving in the heart of the city of London, is one of the etymological mysteries which have not yet been solved. It was the well-known name the Saxons gave to the great Roman road that ran from Dover through Canterbury and London, across the island to Chester and the coast of Wales, and remained one of the principal public thoroughfares long after the Roman rule had ceased. The fact that the Milky Way passed somewhat in the same way across the heavens, led the Anglo-Saxons to transfer the name to the stars, and even Chaucer speaks of it still thus:—

> "So then, quoth he, cast up thine eye
> Se yonder, lo, the galaxie
> The which men yclepe the Milky Way,
> For it is white and some parfay
> Ycallen it have Watlinge Strete."

It is remarkable that no name of the bridges survives, which these magnificent roads must necessarily have had over the rivers they crossed. Undoubted ruins of such bridges have been found, and the ancient names of Roman towns or stations show that they must have been situated near a bridge, but their names have invariably become Saxon. Thus the ancient Pontes on the Thames, near Windsor, survives only as *Staines* (stones), and the famous Pons Actii on the Tyne has been altogether modernized into *New Castle*.

The derivation of *Pontefract* and *Ponteland* from *pont*, is extremely doubtful, so also that of *Bridgeport* from *portus*.

Traces of Roman legions survive here and there in local names, as in *Lexdon*, Legionis Dunum, and *Caerloon*, Isca Legionum (?).

Other races followed in rapid succession, invading the island on all accessible points, holding some parts of the coast for a generation or two, and then disappearing again. Of these only one, the Frisians, have left behind them really valuable and interesting traces in local names. They came from the country between the Scheldt and the Weser, on both sides of the river Ems, but also from the islands on the eastern coast of Denmark. They were so nearly related, in race and in language, to their successors, the Anglo-Saxons, that Wilfrith, bishop of York, being accidentally thrown upon the coast of Frisia, could preach to the people he found there the gospel of Christ in his own native tongue, the Anglo-Saxon, and baptize not only the princes but many thousands of the people. The Frisians are ill-treated cousins of our English, and it is hardly creditable to the latter that they should ignore their relatives merely because they have not succeeded in maintaining their position among the great nations. They were once masters of a large portion of the German seaboard, though now they are much broken up and intermixed with other races. Of all ancient dialects none has a closer connection with Anglo-Saxon than Old Frisic ; and of all modern dialects perhaps none has such strong points of resemblance with English as New Frisic. Thus on all the Continent they alone use the word woman as we do in English. Like all other races, the Frisians also have left their traces most distinctly in those parts of Great Britain where they dwelt longest. There is, to this day, a remarkable coincidence of local names in Kent with those of Frisia, and especially of Holstein, because this country alone, of all the homes of early invaders, has not been in the hands of foreigners, and thus its language has been left comparatively undisturbed. The dialect of West Somersetshire resembles their language more than any other, and their modern words even correspond so closely to our own that some of Shakespeare's plays have been translated into Frisic, almost word for word. They still hold themselves our kinsmen, and show the likeness of the two tongues in the common saying,—

> " Good butter and good cheese
> Is good English and good Friese."

With the exception, however, of the diminutive termination *kin* which we clearly owe to them, it is extremely difficult to separate in modern English what is due to them, and what to the speech of the Angles. For these came themselves from that part of the duchy of Slesvic, which is called Frisia Minor, where the very place is shown at Gundern, from whence they embarked, when they went forth finally to take possession of their conquest in Britain (Westfalia I. p. 58). It must also be borne in mind that long before the Romans finally retired from the island a considerable element of Saxon had already obtained possession of the southeast coast, and that even Cæsar mentions already the great extent of German immigration into England. These settlements must necessarily have affected the nomenclature of these parts of the island, and it is fair to presume that many, if not most, of the Saxon names are at least as old as the time of Alfred.

More remarkable is the influence exercised on local names by the conquerors who next came to carve out for themselves a new kingdom in England. They formed part of that wonderful race of Scandinavians, whose ships made their way into every creek and inlet in the British islands and in Northern France, and who first landed as pirates, and then seized as conquerors, the sway of hapless Sicily, Normandy, and England. In the latter country they were very generally designated simply as Danes, and first appear under the indefinite name of "*Pagani, Normanni, sive Dani,*" in Asser's "Life of Alfred." Their proper name, however, was Vikings, not as is very generally believed from any assumption of the title of king, with which the name has nothing to do, but from the word *wic* or *vik*, which meant in their own language a place by the sea, and the patronymic *ing*. From the days of Egbert to those of the Conquest, the annals of England are fast bound to the history of these Norsemen and to their northern kingdoms. Even before the time of Alfred these daring invaders had settled themselves firmly down in Northumberland, and with that great monarch began the fatal system of buying off their hostility by means of yielding up to them large portions of Saxon soil. One sovereign after another followed this unfortunate and unwise policy, down to Ethelred the Unready, who brought the greatest misfortune of all upon his ill-fated kingdom. After having in vain tried to buy them off, first with ten thousand, and then with thirty thousand pounds weight of gold, he attempted in an evil hour the midnight massacre of St. Boice's day in 1002, and thus delivered England into the hands of the infuriated Danes. Then followed the days of his flight to France, and the subjugation of England by Canute the Great, and Sueno the Blessed, when the laws of the Danes, the *Dane-lag*, became paramount in England. Thus it remained, even after the land was reconquered by the Saxons, and at the time of the Conquest England was still more than half

Scandinavian. Besides the great district of Northumber-land, which reached far across the border into Scotland and the province of Anglia, the nationality reached as far south as Derby and Rugby, in the very heart of Mercia, and all over the land the Saxon language was "laced and patched" with northern words and idioms.

Their language gave, besides, a general and permanent coloring to our English, which now mainly shows in the provincial dialects of the North, and in local names along the coast and the great river-courses, reminding us thus constantly that England owes to the Danes, and not to the Saxons, its fondness for the sea and its ability to "rule the waves." The people, also, with their darker hair, smaller bones, and sterner countenance, betray their descent from a northern race. This applies especially to Northumberland and the North and West Riding of Yorkshire, with its famous old metrical romance of Havelok the Dane, from which we have derived a name that has been made once more in our day immortal by a son of England, whose heroic deeds have been recounted wherever the English tongue is spoken.

Here former Anglian or Saxon occupants had perished in war, or had been expelled from their native seats, unless they submitted to the invaders. Among the different forms of government adopted in this large Scandinavian popula-tion, were not only the usual power of kings and jarls, but also the peculiar one known as the Confederation of the Five Burghs, namely, Lincoln, Leicester, Derby, Notting-ham, and Stamford, with which York and Chester commonly acted in concert. It was here, of course, that the *Dene-laga* had its fullest sway, and the division of the whole of England into the *Dene-laga*, *Myrcna-laga*, and *West-Seaxna-laga*, which designated the several districts under Danish, Mercian, and Saxon law, became of such importance that it continued till long after the Norman Conquest. In the laws published under Henry I., (1109–1135,) " the province

of the Danes'" is especially mentioned as one of the three
parts of England. They were, however, by no means confined to these districts, for we find, *e. g.*, that the Orkneys
as well as Shetland are in name, manners, and language
true Norse. *Sodor* reminds us yet of the Danish for
Souther, and *Sutherland* itself was so called because this
northernmost county of Scotland was nevertheless to the
south of Norway.

As would naturally be expected, the Danes have left
behind them a vast number of names of places which they
bestowed, and which are still preserved. Of these the most
important and the most frequent are *by*, meaning originally
a farm, and then a village or town; *thorpe*, a hamlet;
thwaite, a piece of cleared land; *ey*, an isle, together with
a few similar endings like *holme, top, beck, ness*, &c. The
most frequent of these is *by*, which forms at least one fourth
of all the names of towns in Lincolnshire. The Danes
were fond of adding it to the names of their gods, and thus
made *Thoresby* and *Baldersby*, justifying the poet when he
sings of the Northmen, that they "gave their gods the land
they won." Other Danish names of the same kind make
it, however, plain that these were mere reminiscences of
home, and that Christianity was the religion of the people
when they gave these names. *Kirkby*-underdale and *Kirkby*-
moorside, *Kirkby* in Lonsdale and *Crossby* show that long
since the Christian bishop had driven out the heathen
priest, and the Christian Church and Cross had succeeded
to the pagan altar. Where neither God nor Church stood
sponsor, the name of the owner of the place served instead,
and thus were formed *Rollesby* (Rolf's-by), *Ormsby* (Gorm's-
by), *Grimsby*, (whose vessels, when they enter a Danish
port, can even now claim the exemptions derived from the
Danish founder,) *Haconby, Swainsby, Ingersby* and *Osgodby*.
Even persons who were not Danes supplied occasionally
their names to the place, as in *Saxby, Frankby, Scotby*, and
Flemingby, which must at least have been situated near

7

large Danish settlements, so that the final *by* could be familiar to the people around. Nor did the favorite termination disdain to enter into an alliance with common nouns; thus *Derwentby*, *Appleby*, and *Netherby*, are easily understood, and *Coningsby* is the Danish form of our English Cunningham, meaning literally King's Home. *Digby* is Dike Town, and the only southern place thus named is old Rokeby, now famous *Rugby*. The spelling is Anglicized in *Battersbee*, *Ashbee*, and *Hornsbee*. The "Rape of Bramber" in Sussex preserves to this day the memory of the old Icelandic division of lands by Hreppar, from which the Danish word *rebe* is derived, meaning to measure, from the instrument employed, a *rep* (rope), — very much as we speak in modern English of a "hide" of land, from its being measured by a thong.

Our word *By-law* owes its origin to the same Danish word *by*. The common error which regards a by-law as one of inferior importance, arises from a confusion in the mind of the people, produced by the idea which we connect with the preposition by. The Danes, on the contrary, used the word to designate the laws of byes or towns, as distinguished from the general laws of the kingdom. It may be mentioned in this connection, that a few such Danish names bear record of political changes in the state of the kingdom, by their own verbal changes. Thus the Anglo-Saxon town of Streoneshalch was rebaptized by the Danes as *Whitby*, the White Town, and Northwearthig as *Derby* or Deer Town, in analogy with Derwent and Deerhurst.

Thorpe has in like manner furnished a large number of local names in those districts which were most frequented by the Danes. *Ullesthorpe* reminds us again of a Scandinavian deity, whilst *Bassingthorpe* and *Shillingthorpe* are probably the only two out of all the names in Lincolnshire, compounded with thorpe, which are derived from family names. *Bishopthorpe* and *Nunthorpe* tell their own tale.

How very important these names may be for historical

researches, appears strikingly in the Isle of Man, where, curiously enough, the names which denote places of Christian worship are all of Norwegian origin, and thus clearly prove the late date up to which heathenism must have prevailed there.

The word *ea* for our Island, is not only Danish but also Frisic, and may, therefore, occasionally belong to the latter language. It is at least as suggestive of historic changes as *by*. Thus when the island of Mona, of classic antiquity, which had already once changed its British name into the Saxon Maenige or island of Maen, was overrun by king Egbert, it was called *Angles-ey*, the Englishman's island, and has ever since retained its name as *Anglesea*. The older Celtic name has, however, not entirely disappeared with the Saxon conquest, but survives in the *Menai* Hundred, the *Menai* Strait, and *Menai* Bridge, and in the name of the parish *Penmon*, the Head of Mon. *Sheppy* and *Mersey* are, from of old, the islands of Sheep, and of the Mere or sea. *Roodey*, the name of a meadow near Chester, now used as a race-course, was originally the island of the Holy Rood or Cross, lying as it did between the walls of the ancient town and the banks of the river Dee. *Bardsey* was called the Bards' island, as being the last retreat of Welsh bards. *Ely* has its name of eel-island from the abundance of that fish in the neighborhood, 100,000 of which were annually paid to the lord of the manor as rent; *Elmore* and *Ellesmere* are said to have the same derivation. *Jersey*, however, with its apparent identity with these names, ought to be a warning to overhasty etymologists, as it is derived from Cæsarea and has nothing to do with Dane or Saxon.

Besides these names of localities the Danes have given us also some words for mere features of landscape, as *billow*, *gar* and *elding*. *Gil* is from the old Norse, and means a small ravine; it enters into the formation of the proper names of *Gilbert* and *Gilmore*; whilst *forse*, a waterfall, has helped to form the famous name of *Wilberforce*. A hungry sand-piper is called *knot* from king Canute, as we find in Camden's "Britannia," (p. 971,) and as Drayton's "Polyolbion" confirms it in these lines.—

> " The *knot* that called was Canutus' bird of old,
> Of that great king of Danes his name that still doth hold,
> His appetite to please that far and near was sought
> For him, as some have said, from Denmark hither brought."

As Canute still lives in *Knutsford*, the great Hacon may possibly survive in Hacon's island, *Hackney*, and the children of God, Aesbjörn, in our *Osborne*. In Danish times, moreover, their own northern habit of counting not by days but by nights, from sunset to sunset, prevailed in England, an evidence of which survives in our *sénnight*, *fortnight* and *Twelfth Night*. Among less frequent evidences of this Danish influence may be mentioned occasional allusions to the national standard, the Raven, which occur in some local names. Thus in *Ravenhill*, in the North Riding of York, which claims to be the place on which the Danes planted the Reafn (raven) on landing under Inguar in 876, whilst in other places it may simply recall the worship of Odin, on whom the raven attended, as the eagle on Jupiter. Hence names like *Ravenstone, Ravensworth*, and *Ravenspur*, which has since been swallowed up by the sea, like the master of Ravenswood himself.

As the Devil plays an important part in English local names, calling bridges, caves, and causeways after his name, so the Danes also have bequeathed to us the name of at least one evil spirit, a wild and rough being who played the part of Satyr or Faun in their gloomy mythology. The Old Norse called him *Scratte*, and hence *Scratby* and *Scratta*, on the borders of Derbyshire, which is still so firmly believed to be haunted that no house is built there. The sprite survives even in America as Old *Scratch*, a polite designation for the Devil, taken from Scandinavian mythology, as Old Nick is for the same purpose borrowed from the water sprite of Old-High German.

A much more important relic, however, of Danish manners and customs which survives in our local names, is found in the word *thing*. This was derived from the name the Danes gave to the assemblies which they held, in common with all Scandinavians and Germans, in the open air, and in some place of peculiar sanctity. It survives to this day in the Scandinavian *Storthing*, the Great Court or National Assembly. It is thus that *Thingwall* in Cheshire obtained its name, from being a place of meeting of the Thing; so also are formed the names of *Dingwall*, in the north of Scotland, *Tingwall* in the Shetland Islands, and the slightly modified *Tynewald* in the Isle of Man. Some of the petty courts of this kind, moreover, seem not to have been held in the open air, like the larger assemblies, but in the house, and hence were known under the name of *Hustings*. Such a judicial tribunal met in the cities of York and Lincoln, in a few smaller places, and in London, where it has been preserved down to our own times. It has been suggested, and not without great plausibility, by the great Danish scholar, Warsaae, that traces of these *Things* may be found in the triple division of Yorkshire and Lincolnshire into Ridings. Whilst the word is generally traced back to the Saxon *thrithings* or thirdlings, it must not be overlooked that in Scandinavia the division of provinces into thirds, *tredinger*, is quite common and corresponds exactly to the North English *trithing*.

Every now and then some new Norse word makes its appearance in English writers, but few have become permanently at home there. Among the latter are some which the English soldiers in the Thirty Years' War learnt from their comrades, whilst they served under the great Swede, Gustavus Adolphus. Thus we obtained *plunder* and *life-guard*, which comes, not from the English word life, but from the Swedish *lif*, (German *leib*,) meaning body, and thus is identical with body-guard. *Furlough* also was introduced at the same time from the Swedish *forlof*, spelt sometimes *furloofe*. Among English words recently claimed by Mr. Coleridge for the Danish or Norse we find *bait, bray, dish, dock, dwell, flimsy, fling, gust, ransack, rap* and *whim*.

A great change was produced in British nomenclature, and hence, in English names generally, when the Saxons came into the land. A conquering people, who subdue an indigenous population and reduce them to serfdom, catch only with an ill-will and great reluctance, the names of objects around them. They repeat them as well as they can, and retain them more from haughty indolence than from choice. But when they form themselves new objects of the kind, when they make an inclosure or erect a fortress, they take the elements of the new name, not from the language of the conquered land but from their own. This was the case with the Anglo-Saxon idiom, for the settlers who spoke it gained possession, not of a sudden, in one day, as the Normans did afterwards, but step by step, during an obstinate conflict which lasted for centuries. Besides, they remained long without any centralization of power, and exterminated or expelled a large proportion of the British race before they themselves united under a common ruler. In this fierce conflict they rooted out the British language, as well as the British people, and drove both to the extremities of the island, there to linger and to pine away in helpless isolation. Hence it is that the Saxons have left by far the strongest impress of all on the land and its names.

The race itself shows its blood to this day in those portions of England where their settlements were most numerous; in the midland counties, in inland dales, in all remoter regions, their large frame, muscular and massive now as of old, their fair hair and blue eyes, are easily recognized. The ancient blood is heard in the broad, loud speech of these men, and they can read their title clearly in the names of all leading localities.

> " In ford, in ham, in ley, and tun
> The most of English surnames run,"

says an old ditty, and recent researches have confirmed the
fact that these syllables belong to one fourth of all local
names mentioned in Saxon charters. *Ford* is, of course,
the present word of the same meaning, but it was by so
much more common then, as fords were more numerous
than bridges. It is now mostly attached in local names to
common words, as in *Bradford*, the broad ford ; in *Herford*,
the ford fit for an army ; and in *Oxford*, not the ford for
oxen, but the ford over the river Ouse. At other times it
is added to the names of great leaders, who have made certain fords historical, as in the case of Uffa, in Suffolk, from
whom *Ufford* bears its name ; and in *Knutsford*, from Canute,
the Dane. *Bridgford*, in Nottinghamshire, combines the
new and the old *régime*. *Ham* is our modern *home*, the
word so peculiarly dear to all Saxon hearts, because it is
really the most sacred, the most intimately felt, of all the
words by which the dwelling of man is distinguished. By
its historic associations, it gains, in local names, an additional hold upon our sympathies. Thus the memory of
the first Christian Queen of England, Ebba, lives still in
Ebba's home, now *Epsom ;* nor is it quite unimportant that
in the South of England it should always have its full form,
home, whilst the sterner North has as invariably shortened
it into *ham*. St. Keyna, a saint of whom otherwise few
would know, has left his memory in *Keynsham ;* and Horsa,
the companion of Hengist, protests, by his town of *Horsham*,
against being treated as a simple banner, with a horse for
its emblem. *Farnham* still abounds in ferns ; and *Denham*
lies in a snug and cozy den ; *Langham* and *Higham*, *Shore-
ham* and *Cobham*, explain themselves, while the diminutive
hamlet applies with peculiar appropriateness to the well-
named *Waltham*, the home in the woods or the weald.
Hampden and *Hampton* have admitted an intruding *p*,
which loves to slip in between labials and dentals ; and

the State of New York boasts in its great city of the Goat's home, *Gotham*, of the father of modern humbugs, *Barnum*, whose home is not a barn, but an Eastern palace.

It is very evident, from many of the examples mentioned, that our Anglo-Saxon fathers were peculiarly fond of connecting their family names with their dwelling-places. They remind us uncomfortably of the words of the Psalmist: — "Their inward thought is, that their houses shall continue for ever, and their dwelling places to all generations; they call their lands after their own names." (Ps. xlix. 11.)   But the same habit, still so characteristic of the Saxon race at home and abroad, has prevailed in most ages and in most countries of the world.   Great kings and conquerors applied their name to countries and cities as we do to farms and villas.   Philip of Macedon gave his to *Philippi*, so famous in the history of Brutus and Cassius, and dearer to us all, because here tidings of the Gospel seem first to have been received with gladness by European listeners.   Alexander and Antiochus left behind them *Alexandria* and *Antioch*.   The Cæsars are remembered by name in *Autun*, once Augustodunum, *Saragossa* (Cæsarea Augusta), *Adrianople*, and *Constantinople*.   In the United States the name of the founder of the Republic was bestowed upon the capital city, *Washington*, and the name of the British Queen has been given to *Victoria*, in her great Australian empire.   These examples of the rulers of the world have been very generally followed by the *Dei Minores*, and England, especially, abounds with local names of this nature.   These designations are generally recognized by their termination in *-ing* or *-ling*, and are not unfrequently of venerable antiquity.   It has been ascertained that the names of places like *Billing*, *Tarring*, *Sterling*, *Twining*, and *Basing*, with their derivatives, were originally settlements of several members of the same family.   In some instances, it is well known, this connection between a place and its ancient owner has never been severed through all the intervening centuries, as in High *Legh*, in Cheshire, which has been inhabited from time immemorial by branches of the same old family. Even *Buckingham*, so long called the Home of the Beeches, is no longer allowed its poetical origin, but traced back to an ancient family of Bucks and Buckings, from whose residence the name is said to have been transferred to the surrounding shire.

The sweet name of *Leigh* is the most recent and fullest form of the Saxon *lea* or *ley*, which still survives unchanged in words familiar to every English farmer — the pasture *ley*, the clover *lea*, and even the sainfoin *lea*. Local names in *ley* abound in all Saxon regions, especially in Cheshire, where there are " as many Leighs as fleas," as the proverb bluntly says. *Offley*, near *Hitchley*, recalls the great Offa, king of Essex; *Netley*, so little creditable to farmers who . generally abhor nettles, makes amends by its beautiful abbey, and *Berkley* conjures up before the mind's eye fair fields surrounded by birches.

Of all Saxon names, however, those that denote an inclosure are by far the most numerous. This appears very natural when it is borne in mind that for more than a thousand years England has been known abroad as the land of inclosures of well-protected property. Hence the numerous words the English use to denote something hedged or walled in or inclosed, arising from the love of · privacy and the exclusiveness of the English character. Those constantly recurring terminations, *ton, ham, worth, fold, park, burgh,* all convey this one prominent notion of inclosure and protection.

Tun is, of this class, again by far the most frequent, because its meaning adapts itself most readily to a great variety of habitations. Originally derived from an Anglo-Saxon verb, *tynan*, which meant simply to close or inclose, it was soon adapted to various purposes, now helping to count, when as *ten*, it meant the closed hands, and then as *tyning*, an inclosure, giving a name to a farm which still survives in many counties. Its use became all the more general, as the Celts had already, a fact little known among us, those regular and beautiful hedgerows, which are so striking a feature in English landscapes. These the Saxons readily adopted, giving the name of *tun* to every regularly hedged in, or fenced in, settlement, from whence it came finally to designate a *town*. This is well illustrated in Wickliffe's translation of the Bible, where the invited guest excuses himself with the words, "I have bought a *town*, and I have nede to go out and se it," (St. Luke xiv. 18,) and in the reference to it: "But they dispisiden and wenten forth, oon to his *town*, another to his merchandize." (St. Matt. xxii. 5.) In both places, town is used for the modern farm, whilst the word *wyrt-tun*, (St. Luke xiii. 19,) is employed for "garden of herbs." Its latest and most peculiar meaning is found in *tunnel*, as an inclosed and covered way. *Tunbridge* is one of the few names in which its ancient form is fully preserved; generally it has been either lengthened into *town* and *toun*, as in *Hopetoun*, or shortened into *ton*, as in *Stratton, Leighton* and *Leamington*. *Acton*, in Middlesex, requires the aid of its neighborhood abounding in oaks, and of its once noble "Old Oak Common," as part of the parish is still called, to remind us in its reduced form of the original Oaktown. Almost every county, however, has its *Norton* (North), *Sutton* (South), and its *Newton*. Local names, like the last mentioned, were readily transferred to men, and thus we see in *Milton* the mill, in *Burton* and *Warburton* the burg, in *Walton* the wall, and in *Wotton* the wold, in *Staunton* the stone, and the moor in *Morton*.

Closely connected with this word, and yet different in origin and meaning, is our *dun*, and its many forms, all derived from the Anglo-Saxon *dun*, an eminence stretching out in a gentle slope, and hence applied to the sea-shore sands as *downs*. It is the same as the *dunes* of the Continent, and the first part of famous Dunquerque, the Frenchified Kirk on *the Downs*. We use it likewise in our South *Downs*, in *Landsdowne, Huntingdon,* and *Farringdon.* The Scotch prefer placing it first, hence they say *Dunbar, Dunkeld, Dunrobin* and *Dumbarton.* Its shortest form appears in *Malden* and *Hampden.*

Such are some of the more prominent local names which have come down to us directly from our Saxon fathers. There is only one other of almost equal frequency, that of *wic* or *wick,* which, however, is not found in German, but exists only in old English and Frisic, so that it ought perhaps to be more properly credited to the latter. The Icelandic and Swedish also have *wik,* and etymologists have been fond of tracing its connection with the Latin *vicus* and the Greek οἶκος. Lord Coke tells us, that it means a place on the sea-shore or on the banks of a river, and generally this definition is justified by the local position of places that bear such names. *Alnewick,* pronounced Annick, lies on the banks of the Alne, and *Berwick* is named after the Celtic Aber. *Kerwick, Warwick,* and *Sedgwick,* all remind us, by their hard final letter, of North of England speech, whilst in southern counties the softer *wich* prevails, as in *Sandwich, Greenwich, Ipswich, Droitwich* and *Harwich.*

Careful researches have led to the discovery that the inland *wicks* are generally of Saxon origin, while those on the coast are as constantly derived from stations used by the sea rovers of Scandinavia. Those inland towns, however, which end in *wich,* may have less to do with the Anglo-Saxon *wic,* than with the Norse *vik;* for they are all noted for the production of salt, which was formerly obtained by evaporating salt water in shallow pans, called *wyches.* Hence a place for making salt came very naturally to be called a wych-house, and *Nantwich* and *Dortwich,* and other places where rocksalt was found, took their names from such wych-houses, around which they were built. Hence Drayton says : —

> " The bracky fountains are those two renowned *wyches,*
> The *Nantwich* and the North" (Norwich).

The first part of *Nantwich* is still pure Celtic, and the same which forms the French names *Nantes*, *Nanteuil*, and *Nanterre*, which thus preserve, in name at least, the old family connection long after every other trace of it has disappeared.

The ancient name of *burg*, so frequent in all Germanic countries, is of course not wanting in England. It assumes there under varied circumstances varied names, changing from the full *Scarborough* to the shortened *Edinboro'*, and occasionally appearing as *bury* in *Salisbury* and other names. *Aldborough*, near York, corresponds thus, in its meaning of Old Town, to the Palæocastro and Castelvecchio, which throughout modern Greece, Asia Minor, and the islands of the Ægean Sea, are so generally applied to any ancient site. *Brough*, in Westmoreland, has retained its simple, original meaning, and the same root prevails, but slightly altered, in the more familiar *Brougham* (Burgham).

There are, finally, numerous local names derived from proper names of the Anglo-Saxons. We need not remind even the general reader of the Saxon element in *Essex*, *Wessex*, *Sussex*, and *Middlesex*, or of the many Jutish designations left in the Isle of Wight, and on the opposite coast of Hampshire. The Angle's *folk* survive clearly enough, to the North and to the South, in *Norfolk* and *Suffolk*, and became finally sufficiently powerful to impart their name to the whole land under the national denomination of *Angleland* or England. But individuals also made their name thus immortal. Thus, to mention but one example, the memory of the great and pious Ella survives in this manner in the parishes of *Ellakirk* and *Ellaburn*, in the townships of *Ella* East, *Ella* West, and *Ellerbeck*, and in the chapelry of *Ellard*, all in Yorkshire.

The Norman French, who were the next masters of England, have left us comparatively few names. This is mainly due to the fact, that they by no means conquered the Anglo-Saxon. It is true the language of the invaded

kingdom fled to the open country, to the fields and the
woods, but there it stubbornly maintained its ground, vulgar but strong, degraded but hearty, and, above all, reso-
lutely determined not to be overcome. The Norman-
French, in the mean time, led but a sickly, artificially pro-
longed life in walled towers and gloomy castles. All the
efforts of the Normans to impose their manners and their
language on the conquered race remained wholly ineffective. The mass of the people clung to their old habits and
old words with wonderful energy. Hence, although the
sixty thousand followers of the Conqueror were at once
ennobled by the simple fact of their victory at Hastings,
and large portions of the lands of England were at once
appropriated to them as the reward of past, and an incite-
ment to future, services, this change was not perceptible in
the local names of any but smaller localities. To the
latter belonged first of all the *manors*, into which the
greater part of the country was parcelled out. Not
a few of these manor-houses survive, though we can now
hardly imagine the effect of ten thousand such mansions suddenly appearing as so many marks of the conquest, impressed in effect on every separate locality
throughout the country. Along with these manors the
Normans introduced into the local nomenclature of
England numerous *castles*, which the Conqueror and his
immediate successors caused to be erected in all parts of
the land. They were needed to enable a handful of hated
foreigners to overawe a large and rebellious population ;
hence they were walled with stone and designed for residence as well as for defence. The king himself owned
many ; his barons followed the example, and thus the Earl
of Mortaine built *Montague* in Somersetshire, and another
Norman noble *Beauvoir Castle*. Frequently the Norman
castle took its name from the neighboring locality, and so
there still exist parishes called *Castle Hedingham*, *Castle
Cary*, *Castle Acre*, &c. Most of the castles erected at a

later period, and which had frequently served as mere dens of robbers, were subsequently destroyed under Henry II. In some instances, however, their names survive their existence. Thus, *Castle Baynard* and *Castle Mountfichet*, which stood upon the banks of the Thames, near the cathedral of St. Paul, have ceased to exist since the great fire of London in 1666; but *Baynard Castle* is still the name of·the city ward, in which that castle was once situated. As the Norman noble, even when willing to call his town or village by its old Saxon name, was yet not always able to lay aside altogether his early predilections, we find not unfrequently very eccentric French additions, as Adwick-*le*-Street, Bolton-*le*-Moor and Thornton-*le*-Moor, Laughten-*en*-*le*-Morthen, Poulton-*le*-Sand, Poulton-*le*-Tylde, and Buckland-*tout*-*Saints*, with many others. In very few cases only were entirely new names bestowed, as in *Battle, Beaudesert, Beaumanoir, Bellasis, Belsise,* and *Belleau.* A mixture of old and new produced often not unpleasant effects. Thus *Beaumaris,* in the isle of Anglesea, looks French, but sounds as Bómorris like fair Anglo-Saxon. The old town of *Ashby,* the bye or town of the Essi, is but slightly disguised by its foreign owner's name, *de la Zouche,* who seems to have been desirous to impress upon posterity that he was "of the genuine stock." It was also a common custom simply to add the new owner's name to the Saxon name of the place, and already Camden has Hurst *Pierpoint,* and Hurst *Monceaux,* and Tarring *Neville,* and Tarring *Peverell.* Similar names are Aston-*Turville,* Burton-*Segrave,* Burton-*Latimer,* Melton-*Mowbray,* and many others. There is in the County of Essex a place of great natural strength on a small river, which gave it anciently the name of *Depenbeck* — the deep brook. The French conquerors, finding the castle renowned in many a ballad, called it *Malpas,* and as such it became famous in the annals of later Welsh wars. Other localities have fared worse and suffered sad mutilation of their once fair names. The famous *Y Widdzug,*

Conspicuous Mountain, in Wales, was surnamed *Monthault* by the Normans, and has sunk into inglorious *Mold.* More unfortunate still was the high-sounding Leiton *Beau Desart,* the grassy ground near the beautiful wooded land, which soon appears in public documents as Leiton *Busart,* and now has ignominiously subsided into Leighton *Buzzard !*

Occasionally we find, moreover, among local names in England, not uninteresting allusions to certain striking features of the rule of the Normans. Such are the many names formed with *forest,* which did not mean wood, but indicated privileged localities, created mainly for, and enjoyed by, men of Norman blood. On the sea-coast the *Cinque Ports* are still known by their collective name, though their individual names of Sandwich, Hastings, Dover, New Romney, and Hythe, are of a much earlier date. The Church has, of course, also left a strong impress of its power under Norman rule on numerous localities. They are easily recognized by their ecclesiastical titles, as *Abbas-*Combe, *Abbotsbury, Priors* Hardwick, Leamington-*Priors, Monk-*Wearmouth, *Monkland,* Toft-*Monachorum,* and Toller-*Fratrum,* by way of antithesis to Toller-*Porcorum,* the adjoining parish. On the Tweed the stately rule of the monks of Melrose still lives in the well-known name of *Abbotsford. Bishop's* Lynn became subsequently by exchange King's Lynn, whilst Kingsbury passed into Kingsbury-*Episcopi ;* so also *Bishop-*Auckland, *Bishop-*Stoke, and with double emphasis *Bishop-Monk*ton. Nor ought we to omit, finally, the Knights-Templars, whose large possessions in England are still traceable in local names, and add to the Norman element. They are generally known by the addition of *Temple,* as at *Temple* in Cornwall, *Temple-*Bruer in Lincolnshire, *Temple-*Newsam in Yorkshire, &c. The head-quarters of these soldiers of Christ were in London, and the locality is still known as *The Temple,* now long in the possession of another profession — *Cedunt arma togæ.*

The slight impression which Norman-French has produced on English local names is easily explained by the peculiar nature of the Conquest itself. The new ruler had acquired the kingdom by a single victory; he claimed to succeed lawfully to a kinsman's crown, and promised solemnly to observe the laws granted by Edward the Confessor. The conquered nation remained on their native soil; the nationality was not broken up and destroyed, as that of the Britons had been by the Saxon conquest. Only slight and rare changes have, therefore, taken place in the local names of the island since the Norman conquest, and England is still, as she promises to remain for many a century to come, in name and in deed the champion of the Saxon race.

The case of American local names is entirely different from that of the names in Great Britain. There, succeeding races left their impress on hill and dale, city and village, river and lake, now in rude and uncouth terms, and then again in modern speech, but always intelligible, always in some way connected with the life of the people, and never wanting a historic basis. Here, on the contrary, a body of civilized men, who had already learnt to appreciate the advantage of an established nomenclature, came to a new country, and felt few wants more urgent than that of giving proper names to their future dwelling-places and the prominent objects that surrounded it. Now it seems to be beyond the power of man, under such circumstances, to invent new names. The Greeks, with all their fertility of invention and a wondrously pliant language, proved this in their colonies. In America, certainly, the poverty of imagination and the awkwardness in applying English names to new localities is perfectly astonishing, and has led to countless inconveniences and frequent ambiguities. The Canadians once had the matter made a subject of official complaint. A member of the House of Commons, we are told, who was born in the colonies, stated with much feeling, that the ill-treatment of her dependencies by the mother country had gone so far as to induce a governor of Canada to name four new townships after his wife's pet dogs, and that two of them, called Flos and Tiny, still remained there! In the United States things are infinitely worse. The census of 1860 shows an overwhelming number of Athens and Spartas, thirteen Romes, and as many Rochesters. A facetious Englishman expressed lately in an American paper his doubts whether the name of Washington appeared on the lips of Americans as frequently now as formerly, when there were more than 133 towns called after the great founder of the Republic. This might be pardoned on the score of patriotism, but what shall we say to the taste that made nineteen Browns and ten Smiths, to say nothing of the trouble this must give to postmasters! There were at the same time more than fifty places or townships called Centre, over seventy that bore the name of Liberty, and nearly one hundred and twenty named Union; but this number also may possibly hereafter be diminished.

CHAPTER VIII.

NAMES OF MEN.

" Bonum nomen, bonum omen."

THROUGHOUT the whole of antiquity, from the first records of the Bible down to the accounts of the early Greeks and Romans, there appears to have existed a mysterious connection between names and their meaning. It is well known that this correspondence is so striking in many instances as to have induced the belief of an inspired or at least unconscious expression of the future fate of persons in their first naming. Thus the fathers of the Church saw in the words, " God called the light day and the darkness he called night," an evidence of the inability of man to name these things or anything else without the aid of the Creator, and others distinctly ascribe man's power of first naming the animals to a prophetic gift. Greek authors abound with instances of the vast importance their countrymen attached to the meaning of proper names, from Æschylus's " Agamemnon," in which *Helena* is alluded to as having both Hell and Heaven in her name, to Herodotus, who mentions the encouragement which the accidental omen in the name of *Hegesistratus*, the leader of an army, gave at a critical moment. The Roman creed on this subject is boldly stated in the lines of Ausonius —

> *" Nam divinare est nomen componere, quod sit*
> *Fortunæ, morum vel necis indicium."*

Cicero tells us that the rolls of Roman levies were sure to begin with favorable names like *Victor, Felix, Faustus,* or *Secundus*, and if they could obtain a *Salvius Valerius* to stand at the head of the list, the omen was hailed with delight. An obscure *Scipio* once obtained the command in Spain merely upon the strength of his name; while the great Scipio, as Livy tells us, reproached his mutinous soldiers for having obeyed an *Atrius Umber*, whom he calls a " *dux abominandi nominis.*"

The superstition was natural enough when we remember that originally all names had a meaning suggestive of some peculiarity of the bearer, or of some remarkable incident connected with his history. Thus the oldest known to us, *Adam*, meant Red, probably indicating that man's substance was taken from the red ground; and *Moses*, drawn from the water. In like manner were all our Saxon names once significant, and no doubt they also were frequently given to children with an open conviction or a secret hope that the meaning of the word might in some mysterious manner influence the future destiny of the infant. *Alfred* is thus all-peace (Germ. *Friede*); *Egbert*, eye-bright; *Bernard*, the great bear; *Biddulph*, the slayer of wolves; *Edward*, the guardian of truth, like *Gertrude*, which has the same meaning; and *Bertha*, the bright. These simple names, however, naturally soon became so common to many owners as to fail in conveying individuality, and this led to the addition of other designations now known to us as surnames.

The oldest of these with which we are familiar, are again those of the Bible, which in their earliest form represent invariably true patronymics. We read of Caleb, the son of Jephunneh, and of Joshua, the son of Nun. For the father's name was soon substituted an ordinary word. Thus dying Rachel had called her child Benoni, the son of my sorrow, but Jacob gave him the name of Benjamin, the son of my strength. The same custom prevailed in Greek, where we read of Ἴκαρος τοῦ Δαιδάλου, and of Δαίδαλος τοῦ Εὐπάλμου. The custom survives in our Isaac *Jacobson* or Stephen *Fitzherbert.*

Such names were the rule in England before the Conquest, when as yet proper names, in the modern sense of the word, were as little known as they were even in the last century in Wales. Only about a thousand surnames began to be taken up by the most noble families in France and in England, when the language was gradually Frenchified, about the time of Edward the Confessor. The lower nobility did not follow this example before the twelfth, and citizens and husbandmen had no names of their families before the fourteenth century. It is probable, though not absolutely certain, that surnames were at first always written, "not in a direct line after the Christian name, but above it, between the lines," as Ducange says, and thus were literally "*supranomina*," or surnames.

Our English names, most of which have arisen subsequently to the Norman Conquest, have recruits among them from almost all races and languages known upon earth. The Hebrew itself is largely represented in its ancient *Ben*, which means son. It has given us *Benjamin* and the shorter *Benson, Bendigo*, and *Benari, Bendavid*, and *Benoni*. The corresponding word in Syriac, *Bar*, is of less frequent occurrence, and mostly modernized, as in *Barron*, which now stands for Baruch; and in *Bartholomew* and its descendants. This tendency to disguise old testamentary names has led to much ludicrous sham-work, both in the attempt to conceal and to discover the ancient forms. Abraham is shortened into *Braham*, and Moses into *Moseley* or *Moss*. Solomon becomes, according to fancy and taste, *Salmon* or *Sloman;* Levi is transformed into French *Lewis*, and Elias into *Ellis*. Our French neighbors are as skillful as we are in this operation. Few readers of history will recognize in the great Republican *Manuel*, the sweet name of Emmanuel, or in the famous banker *Mirès*, the simple German-Hebrew Meyers. Valiant Manasseh proves its valor on Italian battle-fields as modernized *Masséna*, and the vain composer, Herz Adam Levy, adds his initials to

his father's name, and calls himself *Halevi*. This tendency
is pleasingly illustrated in the great novelist D'Israeli, who
loves to convert every great man of our day into a descendant of the chosen people, as the Irish affirm, with great
good faith, no doubt, that all the heroes of recent date
belong to the favored isle. *Cavaignac* is, in their eyes, but
bad French for Kavanagh; *Pélissier*, of Crimean fame, belonged to the Palissers, and even *Garibaldi* was originally
Garry Baldwin.

Dutch names are but rare in English families, and more
frequently to be met with in those parts of the United
States where early Dutch settlers acquired large tracts of
land, and left numbers of *Van Renselaers*, *Van Schaiks*,
and *Van Benthuysens* behind them.

The three most numerous patronymics of Celtic origin,
now in use among the English and their descendants, are,
of course, the *O*, the *Mac*, and the *Ap*, of the three Celtic
branches settled in the United Kingdom. The Irish *O*, or
Oy, is said by their own writers to have originally meant
grandson; it is certain that the old Irish *Ui* was formerly
quite frequent, though it must now be considered extinct.
Mr. Lower, in his charming book on surnames, tells us of
an old Scotch dame, who boasted that "she had trod the
world's stage long enough to possess a hundred *Oyes*." It
cannot be denied, that the unhappy differences between the
Emerald Isle and the ruling island have frequently led to
very unjust prejudices against this *O*. Thus Pinkerton,
who argued so vehemently the inferiority of the Celtic race,
said contemptuously, " Show me a great O and I am done."
The prejudice, however, is gradually wearing away, as the
O itself is disappearing more and more; while, on the other
side, more careful researches lead constantly to the discovery of facts highly creditable to the ill-treated race.
The most interesting among them is, perhaps, Mr. Marsh's
ingenious interpretation of an expression in the Elder Pliny,
from which it would appear that the Celts had reaping ma-

chines, a fact which certainly overthrows the presumed inferiority to Roman or Anglo-Saxon civilization. Nor ought it to be overlooked, that the *O'Connels* and *O'Connors* have made their mark in English history, and the *O'Donohue* is still ever heard where Erin's wrongs are rehearsed. In France their *O* has been slyly incorporated into the name, and a son of the O'Dillons has there become famous as *Odilon* Barrot.

That the *O* itself is gradually becoming rarer, is partly due to the voluntary action of many Irishmen, but mainly to certain violent acts of the British Government, which in Ireland as in Scotland did its best to destroy the nationality of the subjugated race. The cruelest act of all was passed by the Irish Parliament in the fifth year of Edward IV., and is entitled: " An Act that the Irishmen dwelling in the counties of Dublin, Meath, Uriel, and Kildare, shall go appareled like Englishmen, wear their beards after the English manner, swear allegiance, and *take English surnames.*" Each such Irishman was to " take to him an English surname of one town, as Sutton, Chester, Trim, Skrym (sic), Cork, Kinsale ; or color, as White, Black, Brown ; or art or science, as Smith or Carpenter ; or office, as Cooke, or Butler, and that he and his issue shall use the name under pain of forfeiting of his goods yearly till the premises be done." It was then the McGowans became Smiths, and the McIntyres Carpenters.

For it need not here be explained that the Irish use frequently the cognate *Mac*, so that there was, in former days at least, much truth in the well-known lines :

> " Per Mac atque O tu veros cognoscis Hibernos,
> His duobus demptis nullus Hibernus adest."

This *Mac*, now generally looked upon as Scotch, meant also, originally, nothing more than son, or male descendant. *Macaulay* and *M' Culloch* have made the prefix renowned all over the world, whilst poor *McGowan*, once famous, has sunk into obscure Smithson, to rise once more in

America, through his munificent endowment of the Smithsonian Institute at the seat of government. *McPriest*, *McBride*, and *McQueen*, look like evidences of a sad disregard of the vows of celibacy, but fortunately their first meaning is rarely present to the mind. *McQuaker*, a name of more recent origin, has a spice of the ludicrous. *McNabb* meant, after the same manner, the son of the Abbot, and the origin of the name *McPherson* has been historically ascertained. During the reign of David I., king of Scotland, we are told, a younger son of the powerful clan of Chattan, became Abbot of Kingussie. The elder brother died afterwards childless, and the chieftainship fell to the share of the venerable father. He procured the necessary dispensation from Rome, and married the fair daughter of the Thane of Calder. A swarm of little Kingussies followed, and the good people of Inverness-shire, in their quaint, straightforward way, called them *McPhersons*, the sons of the parson.

This instance stands by no means alone, but similar vicissitudes led more than once to the same results. Thus we find that the uncommon name of *Archbishop* arose in a like manner. It originated in the person of the well-known Frenchman, Hugh de Lusignan, who was an archbishop. By the death of one of his brothers he became the heir to the family estates and the lordship, and applied to the Pope for a license to marry, in order that the noble family might not be doomed to become extinguished. The permission was granted, but coupled with the condition that his descendants should bear the surname of Archevesque and a mitre over their arms. The family is quite numerous in France, and still use the prescribed crest.

Occasionally the word *Mac* gives way to the more pretentious *Clan*, the Gaelic for offspring or descendants, and this furnishes illustrious names like that of *Clanricarde*.

The Welsh *Ap* is the Celtic word *Mâb*, meaning son. Mr. Lower tells us that its earliest form known in names

was *Vap* or *Hab*, as it is written in the days of Henry VI.
Under the seventh Henry we find it used thus: (15 Henry
VII.) "*Morgano Philip alias dicto Morgano* Vap *David* Vap
Philip." Subsequently the first letter being lost it became
simply *Ab* or *Ap*, and was, first in pedigrees, placed between
the son and the father's name, by which means it gradually
came to serve as a surname. This survives in modern
names as in Thomas *Ap Thomas*. But since the Welsh
have taken to the use of surnames, after the manner of
their English neighbors, they generally drop the *a* and connect the *b* or *p* with the father's name, thus producing regular family names. In this manner:—

Ap Evan is now Bevan, Beavin or Bevins.
Ap Henry   "   Penry, Perry, Barry or Parry.
Ap Howel   "   Powell, though the same name may have been
derived from Paul, as we find it spelt in Chau-
cer (7220) thus: "After the text of Christ, and
Powel and Jon."
Ap Hugh   "   Pugh and later Pye, as *u* in Welsh often has the
sound of *y*.
Ap Lewis   "   Blewis, Blues.
Ap Llwd (Lloyd) is now Blewitt, Blood or Floyd.

Ap Llewllen has early become *Fluellen* — a name which
actually existed in Stratford during the lifetime of Shakespeare. Ap Owen is *Bowen*, Ap Richard *Prichard*, and
probably also *Pickett*, unless the latter is derived from the
French Picoté. Ap Roderick is *Broderick* and *Brodie*,
Ap Roger, *Prodger*, Ap Ross, *Prosser*, Ap Rhys (Rees)
Pryce, *Brice*, and *Breese*, and Ap Watkin *Gwatkin*.

The exaggerated importance which Welshmen are reported to attach to their patronymics has given rise to many
an unfair jest at their expense, which the weakness of a
few of their race would hardly seem to justify. Already
in the reign of Henry VIII. a judge, to whose question
how he was called, an ancient worshipful Welshman gravely
replied: "Thomas Ap William, Ap Thomas, Ap Richard,
Ap Hoel, Ap Evan," &c., suggested to the irate owner of
the endless name the propriety of contenting himself with

the name of Mostyn, after his chief residence. A like
advice might have benefited the happy man who deduced
the name of Apollo, to his own satisfaction at least, from *Ap
Haul*, the son of the Sun. Hence the bitter lines —

> " Cheese, Adonis' own cousin-german by birth
> Ap Curds, ap Milk, ap Cow, ap Grass, ap Earth."

In the year 1299, we find there was a proud Welshman
summoned to Parliament, by the name and title of Lord
Ap Adam, though it is not stated whether he traced his
descent in an unbroken line. This baron of so ancient a
family left a son, but neither he nor any of his descendants
seem ever after to have been summoned again. Later
descendants, however, have carefully noted every step in
the pedigree of the Ap Adams, and may yet establish their
claim to a seat among their post-diluvian brethren.

There is another *a* occasionally prefixed to names which
must be carefully distinguished from its Welsh namesake.
It occurs much among the humbler classes in Cumberland
and Westmoreland; as in William *a* Bills, John *a* Toms,
Billy *a* Luke, where it seems to stand simply for the English *of*, with the father's name. In other cases it appears
to have been used, after the fashion of the Norman *de*, for
the Latin *ab*, as in John *a* Gaunt (*ab* Ghent), and in the
name of the first grand-master of the Teutonic order, whom
Fuller calls Henry *a* Walpole (Holy War. II. ch. 16). We
are all familiar with Thomas *à* Becket, Anthony *a* Wood,
and Thomas *a* Kempis, though few may be aware that the
fictitious name of John *a* Nokes and Tom *a* Styles have
been handed down to us from " Jack Noakes and Tom
Styles," who formerly served as representatives of the
profanum vulgus or our more fastidious Tom, Dick, and
Harry.

The Normans added to these three patronymics their
own *Fitz*, the much abused *filius*, (*fils*,) of the Romans.
It is somewhat strange, however, that the use of this word
is now unknown in France, and does not occur in the

ancient chronicles of that country. The name came, we believe, more probably from Flanders, and was only subsequently adopted by the Normans, who were strangely proud of names and surnames. Like the old Romans, of whom already Horace said, "*Gaudent prænomine molles auriculæ*," (Sat. II. 5–32,) whilst he satirizes one as "*Tamquam habens tria nomina*," they loved to add name to name, so that Fitzhamon's daughter could justly complain, as of a great wrong, that the natural son of Henry I., whom he gave to her as husband, had but one name. The king thereupon bestowed on him the proud name of *Fitz-Roi*, for, says she in the poetical version of the event, —

> "It were to me great shame
> To have a lord withouten his twa name."

Henry II., to recall his being born in imperial purple, called himself *Fitz-Empress;* and at one time it was the fashion among old Anglo-Saxon families to exchange their ancient *son* for the modern *fitz*. The Sveynsons thus became *Fitz-Swains*, the Hardysonnes *Fitz-Hardinges* and the ancient Ethelwulfs, the noble descendants of the Wolf, whom they called farther south Guelph, became *Fitz-Urse*. Occasionally the process was reversed. Thus King Edward I., who disliked the name of Fitz, ordered the Lord John Fitz-Robert, whose ancestors had for long generations used each his father's Christian name as a surname, to "leave the manner and to be called John of Clavering, which was the capital seat of his barony."

Even now the eldest son of the Earl of Malmesbury is by courtesy called Viscount *Fitz-Harris*. It will be seen from this, how erroneous the general impression is, that Fitz was always a sign of illegitimacy. On the contrary, it was probably not before the times of the later Norman kings that the name was at all applied to bastards. Since that time, however, this custom has been regularly kept up, as in the comparatively recent case of the children of the Duke of Clarence and Mrs. Jordan, who bear the name of *Fitz-Clarence*.

The very large number of English names which are derived from saints, have mainly come down to us from the Normans, though some, no doubt, are derived more directly through the Church. A few have been preserved in their purity; others are sadly mispronounced, as St. Leger and St. John. The majority, however, have been so fiercely mutilated that but for authentic documents showing the gradual change, their present form would scarcely suggest their original formation: —

Thus St. Paul is now		Sampole, Sample, or Semple.
St. Denis	"	Sidney.
St. Aubin	"	Tobyn or Dobbin, a degradation due, like so many others, to the desire of certain English settlers in Ireland to become thoroughly Hibernicized.
St. Clara	"	Sinclair or Sinkler.
St. Leger	"	Sillinger.
St. Pierre	"	Sampire, Sampier, and even Yampert!
St. Oly	"	Toly.
St. Ebbe	"	Tabby or Tebbs.
St. Amandus is now		Samand.
St. Edolph	"	Stydolph.
St. Barbe	"	Simbard.

Most of these changes took place as soon as the loss of Normandy cut off English noblemen from their constant intercourse with France, a time at which the Saxon element began to get the better of the Norman French, and to fashion it to its own laws of euphony. It was then, also, that other French names, not derived from saints, underwent similar mutilations, when *La Morte Mer* gave us *Mortimer*, and *Le Mort Lac* our *Mortlake* or *Mortlock*, when *Beauchamp* began to sound like Beachame, as Troissart spelt it by ear in 1400, *Belvoir* became *Beever*, *Cholmondeley*, *Chomley*, and the French-English word skirmisher, from *escrime*, appeared first as *Scrymgeour!*

Among the early Saxons, the good old rule, "One person one name," seems at first to have prevailed, as even before their arrival in England, neither the German hero Herrmann nor the Celtic Caractacus had been distinguished by any additional epithet. Very soon, however, surnames came into fashion among them also, and were probably first taken from some outward peculiarity, as the ancient *Mucel*, big, which has come down to our day as *Mitchell.* Others were taken from occupations, and form a class so overwhelmingly numerous as to require here no special explanation. It will suffice to quote the quaint words of an old writer on the subject, which cover the whole ground: "Touching such as have their surnames of occupations, as *Smith, Taylor, Turner*, and such others, it is not to be doubted but their ancestors have first gotten them by using such trades, and the children of such parents being contented to take them upon them, their after-coming posterity can hardly avoid them, and so in time cometh it rightly to be said, —

'From whence came Smith, all be he knight or squire,
But from the smith that forgeth at the fire?'

"Neither can it be disgraceful to any that now live in very worshipful estate and reputation, that their ancestors in former ages have been, by their honest trades of life, good and necessary members in the Commonwealth, seeing all gentry hath first taken issue from commonalty." Certainly a Chaucer had no cause to blush for his descent from a hosier, as Camden calls his ancestor, from its being the same as *Chausier*, the name of the man, who made the chausse or hose, which in those days served to clothe both the leg and the foot. This tendency toward the addition of a surname seems to have been occasionally exaggerated, else Lord Coke would not have felt called upon to say, "that special heed was to be taken to the name of baptism, because a man cannot have two names of baptism, as he may have divers surnames." Modern usage is apt to sin in the opposite direction.

Together with these fertile sources of surnames, patronymics also were employed by the Saxon race to obviate the difficulty. It is held by many, that the oldest of this stock is *kin*, a Flemish or Frisic termination, but probably so

closely connected with the pure Saxon *kin* as to make it
almost impossible, at this period, to decide to which source
each name is due. From the occurrence of the same words
on the continent, we may presume that especially the abbreviated names are of Frisic origin, such as *Watkin*, *Simkin*,
Jenkin, *Perkin*, and *Hodgkin*, from Walter, Simon, John,
Peter, and Roger.

The most fertile of all is, of course, the good old Anglo-
Saxon *son*, and mixed up with it, now inseparably, the
characteristic letter of the genitive, our *s*. Thus we have
obtained from

Harry :	Harrison, Harris, Herries, Hawes, and, with the aid of *kin*, Hawkins;
Andrew :	Anderson, Andrews, Henderson;
Michael :	Mixon (Mike's son) and Oldmixon;
Walter :	Watson, Watts, Watkins;
David :	Davidson, Davies, Dawson, Daws;
Hodge :	Hodgson, Hodges, Hutchins, Hutchkinson;
William :	Williamson, Williams, Wilson, Wills; Wilkin, Wilkinson, Wilkes;
Richard :	Richardson, Richards; Dixon (Dick's son), Dickens, Dickenson;
Adam :	Adamson, Adams, Atkin, Atkins, Atkinson;
Elias :	Ellyson, Ellis, Ellice, Elliot;
Anna :	Anson; — Nelly: Nelson; — Patty: Patterson.

A similar contraction led to the derivation of *Megson*
and *Mixon* from Meg (Margaret), of *Lawson* from Law
(Lawrence), *Jackson* from Jack (James), *Watson* from Wat
(Walter), *Gregson* from Gregg (Gregory), *Gibson* from
Gibb (Gilbert), and *Samson* from Sam (Samuel). Philip,
which in a similar manner appear as *Phillips*, has been
contracted into *Phipps*, a name of aristocratic import in
spite of its extreme brevity; whilst in another direction it
has expanded into *Philipot*, and thus furnishes the name of
the well-known Bishop, Dr. *Philpotts*.

Occasionally, however, the termination *son* is rather due
to Danish and Norse influence, numerous names of this
kind being distinctly traceable to Northern men, as *Swain-
son* (Sveyn-sen), *Ericson* and *Andersen*. It must, also, be

borne in mind, that the final *s* frequently does not represent the genitive of the father's name, but the plural of some ‘outward peculiarity, from which the name is derived. *Bones* thus belongs not inappropriately to a medical practitioner of some fame, and *Shanks* seems to have the power of attracting public attention in an uncommon degree, if we may judge from the number of *Shanks, Longshanks, Cruikshanks,* and *Sheepshanks* we meet with in history and in actual life. Common people, it is well known, have a strange partiality for this plural form in *s,* adding it even to the verb in the vulgar "says I." To this tendency we are probably indebted for names like *Flowers, Grapes, Crosskeys, Briggs* or *Bridges, Banks, Boys, Brothers, Cousins,* and *Children.*

A different process has led in Italian to the designation of whole families from some peculiarity of appearance or some profession, as in the case of the *Medici,* who had long ceased to be physicians, when they were still so called after an ancestor of fame, and of the charming Bello or Rosso, who left behind them families of Rossi and Belli, and little Rossini and Bellini.

The old Saxon derivation *ing* has left us unfortunately but a small variety of proper names in daily use, such as *Manning* and *Dunning;* still it is said that there are upwards of two thousand names which contain this pure Anglo-Saxon patronymic. Sometimes it becomes the termination of a local name, but generally it is placed before the part which signifies dwelling, as in *Kensington* and *Islington.* In *Harlington,* for instance, it means the town or the settlement of the Harlings, the descendants of an ancient Harl or Jarl (Earl), and it has already been mentioned that the Billings, one of the royal races, have in all probability left their name attached to *Billingsgate.*

The expressive *kin* is much more largely represented. Derived from the ancient *cyn,* it meant originally race, and hence gave us *cyning,* now *king,* the descendants of the race by eminence, as the sons of the French king were with like exclusiveness long known as *fils de France*, the children of France. Thence came also *cyned*, now *kind*, comprising all who belong to the same race or class. This is the true meaning to be given to the biblical expression of " trees bearing each after its own *kind ;* " and to Hamlet's words, " a little more than kin and less than *kind."* In its secondary meaning we find the suggestion, that what is of the same race and blood must needs feel affectionately one to another, and thus *kindness* became equivalent to benevolence, brotherly love, &c. Added to the father's name, it has, from the earliest times, served to designate the descendants, and thus we have obtained *Wilkin, Tomkin, Perkin* (Peterkin), and their derivatives *Wilkins, Wilkinson,* &c.

Of equal antiquity, but of much rarer occurrence, are the names obtained by means of the Saxon termination, *ock*, as in *Pollock*, from Paul, and contracted into *Polk*, which is often connected with the first name by an inserted *c,* as in *Wilcox* (Will-c-ock's) and *Philcox.*

It speaks well for the religious sense of the people, that names derived from the Creator are so much less frequent in English than in other languages. Nothing exists among us like the French *Dieu,* which occurs in the history of France from the oldest times down to the Crimean war, or the German *Herrgott* (Lord God), the name of a well-known author. Spain and Italy abound, besides, in *Jesus, Gesù,* and *Gesù Maria.* Our *Goddard, Godfrey,* and *Godwin* have all come to us from Germany, and hardly convey, in their present form, any suggestion of irreverence. It is questionable if our Old English *Bigod* has any thing to do with the habit of the first owner to take the name of the Lord in vain, although it is well established that the Normans obtained this name from the French on account of the frequency of their oaths, as the English are still occasionally called *Goddams,* or *Jean Gottam,* for a similar reason. The true origin of the name is probably identical with that of bigot.

We make more free with the names of Pagan gods, and

borrow especially largely from Scandinavian mythology. Wodan gives us thus not only our *Wednesdays*, but also *Wodnesbeorg*, now called *Wanborough* and *Wansborough* as a surname. Thor, from which we have *Thursday*, occurs quite frequently, as *Thoresby*, *Thursby*, and *Thurlow*. The ancient goddess Freia, to whom we owe *Friday*, reappears fully in *Fridaythorpe*, and in the surname *Frewin* it is found analogous to Godwin. The god Saster, preserved in *Saturday*, has given his name in like manner to several localities, and to *Satterthwaite*.

It is not our purpose here to enter into a full explanation of the host of English surnames. The work has been admirably done by men of great learning and research, and yet, as a matter of course, but a small proportion of the thirty or forty thousand surnames in our language have been fully explained. They are derived from almost every possible condition of personal qualities, natural objects, occupations and pursuits, localities, and from mere caprice and fancy. We will here only allude to a few peculiarities connected with certain classes of names, which deserve fuller investigation.

The Norman-French brought with them a large number of names which were either derived from places on the continent, and marked as such by having a *de* prefixed, as *De Quincey* and *De Vere;* or, not being local, they were characterized by *Le*, as *Le Marshall*, *Le Latimer*, *Le Bastard*, *Le Strange*, *Le Vert*, and *Le Fevre*, the most aristocratic form of the universal Smith which we possess. A large number of both of these classes have lost, in the course of being Anglicized, both in form and meaning so much that it is not always easy to retrace them now to their first origin. Thus,

Le Dispensier, subsequently known as *Le Spencer*, was originally the " dispensator " or steward to the household. The officer, who accompanied the Conqueror became of course a great baron in England, and at the same time the father of the illustrious house of *Spenser*, now represented by the Duke of Marlborough.

Le Gros Veneur, anciently the great huntsman to the Dukes of Normandy, founded in like manner the house of *Grosvenor*.

Le Naper, now known as *Napier*, was the officer who took charge of the Duke's "napery," his table-linen, &c. This derivation of the noble house of Napier, is certainly less romantic than that which ascribes it to the grateful monarch's eulogy of "No Peer," but, on the other hand, far more authentic. He was the officer who had charge of the Duke's table-linen, and especially of the "nappe" used in washing hands before and after meals, which it was his especial privilege to present to his Lord. Another part of his duty in the royal household was to hand over to the king's almoner the old linen of the king's table for distribution among the poor.

De la Chambre, the first Chamberlain known to England by that name, soon dwindled into *Chambers* in England, and the corresponding *Chalmers* in Scotland.

Summoner became curt *Sumner ;* the Falconer, simple *Faulkner ;* and other French names were treated still worse. The heroic Taillefer, who marched before the Conqueror's host, singing ancient war-songs, survives now only as *Telfair* with us, whilst in Italy his name has been softened into Tagliaferro, which they pronounce in the Southern States as if it were written Toliver. The fair De Champ is now ill-sounding *Shands ;* Belle Chère, taken from what Chaucer means when he says, —

"For cosynage and eke for bele cheer," (4820)

is now unpleasantly suggestive as *Belcher.* Molyneux, in humble life, is written, as well as pronounced, *Mullnicks ;* and saintly Theobald, as *Tipple !*

Many Norman names, taken from the bearer's native land or town, have suffered in a way to make us tremble for the future fate of many of our own names. The Paga-

nus became first a Painim, and then, shorter still, *Payne;*
the Genoese is now a *Janeway*, and the man from Hog-
stepe calls himself *Huckstep*, or even *Huck.*   In like manner the man from Bretagne became a *Bret* or *De Brett,*
Debrett; he from Bourgoyne, a *Burgogne* or *Burgwin;* from
Gascoyne, a *Gascogne* or *Gaskin;* from Hainault, a *Hane-*
way; from Lorraine a *Loring*, and from the East generally, a *Sterling*, through *Easterling.*   But the worst fate
befell three unlucky wights, who came over from three little
towns in Normandy.   One was called *de Ath*, and is now
Death; another, *de Ville*, and became briefly *Devil;* and a
third, from Scardeville, branched off into two lines of descendants, peaceful *Scarfields*, and terrible *Scaredevils.*

This process of changing foreign names is actively going
on in our midst, thanks to the variety of European elements
which flow into the great mass of our people.   Occasionally, the change can be clearly traced, as in local names.
Thus we find the river *de la fève*, as the French settlers
called the tributary of the Mississippi, which passes by Ga-
lena, soon changed into the more familiar name of Fever
River.   The same takes place among our Canadian neighbors, where a French population is slowly giving way to
English settlers, and the old French names undergo strange
alterations.   Thus, a place on the Ottawa, formerly called
Les Chéneaux, or The Channels, has become in pronunciation *The Snows*, and the spelling will probably soon follow
the sound.   Another settlement, which for some reason or
other was called *Les Chats*, is rapidly changing into *The*
Shaws; and a third, *Les Joaquins*, is altogether transformed
into *The Swashings.*   A hill near the Bay of Fundy, once
poetically designated by the Acadians as *Chapeau de Dieu*
(God's hat), is now called *Shepody* Mountain!   Nor are
these changes confined to French names under English
rule only, but foreign words of any kind, when used by
ignorant men, have suffered in like manner.   Thus the
Indian name of a river in New Brunswick, *Pekantediac*

(river in white birch land), is there popularly known as *Tom Kedgewick*, and numerous instances of like transformations are found in every section of the United States.

By the side of such unmerciful treatment, the most violent contractions in sound appear but trifling injuries done to a name. The noble owners of Cholmondeley, Marjoribanks, and Tollemache may, after that, well bear their curtailment into *Chumley*, *Marchbanks*, and *Talmash;* and even the descendant of the Danish monarch's cup-bearer, originally known as *Schenke*, and so called by Shakespeare and Dryden, might be reconciled to his modern appellation of *Skinker*.

Families, moreover, were not the only sufferers by such violence. The names of towns and places, of public and private houses, even though of good English origin, were in like manner ill-treated and changed beyond all power of recognition. It might be pardonable, from the truthfulness of the description, to change St. Dacre into *Sandy Acre*, a parish in Derbyshire; and the *Chartreuse*, a former Carthusian monastery of great renown, suppressed during the Reformation, into *Charter-House*. There is no harm in turning *Boulogne Mouth*, the sign of a tavern much frequented by sailors from that locality, into *Bull and Mouth;* or *La Belle Sauvage*, the name of another inn, the lease of which had been granted to Mrs. Isabella Savage, into *Bell and Savage*, although the pictorial illustrations which accompany the names are enigmatic enough to puzzle the most cunning antiquarian. The frequenters of the alehouse of the *Cat and Wheel*, will be little disposed to quarrel with the owner because he substituted those simple words for the more pretentious *Catharine on the Wheel*, of his predecessor; and the *Bag of Nails* of a well-known public-house in Pimlico is deservedly more popular now than it was under its classic name of *Bachanalia*. But we think we have a right to complain when St. Mary on the Bourne, *i. e.*, on the river, is travestied into *Marylebone*,

as Old Bourne was into *Holborne*; and when the memory
of the gentle *nuns* of St. Helena, whom our forefathers
revered as *Mincheons*, is drowned in the change from
Mincheons' Lane, which passed their ancient house, into
Mincing Lane. Few of us would recognize in the sign of
George and Cannon, a tribute to the fame of George Can-
ning; in the *Plum and Feather*, the Prince of Wales's Plume
of Feathers; in the *Bull and Gate*, the Boulogne Gate, a
trophy taken by Henry VII.; and still less is it suspected
by many admirers of that ancient play, Punch and Judy,
that the names represent nothing less than *Pontius cum
Judæis*, a relic of an ancient Mystery taken from St. Matthew xxvii. v. 19.

The derivation of the oft-quoted sign of the *Goat and
Compasses*, from the supposed Puritan inscription, " God
encompasseth us," has fortunately given way to a more
simple and more correct explanation. It has been ascertained that a company of wine-coopers in Cologne bore in
its arms a pair of compasses in allusion to their craft, and
two goats as supporters. Now it is but fair to suppose that
these arms were branded on casks containing Rhenish wine,
as is the custom to this day, and that they were, very naturally, transferred thence to the sign-board of an inn or a
vintner's house.

Compound surnames are plentiful, and often ludicrous
enough, when looked upon apart from the time and the
circumstances which first suggested their formation. *Mas-
singer* ought ever to be a Catholic, to sing masses, and
Shakelady would hardly be admitted into good society, if he
should presume to make his name good. How *Doolittles*
get along in life is a mystery; a greater one yet the pa-
tience with which men submit, generation after generation,
to be called *Gotobed, Popkiss,* or *Stabback*. Total abstinence
seems to have been in vogue from of old, if we may judge
from the fondness of all nations for the name of *Drink-
water*, which has given us Bevilacquas in Italy, and Boileaus

in France. Sir Thomas *Leatherbreeches* had weight enough to carry his uncomfortable name into the best company, and whilst *Winspear* has become a great name in Naples, *Shakespeare* is immortal. Our Puritan fathers, it is well known, indulged in a sad fancy for Scriptural names, which became unpardonable when extended to whole phrases. On Hume's roll of a Sussex jury, we find, among others, Mr. "*Fight-the-good-fight-of-Faith White*," of Ewen, and Mr. "*Kill Sin Pimple*," of Witham. The most unfortunate of all was, perhaps, the brother of the famous dealer in leather who presided over the Rump-Parliament. His pious parents had had him christened as "*If-God-had-not-died-for-thee-thou-hadst-been-damned;*" and, as no mortal man could utter the whole each time that he spoke of or to the good man, he was universally known as "Damned Barebones."

Such vagaries, however, are by no means of recent origin. The great dialectician, Diodorus, in order to show that language was the result of an arbitrary choice of words, and not a living organism, pointed in triumph to his slaves, to whom he had given new names, calling one Ὅς, and another Ἀλλάμην, in order to prove that any word might be made significative at will. There was, of course, as little connection here between such names and the owners, as there is between the poor slave and his name, chosen by caprice from those of free and famous Romans. A German author of considerable fame, imposed, in similar manner, his pseudonym of *Posgaru* for many years on the world, which admired his works and believed in his name. He was enjoying much reputation, even in England, as the successful translator of Manfred, before it was discovered that he had hidden himself behind the question "Πῶς γὰρ οὔ?"

Double names are not frequent among us. They occur mostly when Norman names have been Anglicized; we have thus *d'Anton* and *Danton; d'Aubry* and *Dobree; d'Aubeny* and *Daubeny.* Other foreign names have been translated and modified.   The French Le Blond reappears as English *Fairfax*, and mutilated *Blount* and *Bland*.   The German Schwarz is now *Black*, and now *Swart* or *Swarts ;* Klein is *Little* or *Small* or *Kline*.   A curious class of double names belong to families who bear them on the pretext of an *alias*.   Documents abound in which the same name occurs not once, which might have been accident, but continually accompanied by its shadow.   Thus, under the date of 1535 already we meet with a " Ricardus Jackson, *alias* Kenerden*.*"   In Scotland the custom prevailed for some time to use the Gaelic name with the English translation superadded.   Men called themselves McTavish *alias* Thomson, McCalmon *alias* Dorr, or Gow *alias* Smith. Hence, probably, arose the eccentric, and otherwise inexplicable custom of some families to write themselves by one name and to call themselves by another, as with the *Enroughty's*, who are called Derby.   The *alias* was gradually omitted, and the two names remained to be used for two distinct purposes.

As the oldest coats of arms in the nobility of almost all countries are the simplest, consisting generally but of a single device, so the oldest names, also, may be presumed to have been extremely simple.   " *Nomen olim apud omnes fere gentes simplex*," says an excellent authority on the subject.   Notwithstanding this prestige, however, there seems to have prevailed, from olden times, a dislike to very short and simple names.   Lucian tells us of a man called Simon, who, " having now gotten a little wealth, changed his name into Simonides, for that there were so many beggars of his kin, and set his house on fire, in which he was born, so that nobody could point at it."   A slave, Pyrrhius or Dromo, on succeeding to a rich inheritance, changed his name to Megacles, just as Diocles, upon becoming Emperor, felt called upon to lengthen his to Dioclesian.   Early French history tells us of Bruna, who became Queen of France, when it was thought proper to convey something of regal pomp in her name, and so she was called Brunehault. A somewhat similar reason induces the popes to change their name as soon as the fisherman's ring is placed upon their forefinger, a custom they have observed ever since the name of one of their number, Sergius, which meant Hog's Mouth or Groin, made it necessary for decency's sake.

Louis XI. had an even better reason for changing the name of his favorite, Olivier le Diable, which he first altered to Olivier le Mauvais, and when that also suggested the truth still too forcibly, to *Olivier le Daim*, forbidding at the same time the former names ever to be mentioned! It is quite a comfort to compare with this the change of a man as great and virtuous as Olivier was mean and wicked. Maria Theresa had an excellent minister, who suffered under the misfortune of an ill-omened name, Thunichtgut, Do-no-good; the great Empress, in acknowledgment of his virtues and his signal services, ordered it to be changed into *Thugut*, our Dogood.

In England also the change is not rare, though a happy excuse was made for short names by worthy John Cuts, an opulent citizen of London, to whose house and care the Spanish ambassador had been assigned. The proud Spaniard complained officially of the "shortness of name" of his host, which he thought disparaging to his honor. "But," says Fuller, "when he found that his hospitality had nothing monosyllabic in it, he groaned only at the utterance of the name of his host."

An entire change of name was not unknown to our forefathers. Even Camden tells us that this was quite frequently done in his time "to modify the ridiculous, lest the bearer should be vilified by them." This wish to get rid of a vulgar or ill-sounding name created, at an early period, the habit of giving Latin and Greek forms, which meet us so frequently in history. The great theologian Schwarzerd, Luther's friend, became thus familiarly known to us as *Melancthon* (Black Earth); and the great *Neander* of our day was, before he became a convert to Christianity, known as the Jew Neumann, just as a former Hosemann (man of hose) called himself *Osiander*. The English physician Key, in like manner, Latinized his name into *Caius*, suggestive of some relationship to the great Roman jurist, and perpetuated it handsomely in the College of Gonville and Caius of Cambridge, although everybody now calls it, regardless of the founder's pardonable vanity, simply Key's College. The same period gave birth to the two names of *Caius* and *Magnus*, both still famous in England and Germany.

It is less easy to account for the wish of Lord *Byron* to be called, not by his English name, but by that of the French family of *Biron*, than to appreciate the reasons which induced Napoleon, at the very beginning of his marvelous career, to denationalize his Italian name of Buonaparte, and to make it French as Bonaparte. We can understand, also, why the *O'Briens* of Ireland should be willing, in our day, to exchange their name for that of Stafford, since the famous conspiracy in the cabbage-garden has given an unenviable notoriety to the former. We all know why our friend *Smith* writes himself *Smythe* or *Smeeth*, or even *Smijthe*, and when driven to the wall has been known to change it into *Furnace*. This recalls to us Swift's sneer: "I know a citizen who adds or changes a letter in his name with every plum he acquires; he now wants only a change of a vowel to be allied to a sovereign prince (Farnese) in Italy."

The Taylors, in the same way, are apt to become *Tayleurs*, of whom Mr. Lower tells the following good story: A Mr. Tayleur, who had been thus modified, asked a farmer somewhat haughtily the name of his dog. The answer was, " Why, sir, his proper name is Jowler; but since he's a consequential kind of a puppy we calls him Jowleure." If Plato was right in recommending parents to give happy names to their children, because the minds, actions, and successes of men depended not on their genius and fate only, but also on their names, then we can certainly not blame those who desire to rid themselves of an ill-omened name. They may remember what befell the unlucky princess of Spain, whose name cost her a throne. For when the good King Philip of France had determined to seat a queen by his side, he sent ambassadors to his neighbor the King of Spain, and gave them license to choose one of his two daughters for their sovereign. They were struck with the beauty of the elder sister, and decided among themselves that both on account of her age and her charms she would be a fit bride for their master. But of a sudden their opinion was changed. They had been informed that the beauty was called *Uracca*, whilst her younger and less attractive sister's name was *Blanca*. That name of Uracca destroyed all other charms; they gave up their own preference and led the younger princess back with them to rule over France. History has more than one such answer to the oft-quoted "What's in a name?" Perhaps parents would be more guarded in naming their children if they thought how much more pleasing *Mary*, *Anna*, and *Lucy* sound, even to the uneducated ear, than barbarous *Barbara*, the little bear *Ursula*, or the heathen *Apollonia*, to say nothing of American eccentricities. It is not too much to say that men might possibly even guard their names more jealously from every stain and bad repute if they gave more attention to their meaning and their history. But as we have, unfortunately, little to say when our names are given us, we ought at least be permitted to change them when they are too atrocious and prove intolerable burdens. First names can generally be hidden under mysterious initials, but the family name asserts its rights, and may prejudice all the world against the unfortunate owner.

We cannot help sympathizing, therefore, with poor Mr. *Death* of Massachusetts, who petitioned the legislative body of his State to change his name to Dickinson, and we do so all the more because malicious Fate would have it that the member who presented his petition was a Mr. *Graves.* A Mr. *Wormwood* supported his more ambitious desire to assume the name of Washington by the argument that "no member of taste would oppose his request," and that "the intense sufferings of so many years of wormwood existence deserved the compensation of a great and glorious name."

CHAPTER IX.

HOW NOUNS ARE MADE.

" Non enim ut fungi nascuntur vocabula." — *Ihre.*

WORDS share the dualism that seems to pertain not to human nature alone, but to pervade the whole creation. As man consists of a heaven-born mind and a body, of the earth, earthy, so words also have their immortal part, an idea, and their perishing, changeable body, the outward form and its sound. The ever-active mind of man creates incessantly new ideas, and the frail and subtle material in which they are clothed and of which the body of all words consist, the air we breathe, suffers a thousand varying influences from outside. Thus words have a physical history which explains the growth of their form, as well as a mental history belonging to the idea they represent. Both go, of course, hand in hand, though but too often the clumsy, awkward body remains far behind the subtle idea, and is not unfrequently left in the end an empty shell, a mere sign and symbol. Of no class of words is this more true than of the names of objects, as they are necessarily the oldest, and, with the verb, the only essential part of speech ; these two, noun and verb, sufficing to constitute language. To name an object, by a noun, and to affirm something concerning that object, by a verb, is all that is needed to convey thought from one mind to another. The other parts of speech are mere luxuries and asses' bridges ; they grow in number and importance, as articles of luxury grow with prospering nations ; but when passion drives our thoughts at a tempest's pace, or terror chills our tongue, the master-words alone appear and are found amply sufficient.

Fortunately we have in English the rare opportunity of tracing nouns from infancy to full manhood; we can follow the varying fate of some with unfailing certainty and in unbroken line, from the cradle to the grave. Our language is just pliant enough now to form new nouns as the necessity arises, and to allow us to watch their success in life. Some come upon the stage with a dash and an air of triumph which soon gives way to utter discomfiture, and they are seen no more; others creep in stealthily; they have no famous poet or brilliant essayist for their godfather, but they do their duty so well, and are such useful hewers of wood and drawers of water that, before we are well aware of it, they are admitted to every house, and finally hold their own among the oldest and proudest of words.

If we go back, for the purpose of thus tracing the history of nouns'to the oldest forms of English, we will there find the method of forming them from the first and simplest elements. A single vowel, *a*, served in primitive times to convey the idea of eternity; it has since grown up with our people, it has spread out and is now known as *aye* (for ever and aye), still bearing its striking resemblance to the Greek ἀεί. Two vowels joined show already some progress, as in the ancient word *æ* for law; then a consonant was added to a vowel, and we have *ac*, our modern *oak*, but still surviving in many a name, as in Acland and Acton, the town and the land of oaks.

It is not to be presumed that these most simple words should have long existed alone, or even been allowed to retain their primitive forms. Some were lengthened out; in other cases, from rapidity of utterance, convenience or inattention, two were run together so as to form one word. The latter process is still continually going on. When we first hear a foreign language spoken, the most striking impression is that it seems to be all one word, and nothing is more difficult for the ear than to learn how to divide the continued sound correctly into words and syllables. Even in English, certain words now written in one were carefully separated as late as the days of Byron, and others are now in the very act of being contracted. We derive from this experience the simple law that every English noun consisting of more than one syllable has no longer its first form, but has had other words or particles added to the original root of one syllable.

We may follow, in like manner, the mental process by which nouns were formed, in our vernacular. The first use of language was always and everywhere to give names to material, sensible objects, as the five senses are after all the one great inlet of human knowledge. "*Nihil in oratione quod non prius in sensu,*" is a dogma of practical truth. Adam proceeds in this manner in the Bible narration, and every newborn infant does it afresh. Gradually, however, the mind becomes more active in itself and more deeply interested in the nature of these tangible objects, first observes qualities, color, size, life, &c., in them, then thinks of them abstractly, aside from the object which first suggested them, and finally gives them names. Last of all come abstract nouns, the names of ideas, which have neither a substance of their own nor any connection with the tangible world. Rude, barbarous races are almost altogether without this class of nouns; speculative nations admit them in burdensome numbers.

This process of forming nouns is by no means exhausted in the modern form of languages; in none perhaps is it completely ended. We judge so not from abstract reasoning but from the very evident fact that the three classes we have mentioned are, even in English, not yet absolutely defined and separated from each other. Many nouns have yet, with us also, to answer for an abstract idea, and at the same time for its special representative. *Youth* is a time of life, and a young man; *acquaintance* is a state and a person ; *witness* means as much the evidence given as the person from whom it is elicited. Every now and then we can trace the gradual transition, as in the word *fairy*, which was formerly used only like its parent *féerie*, whilst now it is also employed for what of old was called a *fay*, a middle-being of Gothic mythology, as in

> " Delightedly dwells he 'mong fays and talismans
> And spirits.''

The stock of English nouns in use at present comprehends every class and kind of words, from the simplest to the doubly compound, from the original form to one which has not a single letter left. One of the most striking peculiarities of our language in this respect is, that it can use any word, any part of speech, as a noun. Large numbers of verbs like *hate, love, fear, turn, draw*, &c., are, without any change, used as nouns also. University men have made us familiar with " the little *go*," and modern authors, especially in this country, have multiplied the number of substantives drawn from verbs with almost appalling license. Thus we read of a hard *freeze*, a fine *swim*, a long *run*, a good *haul*, a long *pull*, a big *scare*, a bold *dash*, a long *talk*, a regular *flare-up*, a *ride*, a *stroll*, and a *saunter*, and even of a soapy *feel* in Mineralogy.

The wealthy of the land show us " a splendid *turn-out*," whether it be a *Brougham*, a *Clarence*, or a swift *Hansom*. We speak familiarly of *Philippics*, as if we had a Demosthenes to thunder against Philip of Macedon, of *simony*, bequeathed to us by Simon Magus, of *dunces*, the unworthy representatives of worthy Duns Scotus, of an *orrery*, so called after their first patron, the Earl of Orrery and Cork, of *rhodomontades* after the famous hero of Ariosto, of *Spensers, Mackintoshes*, and *d'Oyleys*, showing us that proper names furnish an abundance of common nouns, to which they have been godfathers.

This is especially the case with the names of foreign countries and cities, which have added largely to the class

of nouns used to designate materials or manufactured articles. Thus the towns of Calicut (Calcutta) and Damascus
have given us *Calico* and *Damask;* from Moussul in Asia
Minor we have *Muslin* in its various forms of spelling, and
from Gaza, probably *Gauze*. *Dimity* does not come, as is
generally stated, from Damiette, but from a Greek word,
which originally meant "two threads." For Du Cange
quotes an ancient writer on the affairs of Sicily, who mentions a factory in the island which produced " Amita, Dim-
ita, and Trimita," as also " Exhimita,". made thick by an
abundance of thread, and thus explains to us the different
stuffs made up respectively of one, two, three, and many
threads. While *chintz* finds its origin in the Hindustanee
word cheent or cheet, which means a spotted stuff, *cambric*
comes from the town of Cambray, *diaper* from d'Ypres, and
arras from the city of that name. Cordova in Spain has
given us our *cordwainers*, Armenia our *ermine*, Cyprus our
copper, China our porcelain of that name, and Creta our
crayon. *Indigo* is so called as an Indian dye through Indi-
cus, as the *cherry* came from Cerasus, and the *peach* from
Persicum (malum). Pergamum in Asia gave us, indirectly,
the word *parchment*, and Phasis the name of the Phasian
bird, a *pheasant*. To Morocco we owe the best leather, to
Lazarus, through the Italian, our but half-naturalized *laza-
retto*, to Livorno the Anglicized *Leghorn* hats, and to the
Croats of the seventeenth century, through the French, our
cravats. *Baldaquin* comes to us through a series of changes
from the city of Bagdad, known to the Italians at one time
as Baldacca, and in the adjective form Baldacchino, because canopies were generally made of a costly stuff, manufactured in that Eastern city, and known even in England
as Baldach. *Varnish* is traced back either to the golden
hair of Berenice, or to the city of that name, where a peculiarly beautiful, amber-colored nitre was found. *Worsted* is
derived from no foreign country, but from the English
town of Worstead, where woolen goods were largely manu-

factured. Weapons, also, take their names from places famous for producing the first or the best of their kind, as Damascus and Toledo blades, *bayonets* from Bayonne, and *pistols* from Pistoja. *Velvet* traces its origin to the Italian word *velluto*, descriptive of the peculiar nature of its surface, and *satin* from the Latin *seta*, which subsequently formed *setinus*. The word *dollar* has an obscure beginning in the mines of the little town of Joachimsthal (Valley of St. Joachim), in the heart of Germany, as the productive silver mines of that region led to the coining of a large silver coin, which from the place was called the Joachimsthaler. The uncouth word was speedily reduced, in German, to Thaler, which is now the name of the coin throughout Germany, and then Anglicized into dollar.

With greater license still the English takes up words of any kind and class, and transforms them, at will, into nouns. Thus Shakespeare, using his language with masterly indifference, says in King Lear:—

> " Thou losest *here*, a better *where* to find,"

and elsewhere

> " Henceforth my wooing shall be expressed
> In russet *yeas* and honest kersey *noes*."

There is, however, some limit in this apparently unchecked freedom, for good taste and established usage become in language as arbitrary tyrants as fashion in society. Adjectives, for instance, cannot be promiscuously raised to the dignity of nouns. We speak of the *black*, the *white*, and the *native*, but only with regard to man ; "the *grey* I own" can only be said of a horse, and the *main* means only the ocean.

Others again are limited to a plural meaning, no other reason being perceptible than the dictates of usage. The *good* and the *bad*, the *rich* and the *poor*, the *wise* and the *learned*, the *quick* and the *dead*, all are singular forms applied only to numbers of men. In the *ancients* and the *moderns*, the *nobles* and the *commons*, the form goes with the meaning.   The last is used already by Shakespeare when he says,—

> "Let but the Commons HEAR this testament,"

where he means, of course, the commonalty, the common people and not the House of Commons.   In a still more whimsical manner we find some adjectives, when used as nouns, invariably accompanied by the possessive pronouns; thus we only speak of my or his *superior* and *inferior*, *junior*, *senior*, and *equal*.   *Better* also is most frequently thus escorted, although not, as is commonly imagined, limited to a plural meaning, for we read in Shakespeare :—

> "The Cardinal is not my *better* in the field;"

and

> "His *better* does not breathe upon the earth;"

as well as

> "If our *betters* play at that game." — *Timon*, I. 2.

Some again do not venture forth, as nouns, without the protection of an additional *one*, as when we mention our *little* ones and our *dear* ones.   Still more strictly limited is the meaning of a numerous class, each of which is but applied to a special subdivision; such are *greens*, *sweets*, *bitters*, *eatables* and *drinkables*, *movables*, *odds*, &c.   Ben Jonson already says—

> "*Contraries* are not mixed." (741.)

And in the "Spectator" we find —

> "Not to confine itself to the usual objects of *eatables* and *drinkables*."

If we regard, on the other hand, the different stages of development in which we find our present nouns, it appears at a glance that they still represent the three stages through which all nouns have to pass.   There are our simple nouns, consisting of nothing but a simple root, as *man*. *day*, or *house*.   Then we have derivatives, which boast of a root adorned by a little syllable added before or after, as

10

in *become* and *winter*. We have, lastly, compound nouns, in which two distinct roots have combined to form one word, as the two ideas they respectively represent have coalesced into one. Such are *housewife*, *wristband*, &c. Simple nouns, which have really no element but a single radical, are comparatively few in number. There are many nouns, however, which appear very innocent of any connection with particles, and which still, when examined more closely, have to acknowledge their borrowed feathers. For of all languages the English has allowed its derivative nouns to be most obscured and contracted, thanks to the general tendency of our language to shorten and curtail all apparent superfluities. Words like *sail*, *fair*, *soul*, *main*, and *stair*, seem to be quite simple until we compare them with their ancient forms, which generally still survive in modern German, and then find them to consist truly of two syllables, viz: *saegel*, *faeger*, *savol*, *magen*, and *staeger*. Very rarely the full and the contracted form continue in use, side by side, as in our *havoc* and *hawk*, if they really are the same word.

The most fertile of derivative syllables, which thus serve to make new nouns, is probably *er*, the remnant of the Anglo-Saxon noun *wer*, a man, and thence conveying the idea of male sex and male agency in addition to that expressed by the root. The word seems to have belonged alike to almost all languages; the Sanscrit *virah* reappears in the Armorican *air* as well as in the Celtic *fear*. *Ver* is universal throughout the North, and, as Rask tells us, found in Runic inscriptions and the oldest writings. The syllable *er*, therefore, occurs in all Northern European languages now, and so great and so evident is its convenience, that it holds its ground in our own idiom in spite of the strong tendency of the latter to rid itself of all grammatical characteristics. The very fact that it existed in all the idioms, Celtic, Saxon, and French, from which the English has drawn, has enabled it to adapt itself to so many different classes of words. It must not be overlooked, however, that on account of this very circumstance it has not always preserved its pure form, but yielded often to the influence of the foreign element, with which it has been combined. In Scotland we meet occasionally with the full form of the originally *wer*, as in *lawwer*. Then the *w* softened into *y* and we read already in the " Chevy Chase : " —

> " And long before high noon they had
> An hundred fat buckes slaine,
> Then having din'd, the *drovyers* went
> To rouze the deere againe."

Our own *lawyer*, *Sawyer* and *Bowyer*, bear evidence of the same change. *Reader* and *writer*, *fisher* and *fowler*, *glover* and *hatter*, *hearer*, and *seer* with its special, beautiful meaning, are old Saxon words so formed. In our day there prevails a fashion to make such nouns from verbs, and *maker*, *founder*, and *doer*, are of comparatively modern origin. *Beggar* and *sailor* are due to the same process.

The Latin *tor* having undergone a frequent change into *eur* in French, words derived from that language present a strange variety of spelling, which is due to the fact, that *er* has since been continually confounded with the French *eur* or *er*. Thus we have now *actor* and *sponsor*, but also *volunteer*, *auctioneer*, *mutineer*, *mountaineer*, *muleteer*, *buccaneer*, and *pioneer* (from the Spanish *peon*, originally *pedone*, men on foot who cleared the way before an army of knights) ; but *engineer* is from *ingénieur* (ingeniator), and *chanticleer* from *chante clair*. In other words we spell it *or*, as in *bachelor* from *bachelier*, *savior* from *sauveur* (salvator), and wrongly, in *sailor*. *Glazier*, *hosier* and *spurrier*, are Saxon words with French terminations, whilst *barrier*, *carrier*, *courtier*, and *courier*, have nothing at all to do with the Saxon *er*. *Soldier* has assumed it, we know not how, although it comes originally from *solidarius*, the man who received for his fighting-wages a *solidus* (nummus), the standard coin of the Romans. *Collier*, on the other hand, looks quite foreign, and is yet nothing but good Saxon *coal* and *wer*, coalman, just as we say milkman; it was in old writings called *colger*, and hence the contraction. In the same relation to each other stand *hostler*, from the ancient hospitaller, a word sadly reduced alike in form and in meaning, and the curious word *brother*, literally one of the same brood. It is not to be wondered at, that in the course of time, especially under Norman influence, the force and meaning of this little syllable should have often been forgotten, a circumstance which led to its occasional repetition in the same word. Thus we have *fruiter*-er, and *sorcerer* from the French *sorcier* (sortiarius). Shakespeare uses for our *poulterer* the simple form *poulter ;* and when Henry VIII. was visited by Charles V., the accounts had it : — "Item, to appoint four *pulters* to serve for the said persons of all manner of *pultry.*" The same word occurs in Stat. 2 and 3 Edward VI. ch. 25, and Henry VIII. incorporated the "Poulters' Company." *Caterer* is a mere mis-pronunciation of the word *acheter* in days when *ch* was sounded like *k*, and Rocheby was the name of modern *Rugby*. *Saunterer* only looks like a word derived in this manner, but it really comes from Sainte Terre, and was a name given to those who, after the Crusades, went to the Holy Land without any definite business, which finally became equal to going no where in particular. In other words the *er* is purely French, as in : —

barber,	from	barbier,	from	barbarius;
river,	"	rivière,	"	ripuaria;
prayer,	"	prière,	"	precaria;
danger,	"	danger,	"	damnuarium;
manner,	"	manière,	"	maneries;
matter,	"	matière,	"	materia.
gardener,	"	jardinier.		

Draper comes to us from the French for cloth, *drap*, which we preserve in *drab*, the original color of cloth. *Grocer* was at first *grosser*, from *gros*, meaning a man who sold by the gross, although curiously enough they were formerly called pep-

·perers. Statutes, prescribing that English merchants must choose one ware or merchandise and deal in no other, say, " *De ceo que les Marchaundy nomer* Grossers *engrossent totes manières des marchandises vendables.*" *Stationers* had at first nothing to do with paper or printing, but derived their name from their regular station, which distinguished them from the mass of itinerant vendors. *Butchers*, from the French *bouchers*, were long called *bochers.* " A *bocher* that selleth swyne's flesh that is anywise mesele, corrupt or in morrayne" is threatened by law (Stowe, Vol. II. page 445), and Wickliffe says, " Al thing that is seeld in the *bocheri*," (1 Cor. x. 25,) using it for our " shambles." Skelton prefers the French form and says —

> " For drede of the *Boucher's* dog
> Wold worry them like a hog.''

We ought not to forget that the name of Boucher is derived in a far more honorable way, for Saintfoix tells us in his " Historical Essays," that " anciently Le Boucher was a glorious surname given to a general after a victory in acknowledgment of the carnage which he had caused." It is a pity the fact should have been forgotten, whilst on the other hand we are more grateful for such oblivion in the case of *Fletcher*, the original form of which was in England Flesher. The origin of the name of *Tucker* is quite peculiar. It is derived from the town of Toucques in Normandy, near Abbeville, whence the manufacture of cloth was first brought to Bristol and the West of England. In Stat. 2 and 3 Philip and Mary, ch. 12, 1555, the cloth workers are called *tuckers* and the mills *tucking mills.* *Currier* comes from the French *cuir* (corium), and so it is spelt in Stowe. " Also the assize of a *coryour* is that he *cory* no manner of ledder," and Wickliffe has " This is herboride at a man symount *couriour.*" Acts x. 6. *Usher* is the Anglicized *huissier*, and among proper names we find *Jenner*, the old form of joiner, *Butler* or *Boteler* from bottler, and *Milner* from the Anglo-Saxon *miln*, our mill. Nothing but the forcible law of analogy, the power of the majority to coerce the minority in language, can explain why the Latin *charta* should be *charter* and the Spanish *daga* our *dagger*. It is a clear abuse, on the other hand, where the truly masculine *er* has been added to feminine nouns, as in *drake* from andrake, the German *enterich*, in *gander* from Gans, now goose, and in *widower*.

In many words the syllable *er* has met very strange company; and thus it can hardly feel quite at home by the side of a Latin subjunctive or the name of a Spanish city. Still, such is its fate in *Sumner* and *cordwainer*. The former is derived from *submoneas* (thou shalt summon), the order given to a certain officer to cite delinquents before an ecclesiastical court. From the first word of his order, used like the lawyer's *fi. fa.* or the statesman's *habeas corpus*, he was probably once called a *submoneas-er*, though the earliest mention in the Coventry Mysteries gives him already a more modern name —

> " Sir *Somnor* in hast wend thou thi way
> Byd Josef and his wyff be name
> At the coorte to apper this day," ·

whilst Chaucer writes it sumptuously *Sompnoure*. The other word, *cordwainer*, takes its origin from the city of Cordova and its celebrated goatskin-leather. The same Mysteries say —

> " Of ffine *Cordewan* a goodly peyre of long pikyd schon,
> Hosyn enclosyd of the most costlyous cloth of crenscyn."

As the famous material is now only manufactured in Morocco, that city in its turn gives its present name to this kind of leather. Another city gave us anciently *Roamer*, a man who makes a pilgrimage to Rome, the same as the Italian Roméo, which still survives in our verb to *roam*. A ludicrous mistake is hidden in the word *bumper*. Once upon a time the great toast of every feast was *le bon père*, meaning of course the Holy Father, and as it was generally the final toast it was considered that the glasses would be

desecrated by being ever again used. The contraction of
Bon Père into Bumper hardly requires the apology of a
protracted feast; but being accompanied by this general
smash it was as frequently designated as *la Brise Générale,*
the ancestor of that " General Breese " to whom, as to a
famous warrior, many an enthusiastic toast has been drunk
since the earlier popes.

The corresponding feminine termination of our language
is the much rarer *ster*, by some traced back to the Sanscrit
stre, meaning woman. Older authors abound in words
formed by such means. Sir John Mandeville, and others
after him, speak of *tombestres* and similar professions, which
by charter or monopoly were practised by women only.
At a later date, however, men began to invade these
branches of industry and yet to retain the female appellation for some time. After a time the masculine terms
drove the old ones out of the language, even as the men
had driven the women out of the employments. The fact
is, that in oldest times war prevailed everywhere, and
almost constantly, and claimed for the service all able-
bodied men. When peace was restored, large numbers of
the latter came home and turned out the women who had
in the mean time filled their places. Hence we have in
modern English the forms in *-estre* yet, but without the
original meaning. This transfer from the feminine to the
masculine gender is all the more easily explained, as there
are nearly a hundred words in *-ter* derived from foreign
sources, and all masculine, which naturally aided in effacing
the original grammatical force inherent to *-ster*. Thus we
find already in " Piers' Ploughman," (434) —

> " *Baksteres* and *Brewesteres*
> And *Bochiers* manye;
> Wollen *Webbesteres*
> And Weveres of lynnen,"

without any indication of sex or gender. *Songster* is one
of the few words of this class which, even in our day, may

be used for both genders, although songstress occurs not unfrequently. To hawk goods about was the privilege of men who were then called hawkers, and of women who became hawkestres, from which our *huckster*. In like manner women long monopolized the right to brew beer, and hence *tapster* is used by Chaucer as another word for hostess, and Shelton says —

" A *tappystre* like a lady bright." — I. 239.

Whether women ever drove teams by the same right is not ascertained, but in the days of Henry VIII. they were certainly still called *teamsters*. The much abused *spinster* derives her name from the legal fiction which presumes all elderly unmarried women to spin, as well as all good wives to weave, the words *weave, woof,* and *wife* all coming from the same common ancestor. It seems a delicate irony that the bar of the inn should have been transferred to the court-room, and that thus the *barrister* still bears the feminine ending under his wig and gown. In one word at least the Saxon *-stre* has joined a Danish word. This is the case in Danish *svein*, the swain of our poets, the boatswain on board ship; the feminine was made as *sweoster*, and has given us our modern *sister*.

Large numbers of such words are used as patronymics for men, because these are generally derived from male and not from female ancestors.' Thus we have *Webster* from web and weave, and *Brewster*, which still survives as a common noun in Hull, where in public court publicans are licensed and advertised by that name. Many of these names, however, are no doubt to be ascribed originally to cases in which the father did not choose to acknowledge the paternity, according to the old saying, " *Cui pater est populus non habet patrem.*" In old times it is by no means rare to find names pointing to the conduct or the character of the mother, who founded a family. Thus, William the Conqueror boastfully used his name of *Bastard*, and even in lower

ranks we meet frequently with names like *Leeman*, sometimes changed into *Lemon*, *Hussy*, *Paramore*, and *Trollope ;*
of this kind is also *Baxter*, which comes from *bakestre*, the
ks being changed into *x*, just as *cockscomb* is now *coxcomb*,
and *pokkes* are now *pox* in small-pox. *Bakestre* also is still
used in some parts of Scotland for baker. *Wooster* is from
' the happy profession of wooing, as *Songster* from singing ;
the humble work of thatching roofs has given us *Thaxter ;*
and, according to Mr. Lower's ingenious suggestion, the still
harder work imposed upon women engaging themselves
by the day, the name of *Dexter* from *daegestre*. *Foster* is
the same as *Forster* from the fuller forester, though occasionally it seems to have been derived from *foodster*, as in
foster-mother. *Dempster* comes from *deeming*, the Saxon
word for judging ; hence the judges of Jersey and the Isle
of Man are still called Deemsters, whilst unfortunately in
Scotland the legal name for the common hangman was formerly Dempster.

Occasionally we meet with regular forms, representing
both genders. Thus we have *Weaver* and *Webster*, *Fibber* —
used by Thackeray in " Vanity Fair " — and *Fibster*, and
Singer and *Sangster*. The two words *Younker* and *Young-
ster*, originally standing in the same simple relation to each
other, are now used, the first with contempt, the second for
a young man, having its meaning transferred from one sex
to the other.

The Scotch seem to have a peculiar preference for this
ending, for we find among them a large number of words
in *ster*, not used in England, such as *brandster*, *bangster*
(from bang !), *dyester*, *landmetstre*, *mawster*, *kemster*, (wool-
carder) and *cogster* (flax-breaker.) On the other hand we
notice, since the days of the " Spectator," which uses *roadster*,
a disposition to use *-ster* as an expression of contempt,
perhaps from an instinctive association with the Latin *aster*
in *poetaster*. Thus we use *punster* and *fibster*, *gamester* and
trickster.

As soon as the original meaning of *-ster* was lost to the perception of the mass of the people, there arose a tendency to add another feminine termination for the better expression of the gender. Although, therefore, Ben Jonson still uses both *seamster* and *songster* of women, we find the French termination *esse* added to the former, as *seamstress*, as early as 1699, and Thompson speaks already of a *songstress*. *Upholster*, from upholder, is an older form than either.

This same termination, *-ess*, the representative of the Latin *-ix*, and surviving in *executrix* and the rare *directrix*, is, of course, a gift of our Norman masters, but never very freely used in English, and applied to but few Saxon roots. In some words it has almost vanished in the process of being Anglicized, as in *nourrice* (nutrix), which we now call *nurse ;* in others, even in foreign words, it has been entirely dropped, as in the once generally used *cousiness.* We find it, therefore, although an important feminine ending of our language, most frequently in pure Latin and French words, as in *peeress, heiress, lioness,* and *princess,* which, by the way, is by some learned men considered the only word in English with an accent not on its legitimate syllable, the radical. The exception is made, it is said, in order to distinguish it from the plural of prince. It is not quite clear why this syllable, among so many of its kind, should have been so particularly unfortunate as not to harmonize with the Saxon character of the language. It cannot be denied, however, that older authors used it frequently and fondly in cases in which it is now utterly unknown. In Wickliffe's New Testament, we find *spousesse, cosinesse, synneress, friendess, servantess,* and *leperess.* Bishop Fisher's works abound with *saintesses.* Milton has *auditress, cateress, chantress,* and *tyranness,* whilst in Shakespeare we meet with *cloisteress,* and *fornicatress.* Sterne uses *deaness,* and Addison *detractress.* All these forms are unknown to our generation. A curious word of this class

is derived from the French *lavandière*, a washer-woman,
which first gave us *lavender;* from this a new feminine
was made, in a contracted form, belonging to the days when
v and *u* were written alike, the modern *laundress*, and from
this again an artificial masculine *launderer*. From *negro*
and *votary* we obtain, with a loss of the final vowel, our
negress and *votaress*, and some will have it that *lad* made,
once upon a time, a feminine *laddless*, which subsequently
shrunk into simple *lass*.

A still rarer termination of this class is the ancient *-in*,
commonly traced back to the Northern *cvin*, a woman, from
which our forefathers' *quean*, and our own *queen*. It was
formerly much employed, and is in German still used, as the
principal feminine ending ; in modern English it is, however, scarcely ever met with. The Scotch *carlin*, the feminine of carl or churl, is well known through Burns' —

> " There were five *carlins* in the South,
> That fell upon a scheme,
> To send a lad to London town,
> To bring them tidings heme."

The *gyre-carline* of Scotland is nothing less than the mother
of witches, of whom the Ballad of Glenfinlas sings :

> " Thair dwelt ane grit *Gyre-Carline* in auld Betokio-bour,
> That livit upoun Christiane mene's flesche."

It is curious that this strange-sounding word is, in reality,
the same word as our familiar *girl*, the latter being nothing
more than the contracted form of ceorl-in, ciri-in, *i. e.*, a little churl, and originally in old English, of both genders. We
are unfortunately more familiar with a *vixen*, a name which
hides to the superficial observer its connection with *fox*, from
which it is derived by a change of vowel as *filly* is from *foal*.
Maiden is suspected of being formed by the aid of *-in*, as
maegd was in Anglo-Saxon used for both genders. The
adopted titles of Margravine, Palsgravine, and Landgravine
have, however, nothing to do with the derivative syllable ;
they are merely English imitations of the German *Gräfinn*,

whilst heroine, which is often counted in under this head, is pure Greek (ἡρωίνη.)

Intimately connected with these means of forming nouns expressive of sex, are similar ones employed to convey the idea of diminution. Unfortunately, the English language possesses but few of these, which deprives it of the many charms and endearing expressions, for which German and especially the Sclavonic languages are so famous. It seems as if the Englishman's national reluctance to let the world become aware of his inward feelings — that apparent coldness which makes him in the eyes of foreigners the most reserved and least amiable of men — had affected the language also. Those that we possess are chiefly of Saxon origin; there are a few we owe to the French, but not one has survived from the Latin.

The oldest of all, if we may judge from its absence in Scotch, and most probably of Frisian origin, is the word *kin*, closely connected, though probably not identical with the ancient *cyn*, our modern kith and *kin*. The transition from that which is not the thing itself but only akin to it, to the idea of diminution, is common to all languages. Thus we use *lambkin* and *catkin*. *Mannikin* is both the lay figure of the artist and the dwarf in actual life, which latter meaning agrees with the Latin *homunciones* and the Italian name *Piccoluomini*, famous in history. *Minnikin* does not, like the former, come from *man*, but from the same root with Latin *minus* and German *minder*, which reappears in *minx* and *minion*. As we have obtained *Alaric* from the German Ulrich, so we take their word Gurke and make from it our diminutive *gerkin*. *Jerkin*, on the other hand, is from the Frisian-Dutch *jurk*, a frock or short jacket; *bumpkin*, from the Dutch *boom*, our beam, means not only a man of small sense, whom, substituting block for boom, we often call a blockhead, as the Spaniards call him a *juez de palo*, but is even now used in its original signification, as a naval term to designate a bar of timber. *Pipkin* is a little pipe, such as contains madeira, and hence often, in the descending scale, nothing more than a little pot; *finikin* comes in like manner from fine, and *firkin* from four, meaning the fourth of a barrel, as *farthing* meant originally the fourth of a penny. *Monikin* is a malformation from monkey, as *Malkin* is from Mary, whilst the diminutive of Lady in the sense of the Holy Virgin, has given rise to the oath " By our *Lakin.*" In like manner arose " God's *bodykin* " or " Ods *bodikins*," and even " Ods *pitykins*," as we find it in Shakespeare. The only important case in which *kin* has been added to a foreign word is *napkin*, which contains the old Frisian word tacked on to the French *la nappe*, from the Latin *mappa*, which originally meant any cloth, and hence is still the common name for handkerchief in Scotland, in the same manner in which it is used by Shakespeare in " Othello."

Perhaps quite as old is our *y*, which appears in Scotch exclusively as *ie*, and hence has produced so great and unpleasant variety in the spelling of proper names. We have *Betty* and *Betsey*, *Billy* and *Barney*, (from Bernard,) *Molly* and *Fanny*, *Sally* and *Sadie*, the latter already pure Scotch. The Scotch have many more, and add to *Willie*, *Davie*, *Peggie*, *Tibbie* and *Annie*, also *lassie* and *laddie*, *daddie* and *wifie*, even *sternie*, *coatie*, and *housie*. Occasionally they love, we know not why, to insert an *uk* before the *ie*, and thus Whitelaw among his Scotch songs has one called " The wee *wifukie ;* " and Burns uses *droppukie*, *housukie*, and *Bessukie*. Their number in English is much smaller, and some seem to have been lost more recently, for in Shakespeare we find repeatedly *county*, for little count (Romeo, III. 5, and alias), which is now no longer in use. *Ninny* and *noddy* occurs but rarely now in comparison with older authors ; *dummy* is from thumb, and *granny* from grandame, formed like beldame. *Baby* is of course from babe, but its meaning is modern ; for formerly it meant pictures in books as in these lines : —

> " We gaze but on *babies* and the cover,
> The gaudy and flowered edges painted over,
> And never further for our lesson look
> Within the volume of this various book."
>> *Sylvester Dubartas*, ed. London 1621, p. 285.

Another diminutive, which is much more popular on the northern side of the Tweed than south of it, is *-ock*, which occurs but in a few words in English. Thus we have *hill-ock* and *bullock ; paddock* means both a small enclosure and a toad, derived in the latter case from the Dutch *padde*, the Anglo-Saxon *pada*. *Hummock* is from hump, *buttock* from the French *bout*, the end, and *ruddock* represents the little *red* one, viz : Robin Red-breast. In Scotland, on the contrary, *ock* is still used as a common diminutive, and occurs in *wifock* and *mannock*, in *laddock* and *lassock*, in *willock* and *mannock*. It is not improbable that this same termination, so fertile in names like *Davock, Jamock, Bessock*, and *Jeanock*, may have softened into the above-mentioned *uk* under the influence of the affectionate *-ie*, which has been added. Names in *-ock* are more common ; Baldwin has given us *Baldock*, Paul, as has been mentioned before, *Pollock*, and finally Polk ; Matthew is often *Mattock*. Care must be had, however, not to attribute all similar names to the same origin, for *Bowcock*, which resembles the class very much, is the Anglicized Beau Coq of the Normans ; *Havelok* is a pure Danish name, and *Gavelok* is derived from the Anglo-Saxon *gaveluce*, as in the verse —

> " *Gavelukes* also thike flowe
> So gnattes, ichich avowe."
>> *Arthour and Merlin*, p. 338.

Our Anglo-Saxon fathers have bequeathed us their favorite *-ing*, which originally expressed descent, as in the great name of their Aethelings, the sons of the noble, and only secondarily acquired the power of diminution. The Germans also have their kindred *-ung*, and the connection of this syllable with our *young* is not to be doubted. In ancient times it often meant simply *son*, and already, in

824, we read of "*Eadberht Eadgaring*" (son of Edgar), and "*Aethelheah Esning*" (son of Esna). Hence it served often to form patronymics, many of which survive, like *Manning, Dunning, Browning, Whiting, Waring*, and *Dering*. *Herring* is derived from *here*, the German *Heer*, a host, and expressive of the number and order in which the enormous shoals of herrings arrive in English waters. It is curious to notice how this syllable has been used in the names of English coins. *Penning*, from which our *penny*, may be from *pan*, the form of the ancient Bractata, which resembled hollow pans, and were first known in the lands of Ina, king of Wessex, in 688. Four of them made a *shilling*, literally a small shield or coat of arms, exactly as the French *écu* comes from the Latin *scutum*, still called in Italian a *scudo*. The full word penning has been shortened into *penny*, and when Edward I. reduced its weight to a standard of thirty-two grains of wheat, taken from the middle of the ear, it gave its name to a *pennyweight*. Before that king each coin had been marked with a cross so as to admit of its being easily and justly cut into four quarters, and hence the *farthing* or fourth-ing of those days. To avoid fraud, however, Edward I. caused round pieces to be coined, especially for half and quarter pennies. Hence the sad degradation of the farthing, which is now the fourth part of a penny, whilst formerly it was the same fraction of a gold noble. Stat. 9 Henry V. and Stat. 2, ch. 7 (1421), say, "that the king do to be ordained good and just weight of the noble, the half noble and the *farthing* of noble." This was done, therefore, precisely in the same manner in which the Roman quadrans was made to express the fourth part of an *as*.

It must not be overlooked, however, that every now and then the termination *-ing* appears also as a mere augmentative, after the manner in which *-ain* was added to French words. For as mount made *mountain*, and fount, *fountain*, so even makes *evening*, and morn, *morning*.

The diminutive *-ling* has also passed through two distinct

stages, expressing at first simply small size, and then passing into the idea of subjection. Words of the former kind
are our *seedling, nurseling, stripling,* and *bantling,* from the
band in which children were wont to be swathed. In animals it indicates with smallness also youth, as in *yearling,
nestling, starling, groundling,* (of fishes,) *duckling, suckling,
firstling,* and even of trees, *sapling,* because it has as yet no
heart but only sap. Added to dear, it has become, as *darling,*
an expression of tenderness. The transition from smallness
of body to smallness of soul was here also easy enough; thus
we have *lordling, underling,* and *worldling.* It is somewhat
strange that *hireling,* which means, just like soldatus, one
who serves for coin and not for his love of master or country, should now be used with contempt, and *soldier* with
honor. *Fondling* has undergone a change for the better.
In former days it meant a weak man, a fool, and in this
sense it is used in Burton's "Anatomy," III. 3. "We have
many such *fondlings,* that are their wives' pack-horses and
slaves." The origin of *sterling* is curious. It was anciently
written *Estarling,* and meant an Easterling, *i. e.,* a man from
the East, especially from the Hanse towns. These thrifty
merchants introduced their pure coinage under Richard I.,
and their coins being called after them, this gave rise to
the expression "*sterling* money." Subsequently the name
was transferred to everything in its way excellent and genuine. The loss of some of these words in *-ling,* used by our
ancestors, is much to be regretted; our *vagabond* is but a
poor substitute for the ancient *scatterling,* and *lunatic* is
much less suggestive than *moonling.*

Besides these diminutives of the German part of our
language we have a few that belong to the French addition.
Among these the most fertile is *-et,* the older form of the
more frequent *-ette,* which occurs quite early, as in —

"Et se li prend de rire envie
Si sagement et si belvie,
Qu' elle descrive deux fossettes
D'ambedeux parts de ses *joettes.*"
Roman de la Rose.

Being French, and apparently not very easily joined to true Saxon words, this syllable has either come into use only lately, or in other cases lost its first meaning. Instead of the modern *pocket*, we find that Henry VIII. put a certain "book into his *poke*," and even as late as Shakespeare, melancholy Jaques, in the "Forest of Arden,"

> " Drew a dial from his *poke*
> And looking on it with lacklustre eye.
> Says very wisely: It is ten o'clock."

Now, the diminutive meaning is entirely lost, for we speak of vast and capacious pockets; so it is in *packet, pullet, trumpet,* and *lancet* from the French words *poule, trompe,* and *lance.* In *russet* from *roux,* and in *owlet,* its diminutive power is still felt; in *martinet* and *islet* at least in a moderate degree. *Varlet* is the French *valet,* which again is the substitute for the older *vaslet,* the diminutive of *vassallus.* In the single word *linnet* it has not only been added to an old Saxon word, but actually superseded the original Saxon diminutive, for before the invasion the word was *linece.*

Our diminutive *-el* is mainly derived from the old French ending *-el,* which was subsequently very generally softened into *-eau.* Our English words having been imported from the French at the time that *-el* was still in use, they have preserved the old form with us, whilst they have changed on the Continent. Thus we say —

mackerel,	the old French	maqueral,	for the modern	maquereau;
pommel,	"	pommel,	"	pommeau;
castle,	"	chatel,	"	château;
prunel,	"	prunel,	"	pruneau.

As a true diminutive it is rare in English. ·We have from cock, *cocker,* and then *cockerel.* Thus in Shakespeare: —

Ariel. Which of he or Adrian, for a good wager, first begins to crow?
Seb. The old cock.
Ant. The *cockrel.*   *Tempest,* II. 1.

From pike we make *pickerel,* and from sour, *sorrel.* *Satchel* stands alone. *Bottle* and *corbeil* in fortifications come to us from the original German forms *butte* and *korb*, through the pseudo-Latin diminutives *boticula* and *corbiculus* and the French *bouteille* and *corbeille*. Here also care must be had not to confound with these true diminutives words terminating now in *-el* and now in *-le*, which are derived from Latin plurals, such as : —

battle, from the French bataille, and the Latin batualia;
entrail,	"	entraille,	"	entralia;
marvel,	"	merveille,	"	mirabilia.

Occasionally an additional *r* is inserted before this *-el*, as in mong*r*el from the Saxon *meng*, which we have in *mingle* and in *among ;* in *wastrel* from waste, a common, and provincially at least, and in Scotland, *hangrel*, a small hook, and *gangrel*, a vagabond. Unlike the before mentioned *-et*, this syllable combines quite readily with certain old Saxon words, as *shovel, bundle* from bound, *needle*, and *muzzle* from mouth. In *flail, fowl,* and *nail* we see a mere contraction from the original *flaegel, faegel* and *naegl*, still preserved in the German words *Flegel, Vogel* and *Nagel.* The termination *-let*, which is occasionally used for similar purposes, seems to be nothing else but a combination of *-el* and *-et*, such as appears in the French words *oiselet* and *œillet*, and the Italian *manteletto*, although there is some possibility that it might have originated in the Anglo-Saxon *lyt*, our little. The old French *hamel* (now hameau) became thus *hamlet ;* other examples are *crosslet*, and *sparklet* and *streamlet*, in which the foreign termination is added to Saxon words.

Diminutive endings of classic origin are found in *ferrule* and *chapel*, and compound in *ret-ic-ule*, a very small net, *particle, article,* and *curricle*, while *vermicelli* and *violoncello* have come to us through the Italian.

Other diminutive endings of this kind are still so far foreign to our ear and mind that we generally use them without a clear perception of their original meaning. When we speak of a *libel*, we rarely think of a small book, nor do words like *vehicle* and *obstacle* convey to us the idea of diminution. *Globule* and *animalcule*, being scientific terms, are more likely to be correctly appreciated; *circle* suggests but a certain figure. Still less are Greek forms of this kind likely to be understood, and few ever think of a little king or a small star, when they use the words *basilisk* and *asterisk*; nor is *obelisk* apt to be more suggestive.

A third class of such terminations are employed to form augmentatives, and these also are generally of foreign origin. Thus from the French we take *mountain* from mount, and *fountain* from fount, *standard* and *bombard*; from the Italian *trombone* from trump, *balloon* from ball; and from the Spanish *barracoon*. But there is no lack of old Saxon syllables, also, which were once used for this purpose, and can easily be traced back to the word from which they descend. Thus we find that *wold*, the German *wald*, enters into common nouns and proper names alike, soon losing, of course, its delicate initial. *Threshold* meant at first the thresh wold or wooden floor for threshing, which was almost always just before the house door, where it may still be found in many countries. *Arnold* and *Reynold* are made in like manner. Then we have *wolf*, which, however, already of old seems to have lost both its first letter and its original meaning. It now survives only in the mis-spelt names of *Bardolph, Marcolph, Randolph*, and *Adolphus* with their inorganic *ph*. The more frequent termination *-ard* owes its origin probably to more than one ancestor, as its many different meanings can only be explained by ascribing them to as many different sources. In some words it is no doubt the same as *hard*, and was derived from the German through the French. This meaning we find in *Bernard, Reynard*, and *Leonard*, from the bear, the fox, and the lion; in *wizard*, whom Dr. Angus facetiously describes as too wise by half, from *wise*, in *staggard*, a stag of four years old, in *buzzard*, and in *haggard*, which probably meant looking hard as a hag. *Pollard* is not yet explained, though it may come from Paul, and *dastard* is not made of hard, but is only the Anglo-Saxon participle of the verb *dastrian*, once spelt *dastrod*, although it has also been explained as a contraction of *dared* and *hard*. In other words it may be traced back to our Saxon word *ward*. This explanation would give a sad blow to some of our finest names, as *Hayward* would become but the ward or guardian of hay, *Stoddard* of the stud, *Durward*, of the door, *Kennard* of the kennel, and *Steward* of the (house) stead or the stow. *Goddard*, the goat-ward, is still at the North pronounced Gotherd, and there means a fool, which adds some probability to the surmise that *coward* might, in like manner, be simply the cow-ward. Poor *Hogarth* would become a hog-ward, and sink still lower, as Swift says of him in his clever satire of the Legion-Club : —

> "How I want thee, hum'rous *Hogart*,
> Thou, I hear, a pleasant rogue art."

Of *Bastard* nothing more is definitely known than the association with base birth, as in " King Lear," I. 2 —

> " Why bastard ? Wherefore base ? "

In Old English the termination was frequently used in a depreciatory and contemptuous sense; thus we find *blinkard* in the Homilies, *dizzard* in Burton's " Anatomy," *dullard* in Shakespeare's " King Lear," *puggard* and *stinkard*. The majority of these words are no longer in use; we still have, however, *braggard* and *luggard*, *drunkard* and *dotard*, *dullard* and *niggard*, which Shakespeare in " Julius Cæsar " even uses as a verb, saying of the night, —

> " Which we will *niggard* with a little rest."

To derive *Gifford* from " give hard " is probably too violent a presumption, but in changing *sweethard*, as it originally was, into *sweetheart*, no great harm seems to have been done to the meaning.

French augmentatives can hardly be said to be in use in modern English. The only genuine syllable of the kind is perhaps our *-ee*, which comes down to us indirectly from the Latin *-atus*. The latter survives, oddly enough, in some of our words as *-ate*, even where the same words have been essentially modified in French. We still have *state, curate,* and *advocate*, from the corresponding Latin words, where our neighbors have now *état, curé,* and *avocat.* True French terms of this kind are *feoffee, referee, legatee, jubilee,* and *debauchee*, retaining, as may be seen, the French accent on the last syllable, with the exception only of *cómmittee* and *ópogee.* *Levee* may come from the Latin *levata*, though it is more commonly derived from the French verb *lever ;* *grandee* owes its last syllable simply to an effort to imitate the Spanish pronunciation of *grande.* The *-ee* is not unfrequently exchanged for a simple *y*, which represents, however, the same Latin *-atus*, as in *country* from *contrata, duchy* from *ducatus, journey* from *diurnata, clergy* from *clericatus, beauty* from *bellitatem, city* from *civitatem*, and *bounty* from *bonitatem.* The same *y*, it must not be overlooked, stands quite as often for the Romance termination *-ie*, as in *cavalry* and *infantry, fancy* and *courtesy.* A curious feature of this class of words is, that they often assume an *r* before the *y*, for no other ostensible reason than from the force of analogy with some word like *artillery*, aided by a few Saxon words with a natural *r* as *buttery.* Such are, *e. g.,* of Saxon words: *fishery, shrubbery, rookery* and *midwifery*, and of Norman-French words: *peasantry, bravery* and *debauchery.*

Besides these three important classes of nouns, which convey, in addition to the meaning of the radical part, the ideas of descent, diminution and augmentation, followed by nicer shades of signification, we find in English certain derivative nouns, in which the addition does not produce so clear a change of meaning. This is especially the case when the suffixes, though once full and significant nouns, are no longer used as such, and now appear only as parts of other words. The Anglo-Saxon had thus from the verb *deman* to deem, a noun *dom*, which survives in the modern *doom.* We speak still of " dooms-day " as the day of final judgment, and of a " Domes-day Book," not only of William the Conqueror, but such as King Alfred already made, when he divided his kingdom into hundreds and tithings. The *Dooms* of Ethelbert are dear to us as first recognizing Christianity and establishing the Church in Kent. The *doom* of a traitor is still expressive enough; but nouns made up by the aid of this word do not profit any longer by its special meaning. *Freedom* and *thraldom* are old Saxon words; *birthdom* is now rare; *kingdom* and *earldom* are as recent as *Christendom* and the less frequent *Heathendom.* It will be seen that in most cases *dom* is added to the names of persons or their peculiar qualities, and thus serves, very generally, to designate the corresponding state, office, or dignity. In *wisdom* and *freedom* it has been added to adjectives; *dukedom* and *martyrdom* are the offspring of a Saxon and a Norman word united.

The curious suffix *-ric*, derived from the Saxon *rican*, to rule, bears on its face clear marks of its ancient connection with the Greek and Latin root *reg*, which we preserve in words like *regal* or *direct.* It conveys the idea of rule and of its extent, the former *e. g.* in *Aelfric*, he who rules with elf-like wisdom, the latter in Surrey, formerly *Southric*, the kingdom south of the river Thames. The two words *hood* and *head*, which we meet with so frequently in English, are alike from the old verb *haebban*, our to have, and express vaguely the state or condition of things. Its corresponding form in German is *heit*, and in Bavaria and other parts of Germany, the common people speak even in our day of the good or bad " Heit," or state of affairs. In an ancient metrical version of the Athanasian Creed, copied in Hickes' " Thesaurus," (I. 233,) we find " Ne the *hodes* auht mengande," *i. e.*, neither aught confounding the persons. *Priesthood, monkhood, knighthood,* and *childhood* occur very early in our language; *womanhood, neighborhood,* and *widowhood* from nouns, and *likelihood, falsehood,* and *hardihood* are comparatively modern. Here also hybrids occur frequently, as in *falsehood* and *squirehood*. *Head* seems to have been employed when the full meaning of the original noun was to be conveyed, for which reason we probably say *Godhead* and *manhood*. *Maidenhead* does not belong to this class, as it refers literally to a head of the Virgin Mary, an image which stood in that locality, as Bagford writes to Hearne. Our modern *-ship* comes from the Saxon verb *scaepan*, to shape, and expresses but rarely any thing more than the general idea of form and fashion. It is, however, interesting to notice how, in the only two instances in which the original spelling of the word is preserved, the precise meaning also survives. They are *landscape*, occasionally written *landship*, and *foolscap*, which does not mean, as is generally believed and even conveyed in the water-mark, a fool's cap, but the shape of folio, a large leaf. The term is as old as Queen Anne, whose statute laid a tax on "Genoa *foolscap* fine and second," in order to protect the home-manufacture of paper against the competition of Italian importations. From the same root in folium (the Greek φύλλον) we derive our "foliage," the leaves of a tree, and at least the idea, when we speak of turning over the leaves of a book. Of modern forms *worship* deserves an explanation. It consists of worth and shape, meaning "to hold worthy," in esteem and in honor, and is thus used in the much-abused words of our beautiful marriage-service, "and with my body thee worship." As this part of our church service has been handed down, almost unaltered, from the days of our Anglo-Saxon forefathers, this word, like a few others, has here retained its original, simple meaning, and has of course nothing to do with the now current signification of worshiping God or idols.

Shire comes in like manner from a Saxon verb *scearan*, which has given us a perfect host of descendants, all of which retain just enough resemblance to their ancestor to be able to prove their legitimacy, and yet have branched off into widely different meanings. The fundamental idea is, of course, to cut off; hence the severed part is a *share* in business, or a *shore*, when separated by sea; the instruments for doing the act are *shears* and nautically *sheers*. What has been cut off is called a (pot)*sherd*, or with a transposed *r* a *shred ;* the mutilated remains are *short* or *shorn ;* when healed there remains a *scar*, as the cut-off piece of stuff may be either a *shirt* or a *skirt.* Ignorance is *sheer*, when it is cut off from all knowledge, and even *sharp* may belong to the family, if we accept the analogy of words formed like *help* and *damp*. The use of *-shire* is now almost exclusively limited to its meaning of cut-off portions of land and their local designation. In *sheriff* it has been sadly mutilated; the word contains *shire* and *reeve*, its superior officer.

The syllable *-ness*, for which no legitimate pedigree has yet been found, is therefore suspected of being an impostor, consisting at first simply of double *s*, as in Greek and Latin words we find them added to certain roots, *e. g.*, in θάλασσα and μέλισσα, or mantissa and vibrissa. At a very early period of our history, however, an inorganic *n* seems to have crept in before the final letters, and thus it appears now in all Germanic languages. We have *business, greatness, kindness,* and *likeness, righteousness,* and *lonesomeness ;* and in dialects even *drouthiesundieness*, fondness for drink. None of these words can be used as verbs except one, and that is *witness.* The number of nouns formed in the same manner in foreign languages, and thence imported into English, is of course very great, but of comparatively less importance for modern English, as they did not grow on English soil, but were brought in ready made. Such are words like domin*ion*, hom*age*, sanctim*ony*, somnolency, verd*ure*, mot*ion*, and just*ice*, from the Latin, and eu*logy*, pan*orama*, hero*ism*, tri*ad*, and analys*is* from the Greek.

Nouns have thus been shown to be either simple or derivative ; it remains but to say a few words with regard to compound nouns. Properly speaking, no real composition has taken place unless actually two distinct words have been joined in such a manner as to produce by their joint meaning a third and new signification. In the modern form of languages, however, great license is allowed in this respect, and we find now all nouns called compound which contain two distinct roots. Our Anglo-Saxon fathers were particularly fond of this class of nouns, as the nation was then still in the state of a child which cannot and will not form abstract ideas, and consequently does not use abstract nouns. As any such idea became clearer to all and entered into daily conversation, it became, of course, necessary to find an adequate expression for it, and this was at first done by compound nouns. The Saxons were as poor mariners as the majority of Germans are to this day, thanks to their remoteness from the sea, and hence a ship was to them a *mere-hus*, or sea-house. *Gast-gedale*, the parting of the ghost with the body, was their nearest approach to our abstract " death ; " *æsc-plegan*, the playing of ash (spears), suggested to their mind, familiar with the sight, the idea of " battle ; " and the Saviour was to them touchingly, as he is to the Germans to this day, the *Healand*, the " Healing " one. Unfortunately, but few of these beautiful and suggestive words survive ; and the loss is great, for they spoke clearly and appealingly to the minds of the mass, and almost always suggested a poetical idea to the educated. The language, even, seems to have parted with them most reluctantly, for we find that Old English long adhered to them, even when they were already sorely beset by our modern Latin terms. In those days writers would often use both the ancient and the new-fashioned term, as it suited the occasion. Thus Wickliffe has agenrysynge (again rising) and resurrection, out-taken and except. Gascoigne uses now star-conner and then astrologer ; Golding hesitates between half-god and demigod.

The few that survive are not always as well preserved as *witchcraft, handicraft*, and *bookcraft* are, to which in Holland's

" Plutarch," *leechcraft* is still regularly added. Many are so completely disguised that they have to be carefully studied and built up again, like the scattered skeleton of some ancient fossil. In *gospel* we may thankfully recognize the "good spell" or good message of our pious fathers, the εὐαγγελία of the Greek. *Acorn* barely suggests the oak-corn or fruit, for corn was in those days used for all kinds of fruit, and not, as now, only for the particular staple of each country, by which abuse corn now means maize in America, wheat in England, rye in Germany, and barley in Sweden. *Acton* in Middlesex is, in like manner, the oak-town. Two compounds of the Saxon word *eage*, our eye, are interesting. Our ancestors spoke of a *wind-eage*, or wind's eye, which we call obscurely "window," and most poetically named our unmeaning "daisy," as Chaucer explains in his charming verse:—

> " That well by reason men callé it maie
> The *daisie* or else the cie of the daie."

Emerson says very truly of these and similar words : "Is it not true that language is fossil poetry, made up of images and tropes, which now in their secondary use have long ceased to remind us of their poetic origin ?" One of the worst-treated words of this kind is *deal*, which has continually dwindled down into simple *dle*, so as to be mixed up with the diminutive *-el*. Where our fathers spoke respectfully of a *lyt-deal*, a *mid-deal*, and a *bound-deal*, we say curtly little, middle, and bundle, as was done already in 1559, when a political pamphlet had it thus : " Papistrie being an heresie or rather a *Bondle* made up of an infinite number of heresies." The same fate has befallen *dale ;* Kent-*dale*, the place where the river Kent passes through a fair dale, is now Kendal, and Sleddel was originally *Slate-dale*. The oft-misquoted *bridal* has an entirely different origin : it is a mere reminiscence of the nuptial feast associated with the specially strong bride-ale.

Originally the language possessed a guard against such

corruption in the rule that compound words invariably threw the accent on the first part of the compound. Thus a *bláckbird* is easily distinguished from a black bird, and *Néwport* from a new pórt; but the rule suffered, at an early period, certain exceptions in the case of words in which such an accent would have made distinct pronunciation impossible, as in *monks-hood* and *well-head.* Hence the distinction became less marked and the integrity of compound nouns was destroyed by the effect of this apparently insignificant agent.

Large numbers of genuine compound nouns, again, have lost their compound meaning, and now represent, at least to the unlearned, but one single idea. These are mostly of foreign origin, which accounts for their dimmed signification. To this class belong *vinegar*, from the French vin aigre, sour wine; *verdict*, from the Latin vere dictum; *bachelor*, from the French bas chevalier, a lower knight, — although many maintain the connection with the barbarously formed baccalaureus; *biscuit*, from the Latin bis coctus, twice baked, the Italian biscotta; and *mildew*, from the spurious German Mehlthau.

The abuse of compound nouns is fortunately checked in English by the terse and concise nature of the language. The incontinence of other idioms in this respect is, however, well known. The Sanscrit is reported to own at least one word of a hundred and fifty-two syllables. Aristophanes made one, for a special purpose, of seventy-seven. The Germans are proverbially fond of formidable words, which suit, admirably, sentences of forty and fifty lines. Occasionally even our English indulges in a monstrous combination, as when Miss Burney speaks of " the-sudden-at-the-moment-though-from-lingering-illness-often-previously-expected-death of Mr. Burney's wife."

CHAPTER X.

"How many numbers is in Nouns? Two!" — *Merry Wives*, Act IV. Sc. 1.

OUR Saxon forefathers had as artistic a fabric of cases
for their nouns as Greek grammarian ever recorded.   It
is true they did not quite rival the accuracy and exuberance
with which the Algonquin languages of the North American continent form almost as many cases as there can be
relations of nouns in a sentence.   Still, grammarians differ
even now as to their number, and rarely admit less than six.
It seems unfortunate enough that we should in our day,
and in a living, actively thriving idiom, yet resort to the
quaint artifices and the almost childish language of the
ancients who knew no grammar.   It was all very well
for Peripatetics and Stoics to imagine an upright or direct
line which was to represent the name of the object, the
nominative, whilst a number of declining lines, (*declension*,) approaching a horizontal line, were to represent the
different relations of one noun to another.'   These falls,
or direct and oblique *cases*, suggest nothing to our mind,
and yet we are set to work, at an age when we are least
likely to appreciate the illustration, to learn all the tech·
nical terms of early Latin grammarians, and to burden our
memory with numerous useless names.   Surely, it is high
time that a grammar should be written, English not only
in name but in spirit.

The more refined than useful system of Anglo-Saxon
declensions shared the fate of all similar contrivances.   It
was tacitly and almost universally abandoned, as soon as

another language came in contact with our own.   As the Latin inflections were disregarded by the barbarous conquerors of Rome, so our Saxon declensions were summarily thrown overboard by our Norman masters.   Their ear, familiar only with their own Norman sounds, was not easily enabled to catch the nice distinction of vowels and final consonants which constituted the many inflections of Saxon nouns.   They were the masters, moreover, and with rude insolence used only so much of their subjects' speech as was absolutely necessary to make them fulfill their commands.   It was the vassal's duty to guess and supply what might be wanting ; they cared not to take the trouble of learning the numerous varieties of form, which to them had neither life nor interest.   Thus the language returned to an almost primitive simplicity, and for the delicate, hardly perceptible modifications of sound at the end of nouns which characterized the highly developed Saxon, were substituted clear, unmistakable words, which were placed before them, prepositions and pronouns.

This violence done the language of our fathers was all the more effective as it came at a time when, as the history of all idioms teaches us, certain terminations are losing their precise characteristic sound, and with it their first clear meaning.   They become then apparently, if not really, useless and inconvenient to the mass of the people. What was before the case with the foreigner, is now equally so with the native : they convey no longer any precise idea to his mind, and awaken no interest in his heart. He first neglects, and, after a while, abandons them altogether.   "Besides," says an unknown author quoted by Dean Trench, "in all languages there is a constant tendency to relieve themselves of that precision which chooses a fresh symbol for every shade of meaning, to lessen the amount of nice distinctions, and to detect, as it were, a royal road to the interchange of opinion."   As the child learns to walk without leading-strings or other assistance,

so men begin to find that they can commune with each
other without supplying all the little helps to understanding which were first required. A hint now supplies an
idea, and more is conveyed by suggestion than by fully expressed words. The people gradually find out that they
can do as well without a large number of grammatical
forms, and therefore cease to employ them. This process
is aided and accelerated by the general tendency to greater
uniformity. It is true that this leads often to a loss of
what had real, intrinsic value, and the greater simplicity,
the higher mechanical perfection of an idiom, is but a
sorry compensation for the means of setting forth in a
more lively, if not a clearer manner, the inner feeling of
the speaker. Still, such is the fate of languages, in which,
as in all mechanical contrivances, every thing tends toward
the one great end, — to obtain the greatest result by the
smallest means.

Our English, has, therefore, preserved but very few
traces of the large number of inflections which trouble us
so much in reading the sadly incorrect remnants of Anglo-
Saxon literature. The dative plural, for instance, which
always terminated in *m*, survives only in *him* (originally
heom), *them*, *whom*, *seldom*, and *whilom*, which latter word,
however, is now but rarely used, except for some special
purpose. Spenser says yet in all sincerity and good earnest, —

> "Where now the studious lawyers have their bowers
> There *whilom* wont the Templar knights abide."

But when we meet with it in a connection like the following : —

> "In Northern clime a valorous knight
> Did *whilom* kill his bear in fight
> And wound a fiddler," — *Hudibras.*

we feel that the waggish poet has adopted it merely for its
antiquated sound, and to render the verse more ludicrous.
After it has thus continued to exist for a time, like some

fossil among the alluvium of the language, with all its original characters unobliterated, it seems now to have been entirely worn out with old age.

With these exceptions, nothing has come down to us of Anglo-Saxon declensions but a single termination, the *s*, by means of which we now form all our genitives. It is, moreover, the only sign of a case which we now possess. Even the old form of *es* in nouns which end in *s*, *z*, or *x*, seems to become burdensome, and, except in a few cases like "the foxes tail," we supply its place now by a simple apostrophe, as in "Eblis' self" and "Tigris' shore." Shakespeare seems yet to have hesitated about it, for he says now "his mistress' eyebrow," and now "St. Jacques's pilgrim." The apostrophe we insert nowadays before this letter *s* as an apparent note of elision, has no such meaning, but is simply a modern expedient, a late refinement, to distinguish the genitive from the plural. What we have thus gained in uniformity we have lost in expressiveness; we are now without the means to convey by the outward form of nouns any suggestion as to gender. It was not so of old, when every noun had a different declension according to its signification; the first effect of this tendency to abolish all such distinctions being noticeable in the days of Chaucer, who uses himself the first feminine genitive in *es*, in "The Prioress*es* Tale," 13383, and "with modr*es pitee*," 13253.

A similar fate has befallen the variety of forms by which our fathers endeavored to express the plural number. It is well known that this was in almost all languages accomplished by the addition to the root of a word denoting multitude, folk, etc. Thus in Bengalese the very word *loc*, which means people, is added to all nouns to make a plural. The Hebrew, in like manner, took *im*, a multitude, and joined it to the singular in order to make it plural; hence our English plural of Cherub and Seraph in "*Cherubim* and *Seraphim* continually do cry," where we use unconsciously a Hebrew declension. In other languages, as in the Chinese and some of the languages of the north-western Indians, the same end is attained by a mere repetition of the word. Thus the Chinese say, tree-tree for our "trees," but this leaves it undecided whether several trees in their individuality are meant or a whole forest. The same mental process is familiar to most southern races, especially the Italians, who endeavor to increase the force of a word by repeating it, as in their "bel bello" or "presto presto." A curious distinction exists in some languages, as in the Persian, between the plural of animate and that of inanimate objects, the one being made in *ân*, the other in *hâ*.

The Anglo-Saxon, like all German dialects, had its strong nouns, that made their plural by a change of the radical vowel, and their weak nouns, that required the aid of an additional syllable for the same purpose. Of the former class but few remain in our day, such as the plurals *mice, lice, feet, geese, men*, and *women;* for here, also, the Norman conquest made an end to the existing variety of forms. The illiterate masters, at least, did not catch the nice distinctions of sound; and where their ear really caught them, they were unwilling to take the trouble of committing them to memory. They found one very largely used termination, the masculine form of *-as;* this appeared simple, and was all the easier to them as it was so much like their own familiar *s;* so they adopted it as their favorite ending for the plural, and soon, by the force of the principle of analogy, it extended to nearly all nouns. The process was aided by the many new words that were introduced, with which the Saxon forms did not blend readily, and thus all plurals were gradually made in *s*. The change was, of course, neither violent nor immediate. In our oldest documents, *e. g.*, in the famous proclamation of Henry III. 1258, and in the first political songs, found in Wright's collection, the majority of nouns do not yet make their plural in *s*, but retain a variety of different forms from the

Anglo-Saxon. The uniformity of our days begins only to show itself toward the end of the thirteenth and the first part of the fourteenth century. In " Piers Ploughman " it is fully established, with a few exceptions only in addition to those that exist now. This majority begins thus to rule just at the time when French words entered in large numbers into English, at a period of which Harrison's Chronicle says that then " the English tongue grew · into such contempt at Court, that most men thought it no small dishonor to speak any English there ; which bravery took his hold at the last likewise in the country with every ploughman, that even the very carters begun to wax weary of their mother tongue and labored to speak French, which was then counted no small token of gentility." Even in the sixteenth and the first half of the seventeenth century, there is no distinction made between *s* and *es ;* Shelton has *lyppes, buyldynges, princes,* and *lordes, hartes,* and *hartis ;* and in Taylor's Works (1630) we find *peares, plumbes,* and greene *beanes.* But soon after these writers the principle of adding a simple *s* to all nouns, except after sibilants, etc., was fully established, and since that time the once very popular additional *e* has become daily rarer. After sibilants we prefer, of course, *es* as an orthographical remedy, to avoid the meeting of so many hissing sounds, which already abound in the language beyond the rules of euphony. Thus we say *churches, ages, foxes, glasses,* and *horses.* But even *th* takes a simple *s,* one of the most difficult sounds for all foreigners, except only *cloth,* which makes *clothes* for dress or *cloths* the material. Mandeville says still, without such distinction, both " tentes made of *clothes,*" and " clothed in *clothes* of gold." Nor is this the only instance of two plural forms for two different meanings of the same word; for we have *staffs* for sticks, but *staves* for the official wand or the musical measure ; *peas* for the seed, and *pease* for the species. *Peasen,* which John Wallis tells us was still used in the seventeenth century, is now quite obsolete. It is more curious, however, to observe that here the language has made a singular, which originally did not exist. The word was first *peas*, from the French "pois." Spenser says in his "Shepherd's Calendar" for the month of October: "Nought worth a *peas ;*" and Puttenham has, —

> "Set shallow brooks to surging seas,
> An Oriental pearl to a white *peas*."

Our singular *pea* is formed upon a misconception of *peas* being a plural, like the blunder of the good mayor of a town, who was so deeply impressed with his own dignity that he always spoke of a "*claw* of Parliament," and the poet Holmes's humorous expression of the "One-Hoss *Shay*." Many an ignorant countryman still uses *Chinee* as the singular of Chinese; and Milton, in his "Paradise Lost," (III. 437,) sins in the opposite direction, when he says : —

> "But in his ways lights on the barren plains
> Of Sericana, where Chineses drive
> With sails and winds their carry wagons light."

We say, finally, *pennies* for coin, and *pence* for their value, instead of the Old English *pens*, so liable to misapprehension. Mandeville has, (p. 93,) —

> "There caste Judas the 30 *pens* before him."

A few words of Anglo-Saxon origin, not content with the addition of *s*, change besides their final *f* into *v*. This observance is not old, however, for the first instance known of it is the only one that occurs in Mandeville, where he says *theves*, instead of his ordinary plural, like *knyfes*, *lyfes*, and *wyfes*. We say now *lives*, *loaves*, *thieves*, and *wives*, but we except all Norman-French words like *chiefs*, *reliefs*, *briefs*, and *fiefs*, save only *beef*, where the Latin "boves" probably led to the modern form of *beeves*. We except in like manner, for reasons not yet satisfactorily explained, words terminating in *oof*, *rf*, and *ff*, and therefore do not change the *f* in *roofs*, *dwarfs*, and *muffs*, which, in contrast to the modern *wharves*, led an irate author to ask, "Why do we say wharves? Do we speak of the *chieves* of clans and the *rooves* of houses? as if the ladies carried *mufves* to keep their dear little hands warm, or as if Tom Thumb was to be spoken of as big among the *dwarves*." If we preserve the *f* also in *fifes*, *strifes*, and *safes*, it is for the good reason that without such a mark we could not distinguish the first from fives (5), and the others from the similar forms of the verbs, he strives and he saves.

Another peculiarity of our modern plural is the introduction of an additional *e* after the vowels *y* and *o*, to protect the long vowel. This necessity seems to have been early felt, for Shakespeare already writes : —

"In russet yeas and honest kersey *noes*." — *Love's Labor 's Lost*, V. 2.

and —

"All yon fiery *oes* and *eyes* of light." — *Mids. Night's Dream*, III. 2.

Hence we say now, *flies, destinies*, and *soliloquies;* but the necessity ceases where another vowel already precedes the above mentioned, and therefore their integrity is not threatened. This is the reason why we say *valleys, keys, rays, boys, chimneys*, and *monkeys*, for the use of *vallies, monies*, and *monkies* is in reality incorrect spelling, from a want of attention to the principle which underlies these by no means arbitrary rules. For even in verbs the same law is observed, as may be seen in the difference between *he denies* and *he delays*. Thus we also say *heroes, calicoes*, and *echoes*, but, thanks to the additional vowel, *folios* and *nuncios*. The very exceptions which are occasionally quoted against the rule, the words *ladies, sympathies*, etc., find an easy and satisfactory explanation in the fact that their present form in *y* is modern, whilst formerly they were written with *ie* at the end.

Our English, like most languages, limits the use of certain nouns to one number alone, whenever the meaning suggests such a regulation. We use no singular of *bellows*, *scissors, lungs, spectacles, whiskers, drawers,* and *small-clothes,* because their duality instinctively requires and admits of nothing but a plural form. Others, again, are employed in a collective meaning, and then must needs be singular only; such are *sheep, deer, neat, horse,* and *swine,* a usage which was probably strengthened by the fact that most of these words had no plural in Anglo-Saxon and even in Old English. Mandeville, at least, uses *swyn, hors,* and *scheep* for both numbers alike. This does not, of course, exclude their ordinary use; and thus we find, in Levit. xi. 7, "and *the* swine though *he* divide the hoof;" and in Shakespeare, " pearl enough for *a* swine." In like manner are *horse* and *foot* used when they stand for infantry and cavalry, and *sail* in nautical language. A few of our nouns make a nice distinction of meaning in the singular and the plural. *Manner* is a very different thing from *manners,* as when Ben Jonson already says, " wheresoever manners and fashions are corrupted." The *practices* of a lawyer are well to be distinguished from the *practice* he may have in cross-questioning, as the *mean* or average income is not always within the *means* of everybody. A lad of good *parts* may take *part* in an enterprise; and *color* has nothing to do with its plural, as ".I must advance the *colors* of my love." — *Merry Wives,* III. 4. A *minute* belongs to time, *minutes* are written down. The " Spectator " (454) says : " I writ down these *minutes,*" which shows the remarkable change this word has undergone since the days of Old English. Then it meant something very different, as may be seen from Wickliffe's Bible, St. Mark xii. 42, where he says, " But whanne a pore widowe was come, sche cast two *mynutys,* that is a farthing." From this meaning is derived the contracted form, *mite,* of our day, which has since held its place by the side of its richer brother *minute,* just as *mart .* has its special meaning alongside of the fuller *market.*

The only other plural termination of our English which claims attention by the side of the almost universal *s* is *en,*

which seems to have given way 'more slowly than the other
inflections. It begins to be rare in the fourteenth century,
and Spenser uses it together with *s*, employing *eyen* when
he wishes it to rhyme with *pine*, and *eyes*, when there is no
such reason. In Sackville's " Mirror for Magistrates " we
read, —

> " The wrathfull winter, prociing on apace
> With blustering blasts has all ybarde the *treen;* "

and in Fairfax's famous translation of Tasso, (XVII. 49,)
which, to be sure, though later in date, follows Spenser
very closely, we have, —

> " While thus the Princess said, his hungry *eine*
> Adrastus fed on her sweet beauties' light."

Housen, as well as *hosen*, was used, with other similar
forms, as late as the seventeenth century, and in the
" Gilderoy Ballad " of that age we find, —

> " Gilderoy was a bonnie boy
> Had roses tull his *shoone,*
> His stockings were of silken soy
> Wi' garters hanging doune,"

and in another place —

> " Oh sike twa charming *een* he had,
> A breath as sweet as rose."

Shoon is, by the way, a comparatively modern form, frequently used by Shakespeare, very common as a provincial
term in Cheshire and Leicestershire, and used by Byron in
his " Childe Harold : " " He wore his sandal *shoon*."

The south of England is especially fond of these older
plurals, and abounds with *pleasen* (places), *sloen*, *cheesen*,
and *peasen*. *Oxen* is, of course, quite orthodox. *Kine*
comes from the Anglo-Saxon word *cu*, which, being a strong
noun, made its plural in *cyen*, although in Percy's " Relics "
· (III. 120) it appears as *kye* simply. Macaulay indorses the
word by saying (" Hist. of England," V. 30) : " His stores
of oatmeal were brought out, the kine were slaughtered."

A double plural form, arising from the fact that here

also the original inflection no longer conveyed to the
people at large a precise meaning, occurs in many modern
nouns. We say *brethren* from the strong plural *brether*,
with the addition of *en*, and mean by it the same as by
brothers, but use it only in strong and scriptural language
instead of the latter. Thus in Byron, "Call not thy
brothers *brethren!* Call me not mother!" *Child* made
originally only *childer*, after the fashion of the Old Norse
plural, preserved in German neuters. Percy's "Relics"
(II. 94) has, —

" It was no childer game."

Now we add the ending *en*, and contract both into *children*.

A few plural forms are now used with a singular meaning, — another evidence of the readiness with which in a
changing language the first meaning of certain inflections
is forgotten by the people. Our word *kitten* was originally
the plural of *kit*, a diminutive made from *cat*, according to
early Gothic usage, the *c* being changed into *k* to preserve
its hard sound before the vowel *i*, just as we change *candle*
into *kindle*. In like manner *cock* makes first *chick*, and
then in the plural *chicken*, which we now use as a singular
by the side of the former, for "a pretty *chick*," is still a
common expression, and "the old gentleman had neither
chick nor child," used by Warren, shows the former meaning. It was only about the time of Wallis, as he tells us
himself, that *chicken* began to lose its plural meaning; and
we are told that in Sussex, to this day, the people would
as soon think of saying *oxens* as *chickens*.

Twin is the sole remnant in English of the old Saxon
dual; it is the same as our now unfashionable *twain* from
twa. Few of us think of *garden* as a plural, and yet it
belongs as such to *gard* or *yard*, as *stocking* is an ill-treated
form of the genuine *stocken*, as used by Spenser, from the
singular *stock*. Still less is it commonly known that the
poetical word *welkin*, as in Milton's line, —

" From either end of heav'n the welkin burns
With feats of arms,"

is the plural of a now obsolete word *welc*, the German *Wolke*, for which we now substitute *cloud*. In Archbishop Aelfric's Vocabulary, the oldest work of that description in the English language, we find, " nubes : *wolc ;* " but in the days of Shakespeare even, the plural had already an air of affectation. Hence the Clown in ".Twelfth Night" (III. 1) says to Viola, ". Who you are and what you would, are all out of my *welkin*. I might say, element ; but the word is overworn," where of course, welkin is intended to be even more " overworn." In another place, however, the poet says simply, " She is the weeping *welkin*, I the earth ; " now its use is confined to the phrase of " making the *welkin* ring."

Nothing appears at first sight simpler than the plural *men*, made after the manner of strong nouns from *man*, and yet we find in it a curious historical illustration. Whilst we say regularly wo*men*, country*men*, and horse*men*, we employ Ger*mans* and Nor*mans*, not from any difference of origin or nature in these words, but because at the time when they entered the English through the French, the latter were no longer aware and conscious of their derivation from Ger or Wer-man and North-man, and hence treated the whole as a proper name.

An apparent plural, also, is found in many English nouns, and has led to serious errors in some of the best of our grammars. *Alms* is so far from being an English plural, that it is rather a Greek singular ; for the biblical word ἐλεημοσύνη was, by our Anglo-Saxon fathers, already contracted into *almesse*, as in Chaucer, —

" This *almesse* shouldst thou do of thy proper things,"

and thence into the form now in use. *Riches*, on the contrary, is the mutilated form of the French " richesse," and Ben Jonson is incorrect when he says, —

" Riches *are* in fortune a greater good than wisdom is in nature,"

although now it has so completely usurped the force of a

plural that to use it otherwise would appear singular. *Bellows*, from the old French " baleys;" has been more fortunate, for, although frequently treated as a plural, Shakespeare says, correctly, (" Pericles," I. 2,) " Flattery is the *bellows blows* up sin," and more recently Longfellow has, —

> " They watched the laboring *bellows*
> And as *its* panting ceased."

Summons is, like alms, an ancient word, being the contracted " submoncas," a well-known legal term, made of the verb after the manner of " fieri facias," " habeas," " capias," etc., and hence we can hardly approve of Waller's

> " Love's first *summons*
> Seldom *are* obeyed,"

though we ought to be thankful when we are not offended by the worse and vulgar, but by no means unfrequent, form " summonses."

Among the doubtful words which even now are found used in both numbers, must be counted *News*, derived from " nouvelles," and hence of old always a plural. Roger Ascham says, about 1550 : " There *are* many *news ;*" and Milton has, in his " Samson Agonistes ": " Suspense in *news* is torture, speak *them* out." But already Shakespeare showed both forms. In "Henry VI.," Part I. I. 4, he has: " Whither *go* these *news ;* " and in the same play, V. 3 : " *This* news." The latter is now probably the more general form, and we hear rarely otherwise than " *This is* good or bad news," or, as custom, in the words of Trinculo concerning necessity, makes words " acquainted with strange bedfellows," even " old news." *Tidings* are, we ought to say is, in the same predicament, for it also is used by Shakespeare now as a singular and now as a plural, though neither *new* nor *tiding* exist in English.

A common error limits us in the use of *hair* to the singular ; the plural has no less authority in its favor. " His *hairs are* gray," in the " Last Minstrel," and " *These hairs* of mine," in Byron, are not merely poetical licenses, for we have also "His [Cicero's] silver *hairs* will purchase us a good opinion." *Wages* and *dregs*, *ashes* and *pains*, belong to the same class of words. The few foreign plural forms which have still held their own in English are all the more interesting because they must have possessed peculiar strength to resist the influence of a language which has shown such unsurpassed power of receiving foreign ingredients, and of naturalizing and converting them from aliens into useful citizens. This seems a peculiarity not only of the Saxon tongue but of the Saxon race. The most striking evidence of this quality may be seen in the truly marvelous power of absorption which it shows especially in the Western States of North America. In the Union the German lays aside his Teutonic character, the Celt forgets his own feud, and sees his son assume the garb, the principles, the very name of the Saxon. Here, most striking of all, the Jew even loses his ancient marks, because here alone, on the whole globe, he is not persecuted by the Saxon, and thus is stripped of that strength which is everywhere else mainly derived from the ever-pressing necessity of resistance.

We have French plurals, as in *beaux*, *messieurs*, and *mesdames*, and Italian plurals in *virtuosi*, *banditti*, and *conversazioni*. The form of the plural is, moreover, frequently a sure sign of the naturalization of a foreign word. When we find that Holland makes "ideæ," we may safely assume that it was to him yet a Greek word; to us it is English, and we make *ideas*. Hammond has "dogmata" for our *dogmas*, though the former is still in use, together with miasmata and lemnata. Spenser makes, after Greek fashion, three syllables of *heroes*, where we have but two; and even the metrical accent alone betrays Pope's views on *satellites*, when he says, —

"Why Jove's *satellites* are less than Jove."

When we, in our day, use a foreign word as such, we

give it the plural it had in its own tongue; and thus we say *errata*, *hypotheses*, *phenomena*, *appendices*, *vases*, *bases*, *formulæ*, *larvæ*, *magi*, and *data*. Where we treat them as naturalized, they have an English plural, as *waltzes* and *bandits*. Many are, even now, in a transition state; our railways have accustomed us to the use of "terminus" and many say, already, *terminuses*, while others still adhere to *termini*. In a few instances we meet with a foreign and an English plural in the same word, attributed to two different meanings; thus *indexes* are tables of contents, but *indices* only signs, and *geniuses* are men of genius, *genii* fabulous beings.

Hardly less important than the consideration of case and number is the gender of nouns, although this feature seems to be fading away entirely from our language. In this disappearance of one of the most striking features lies a marked difference between ancient languages, and with them modern French, on one hand and English on the other. There the gender is permanently fixed and of paramount importance, here it is barely perceptible and frequently changeable at will.

The mature and severe character of our English furnishes a partial explanation of this remarkable restriction. An abundance of forms of gender, in fact the use of a transferred gender altogether, belongs exclusively to two classes of nations. They are either still so young as to ascribe, from ignorance and the abundance of their own life, a sex to lifeless objects, as men do in their infancy; or they are, even in maturity, endowed with such activity of fancy that they live rather in an imaginary than in the real world. The former find their representative in some of the Algonquin tribes, the latter in the German. The English, as a people, are no longer children, nor are they endowed with unnatural liveliness of imagination. Hence they have abandoned gender as they have approached maturity. For when the quick fancy of childlike nations gradually shrinks back into its legitimate dimensions, and the cooler judgment of fuller knowledge assumes the control, the artificial gender is everywhere seen to disappear by itself or to be discarded as a useless incumbrance. The sensuous element loses its influence, and the power of abstraction asserts its claims more and more. This does not, by any means, exclude the legitimate use of fancy as one of the powers of the national mind reflected in the language. Even in English, although we have nearly abandoned the idea of gender altogether, we are by no means without numerous instances of qualities, limbs, or even agencies, which we daily attribute to lifeless things, especially to features in the landscape that surrounds us. A chair has its legs, a hill a foot, a mountain a shoulder, a head, and a crest, it may even boast of one or several spurs. The needle has an eye, and a sofa two arms; a saw has its teeth, which it shares with a comb, and a bottle a neck; the waves have a breast, the ships their ribs, and even cabbage has a head. In like manner we ascribe functions of various kinds to mere helpless instruments, and give them names accordingly. Thus we speak of monkeys, hydraulic rams, and *chevaux-de-frise.* We cut figures and letters in the living rock; the earth breathes; and mercury is to our eye quicksilver. The hungry ocean demands its victims, and the thirsty earth eagerly drinks in the welcome rain. A lane may be a blind alley, and a trial of swiftness often ends in a dead heat. What would our poetry be without such license and such play of fancy, and how could we, without it, appreciate the beauty of the Psalmist, who makes the hills clap their hands, and the valleys laugh and sing?

Notwithstanding this, our English surpasses in the simplicity of gender all other languages, and has established its claim to be considered the most philosophic among idioms. It has, alone, succeeded in freeing itself perfectly of all control in point of gender by the mere form of words, and with it of a genuine incumbrance of speech. For the three personal genders of words conduce neither to perspicuity nor to energy; the distinction must needs be a purely artificial one, a mere fiction, in a large number of words, that is in all that express inanimate objects, having no real ground in the nature of things. Now our English is a practical, business-like language; it is not imaginative, like its German sister. It rejects, therefore, all mere mechanical attributes of gender, without abandoning in any way its clear right to ascribe sex to lifeless objects for special purposes. By means of thus discarding gender as a common rule, it has gained for its poets and orators the right of personifying abstract ideas and giving life to inanimate objects. Making a sparing use of this power to invest them, for the moment, with a gender, they present them far more vividly and impressively to our imagination than can be done in any other language. How graphic and striking is, for instance, the following description of law, by the aid of this power of our language: "Of law no less can be acknowledged than that *her* seat is the bosom of God, *her* voice the harmony of the world. All things in heaven and earth do *her* homage; the very least as feeling *her* care, and the greatest as not excepted from *her* power." Substitute here *its* for *her*, and the beauty and force of the sentence are seriously impaired.

This manner of giving gender is far more rational, as will be seen from the simple fact that almost every nation has its own peculiar notions connected with the sex to be attributed to certain lifeless objects. Now mythology suggests one, now history another. This is the case, among many others, with the words *sun* and *moon*. To Greek and Roman the former was masculine, represented by Phœbus or Sol, and the latter feminine, as Diana or Luna. Euripides, on one occasion, calls them father and mother; and Virgil makes them brother and sister: —

"Nec *fratris* radiis obnoxia surgere Luna." — *Georg.* I. 396.

In Hebrew, Sanscrit, and German, the result is reversed, the sun becoming feminine, the moon masculine; in modern Russian the former loses its sex altogether, and becomes neuter. The German notion is based upon Northern mythology, as we learn from the prose Edda: "Mundilfora had two children: a son, Mani, and a daughter, Sol, and she became the wife of Tuisco." This influence determined the gender of the two words in Anglo-Saxon and Old English. In a Saxon treatise on the equinox we find: "The moon has no light but of the sun, and *he* is of all stars the lowest;" and in one of the Cott. MSS., Tit. A, 3, p. 63, we have: "When the sun goeth at evening under the earth, then is the earth's breadth between us and the sun, so that we have not *her* light, till *she* rises up at the other end." But when the classic languages began to make their influence felt, first through the Norman-French and afterwards directly, the present gender, taken from ancient mythology, established itself. This is, however, rare yet before Shakespeare, and even he calls ("Henry IV." I. 2.) "the blessed sun a fair hot *wench* in flame-color'd taffata." Now, when we speak philosophically, we designate sun and moon by *it*, as already Mandeville ventured to do, saying, "God loveth *it* more than any other thing." When we treat them poetically, they are *he* and *she* to us, as in Milton: —

> " As when the sun, new risen,
> Looks through the misty, horizontal air
> Shorn of *his* beams; "

and in Pope's Homer: —

> " As when the moon, refulgent lamp of night,
> O'er heaven's clear azure shed *her* sacred light."

In this aspect the English differs from all other languages. The old Greek had its masculine and feminine, and by their side the οὐδέτερον, our neuter, but originally meaning simply neither the one nor the other. In similar manner we find the North American Indians speak of a third gender; as eunuch, because they look upon it in the light of a weakened masculine. The Mongolian idioms know no difference of gender. The Romance languages include the neuter of the Latin in their masculine, except in article and pronoun. The Danish has one common gender for masculine and feminine, which it calls the personal gender, and another, in its nature neuter, which it calls impersonal. The German alone has preserved all three genders, both in inflection and in article. The English, on the other hand, shows no difference of gender at all except in one single form, the personal pronoun.

Saxon words lost their gender with their termination. In Anglo-Saxon most final vowels and some consonants were attributed to one or the other gender; but already in Old English all these vowel-endings were represented by a uniform *e*, — *e. g.* Anglo-Saxon, nama, ende, and wudu; Old English, name, ende, wode. At a still later period even this *e*, already mute, was generally laid aside, and with it the last visible means by which outwardly to distinguish gender.

Foreign words lost their gender in the process of naturalization. As they underwent this, they often became so obscured that the precise original meaning was no longer sufficiently clear to determine the gender. Where this was not the case, their form at least was so changed that they, like the Saxon words, lost the gender with the termination. We find, upon closer examination of Latin words, that wherever the nominative disguised the true root of the noun, the English has not adopted that case, but an oblique case, in which the true and full root makes itself felt. Thus we find we have adopted,

not comes, but comitem, and hence our (comte) count.
"   margo " marginem   "   margin.
"   frons " frontem   "   front.
"   cohors " cohortem   "   (cohort) court.
"   flos " florem   "   flower.
"   actio " actionem   "   action.
"   vox " vocem   "   voice.

In these new forms there is no trace left of the ancient gender as determined by the Latin rules. Besides, such words as have come to us, not from the Latin directly, but through the French, had often there already changed the gender and thus increased the confusion.

Whatever gender, therefore, can be found in modern English, is exclusively artificial. By the common consent of the people it is attributed to some words ; where necessity calls for a designation of a sex, it is made for the purpose, but without ever becoming inherent. A gender merely attributed is of course neither permanently fixed nor absolutely decided. We say of *time* that *it* is out, and the poet says that

> " Time maintains *his* wonted pace,"

as soon as he ascribes human powers or qualities to time. The philosopher tells us of *thunder*, that "*it* arises when the air is surcharged with electricity ;" and the poet again, personifying it, says,

> " the thunder,
> Winged with red lightning and impetuous rage,
> Perhaps has spent *his* shafts." — *Paradise Lost*, I. 174.

Love. even, is sometimes calmly defined, and we are told that "*it* is one of the affections ;" but poets, following, probably, the example of classic writers, think of the god Amor, and thus say :

> " Love in my bosom like a bee
> Doth suck *his* sweet;
> Now with *his* wings *he* plays with me,
> Now with his feet." — Lodge's *Rosalind's Madrigal.*

A beautiful use of attributed gender occurs in connection with the word *night*, in the Book of Wisdom, xviii. 14: "While all things were in quiet silence and that night was in the midst of *her* swift course, thine almighty word leaped down from heaven, out of thy royal throne, like a fierce man of war, into a land of destruction." We fancy we can listen to the soft and silent step of night in *her* swift course, while the *word*, almighty, leaps in *his* power down from heaven. What language, with a permanently fixed gender, could have produced so powerful an impression by such simple means?

The ways by which in English a distinction of sex is represented externally in words are as various as they are numerous, some agreeing with those employed in most languages, others quite peculiar to our own. Not unfrequently we possess two distinct words for the masculine and the feminine of the same being. We have *man* and *woman*, the ancient wifman, to which the German in its abundance adds a neuter form, Weibsbild, used only in contempt. We might add *father* and *mother*, *son* and *daughter*, *brother* and *sister*, *king* and *queen*, *nephew* and *niece*, *lad* and *lass*, *sloven* and *slut*, *wizard* and *witch*. The same applies to animals, where we meet with *ram* and *ewe*, *horse* and *mare*, *cock* and *hen*, *milter* and *spawner*, *drone* and *bee*. In a few cases here a third gender, a neuter, is developed to designate the young, in whom the sex does not matter as yet, and thus we obtain *bull*, *cow*, and *calf*, *dog*, *bitch*, and *whelp*. There seems to be a tendency in modern English to make this distinction in gender much nicer and more careful. Thus we find that *shrew* was formerly applied to males as well as to females, while we, ungallantly, confine it to the latter. *Lover*, on the other hand, and *paramour*, now only used of men, were formerly used of both sexes. Smollett's " Count Fathom," published in 1754, says still : " These were alarming symptoms to a lover of *her* delicacy and pride." Something of the old freedom survives in our " pair of lovers," or " they were lovers."

Sometimes the expression of sex is accomplished by the addition of certain syllables, such as have been explained in a different connection. The Saxon *er* gives us masculines, the Latin-French *ess* feminines. Where one and the same form has to serve for both genders, great want of clearness and often confusion is the necessary consequence.

Dancer and *singer, rival, cousin, witness, parent, student,* and many others, lead to that difficulty which Crabbe in his " Lover's Journey " points out : —

> " Gone to a friend, she tells me — I commend
> Her purpose, — means she to a female friend ? "

Quite peculiar to English is the use made of personal pronouns for this purpose, but its extreme awkwardness has led to its gradual abandonment. In older authors it is quite frequent. Fuller, in his " Comment on Ruth," (104,) speaks of a *shee-saint,* and elsewhere of *she-devils.* Shakespeare, jocosely, in his " Merry Wives of Windsor," says: " Be brief my good *she-Mercury.*" The " Spectator " does not disdain using *she-knighterrant* and *she-Machiavels.* Byron goes even further, and ventures upon " on their *she-parades,*" and " the real sufferings of their *she-condition.*" A *he-friend* would seem to be a most objectionable expression, and yet it occurs not unfrequently ; with animals the result is less unpleasant, and we can pass a *he-* and a *she-goat,* a *he-* and a *she-bear,* etc. Generally, however, better words exist for this very clumsy contrivance, which is now no longer found in careful writers.

The increasing influence of the German has led to the adoption of a system which is there very common, — the addition of a word, which, in itself, expresses clearly sex or gender. Isaac Disraeli was probably the first who introduced, from the Dutch, the word *fatherland* for native soil ; the experiment succeeded, it was adopted by Byron and Southey, and the word has now obtained citizenship. Then followed *mother-tongue* and kindred compounds ; besides these we speak of *mankind* and *womankind, man-* and *maid-servant, beggar-man* and *-woman, bondman* and *bond-maiden, gentleman* and *gentlewoman,* even of a *man-milliner,* and, upon the authority of the " Tatler," (226,) of a *man-mid-wife.* Then we have land*lord* and land*lady, lady*bird and *lady*clock (the coccinea septempunctata). Among animals names are favorite means to mark the sex, besides the words.taken from their own order, as *cockrobin*, *cockchafer*, *cock-* and *hen*-sparrow, pea*cock* and *hen*, roe*buck* and *doe*, *buck*-rabbit and *doe*, *buck*-hare, boar-*cat*, *buck*-goat, *buck*-coney, and, in Halliwell, even *dog*-bee. A *dog*-fox and a *bitch*-fox are well known to hunters; and Moore in his Suffolk words tells us quaintly that —

<blockquote>
" Cock *robin* and *Titty* wren
Are the Almighty's cock and hen."
</blockquote>

The employment of proper names extends, of course, only to the usage among the people at large, in familiar language and provincial dialects. The common people dislike, in all cases, the abstraction of the neuter gender, which requires, as it were, a mental effort on their part, for which they have little relish ; hence to them every thing in Nature is *he* or *she*, and this tendency has led them to give proper names even to lifeless objects. Among men they have a *Tomboy*, a *Tomfool* and his tomfoolery, and *Tom* Thumb ; *Tom*cats and *Tabby* cats are familiar terms. *Tom*tit and *Jenny* wren among birds, and *Tom* and *Jenny* simply, to designate male and female swans, are quite vernacular on the Thames. *Robert*, or the more familiar *Dobbin*, serves, we know not why, very generally for horses, and for our friend, *Bob* Robin or *Bob* Redbreast. In Suffolk we hear much of *Harry* Longlegs or Father Longlegs for spiders, and of King *Harry* for the goldfinch. Edward appears only as *Neddy* for the patient donkey, and *Will* for the sea-gull, or as *Billy* goat coupled with *Nanny* goat. Michael reappears as *Hedge Mike* for sparrow ; Gilbert, as *Gib*, is common in Northamptonshire, and used by Shakespeare in " Henry IV." : —

<blockquote>
" I am as melancholy as a *gib* cat ; "
</blockquote>

and St. Martin has given his name to the swift *martins*. Of all names, however, the most frequent in these combinations is, as might be expected, John, or, more familiarly, Jack. We have, in our own order, *Jack*-of-all-trades, *Jack*-a-lantern, *Jack*-a-lent (a dolt), *Jack*ass, *Jack*anapes, *Jack*-

pudding (a clown,) *Jack*-tar, and *John*-a-dream. *Jackass*, belonging to our friend Neddy technically, a *jack*-hare, and a *jack*-rabbit among quadrupeds; *jack* simply, a *jack*-pike, and a *johndory* among fishes; and a *jack*-heron, *jack*-snipe and *jack*-curlew among birds. The centipede is more commonly known as *Jock*-with-many-feet; and even among plants we meet with *Jack*-i'-the-Bush, or *John*-behind-the-garden-gate. A still more remarkable use of these names is their attachment to lifeless objects, which gives us *jack*-boot, *jack*-chain, and a roasting-*jack*, the companion to a spinning-*jenny*. The feminine is not so well represented in this class; we find, however, *Jenny* wren, occasionally *Jenny* ass by the side of *Jack* ass, and the hated centipede once more familiarized as *Jenny*-spinner or *Jenny*-nettles in Lanark, as *Maggy* Monyfeet in Scotland. Then we have *Poll* parrots, *Magpies*, the " Margots " of the French, (from Margaret,) and *Madge* or *Madge*howlet for a small owl. In Norfolk, and probably elsewhere, the five fingers are humorously endowed with proper names, as Tom Thumbkin, Will Wilkin, Long Gracious, Betty Bodkin, and Little Tit.

Quite a curious usage belonging to this class of expressions is the tendency to add *horse* to other words, in order to indicate their strength, large size, or coarseness, as in *horse*-radish, *horse*-walnut and -chestnut, in *horse*-emmet, *horse*-leech, *horse*-muscle and *horse*-crab, until it is transferred even to a *horse*-laugh and a *horse*-medicine. The gigantic size and defiant attitude of the largest rush has procured for it the name of *bul*rush, but it is not quite as clear why another plant of almost equal dimensions should have to be contented with the name of *cow*-cabbage.

CHAPTER XL

"Sunt fata verbis."

As we have seen that words consist, like ourselves, of a body and a soul, the outward form and the inner meaning, there is, of course, also a double history connected with these two parts. The form, being dependent on the uttered sound or its written sign, is subject to a number of external influences; and the meaning given it by a nation which passes through its childhood, youth, manhood and old age, will naturally in like manner, undergo various changes, keeping pace with the changes in thought and feeling of the mass of the people. In many cases these modifications amount to so little, perhaps only to a slightly altered spelling, a contraction or a widening of sound, that we pass it by as a necessary and natural effect of the influence of time. In other cases, however, violence has apparently been done to words: their form has been twisted, their dimensions have been curtailed, or their meaning has been so completely changed, that it requires diligent search and careful comparison to establish the identity of the original form with its modern descendants. Such cases are, if not always interesting, yet rarely otherwise than instructive; they give evidence of what might be fairly called the inner life of a language, and as the English language presents some of the most remarkable changes of this kind, it may not be amiss to look into the history of some at least with greater care.

A large and important number of words in English have

undergone a serious contraction either from misapprehension of their original form or from sheer caprice and abuse. This applies most naturally, perhaps, to French words introduced at various periods, and used by persons not familiar with the idiom from which they were borrowed. There has been no period in England's history when her French scholars have not been more or less in the predicament of the nun whom old Dan Chaucer introduces to us so quaintly as, —

> "A Nonne, a Prioresse,
> That of hire smiling was ful simple and coy ...
> And frenche she spake ful fayre and fetishly
> After the schole of Stratford atte Bowe,
> For frenche of Paris was to her unknowe."
>
> *Cant. Tales*, 118.

What with mispronouncing first and misspelling afterwards, French words soon lost their native graces and became unmeaning in English. Thus pierre (stone) became *pier ;* peluche, *plush ;* gueule, *jowl* or *jole ;* châssis, *sash ;* issuer (exire), *issue* and *sewer ;* vestiaire (vestiarium), vestry ; chauffer, *chafe* and *chaff ;* fatigue, simple *fag ;* and blasphème, either *blaspheme* or *blame*. Feuille was Anglicized into *foil*, tuile into *tile*. Linon was made *lawn ;* volée, *volley ;* and triomphe was already in the days of Norman rule reduced to *trump* and *trump* cards. Baluster, from the French balustre, is now universally called and spelt *banister*, tourniquet is shortened into *turnkey*, and pêle-mêle into *pell-mell*, if not even into *Pall Mall*.

This is, after all, but the common fate of foreign words, ill understood and hence ill pronounced. The same process changed the mystic words of our religion, Hoc est corpus, into vulgar *hocus pocus ;* the Latin hilariter et celeriter into *helter skelter ;* postumus into a fabulous *posthumous ;* the Spanish cigara into anomalous *segar ;* and carnelian, from its resemblance to the color of flesh, (caro, carnis,) into *cornelian*.

Where the French has furnished us with special or technical terms, and these have undergone similar changes, the derivation is of course not always quite so clear, and must be accepted with some caution. *Tennis* comes to us, we know well, from the exclamation Tenez! used at hitting, as *Tally ho !* is the naturalized form of the Au Taillis! of the French. Whether *omelet* really represents the œufs mêlés of the French is more doubtful; and *jeopardy* has more than one pedigree, that of " jeu perdu " or " jeu parti," the game is gone, being the most probable, from the following lines of Chaucer : —

> " And when he through his madness and folie
> Hath lost his owen good thurgh *jupartie*
> Then he exciteth other folk thereto."

Many French terms have been much disguised by the simple loss of an initial *é*, frequently, no doubt, caused by an indistinct impression of its being an article. Thus we have *proof* from épreuve, *tin* from étain, *scum* from écume, *pin* from épingle, and *escheat* as well as *cheat*. Etiquette has become *a ticket*, and the old French word estrange retains its double form, as in

> " How comes it my husband oh !
> How comes it,
> That thou art thus *estranged* from thyself? "

and

> " Thyself I call it, being *strange* to me." — *Shakespeare.*

The same errors which in olden times caused so much injury are committed by the ignorant in our own day with French words that are now creeping into English, and there is good reason for us to pray still, with our Saxon ancestors of yore in their Litany, " A furore normannorum libera nos Domine ! "

There is perhaps more excuse for the contractions which Latin and other foreign words have undergone in the process of naturalization. That ἀθανασία and πανακεῖα should have shrunk and shriveled into *tansy* and *pansy* is certainly quite pardonable, though it would be very difficult now to trace the gradual change from step to step. We

know better how *proxy* came from procuracy, as *proctor*
from procurator, and *palsy* from paralysis, as we still retain
both the full and the shortened form. The French "fan-
taisie," or the Greek original, gave us *phantasy*, which in
Sylvester's translation of Du Bartas is already " phantsy,"
and thus shows clearly the gradual subsiding into modern
fancy. When Hollingshed says of brandy ": it lighteneth
the mind, it quickeneth the spirits, it cureth the *hydropsy*,"
he gives us the ancestor of our shortened *dropsy*. A curious derivation is that of *quinsy*, which is in reality the same
word as "synagogue," coming like the latter from σύν and
ἄγω, to draw together, which became afterwards "synanche."
In Holland's Pliny, x. 33, we find: "The young birds of
these martins, if they be burnt into ashes, are a singular and
sovereign remedy for the deadly *squinancie;*" whilst Jeremy
Taylor, in his "Holy Living and Dying," has: "Without revelation we can not tell whether we shall eat to-morrow or
whether a *squinancy* shall choke us." *Furlong* is of course
but a "furrow long," as *syrup* and *shrub* are the same.
Cadet is from capitellum, as it were, a little captain, as
cousin is from consanguineus, through the French cousin,
familiarly contracted further into *cozzen*. *Grant* comes in
like manner from garantie, whence also our *warrant ;* and
the law terms *livery* and *seizin* are nothing but our ordinary
delivery and *possession*.

The same unfortunate tendency to save breath and time
has led to a worse treatment of another class of words,
which have not been merely contracted but actually deprived of a part of their substance. The instances in
which proper names have suffered thus are best known.
Great and noble names have been corrupted to mean and
base uses. There is said to be a family in existence now,
lineal descendants of the Plantagenets, who have degenerated into *Plant*. Everybody has heard how Admiral
Vernon, in 1739, first ordered spirits mixed with water to
be dealt out to his sailors, and how, being commonly dressed

in a stuff largely used in the West India islands and known as grogram, he first earned that nickname for himself, and then bestowed it, in its shortened form of *grog*, upon his unpopular beverage. *Tram* roads may possibly recall to us the full name of their inventor, Outram, though the word is said to occur already some time before his day ; and *gin* is perhaps the first part of Geneva, where the best drink of the kind was distilled in former days, as it is now in Holland, which gives us the name of *Hollands*. St. Mary over the River, has thus dwindled into St. Mary *Overy*, as poor Magdalen, the repentant sinner with her abundant tears, has gone, through the abbreviated form of *Maud*, finally into *maudlin*.

The process is, however, by no means limited to proper names, and is still going on, in our day, in numerous common nouns, although here also foreign nouns have naturally suffered most. This is all the more to be regretted as the loss of a part of the form almost unavoidably involves the loss of a part of the meaning, and in language, as in society, half words are the perdition of women, and not only of women but of all who employ them. The very recklessness of the changes which Addison so humorously attributes to the " English delight in silence " and their tendency " to favor their natural taciturnity and to give as quick a birth to their conceptions as possible," is remarkable, for it seems to be a mere chance whether the first or the last part of a word is to be sacrificed. The former is the case in words like omnibus and *bus*, or caravan and *van*, which are fast becoming legitimate, the latter in cabriolet, citizen, and gentleman, which are as rapidly subsiding into *cab*, *cit*, and *gent*. Thus the simple *aid* was once the aide-de-camp of official language, and *plot* used to appear in full dress as *complot*. *Mob*, from the " mobile vulgus," belonging to the age of Charles II. and first applied, as Lord North says, to members of the Green Ribbon Club, together with *sham*, Macaulay very justly called " remarkable memorials of a season of tumult and imposture," though the connection with Whigs and Tories at which he points has not yet been fully established. We can see, however, how slowly admission is gained to the body of orthodox English words, from the hesitating way in which Addison speaks in the "Spectator" of *mob* and *incog:* "As all ridiculous words make their first entry into a language by familiar phrases, I dare not answer for these, that they will not in time be looked upon as a part of our tongue." His apprehensions have been fulfilled with regard to *mob*, though *incog* can hardly be considered yet as authorized by classic writers. The same process of curtailment has reduced the buffalo of the American continent, perhaps through the French "buffle," to the simple *buff*, now the color of tanned leather. The Latin "erinaceus" shows a curious process of gradual reduction. It became in French "hérisson," which Mandeville already Anglicized into *urchoune;* then it became Chaucer's *urchon*, and thus finally our own *ur-chin*. Another animal thus ill treated is the young of the frog and the toad, which was once ceremoniously "toad-pullet," and has now sunk into *tadpole*. *Phiz* is a very early abbreviation of the awkwardly long physiognomy, as primitive manners are now more frequently called *prim*. A *navvy*, whose labors on countless canals and in the Crimea have earned for him a world's respect, is but the half of a "*navi*gator;" a *wig*, the sad remnant of the stately periwig, the French word perruque, first made Dutch in the quaint form of *parruik*. The handiwork, or χείρ ἔργον, of the early leech gave rise to the unintelligible "*chi*rurgeon," whom we now simply call a *surgeon;* his hospital has likewise been shorn, and is now often *spital* only, as in *Spital*fields and *Spital* Inn, an asylum on the wildest parts of Stainmore Fells, erected there, as in other waste parts of the kingdom, to serve as a traveler's refuge. Slang terms of this kind abound in all directions; of the more admissible among them Dickens's "whenever I saw a beadle in full *fig*,"

refers, of course, to *figure*, as " to go " or " to live on *tick*,"
has reference to the *tick*et received at the pawnbroker's,
from which is derived the old phrase " on tick and on bill."
Flirt is not unlikely a mutilated form of the French *fleu-
rette*, which an ingenious writer in " Notes and Queries " com-
pares to the Greek rose, of which Aristophanes in the
" Clouds " says, ῥόδα μ' εἴρηκας, the exact counterpart of the
French, *vous m'inventez des fleurettes*.

One of the most interesting features connected with this
maltreatment of certain classes of words, is the quaint and
often exceedingly amusing manner in which the people at
large have endeavored to make foreign words more easy of
understanding by twisting them into some resemblance of
English words. This tendency ought to serve us as a warning against the too free adoption of foreign words, the form
and meaning of which have often not the slightest analogy
to our own. This must needs produce a certain confusion,
especially in the minds of the uneducated; and where this
is not the case, there will still remain, for the masses at least,
little more than a conventional meaning, an empty and un-
real signification. What is a *Pantheon* to us, who believe
either in one God or none at all, that we should place it
in the midst of our towns, by the side of Christian churches?
If we attend a debating club at a *Colosseum*, we must prepare ourselves to meet *colossi* only in their own estimation;
and wolves, it is to be hoped, have long since ceased to be
found in our *Lyceums*, as long since as Minerva, we fear,
has abandoned our *Athenæums*. The French are precisely
in the same predicament; there is something irresistibly
ludicrous to an Englishman in their advertisements of a
boulingrin vert before a country-house, or of *rosbifs de mou-
ton* in their eating-houses, terms of which already Voltaire
felt keenly the ridicule. So do their modern *Panorama
Universel*, their *feux pyriques*, and above all the *guerre
polémique* of the clever Ste. Beuve incur the sharp but well-
deserved criticism of their distinguished philologist Nodier.

These difficulties are peculiarly great, and the bad results make themselves more immediately felt in the case of French words imported into our tongue, because the French language has itself, long ago, lost all consciousness of its own history. What Frenchman thinks nowadays of the Latin *vir*, when he speaks of *vertu*, of *sus Troja* in his *truie*, of *jecus ficatum* in *foie*, or of *Gehenna* in his verb *gêner?* If this be so in France, how much more obscure must such words become when they are transferred to another tongue!

Everybody knows our dandelion, or dandy lion, as it was recently printed in a book for the "instruction of youth." Its derivation from *dent de lion* is evident. The fair apple of France there known as *belle et bonne*, is vulgarized into *belly-bound;* the beautiful rose *des quatre saisons* into one of *quarter sessions*, whilst the polianthes tuberosa, in French *tubéreuse*, which was nothing more than a tuberous plant, is forced into a *tuberose*. The admirable *chaussées* of the Empire are in England *causeways;* their *ancien*, the "Ancient Cassio" of Shakespeare, our *ensign;* and their *frère-maçon*, we hardly know how, with us a *freemason.* Their *contre danse*, so called from the couples dancing opposite each other, has become a *country-dance*, and the *hautbois*, that serves in the orchestra, by a ludicrous association with a boy, a *hautboy.* Animals have not fared any better: the *langouste* of the French coast is on English shores a *longoyster;* the hogfish, or *porcpisce* of Spenser, becomes a *porpoise;* and the *écrevisse* of our French neighbors had to go through a series of transformations in three languages before it reached its present form. It started from the Old High German *krebiz*, which reappeared subsequently in English as *crab*, and in German as *Krebs.* In the latter form it crossed the Rhine, and became in its new home *écrevisse;* it returned from there once more to its German kindred in England, appearing as *krevys* in Lydgate, as *crevish* in Gascoyne, as *craifish* in Holland, and merging finally, with a double effort at Anglicizing the foreign word into the modern English *crawfish* or *crayfish*.

Another word that has been a sore temptation to hasty etymologists is the recently revived word *filibuster*, which has in a similar manner returned, much reduced in form, like the prodigal son, from foreign lands. It was originally the English word *fly-boat ;* but when adopted by the Spaniards, was softened by them into "filibote" or "flibote." Subsequently it found its way back into English, and the outlandish form was by an off-hand etymology changed into *filibuster*, with some reference, perhaps, to the American slang term, a *buster*.

The sleeping mouse, or *souris dormeuse*, is, in like manner, but, very naturally, transformed into a *dormouse ;* the *farci* of French cooks into *forced* meat; and their *quelque chose* into our *kickshaw*, unless there should be some unknown relation existing between the latter part of the word and our *pshaw*. In a somewhat similar manner the French *quand-aurai-je* became our *quandary*. The transition from the *redingote* to a *riding-coat*, is as amusing as that from the ancient *vertugale* or still older *vertugadin* to a *farthingale*, a word made after the analogy of *nightingale*. The French rope-dancer's *soubresault*, from Latin *supersaltus* and Italian *sobresalto*, was already in Old English *sumbersault*, and thus became with a double association of ideas our *summerset*. Beaumont and Fletcher, in the "Tamer Tamed," have still, —

> " What a *somersalt*,
> When the chair fel, she fetch'd, with her heels upward ! "

but in the "Fair Maid of the Inn" it is already changed : —

> " Now I will only make him break his neck in doing a *somerset*, and that 's all the revenge I mean to take of him."

Where the French saw with the eye of superstition a hand of several fingers, a *main de gloire*, we discover a likeness to a man's two legs, and call the same root *mandragora*, or mandrake. Equally ludicrous is the change from the

rightly spelt *Oyez!* of our courts to the ordinary pronunciation, *O Yes!* and the way in which the men who
were stationed by the king's *buvet* (from *boire*, anciently
buver) to take care of his sideboard and costly wines, and
who in England waited at the *buffet*, a table near the
door of the dining-hall, with viands for the poor, became
first *buffetiers* and then vulgarly known as *beef-eaters*.
Even phrases can be traced to such violent twistings of
words, as the proverbial *dormir comme une taupe*, which
has lost all reference to the mole, and is now *to sleep like a
top*, and the *faire un faux pas*, to commit a blunder, which
is at least provincially *to make a fox's paw!* How not only
a strange form but a whole story may arise from such an
ill-treated word has been very amusingly established by
Mr. Riley in his learned work on the Guildhall in London.
He tells, in the Preface, that in the fourteenth and fifteenth
centuries trading was in London called *achat*, from the
French *acheter*. This foreign word was commonly pronounced *acat*, and came soon to be written so. To *acat*
of this kind the famous lord mayor, Whittington, was indebted for his wealth, but when the word became unfamiliar,
and finally unintelligible to the masses, the desire for some
explanation led to the absurd story of his gaining his wealth
by *a cat!*

Words that have come down to us from the ancient languages have, of course, still less meaning left in their altered
form, and here also many efforts have been made to instill
into them new life by giving them a somewhat English shape.
Greek names of plants furnish γλύκυς ῥίζα (the sweet root),
which was once *glycorys*, and is now *liquorice* or *licorice*,
with a faint reference to liquor; the σταρίς ἀγρία, or flea-wort,
became *staves-acre ;* and the καρυοφύλλον, already in Chaucer
cloue gilofre, instead of the true French form *clou de
girofle*, was first *gilly-flower*, and then, on the lips of the
ignorant, even *July flower*. The Θηριάκη of the Greeks underwent a strange series of changes in form and in meaning.

It had its original name from the viper, whose own flesh was long considered the best if not the only remedy for the creature's bite. As such it became soon a famous antidote, and as leech was once the common name of all followers of Æsculapius, so this preparation became generally synonymous with medical confection. The French called it then *thériaque*, which, however, Chaucer already curtailed to *triacle*; as *treacle* it now designates simply the sweet syrup of molasses, with a slight hint at its *trickling* propensity. Ignorance transformed tragacant gum into *gum dragon*, as even now νεκρομαντία, or *necromancy*, the art of calling up the dead, etc., is often called black art, as if it had any connection with a pretended *Negro*mancy. Our forefathers already mistook the Lydius lapis Graecorum, and called it, perhaps with reference to its unusual weight, or because it attracts iron, *loadstone*, just as they called the North Star the "leading star" or *loadstar*. The translators of Holy Writ made thus *emerods* out of hemorrhoids, associating their infliction with the idea of the *rod* of the Lord; at the same time *hemicrania* was, through the French *migraine* probably, converted into *megrim*. We still speak of the tiny grapes of Corinth as *currants*, as if they were the fruit of our native shrub of that name; and our common people often say *pottercarrier* for *apothecary*, as Jack calls his good ship *Bellerophon* a *Billy Ruffian*.

Botanical names of Latin origin have led to similar unintentional disguises. Asparagus is better known as *sparrowgrass*, febrifuge as *feverfew*, and *ros marinus* as *rosemary*. A frontispicium is a frontis*piece*; and since the *lanterna* of the ancients has been made of thin, split layers of horn, it has become a *lanthorn*. The *rachitis* of the physician is the *rickets* of the masses; the *selarium* of convents is our salt-*cellar*; and the *viridum jus* of the dispensary the ver*juice* of the people. The Latin *viride æris*, or the French *vert et gris*, has become *verdegris*, and vulgarly *verdigrease.* *Petrels*, or Mother Cary's chickens, are, as it were, little St. Peters, because, like the Apostle, they can walk on the water. The *Ligurnum* of Italy was changed into *Leyhorn*, precisely as the Italians themselves made their *Negroponte* out of the Greek name ἐν Ἐγρίπῳ.

We have avenged the old town on the Italians tenfold; we call their *articiocco girasole*, a sunflower artichoke which came from Peru to Italy and from thence to us, with utter disregard to geography, but with a willful appropriation of the *girasole, Jerusalem* artichoke, and even make of it a dish called *Palestine* soup ; we have, in like manner, changed their *renegado*, who denied his faith, into a *runagate*, their *lustrino* into *lutestring*, their *farubala* into *furbelow*, and their coasting vessel *urca* into a simple *hooker*.

The Spanish *cayo*, used to designate a rock or a sand-bank, we transform into a *key ;* and the Indian word *urican*, which has served to make the French *ouragan*, reappears in English as *hurricane* (hurry cane). The Spanish call the commander of a fleet with an Arabic word *amiral ;* and Milton still wrote of a tree fit to become " the mast of some great *ammiral.*" But there seems to have early arisen an idea that the name had something to do with *admirable*, and hence Latin writers of the Middle Ages already are fond of styling the chief naval officer *admirabilis* or *admiratus*, from which we derive our *admiral.*

German and Dutch words have not been exempted on account of their close relationship. The *hysenblas* of Holland, meaning the bladder of the fish called *hysin*, our sturgeon, is now ising*lass.* The German *Weremuth* has become bitter *wormwood ;* the *lindwurm* of noble Siegfried, a mean *blind-worm ;* a prophetic *Weissager*, a contemptible *wiseacre ;* and the harsh name of the Rhenish town *Bacharach* is often found in old English plays as *Backrag.*

The farther we go beyond the members of the family of languages to which the English belongs, the more' difficult is it, of course, to trace the nature of this change and naturalization. The *Mount Vidgeon* pea of our gardeners' catalogues reminds, probably, few readers of its *Montevidean* origin, and the familiar *nightmare* carries still fewer back to distant Finland, where *Mara*, the fearful elf, inflicts that punishment upon the wicked and the scorner. The common *demijohn*, once upon a time spelt *damajan*, has an even more remarkable derivation than the popular but apocryphal *Dame Jeanne*, commonly quoted. The name is the same as that of a city in Persia, in the province of Khorassan, called *Damaghan*, where formerly a famous kind of glassware was manufactured; the Crusaders were struck with certain articles of this ware, and brought the thing and the name together back to their European homes.

The most remarkable feature connected with this process of giving new forms and new meanings to words which are perfectly extraneous and unconnected with their history, is, that even English names should have been made to undergo such a change. This arose, probably, first in names of foreign origin, though borne by English families. The Flemish *Tupigny* became in English *Twopenny*, and the Danish names of *Asketil*, *Thurgod*, and *Guthlac* were changed into *Ashkettle*, *Thoroughgood*, and *Goodluck*. There is a place in Norwich now called Goodluck's Close, which in ancient documents is correctly written Guthlac's Close, and thus allows us to trace the gradual change from one generation to another. In the famous name of Wilber*force* an attempt is made to substitute a familiar word for one less generally known; it was anciently Wilburg*foss*. From names the process was extended to common nouns. A Welsh *rarebit* became a Welsh *rabbit*; *gorseberries* were made *gooseberries*, as *gossamer* is in many districts called *goosesummer*; and Saxon *meregold*, which contained the same old word *mere*, a marsh or water, which appears in *mer*man and *mer*maid, became *marygold*. The diminutive *kin* being no longer effective in connection with the antiquated word *culver*, (from Lat. *columba*,) it was modernized and became *culverkey*. Certain cards in our common games were of old distinguished from others by the long, splendid gown worn by king, queen, etc., according to the gorgeous costumes of the Middle Ages, and hence obtained the name of *coat cards;* afterwards the origin was forgotten, and then these royal personages suggested another idea, and they are now called *court cards*. Old Saxon words have especially suffered in this manner. What we now call *shamefaced* had originally nothing to do with a *face,* but was *shamefast,* formed after the manner of *steadfast,* and printed thus in Chaucer, Froissart, and the first authorized version of the Bible (1 Tim. ii. 9). The Saxon name of that class of plants which contains absinth was *suthewort,* or *soothing wort;* first the latter part became obscure, and gave rise to a change into *soothing wood;* then the first part also was forgotten, and the people now call it *southernwood.* A similar now unknown word *ord,* meaning the first beginning, and preserved in the German *ur,* gave rise to the expression of *ord and end,* for which we substitute the more familiar sounding but unmeaning *odds and ends,* as *topsy-turvy* is but the vulgarized form of *topside the other way.* Shuttle*cock* was not so very long ago used correctly as shuttle *cork;* but *stirrup* has long since superseded the Anglo-Saxon *stig rap,* from *stigan,* to step up, and *rap,* a rope, which in Saxon days served the purpose.

Sadder, however, by far, and yet clothed with additional interest, is the fate of English nouns that have suffered in meaning what those we have mentioned had only endured in form. Here it is the spirit itself that is maltreated ; and the effect is all the more melancholy as the principle of compensation that affords comfort to many a sufferer in life does not seem to apply in like manner to the fate of words. Many have fallen, few only have risen. Horace is either unjust or not well informed when he says : —

14

> "Multa renascentur quæ jam cecidere, cadentque
> Quæ nunc sunt in honore vocabula, si volet usus
> Quem pene arbitrium est et jus et norma loquendi."—*Ars Poet.* 70.

It is strange that terms of war should be almost the only examples of nouns that have risen from an humble to a nobler meaning. Thus *cavalry* comes from the Latin *caballus*, which meant at first nothing more than a pack-horse, from which, however, was subsequently derived the *caballarius*, who finally rose to be the French *chevalier*. *Infantry* consisted once of the *infantes*, the boys and servants, who ran, during the Middle Ages, on foot by the side of their masters on horseback; these formed gradually separate corps, known as *infanterie*, and finally assumed the place of their lords, the knights, in the estimation of great commanders. The humble servant who at first was called in Old German a *schalk*, and whose sole duty was his attendance upon a mare, became known as *marescalk;* he rose to be the superintendent of the royal stables and obtained one of the high charges at court. It was then he was named *marshal,* and distinction in the field procured for him the chief command of the forces. Still, we find, in the French army at least, by the side of the field *marshal* another *maréchal,* who still pursues a profession more akin to the first meaning of the word, for he is a simple farrier. The *knight* himself had a hard struggle before he obtained the lofty position he still occupies in our language. The first of the name known in historic documents was a menial servant, such as the German *knecht* remains to this day. Already in Anglo-Saxon writings, however, the word is used frequently for boy, as in the Southern States of America until our day every slave, of whatever age he might be, was called a boy. Thus we meet with a "tynwintra *cniht,*" a boy of ten years, and in the Anglo-Saxon version of the gospel the Apostles are called "learning *cnihts.*" Certain privileged boys were subsequently allowed to bear arms, and as this honorable distinction was only sparingly conferred, the word gradually acquired a higher application, and finally settled down, in the days of chivalry, into the grade and style of a *knight.*

Unfortunately, it is but too true, as Robertson says, that "names and words soon lose their meaning. In the process of years and centuries the latter fades off them like the sunlight from the hills. The hills are there; the color is gone." Generally the process is this : words are unfamiliar and dignified at first, they become gradually more common and with it more indifferent, until many sink at last into trivial and contemptible by-words. Occasionally the history of such decay is well authenticated, as in the case of *Bridewell.* St. Bridget, or shorter St. Bride, was the name bestowed in olden times upon a well in London, and near it a church of the same name was soon erected. Then a royal palace was added, where King John resided and even Henry VIII. in 1529. After that, however, the mansion was neglected; and when quite decayed, it was converted into a hospital, always bearing the original name of *St. Bride's Well.* This was converted in 1559 into a house of correction, by the agency of Ridley the martyr, then Bishop of London. Ultimately it became a simple prison ; and *Bridewell* is now applied, wherever English is spoken, to denote a work-house, neither blessed saint nor holy well having any thing more to do with the edifice. A somewhat similar fate was that of a priory in London, known as St. Mary's of *Bethlehem,* and founded by Simon Fitzmary, in 1247, for the pious purpose of sheltering and entertaining there the Bishop of Bethlehem whenever he should be in London. Perhaps the fact that such a remarkable visit never actually occurred afterwards, or simpler motives, led Henry VIII. in 1545 to grant it to the city, and thus brought about the conversion of this mansion into a house for the insane. Hence the name of *Bedlam* now almost universally used to designate a hospital for lunatics. As we have mentioned above several military words that had the rare good fate of reaching high honor, we may add here one that has been less fortunate. The noble family of *Merode*, famous in the history of the Netherlands, boasted of one brave member who was unfortunately more successful in making forays into the enemy's land than in obtaining great victories. This uncomfortable reputation gave rise to the term of *marauders*, such as are found hanging upon the flanks and the rear of all armies.

Among common nouns there are again many of foreign origin the meaning of which has suffered sadly in the course of time. Giving precedence to the sex, we find that the *belle dame* of the French was by Spenser already written in shorter English form, but used as yet for "fair lady." Soon after Gallic courtesy transferred the term to grandmothers, and it now appears as *beldame*, a word which afterwards sank to designate a hag or a witch. We are told a moral lesson, characteristic of the change in manners, by the French word *prude*, which originally meant a prudent, honest man, and in that signification survives in *prud'homme*, the title of umpires between mechanics and tradesmen in France. In the other sex, however, it has changed until it is often used to suggest fallen or at least ill-understood virtue rather than prudence. In this connection we may add *respectable*, which derived from its Latin elements the idea of looking back or looking twice at an object, and thus came to mean worthy of respect. Whilst in the United States the older meaning has been preserved in this as in so many English words, it has fallen in England, and refers now generally to mediocre intellect, or fallen gentility, with which we sympathize. *Antique* also conveys its lesson; used at first exclusively for what is old and old-fashioned, it was changed in form and meaning into *antics*, suggestive of the fact that in an age where the young rule, all that is old is objectionable and liable to ridicule. The haughty superciliousness with which the Roman citizen looked down upon the poor emigrant to foreign shores, gave to his *colonus* a dash of contempt, which survived for a time in the kindred feeling of Englishmen toward distant colonies, and led to the contraction of the word into *clown*. The feeling is said to be extinct; the word survives as a sign of its former prevalence. There seems to be an invincible tendency for words to become harsher and more sweeping in their condemnatory meaning, if they but contain the germ of such a growth. Is this indicative of the weakness of the human heart to see the mote in the neighbor's eye and to overlook the beam in our own? Thus we find that *base* meant originally nothing more than low or humble, and even in the old Bible version our Lord was said to be "equal to them of greatest *baseness*;" now it is used only of the scamp and the criminal. In like manner *miscreant* was simply an unbeliever, such as Joan of Arc is represented by Shakespeare; subsequently it became a term of vilest reproach. This leads us to the two words *pagan* and *villain*, both of which are now terms of reproach, after having once had reference only to the residence of certain classes of men. For when first the Gospel was proclaimed abroad in Italy, every town from the blue waters of Sicily to the snow-capped Alps in the north seems to have opened its gates wide to the messengers of peace. But in the villages and waste tracts of land which still were found here and there, the rustics went on in the old path, burning incense on their heathen altars, and slaying white bulls in honor of Jove, as their fathers had done before them. About the end of the fourth century, Theodosius finally prohibited the Pagan ceremonial altogether; from that time no fire was to be lighted in honor of any god, no wine to be poured to the genius, no incense to be offered to the Penates. The sacrifice of a victim to be offered to the gods was to be considered as high treason, and the decoration of a tree or an altar was punished with confiscation. The persecuted wor-

shipers of the ancient gods retired from the city and village
to dark forests and deserts, from the open country to retired valleys. Henceforth the worship of Venus and Jupiter ceased to be that of the great and the noble, and was
gradually more and more confined to the inhabitants of
rural districts, *pagi*. Hence it acquired its name as *religio
paganorum*, and Orosius explains the latter as men " *qui
ex locorum agrestium compitis et pagis pagani vocantur*."
From these despised worshipers of graven images the
name has come down, with undiminished strength, even to
our day. Such is the force of a word, carrying with it on
the stream of long centuries some powerful idea; and well
has it been said of old, " *Credunt homines rationem suam
verbis imperare.   Sed fit etiam ut verba vim suam super
intellectum retorqueant et reflectant*." It is curious to notice,
that, whilst *paganus* has sunk so low, its fellow *compaganus*
has risen to be our modern *companion*. In like manner,
however, fell the name of the Roman master's slave, who
was sent to his villa in the country, and hence received the
name of *villaneus*. This was by no means a word of reproach, and although it may have shared the degradation
of *pagan* to a certain degree, it was not, even in Old English,
used to express more than rusticity or coarseness. At a
certain period the word had acquired a highly offensive
moral meaning; but, by one of those strange fluctuations to
which words are as subject as the ideas which they represent, it was in Chaucer's time used to express nothing worse
than a serf, *glebæ adscriptus*, and, in the general acceptation
of a plebeian, a low-born person with low tastes. Thus
Chaucer employs it when he translates the French *vilonnie*
of Lorris in the Romaunt de la Rose, v. 2175 : —

" *Villanie* at the beginning,
I woll, sayd Love, over all thing
Thou leave, if thou wolt ne be
False and trespace agenst me;
I curse and blame generally
All hem that loven *villany*,

> For *villanie* maketh *villeine*,
> And by his deeds a chorle is seine.
> .These *villaines* are without pitie,
> Friendship, love, and all bountie."

With a somewhat different meaning he uses it, in the Prologue to his " Canterbury Tales," when he says : —

> " But firste I praie you of your curtesie
> That ye ne asette it not my *vilanie*
> Though that I plainly speke in this matere,
> Ne though I speek his wordes proprely."

It has been mentioned elsewhere how pilgrims to Rome became idle *roamers,* and those who went to the Holy Land, the Sainte Terre, were suspected of being *saunterers.* In the same manner the French word *purlieu* meant in England what it literally designates, a *pur lieu, i. e.,* lands taken in from the forest for purposes of cultivation, and hence freed from the strict forest laws of those days. Now it is commonly used for a disreputable neighborhood. Two words of Eastern origin have suffered similar decay. When the Tudors and the Stuarts made their court brilliant with gorgeous displays and cunning masks, dances in Turkish costume were much in vogue and known as *mahomerias,* from their association with Mohammed's followers. Later, the word dwindled down into *mummery,* which means now a low masquerade, a disgusting disguise. Our word *gibberish* has a loftier origin : it comes from a famous sage Geber, an Arab, who sought for the philosopher's stone in the eighth century, and perhaps used unintelligible incantations, — a custom which led to the present meaning of the word..

English words have naturally not so often suffered in this way, as there was always more or less in their sound to recall the original meaning. Still, examples are here also not wanting of words that have fallen from a high estate. There is the Anglo-Saxon *boer,* who tilled the soil and gave his name to the neigh*bor* of our day; his rustic ways, however, soon became known as *boorish,* and the coarse, ill-mannered man is apt to be called a *boor*. Hence, also, through the derivative *boorly*, our less obnoxious *burly*, which refers to external appearance only. The same transition took place in the Saxon word *ceorl*, which once was a title of honor, meaning emphatically a free man, as it still does in the German form, *Kerl*, and which is said to survive in our *Charles*. It is surmised, however, that these free dwellers on their own soil became soon obnoxious to king and nobles alike, and that hence their name soon sank to a lower meaning. The Anglo-Saxon Chronicle says already of King Charles, that he was a " Ceorla Cyng," a *churlish* king, and thus a *churl* has remained to this day a rude boor. The kindred word *fellow* is even now in a state of transition : it still has its original meaning of companionship when we speak of *fellow*-sufferers or *fellow*-citizens, or call a friend a fine *fellow ;* but *fellow* alone is no compliment, and shows the tendency of the word to assume an objectionable expression. *Knave*, on the contrary, is always a reproach. In its earlier days it served to designate a son or boy, and St. Paul was thus called a " *knave* of Jesus Christ." This is the meaning of the German *Knabe* to this day.   But when the sister language-made a slightly different word, *Knappe*, and bestowed this name upon a servant, — even as *serf* differs from *servant*, — our English did not follow the suggestive example, but used *knave* for the same purpose. This meaning accounts for our calling the king's servant in a pack of cards the *knave*, as from the German we have borrowed our *knapsack*, the boy's sack slung over his shoulder.   Hence the curious difference in meaning of the same word at different periods. Wickliffe translates Exodus i. 16 : " If it is a *knave* child, sle ye him ; if it is a woman, kepe ye," and the patient Grisel in the old ballad bore " a *knave* child " to the cruel Marquis, who had robbed her of her daughter.   But already in " Robin Hood " we read ; —

" But now I have slaine the master, he says,
Let me goe strike the *knave*."

The transition is explained by the historic fact, that the name was, at an early period, generally given to the boys in great lords' kitchens; these behaved badly and were treated badly, and thus the word became gradually a term of reproach. Shakespeare shows it to us in a state of transition, using it now for a boy and then for a scamp, whilst in "Julius Cæsar," IV., he even says: "Gentle *knave*, good-night!" It is hardly necessary to repeat that in our day the word is one of earnest condemnation.

Thus it was also with one of the numerous descendants with which the root *bred*, to breed, has endowed our language. Besides the words *breed*, *brood*, *bride*, and *brother*, it has bequeathed to us the unfortunate *brat*, which originally meant nothing but offspring, and is used as such in Dean Trench's quotation from Gascoigne's "De Profundis" : —

> "O Israel, O household of the Lord,
> O Abraham's *brats*, O brood of blessed seed,
> O chosen sheep that loved the Lord indeed."

Then it became usual to designate an ill-favored child as a *brat*, and now the word is hardly admissible in polite conversation. Three names of persons of the fairer sex have had a peculiar fate. *Gossip*, which is at least but rarely applied to men, has the same high origin as *gospel*, meaning *sib* or akin in God, and was originally used to designate all persons who jointly entered into the relation of sponsors for a child about to be baptized. The relationship, it is well known, is considered so close as to constitute, in the Catholic church, an insurmountable obstacle to marriage. Now, the word bears too pointed an allusion to the talking, slandering propensities of certain persons to be any longer complimentary. It is curious that the corresponding word in French, *commère*, has lost its exalted nature in precisely the same manner. The once noble title of *housewife*, in its full form still unsurpassed in its simple and approving meaning, has degenerated into the vile *hussy.* As if to make amends, we find that the ancient word *cwen*, once used in contrast with *gom*, as woman with man, has, from an expression of the mere difference in sex, risen to designate *the* woman by eminence, the *queen*, as *cyning*, of *the* kin, gave us *king*, and as the royal children of Spain and France are to this day called, *fils de France* and *infantes de España.*

CHAPTER XII.

ADJECTIVES.

"THE English is plenteousne enoughe to expresse our
myndes in any thing whereof one man hath nede to speke
with another," says Sir Thomas More, who evidently dealt
much in matter of fact, or despised epithets as much as
modern authors love them by the side of their nouns. For
the English is not particularly rich in adjectives, and resembles, although it does not go quite as far as, the language
of a tribe of North American Indians, the Mohegans, who
have no adjectives whatever, if we may rely on the judgment of Dr. Jonathan Edwards. It is well known how this
statement delighted our democratic philologist, Horne Tooke,
who found in it a strong proof of his doctrine, that adjectives were never original words. They are, at all events,
not a separate class of words, *not* names of persons or
things possessing an independent existence. The mental
process to which they owe their origin is the naming of
qualities, observed in tangible objects but separated from
them, so that they may be applied to others also. One consequence of this want of substantiality is, that they change
their meaning in the process of passing from one language
to another more than nouns and verbs. Nouns are always
more or less intimately connected with the object they designate, and may easily be traced back to it, even after they
have been used figuratively for generations. Adjectives, on
the other hand, express only qualities, and qualities assume

very different aspects as they are applied to different objects. A *brave homme* is by no means a *brave man* with us, and a *virtuoso* need not at all be a *virtuous* man according to our standard of morality. The national respect paid to wealth in England has long since led foreigners to notice the tendency to describe every thing that is praised as a *rich* thing, — rich colors, a rich saying, or a rich joke, even, — and to condemn what is inferior as a *poor* thing, — a poor book and a poor statue. Changes of meaning are shown most in those adjectives we have received from the French. By dint of mispronouncing and misspelling, they have often lost both form and meaning. Thus *écrasé* is now applied to the mind only as *crazy; gentil*, besides the vulgarized *genteel*, the pleasing *gentle*, and the rarer *gentile*, has produced the offensive *jaunty; puisné*, still preserved in our judges, is for all other persons simply *puny;* and *deshabillé* has, not without justice, become *shabby. Aigre* is no longer sharp, as it must once have been, to judge from the line in Chapman's " Iliad : " " Now on the *eager* razor's edge for life or death we stand." It is only in *vinegar* that it has preserved its older meaning of acrid. In other words we find a division of meaning, as in the descendants of the Latin *captivus*, which has given us first *captive*, and then, from the contempt with which early Saxons looked upon the miserable prisoner, the meaner *caitiff.* In Italian the same word, *cattivo*, now means all that is bad ; in French, *chétif* whatever is feeble and fragile. Some of these changes, which are unfortunately but seldom to be traced step by step, are so peculiar as to deserve greater attention than they have obtained heretofore. How came *gros* to be only *gross, petit* to be *petty*, and *joli* to degenerate into *jolly?* The transition has been even more injurious to a number of German adjectives, — a fatality which the learned Dean Trench ascribes to the depression of the Anglo-Saxons after their sad defeat by the Normans. If this can be proved, — and the assertion is well supported,

—their moral deterioration has left a permanent and most interesting record in our language. Some changes are inexplicable, as those of German *emsig* (busy), *klein* (little), *glatt* (smooth), and *dumm* (stupid), into *empty, clean, glad,* and *dumb*. Others show a clear demoralization, as when *taper*, (valiant) sinks into *dapper, rasch* (active) into *rash*, and *prächtig* (splendid) into *pretty*. Among these German adjectives, *bleich* (pale) also became *bleak*, although in Fox's " Book of Martyrs " the latter has still the original meaning: " When she came out, she looked as pale and as *bleak* as one that were laid out dead."

The number of adjectives derived from foreign languages is quite large, that of the natives comparatively small. In return, the English exercises, of all living languages, the greatest freedom in using any word, noun or adverb, as an adjective by merely placing it alongside of another noun. The result, with regard to the former part of speech is, that in our day, of two nouns placed side by side, one, as a matter of course, qualifies or characterizes the other, and thus performs the part of an adjective. We are all familiar with a *gold watch*, a *bottle nose*, a *University man*, an *evening dress*, or a *morning draught*. Some authors go farther, from Campbell's " Like *angel visits* few and far between," to Leigh Hunt's " With her *in-and-out deliciousness*," or Falstaff's advice to Prince Hal, " Go hang yourself in your own *heir-apparent garters*."

Original adjectives can, therefore, scarcely be said to exist in English. Even about the simplest of those now in use there hangs a doubt; our *good* has been commonly traced to the same root as *God*, and *ill* is but a contracted form of *evil*. Others, of course, cannot be so distinctly traced back to their first origin, and pass, therefore, as original.

The number of derivatives is large, and here, as among nouns, we find both Saxon and Norman syllables used for the purpose, although many of them have of late become obsolete. Many Anglo-Saxon and Old English termina-

tions, however, are still clearly known as such, and among them especially the ancient *-en*. Its use must have been very common, for among older writers we meet hundreds of words formed by its aid, which are now no longer in use. Chaucer speaks of *rosen* chaplet and *azurn* sheen; Spenser has, in " Mother Hubberd's Tale," —

> " Or els by wrestling to wex strong and heedfull,
>   Or his stiffe armes to stretch with *eughen* bowe; "

and in his " Fairy Queen," (V. 5, 30,) —

> " Let him lodge hard and lie in *strawen* bed,
>   That may pull downe the courage of his pride."

Sir Thomas More makes good use of the syllable when he says : " In their time they had *treen* chalices and *golden* prestes, and now we have *golden* chalices and *treen* prestes." This word *treen* seems to have been a favorite with our fathers, for we find, that, not to speak of Wickliffe, who has *treen* by the side of *stonen, hairen, bricken,* and *hornen,* Milton speaks in " Comus " of *treen* platters, and Jeremy Taylor recommends a *treen* cup. With true poetic instinct Woodworth still sings of "the old *oaken* bucket" and the noble poem, so full of sweet thoughts of childhood passed in the country, will no doubt preserve the old form as long as Englishmen love English songs.

Now we still use *brazen* and *flaxen, woolen* and *wooden, golden,* and sometimes *leaden* and *silken ;* but there is a manifest tendency in the language to dispense with this class of adjectives, and to substitute for them the simple form of the noun. *Brazen* is giving way to *brass* ornaments, *oaken* to *oak* floor, and *oaten* to oatmeal. *Golden* and *earthen* are still familiar to us, because they are in our Bibles ; but on all other occasions the nouns are employed, and we speak of a *gold* pin and of *earth*-works. *Woolen* holds likewise its own, but its meaning is more limited than before the time when the town of Worstead, in the parish of Norfolk, first established extensive manufactories of *worsted.* The corresponding forms of Latin words in English are

such as *ligneous* and *marine*, of Greek, *cedrine* and *petrine*.
The adjective derived from *austere* has become somewhat
obscured, being shortened into *stern ;* in the ancient ballad
of " Northumberland Betrayed," by Douglas, we find still :—

> " But who is yond thou lady faire
> That looketh with sic an *austeren* face ? "

The termination *-y*, simple as it appears at first sight, is
of great antiquity and original power. It is the last faint
echo of a syllable corresponding to the Greek *-ικος*, from
ἄγω, and to the Latin *-icus*, from *ago*. Only in one single
instance has the fuller form been brought down directly
from the Greek; this is in the word φρενέτικος, which gave
to the Italians their *farnetico*, and to us the modern *frantic*.
Its Anglo-Saxon form had already softened into *-ig ;* the
final *g* was then, most probably, pronounced like a gentle
aspirate, as is the case now in all such words in German,
and, finally, the *g* becoming silent, the English wrote it *y*,
the Scotch *ie*. Thus we have made words like *bloody, any,
holy, mighty, speedy, sorry* (from sore), *ready*, and others,
but not our numerals with the same termination ; for these
the final syllable is *ty*, and has a very different origin and
meaning. When the original word terminates already in a
vowel, we insert, as an orthographical precaution, an additional *e* between it and the final *y ;* this is the origin of our
clayey and *skyey*.

The rarer *-ish*, on the other hand, seems to be of entirely
modern origin, for the Greek did not know it at all, and
the Latin only in verbs, as *viresco* and *pallesco*, from which
are descended the many Norman verbs of the kind, like
garnish and *furnish*. It appears first in Italian adjectives
as *-esco*, and in French as *-esque*, which we have preserved in
picturesque and *statuesque* (?), *arabesque* and *moresque, burlesque* and *grotesque*. The leading idea seems to be that of
likeness, and, as what is only like another object is not the
same as the original, there followed soon the idea of mere
resemblance, and hence of diminution. It differs from *like*

in this, that it refers only to the outside quality, not to the essential character. Thus we speak of *Jewish* and *knavish*, of *bluish* and *grayish ;* and occasionally in connection with a French root, as in *feverish* and *foolish.* The modern *Scotch, Welsh,* and *French* are but contracted forms of the original *Scottish, Walish,* and *Frankish.* We express the meaning of *ish* in Latin words by forms like *rubescent,* and in Greek by *oidal,* as in *spheroidal.*

Of greater importance at present, and of true Saxon origin, is the frequent termination *-ly,* the remnant of the original *lic.* There was yet not only in Anglo-Saxon, but even in Old English, a noun *lice,* which meant, rather technically, the body, and hence often served to designate the corpse. Its German representative, *Leiche,* still in use, has that meaning exclusively, and retains the pronunciation of our Saxon fathers; for the town of Leigh, near Wigan, the name of which is derived from this root, is pronounced by simple and gentle alike with the true guttural sound of the German *ch.* Numerous old terms and local names are derived from the same word, and retain, more or less distinctly, the primary meaning. Halliwell gives us *lichwort* as herb pellitory, and *lychebells* as hand-bells rung for the dead. We are all familiar with the superstitious awe inspired by the uncouth calls of the *lich-owl,* which either accompanies the laying-out of a dead person or foretells the near approach of death. The town of *Lichfield,* the birthplace of Dr. Johnson, is said by Bailey to derive its name of a field of carcasses from the fact that "a great many suffered martyrdom there in the time of Diocletian." In Scotland the same term *lich-field* is frequently used for churchyard as a graveyard; and in some parts of England the gate appropriated specially for the admission of dead bodies before interment is to this day called *lich-gate,* though often misspelt as *leech-gate.* The path leading to this entrance is in Exmoor and the west of England called the *leech-way,* and in Cheshire the *lich-road.*

Chaucer introduces, in the " Knight's Tale," 3959, a similar word when he says,—

> "Ne how the *lichewache* was yhold,
> All thilke night,"

which sitting up with the dead body is now generally a *like-wake*, and, not unfrequently, especially in the North of England, a *late-wake*.

From this ancient word we derive in modern English a double form for adjectives: the full form *like*, the German *gleich*, where we wish to convey the idea of full resemblance in character and all essentials, in the sense, in fact, in which Shakespeare says, in " Julius Cæsar,"—

> "That every *like* is not the same, O Cæsar,
> The heart of Brutus yearns to think upon."

The Scotch proverb, " *Like*'s an ill mark," expresses the same, namely, that to be like a thing is often very far from being that thing. In this sense we form adjectives like *life-like*, *church-like*, and *court-like*. When we wish, on the other hand, to express a mere general resemblance, not in essential qualities but in form or in figure, we employ the shortened form *-ly*, and thus make *lively*, *curly*, and *manly*. In many cases double forms exist, where the full word gives the full meaning, the shortened word the curtailed meaning. The difference is easily perceived between *godlike* and *godly*, *ghost-like* and *ghostly*, *death-like* and *deathly*, or *heaven-like* and *heavenly*. *Clearly*, *durably*, *valiantly*, *voraciously*, and *passively* are examples of French words which have assumed the Saxon ending; they never take *like* with its full Saxon meaning. The original word is obscured and almost concealed in forms like *frolic*, which originally meant nothing more than *freely*, as it came from *freo*, our *free*, and *silly*, which is derived from the word *seld*, strange or rare, still retained in our *seldom*.

The termination *-some* is even now in the act of becoming obsolete, and its primary meaning has so entirely faded away from the memory of men that it is extremely difficult to trace it with certainty to its true origin. The most probable derivation is from a root which has also given us our *sum*, a presumption strengthened by the fact that we use it under the same form of *some* already when we wish to denote an indefinite sum or quantity. Thus we say, "I went *some* twenty miles," or, "He gave him *some* hundred pounds." Here, as in *en*, the former frequency and the gradual disappearance of the termination may be distinctly traced from generation to generation. Wickliffe has *lovesum* and *hatesum*, *lustsum* and *wealsum*, *heavysum* and *delightsum*. Beaumont and Fletcher are fond of the still surviving *toothsome*, Shakespeare has *laborsome*, and Milton *unlightsome*. Even in so recent a writer as Hume we find *playsome*, *gleesome*, and *joysome*, which are rapidly disappearing from the pages of modern authors. We may rest contented with having lost the derivative of *ugly*, which we find in Surrey's Æneid, (II. p. 29,) —

> "In every place the *ugsome* syhtes I saw,"

but the loss of *longsome*, familiar to German scholars as *langsam* (slow) in that language, is much to be regretted. The ballad of " Gilderoy " has, —

> " Wi' mickle joy we spent our prime
> Till we were baith sixteen,
> And aft we pest the *langsome* time
> Among the leaves sae green."

With the exception of a few like *fulsome* (from foulsome), *wearisome*, and *lonesome*, there seems to be a tendency to retain this beautiful and expressive form only for words conveying pleasing impressions, such as *gleesome*, *mirthsome*, *handsome*, and *toothsome*. The Norman hybrids are of a different nature: there we have *venturesome*, *quarrelsome*, and *cumbersome*. *Irksome* comes from the Saxon form *wyrc*, our *work*, and therefore means literally "full of work." *Buxom* was formerly *boughsom*, like a bough to be bent, as in the German *biegsam*, of which Dean Trench gives us the interesting illustration in an ancient profession of submission: "I submit myself unto this holy church of

Christ, to be ever *buxom* and obedient to the ordinances of it." Why it should nowadays be almost exclusively applied to widows is difficult of explanation; it may be that an indistinct association between a bough and a green old age may have led to the connection.

One of the most fertile words of this kind is *-less*, from the Saxon *lease*, to lose, which gives us *fatherless* and *motherless*, *careless*, and *reckless*, literally one who has lost his reckoning. It adapts itself with greater readiness than others to French roots, as in *artless*, *merciless*, *graceless*, *joyless*, and *painless*. Its sense is so manifest and so suggestive that new adjectives of this class are continually made by modern authors; some obtain admission into the body of the language, others are understood but not adopted. Byron ventured far in the lines : —

> " The world was void,
> The population and the powerful was a lump,
> *Seasonless, herbless, treeless, manless, lifeless,*
> A lump of death, a chaos of hard clay."

It is not much to the credit of the people, if we may judge them by their language, that the idea of loss should have produced such numbers of derivatives, whilst the opposite idea of holding fast is met with but rarely. We have but a few, like *steadfast*, and one of the most expressive, *shamefast*, as it is printed in the Bible of 1611, (1 Tim. ii. 9,) meaning protected by shame, is now sadly changed by ignorance into *shamefaced*.

Among these derivative adjectives we must not forget those that have been made negative either by the Saxon *un*, or the Norman French *in*. The former prevailed for a time even after the Conquest; then followed, apparently, a period of confusion, during which *un* and *in* were used without distinction, until, finally, the all-powerful tendency to uniformity made *in* the prevailing form. Thus we use now *incapable* exclusively for the once universal *uncapable*. Shakespeare has *unpossible* (" Richard II.," Act II., sc. 2), and " like a thing *unfirm*," (" Julius Cæsar "). Milton uses

repeatedly *unactive*, and, with strange forgetfulness, says, in
" Paradise Lost," X., " *Uninmortal* made all kinds."   It is
somewhat strange that the disposition to adopt the French
in for all cases, should have affected Saxon words more
than French ; for we still say, *uncertain, unceasing*, and *un-
determined*, and generally use, even now, *un* with French
adjectives. This is all the more remarkable as the language
shows generally a very decided tendency to admit such hybrids only as exceptions, and, as a rule, to combine words
of the same race only, — Latin with Latin, and Saxon with
Saxon.   The state of transition in which the negative prefix now is may be seen from the varied forms in which it
appears in modern English.   We have the pure Saxon elements in *unlike*, a German and a Norman word combined in
uncertain, a Latin form in *insecure*, and finally the softened,
probably French, *ignoble*.

Although we no longer decline our adjectives, as the
Anglo-Saxons did, we still inflect them for the purpose of
forming what grammarians not very appropriately call their
comparative degrees.   As adjectives express but a quality
belonging to some person or object, the extent of being
thus qualified will necessarily differ much in various cases.
Two persons may be endowed with the same quality, but
one will possess it in a higher degree than the other ; and
all languages have made efforts to express this difference in
meaning by a change in the form of the adjective itself,
rather than by additional words.   It is a remarkable fact,
not yet satisfactorily explained, that the oldest of well-
known languages, the Sanscrit, the Zend, the Greek, and
the Latin, all possess double forms for what we now call
the comparative and superlative.

The Sanscrit makes the comp. in *tara*[1] or *iyas*, the superl. in *tama or ishta*.
  " Zend   "   "   *tara* " *is,*   "   "   *tama* " *ishta.*
  " Greek   "   "   τερος " ων,   "   "   τατος " ιστος.
  " Latin   "   "   *ter* " *tus,*   "   "   *mus* " *stus.*

[1] This *tara* is not a pronominal ending, like so many others, but an
ancient root, which means to go beyond, and reappears in the Latin *trans*

Thus we find ἀμείνων and μείζων, ἄριστος and μέγιστος. The Latin, likewise, has *alter, uter, neuter,* (*magister,*) and, for the ancient *tus,* the more recent form *ior,* as in *major* and *firmior;* in the superlative, *optimus* and *maximus* by the side of *venustus, vetustus,* and *robustus.* The example set by these venerable languages has been faithfully followed by more modern idioms, and we find in all kindred languages a similar duality of forms. The English shares, of course, this peculiarity, and we have, to this day, a comparative in *r* or in *s,* and a superlative in *m* or in *st.* The early history of these forms is not quite as clear as would be desirable for the honor of etymologists; we will state here only the most plausible, and, at the same time, best authenticated theory.

It is probable that the forms of our degrees have passed through an extremely simple and regular process. Taking it for granted that the letter *r* is the principal sign of the comparative, common to all Indo-European languages, as is now well established, we find the ancient Saxon word *â,* meaning time, thus treated. It is the same word we meet already in Greek as ἀεί or αἰών, in Latin as *ævum,* and in German as *ewig.* Changed into a higher degree, it appears in Anglo-Saxon as *ær* or *ar,* which has given us our *ere,* more in time, as it were, and hence meaning *before,* or, when used as a derivative, *erely,* our modern *early.* Thus it is still used by Shakespeare : —

> " *Ere* a determinate resolution he did require a respite."
> *Henry VIII.* II. 4.

The same simple and primitive word was next formed into a superlative by the letters *st,* which are in like manner found to be common to all the idioms which belong to the same family as our English. Hence arose the Anglo-Saxon form *aerest,* which has, in its turn, given us our *erst,* first in

and the French *très.* When the latter, therefore, places *très* before an adjective in order to express a high or transcendent degree, it does no more than English does by adding *er* to the end of an adjective.

time. The transition from time to other qualities was easy enough; what was at first only asserted with regard to this one relation, was soon used to express a similar superiority in other respects also, until the two forms *ere* and *erst* became the general means of forming what we now call the degrees. It is in this manner and for these reasons that we, in common with all branches of the German family, make the comparative of adjectives by adding *er*, and the superlative by adding *est*. Irregular forms, however, occur here as in all languages. It is well known how both Greek and Latin abounded with such varieties of forms. In the former, —

ἀγαθός had ἀμείνων and ἄριστος,   κακός had κακίων and κάκιστος,
    βελτίων and βέλτιστος,   χείρων and χείριστος,
    κρείσσων and κράτιστος,   ἥσσων and ἥκιστος,
    λῴων and λῷστος.

In the latter, *bonus* made *melior* and *optimus; malus, pejor* and *pessimus.*

Some of the so-called irregular forms in English are, however, only in appearance such, having merely retained the Anglo-Saxon *umlaut,* or change of radical vowel, which is to this day in German faithfully preserved. Hence we make of *old* the forms *older* and *oldest,* by the side of *elder* and *eldest.* The former we use to designate old age absolutely, and thus speak of that oft-quoted personage, the "oldest inhabitant;" the latter expresses merely relative superiority of age, as in the "Elder Pliny," or the "Elders" of the Church. It is the descendant of the ancient form of the adjective, which was *eld,* as Shakespeare still has it when he says, —

> " And well you know
> The superstitious idle-headed *eld*
> Received and did deliver to our ag
> This tale of Herne, the hunter, for a truth."
> *Merry Wives,* IV. 4.

In like manner we now make of *long* only *longer* and *longest,* but Chaucer has *lenger* for the former, and the original vowel survives in our *length* and in the word *Lent*, so called because at that season the days begin once more to lengthen, so that formerly Lent meant not only the religious season, but Spring simply, as in a poem of the thirteenth century:—

> " *Lenten* ys come with love to toune,
>   With blosmen and with briddes [birds] roune,
>   That al thys blysse bryngeth."

The large majority of so-called irregularities arise from the custom, also common to all known languages, of allowing one or the other form of these degrees to become obsolete, and of substituting another word of similar meaning for it, which produces the appearance as if two entirely different adjectives were closely connected with each other. Thus the Latin language dropped *junis*, which is now only known in the noun *juvenis*, but retained *junior;* its positive *senes* survives only as *senex*, but *senior* is still in use. Thus it is with our *more* and *most*, which are commonly quoted as comparative and superlative of *much*, without having any etymological relation with that word. It is not a little remarkable that *most* seems to be of ancient descent, for it is evidently one and the same word with μεῖστος, used instead of μέγιστος, with the *magsimus* of Latin, and the *meist* of the German. In our own language we trace it back to an obsolete Anglo-Saxon *ma* or *moe*, related to the equally old verb *mawan*, to mow. What was *mown* made a little heap, and *mown* thus naturally used to designate a small quantity, in which sense we still employ it when we speak of *hay-mow* or *barley-mow*, as *mow-burnt* hay is hay which has been burnt in the stack. For this derivation speaks also the use of *maer* and *maest* in Scotland and some of the Northern counties; to which may be added the odd use made of both forms in Scotland, where they speak of *brothermaist*, quite brotherly, and use the equally curious expressions *fartherwaur* and *fatherbetter*. A diminutive form of this word *mae* also survives from oldest times 'in the Anglo-Saxon *micel*, and the Scotch *mickle* or *muckle*,

still surviving in the family name of *Mitchell*, literally the
Great. Hence we say also, "Many a little makes a *mickle* ;"
and in the "Comedy of Errors," III. 1, we read, —

> "The one ne'er got me credit, the other *mickle* blame."

Moe itself is quaintly enough used as a comparative in older
authors. Caxton says, "Many *mo* unto the nombre of ten
thousand and *moo* (were slayne)." The same form occurs
continually in Chaucer and Spenser, *e. g.* : —

> "All these and many evils *moe* haunt Ire." — *Fairy Queen*, I. 4, 35.

Shakespeare also has it as in "Julius Cæsar :" " No, sir, there
are *moe* with him ;" and in " Much Ado about Nothing,"
III. 3 : —

> "Sing no more dittles, sing no *moe*
> Or dumps so dull and heavy,
> The frauds of men were ever so
> Since summer first was leavy,"

where the verse evidently requires it to rhyme with *so*.

The adjective *bad* also has nothing more than a similar-
ity of meaning in common with the comparative degrees
worse and *worst*. These are, on the contrary, derived from
the word *woe*, now used as a noun only, but formerly treated
as an adjective with its Old English derivatives *wyrse* and
wyrst, and its Scotch and North of England forms *waur* and
war. The substitution of these words for the regular *bad-
der* was apparently not completed until a comparatively
recent date, for Chaucer still says, —

> "to this *badder* ende," — 10538,

and Shakespeare was so little familiar with the nature of
worse that he continually uses *worser*, as in " Richard III.,"
where he says, —

> "I wish your grandam had a *worser* march,"

and *worsest* was much affected by all the writers of the fifteenth and sixteenth centuries, not excluding Shakespeare.
Even Dryden says yet, " *worser* far than arms."

In like manner we have lost the once popular adjective
bet, from which, with a doubled final consonant, we derive

our *better*, and *best* by contracting the old form *betest*. The substitution of *good*, also, cannot have taken place very early, or Chaucer would not say, when he introduces his cook, in the " Canterbury Tales : " —   .

> " He loved *bet* the taverne than the shoppe."

Bet also survives in a name which few will now associate with its true origin, *Batavia*, which was originally *Betuwe*, the good meadow, in contrast with *Veluwe*, the bad meadow.

Little is nowadays coupled with *less* and *least*, both of which come from a now obsolete adjective, *leas* or *less*, *least* being but a contraction of its regular superlative, *leasest*. Formerly the comparative was *lesser*, and the substitution of *less* is quite recent. Fuller always uses the former; Shakespeare says, in " Richard III. : " —

> " There is ne'er a man in Christendom
> Can *lesser* hide his love or hate than he; "

and Addison speaks of " the *lesser* Muse." Even the regular superlative of *little* survived still in the days of Shakespeare, for in " Hamlet," III., 2, we read, —

> " When love is great, the *littlest* doubts are fear."

We preserve in the name of the *Netherlands* an Old English comparative, which is even now in the process of disappearing from our language. The adjective *neath*, now surviving only in *beneath*, furnished formerly the derivative *nether*, which is now almost entirely superseded by *lower*. Henry VIII., however, appealed still to " the *nether* House of Parliament," and Milton uses it continually, *e. g.* : —

> " Among these the seat of man
> Earth with her *nether* ocean circumfus'd
> Their pleasant dwelling-place." — *Par. Lost*, VII. 624;

and, —

> " In yonder *nether* world where shall I seek
> His bright appearances, or footstep trace ? "

As in *nether*, so we have in *rather* also a comparative from a lost adjective; the original form, *rathe*, has, howeve'r, only lately become obsolete, for not only Chaucer says, in the " Miller's Tale : " —

> " Why ryse ye so *rathe !* Ey benedicite,
>   What eyleth you ? "

but Milton also says, —

> " Bring the *rathe* primrose that forsaken dies."

It was this use of *rathe* in the sense of early, which led to the use of *rather* as meaning at first *earlier* only.   When Mandeville (46) speaks of " the *rather* Town of Damyete," he means an *older* town, and Spenser, in the " Shepherd's Calendar " for February, means *earlier* when he says that

> " The *rather* lambs been starved with cold."

Ratherest, which Shakespeare uses in " Love's Labor's Lost," IV. 2, can hardly be defended, but *rathest* is used by Bishop Sanderson in his sermons, and, as Dean Trench assures us, even quite recently.

Near is an ill-treated word, which was originally a comparative, the contracted form of *neaher*, from the Anglo-Saxon *neah*, now *nigh*, as in *well-nigh* and *neighbor*.   It lost, afterwards, its comparative meaning, and became a simple positive,—a degradation to which, no doubt, the sad misspelling of the root contributed largely.   It was not unfrequently disguised, as in the following lines from the " Miller's Tale : "

> " Forsooth this proverbe is no lye,
>   Men say thus always, the *nye* slye
>   Maketh the ferre love to be lothe."

In *lief*, on the contrary, we have a positive which has lost, almost beyond recovery, its once very popular comparative degrees, and is itself fast growing obsolete.   It has been so completely set aside that few are aware of its close relationship with the Anglo-Saxon verb *leofan*, our *love*, and its connection with the Old English *leman*, once *liefman* and *lefman*, the dear one, and as such continually used of both sexes.   In Chaucer's time it still had this first meaning of love, as in the " Monk's Tale : " —

> " They lyved in ioye and in felycite,
>   For eche of them had other *lefe* and dere."

The modern use of the word occurs, however, as early as Shakespeare, who says, —

> " I had as *lief* not be as live to be in awe
>   Of such a thing as I myself." — *Julius Cæsar.*

The Germans have preserved it in the endearing word *lieb*, which they connect with the genitive *aller*, (of all,) to make it emphatic; and thus its English form occurs in " Henry VI.," (2) I. 1, —

> " Will ye, mine *allerliefest* sovereign? "

One of the nicest points in English, not only for foreigners, but even for native writers, is the judicious choice between these simple forms of the comparative degrees and those obtained by the addition of *more* and *most*, or, especially before participles, *better* and *best.* In rare cases only, the two forms serve to express an essential difference of meaning; generally it is simply a question of euphony or established usage. We are commonly taught not to add *er* and *est* to long adjectives, but Chaucer, and the best authors down to the seventeenth century, knew no such rule, and modern writers seem to pay it but little respect, if we may judge from Sidney's *refiningest*, and Coleridge's *safeliest*, which, it must be admitted, do not sound well. Another class of adjectives which generally avoid the regular form, are those made by the addition of words like *full, some, less*, &c. This rule was, however, formerly as little observed as the preceding, for we find in Wickliffe *plenteouslyer*, in Fuller *easiliest*, in Dryden *plainliest.* Chaucer has *wofuller* and *fittingest*, Goldsmith in his " Vicar of Wakefield " *cunninger* and *cruelest*, Milton uses *hopefullest*, and even Washington Irving writes *knowingest.* The rule that adjectives of Norman-French origin ending in *ent, ous, ain, al, ive*, &c., refuse to take the Saxon terminations as neither suitable nor congenial, is more generally observed, though here, also, Chaucer indulges in *royaller* and *gentillest.* Even in our day great liberties are taken with certain adjectives, though we admit that if the author of "Master Humphrey's Clock" introduces us to the "mildest, amiablest, forgivingest-spirited, longest-sufferingest female," the man who will pardon such a string of bad superlatives on any other score than that of weak humor, must be the mildest, amiablest, &c., male of a critic.

Occasionally the difference of form enables us to distinguish a predicate from an attribute, as in Byron's lines, —

"Till
Some *worthier* should appear, if I have found such
As you yourselves shall own *more worthy*."

It is not quite so easy to understand Ben Jonson's admiration for the combined use of these double forms, especially those of the superlative. He considered them "as a kind of English atticism or eloquent phrase of speech, imitating the manner of the *most ancientest* and finest Grecians, who for more emphasis and vehemencies' sake used so to speak." It cannot be denied, however, that his fanciful preference is shared by many of our best writers. The Bible has made us familiar with " the *Most Highest* " and " the *most strictest* sect of our religion." Shakespeare has "the *most unkindest* cut of all ;" Milton, in his " Penseroso," " But first and *chiefest* with thee bring," and Addison, " That on the sea's *extremest* border." Byron says in "Manfred," A. I, —

" From thy own lips I drew the charm
Which gave all these their *chiefest* harm."

Whatever can be pleaded in defense of such forms by poets, double comparative forms can hardly be excused on any plea. " *More sorer* punishments " in Hebrews, x. 29, convey no special meaning to us, and Shakespeare's

" Nor that I am *more better* than Prospero." — *Tempest* I. 2,

would justify one of the thousand emendations bestowed upon less objectionable expressions.

It is an open question yet, even with the masters of the

Science of Philology, whether the compounds of *most* with adverbs, like *foremost, inmost, outmost* (utmost), *hindmost,* &c., are really double superlatives ; but no such doubt is attached to the curious forms *innermost, uppermost, uttermost,* and *hindermost,* where, alone in the language, the two degrees are combined in the same word. The Cockney has slyly taken advantage of these eccentric formations, and fashions for his private use new words of the kind, speaking of " the *endermost* house in the street," or of meeting " the *biggermost* man in the parish in his own *bettermost* wig." We shall hardly be justified in complaining much of the liberty he takes as long as even the most fastidious of our authors use such superfluous superlatives as *amongst, amidst, whilst,* and *betwixt,* for which there is no other excuse but established usage

CHAPTER XIII.

PRONOUNS.

" Juvat integros accedere fontes. " — Juvenal.

WELL have pronouns from of old been looked upon as
"venerable relics of languages," for the more we know
of their history, the more clearly can we trace them, not
in one idiom only, but in the whole vast family of Indo-
European languages, up to the very fountain-head.   The
veteran Bopp has proved them to be, beyond comparison,
the oldest of all the elements in our languages, and even
the so-called irregular forms have been shown to be the
most regular, inasmuch as they have preserved the ancient
terminations of the Aryan with greater fidelity than either
nouns or adjectives.   Belonging, as it were, to man himself more directly and intimately, they have been cherished by him with all the partiality and tenderness we are
apt to bestow upon what is thus bound up with our individuality.   For their great and main purpose is to express
personality.   Some express it as it belongs to the speaker
and the person spoken to, and with it, necessarily, to the
relations existing between them.   This applies mainly to
I and *thou*, which, as a matter of course, are inseparable
from the idea of personality.   The others transfer personality and bestow it on whatever is thus spoken of.   Grammarians tell us that they are, as their name indicates, mere
substitutes for the noun, which we do not like to repeat as
often as the same idea is reintroduced.   This is but taking
the very lowest view of one of the most important agents

in the intercourse between man and man. But even in this
aspect we must not overlook the fact that conveniences and
luxuries belong everywhere to a high state of civilization and
refinement. It is not otherwise in languages. The simplest
and rudest are content with expressing what is absolutely
necessary for their general purpose. As new ideas are
evolved, and the minds of the people are more and more
cultivated, additional words not only are required, but convenient forms also are introduced, which at first would have
been deemed superfluous. Hence, when new idioms are
discovered, or known ones compared with others, one of the
first questions asked is after their pronouns. Their number,
and abundant but correct use, is considered at once as the
best evidence of the elegance and the refinement of a language. They are, of all parts of speech, the most distinctive feature of an idiom. They remind us most forcibly of
the intimate connection between the outer and the inner
world, which we can here also observe acting upon one
another. Ben Jonson's words recur almost instinctively to
our mind, when he says that " Language is the mirror of
the soul. Speak that I may see thee! For it springs out of
the most retired and inmost parts of us, and is the image
of the parent of it — the mind. No glass renders a man's
form and likeness so true as his speech." This is eminently
the case with pronouns, and may be noticed even in little
children. At first, being accustomed to hear themselves
spoken of as the baby, or Charles and Mary, they call themselves in the same way, and say " Charley wants to go to
bed," or " Mary loves papa." It is a great step in the
mental development of a child, when it first gives expression to its consciousness of individuality, and uses the proud
I — a step which, in certain imperfect languages like the
Algonquin, has never yet been reached, as they still largely
substitute *she* for *I.*

This remarkable individuality of pronouns is strikingly
illustrated by the historic fact, that even in times of con-

quest and subjugation, they have ever been most faithfully preserved by the suffering nations. All the civilized nations of the world have retained them with unsurpassed tenacity, and our English has given most interesting proof of this conservatism in the days of the Conquest. For among so many thousand words imposed upon the conquered race by the victorious Norman, there is not to be found a single pronoun. No Saxon, it seems, could ever be brought to say *je* or *vous*, for *I* and *you*, though the verb, with which the pronoun was connected, was pure French, as we still say *I vouch* and *you march.*

There lies, however, in this very antiquity and uninterrupted usefulness through so many ages, one of the great difficulties in analyzing pronouns. They are of such hoary old age, that in tracing them up toward the fountain-head, we are soon lost in utter darkness, where history is silent and even inscriptions are wanting. Besides, Schlegel already has observed, that like small change which loses its stamp and impress by continuous transfer, whilst the larger pieces retain it clear and undimmed, these short, much used pronouns lose their substance and characteristic marks until they can hardly be recognized. Without endeavoring, therefore, to trace them in all instances through the various changes they have undergone, we shall confine ourselves here to such hints and suggestions as seem likely to throw more light on their present form and meaning.

The great variety and the strict use made of personal pronouns in English shows, as much as any other characteristic feature of our people, the peculiar value attached by the " free Briton " to his person. His well-founded self-respect, his proud self-consciousness, is embodied as it were in the capital initial, with which he alone, amid all modern nations, adorns the pronoun of the first person, *I.* It is in like manner that he expresses his nationality so very differently from a Frenchman or a German. The latter most modestly says, *Ich bin aus Deutschland,* "I am from Germany;" he belongs to his native land, and all he has to do with it is, that he came from it. The Frenchman rises proudly to the consciousness of his identity with the land that gave him birth ; he says, *Je suis Français*, " I am French," and feels himself a part of the great nation. But the Englishman, more proudly still, at once presents his personal individuality, and says, " I am an Englishman," presenting himself as well defined and as independent as his own sea-girt land, as haughty and conscious of strength as the sea that he loves to rule. Even the slang term, borrowed from naval registers, of "A No. 1," reminds us of the fact that the pronoun of the first person was originally, in Hebrew, for instance, and elsewhere, *ech*, the same as *one* (Ezekiel, xviii. 10). It has passed safely through the Greek ἐγώ, and the Latin *ego ;* it reappears in Old Norse as *ek*, in Anglo-Saxon as *ic*, and has only in later days lost its consonant and dwindled down to simple *I. Ik* is still used by Chaucer, who says in the " Reve's Prologue," —

<blockquote>" But ik am olde, me lest not play for age."</blockquote>

Sometimes he substitutes *Ich* or *Iche ;* which corresponds to the form of the modern German *ich ;* and even Skelton says, (I. 95,) for " I will," *Ichyll*, and (102,) *Ich am*.

As the first person was represented by a word equivalent to *one*, so the pronoun of the second person corresponds to the numeral *two*. The Greek σύ and δύω, the Latin *tu* and *duo*, are clearly one and the same, not to speak here of older forms. The Anglo-Saxon *thu*, reduced in German to *du*, has with us expanded into *thou*. This, it is well known, was once universally used in addressing persons of any rank in life, and it is one of the severest losses the English has ever suffered, that this pronoun is now no longer employed. We have thus lost the voice of peculiar intimacy and special affection, the expression of the tender bond that unites husband and wife, parents and children. How touching is the German *du*, so suggestive of warmer love and closer friendship ! Even the Frenchman can yet *tutoyer*, little as

we may be disposed to sympathize with the use he makes
of the privilege. . Nor must we overlook the fact, that with
the pronoun we have lost another beautiful feature which
adorned Old English — the greater variety of forms in the
verb, like *lovest, lovedst,* &c., which we now only meet with
in the unique *thou wast,* and occasional outbursts of exalted
language. The word seems not to have been entirely abandoned until the seventeenth century, for in 1648, George
Fox says in his journal: "When the Lord sent me forth
into the world, I was required to thee and thou all men and
women, without any respect to rich or poor, great or small.
But ah ! the rage that then was in priests, magistrates, and
people of all sort, but especially in priests and professors,
for though *thou* to a single person was according to their
own learning, their accidence, and their grammar rules,
they could not bear it." It is known from other sources
that in those days *thou* still continued to be used as a sign
of familiarity and love, but it was already considered as
not quite respectful when used with persons of superior
rank or perfect strangers. The Quakers, however, continued it only as they found it, instead of following the fashion which discarded it just at the time at which their sect
became more numerous and influential. There is less to
be said in defense of their habit of using the indirect *thee*
under almost all circumstances for *thou.* It is true that
pronouns generally seem to claim in some manner an ex-
emption from the dominion or the tyranny of Syntax. The
most fastidious authors have taken great liberties with
their grammatical forms, and who would, *e. g.,* think of
rectifying Shelley's bold expression, —

"Lest there be
No solace left for *thou* or me."

Grammatical laws of any kind seem to have so slight a
hold on personal pronouns, that a mere point of euphony is
considered sufficient to justify their neglect, and this universal freedom has been but systematized by the Quakers.

There is, besides, another plea which may be used in their behalf. It is a very old and general custom to substitute an oblique case for the nominative, arising, probably, from the fact that in speaking and in writing, the former are heard so much more frequently than the latter. Whenever, therefore, a foreign language has been adopted by a nation, as the Latin was by the Gauls, they have invariably chosen that form which appears in the different oblique cases, and not the nominative.

Illiterate people especially show the same tendency even now, and all over the world they say, almost without exception, *me* for *I*, *him* for *he*, and vice-versa. Sterne already asks the question, " What can be the reason that all the little children of Great Britain and Ireland universally say *me* for *I?* " (vi. 157.) " It is *me!* " is the almost unfailing answer to the usual " Who 's there ? " and *us* most frequently fills the place of *we*. " Piers Ploughman " (181) sings early —

> " Lord yworshipped be *the*,"

and even Dryden does not disdain saying, —

> " Scotland and *thee* did in each other live."

Shakespeare, faithfully reflecting, in this as in all points, the people's language, makes his fool say in " King Lear " (I. 4), —

> " It would not be *thee*, nuncle,"

but he goes farther than that, and ventures in his " Twelfth Night " (II. 3), upon —

> "Did you never see the picture of *we* three ? "

Mr. Gilpin, in his " Remarks on Forest Scenes," says that he has " oftener than once met with the following tender elegiacs in churchyards in Hampshire : —

> ' *Him* shall never come again to *we*,
> But we shall surely one day go to *he*.' "

The pronoun of the second person is now used only for

specific purposes, such as to give vigor and solemnity, or in earnest appeals. Thus Pope says in his " Iliad." —

> " Ah, wretch, no father shall *thy* corpse compose,
> *Thy* dying eyes no tender mother close ! "

and elsewhere, —

> " Clad in Achilles' arms if *thou* appear
> Proud Troy may tremble and desist from war."

In like manner Milton employs it in " Paradise Lost," where he says : —

> " And *thou*, enlightened earth, so fresh and gay ! "

If we were to venture upon substituting *you* for *thou*, the effect of the whole passage would be, if not lost, at least much diminished and marred. The trite proverb that " Familiarity breeds contempt," finds its practical illustration in this, that we use *thou* for the loftiest purpose for which language can be employed — for our worship of the Creator — and at the same time for the expression of contempt. As soon as *thou* ceased to be heard beyond the domestic circle and the intimacy of friends, it became a sign of disregard, because we are apt to treat those with insulting familiarity whom we do not respect. Thus, at Sir Walter Raleigh's trial, when Coke was at a loss for argument and evidence alike, he fell back upon the easier mode of attack, and said insultingly : "All that Lord Cobham did was at *thy* instigation, *thou* viper, for I *thou thee, thou* traitor." When Sir Toby Belch is urging Sir Andrew Aguecheek to send a challenge to Viola, he says : —

> " *Thou* elfish-marked, abortive rooting hog,
> *Thou* that wast sealed in thy nativity,
> The slave of Nature and the son of hell !
> *Thou* slander of *thy* mother's heavy womb,
> *Thou* rag of honour, *thou* detested : "

and in " Twelfth Night," " Taunt him with the license of ink ; if thou *thou'st* him some thrice, it shall not be amiss."

The so-called first person, representing the speaker, and the second person, the person spoken to, must necessarily bc in presence of each other; hence, in English at least, their respective pronouns require and have no designation of sex. In Hebrew, on the contrary, there is also a feminine form for the second person. The so-called third person, however, of whom something is said and who is spoken of as absent, needs on that account to be more accurately defined. This has led to the only instance in the English language in which gender is actually represented in the form of a word; we have retained for it, in a manner, the Anglo-Saxon participles of the verb *haetan*, (to call,) *he, heo, haet* or *hit*. The masculine has remained unchanged; the feminine, now *she*, survives in the *hoo* of Lancashire; and the neuter has simply lost its aspirate. *He* did not reach our age without a struggle for its existence, for at one time, the old dramatists show us, a simple *a* was threatening to assume its place. Thus we find in " Love's Labor 's Lost " (IV. 1), —

" Who ever *a'* was, *a'* showed a mounting mind."

It still survives among the unlettered, and Goldsmith thus quotes: " A troublesome old blade, but *a'* keeps as good wines as any in the whole country." *She* was first substituted by Chaucer for the *heo* or *he*, which was in universal use before him, and *it* is of comparatively recent origin. Like *that, what,* and similar forms, it represents the true neuter of Old English, to which class may perhaps be assigned, also, one other English word, *athwart*, formed after the same fashion.

The plural form *we* has come down to us almost without change, but its " majestic " use for a single person is comparatively modern. Lord Coke, at least, tells us that it was first so employed by King John, who introduced *Nos* and *Noster* into grants, confirmations, &c., or, as some writer has quaintly observed, thus found out the art of multiplying himself, whereas his predecessors had been content with *ego* and *meus*. Another explanation of this extraordinary substitution is, that kings include in this *we* all their officers and servants, and thus express the collected will of many in one, as editors include all who think like them, and may be charitably supposed to utter not their individual opinions, but those of a party, or at least of many. But what shall we say of our own *we?*

There is a better excuse for the substitution of *you* instead of the old *thou.* When it was first introduced — probably at the ceremonious, etiquette-loving court of Byzantium — it was deemed a courtesy and a sign of uncommon respect, thus to treat one as if he were or represented a large number; as if he were, in fact, a " host in himself." Besides, there is in all respectful ways of addressing others a perceptible tendency to avoid the direct personality ; hence the frequent use which the polite French makes of the indefinite *on* for the direct *vous.* In our own day there has been superadded to these reasons for the use of *you,* a third : the desire to be equally courteous to all, which has led to the gradual supremacy of that pronoun, which more than any other savors of republican equality. It has, however, undergone strange changes before it obtained that general recognition. At first *you,* or rather *ye,* as it was then exclusively written, was considered more polite than *thou,* and thus often mixed up with the singular. Chaucer uses it thus (2256), —

> " And if *ye* will not so, my lady sweete,
> Than pray I *the,* give me my love
> *Thou* blisful lady dere,"

and in 842, —

> " And *ye,* Sir Clerk, let be *your* shamefastedness."

This use of the plural pronoun instead of the singular was by no means contemporaneous in French, nor in any of the other Northern languages, and hence some have supposed that the English may have borrowed it from the Dutch, where it was already common. For some time, however, the two pronouns remained side by side, and *thou* was not set aside for religious purposes until a much later date.

Even in the " Morte d'Arthur " of the year 1485, *you* and *thou* occur in the same line and addressed to the same person. *You* was used regularly for the singular as early as 1503, by Sir Thomas More, who says : —

> " Farewell my daughter lady Margarete,
> God wotte full oft it grieved hath my mynde,
> That *ye* should go where we should seldom mete,
> Now I am gone and have left *you* behynde."

But that it cannot yet have obtained fully seems to appear from John Despanter's Latin Grammar, who, in 1517, criticizes sharply those who used it, and whom he calls " doscitatores." In the sixteenth and seventeenth century it is found without exception, we believe, in prefaces to books, where the author addresses his public. Then, however, a change occurred, and it was not considered as quite so respectful ; at least, William Lee, bookseller, who published in 1640 a book entitled " Youth's Behaviour ; or Decencie in Conversation among Men," says distinctly : " *You* should be used to persons of *lesser* rank, *Thou* and *Thee* to friends and superiors." It may be, however, that he, like many of his profession, was but a lover of the " good olden times," and preferred stating his wishes and preferences in the shape of actual facts.

There arose early, besides, a difference between *ye*, the Anglo-Saxon nominative of the pronoun, spelt *ge*, and *you*, derived from the Anglo-Saxon dative and accusative *eow*. Chaucer observes the distinction with such uniformity, that we may well assume it to have been the rule in his day. At a later time, however, *ye* gradually usurped the place of the accusative, and gave peculiar force to that case. Thus Shakespeare says in " Henry VIII : " —

> " The more shame for *ye* ; holy men I thought *ye*,"

and Milton almost invariably employs it so, *e. g*, —

> " His wrath which one day will destroy *ye* both,"

and —

> " I call *ye* and declare *ye* now returned
> Successful beyond hope, to lead *ye* forth."

At the same time *ye* seems constantly to have been used to express extreme familiarity, and thus it became gradually comic and burlesque.   Thus we find it in the Prologue, —

> " Show your small talents and let that suffice *ye*,
>   But grow not vain upon it, I advise *ye*,"

and in Pope's " Iliad," (XXII.), —

> " Yet for my sons I thank *ye*, Gods! 't was well,
>   Well have they perished, for in fight they fell."

Finally, the same form occurs occasionally now as a mere expletive, and, naturally, only in familiar style, as when Dr. King uses it, (p. 574), —

> " He 'll laugh *ye*, dance *ye*, sing *ye*, laugh, look gay,
>   And ruffle all the ladies in his play."

It is curious, and to the observant student very suggestive, to notice in how many different ways different nations prefer to address one another among themselves.   The German has not less than three distinct modes: he treats the superior of great distinction with a title instead of a pronoun, and speaks to him as *der Herr Graf*, " the Lord Count," but with the verb falls back to the ordinary way of using the third person plural.   This, the pronoun *Sie*, he employs for all above or on an equality with him ; whilst he grants the friendly *Du*, our *thou*, to those he loves and holds dear ; the lower dependent or subordinate is occasionally still reminded of his inferiority by a rude *Er*.   The French revolution abolished this degrading *Er* in the army, the Revolution of 1848 made an end to the half contemptuous *Du*, and now *Sie* remains almost the exclusive mode of address for all classes of society.   The Danes follow the German rule, but prefer the singular of the verb.   The Dutch have so entirely substituted *you* for *thou*, that the latter has completely dropped out of the language, and the form of the second person of the verb is hardly ever given in grammars even, unless it be for the imperative.   Hence in poetry they address the sun and the moon and all lifeless objects alike with *you*, and the plural of the verb; and even the actor in his monologue has to become a plural to himself. It sounds strange indeed to the foreigner, to hear them use one and the same pronoun for God and king, wife, child, and friend, heaven, and earth, and horse, and dog. The Russian and the Greek use *thou* for all ordinary purposes, but *you*, as do almost all nations now, when they are particularly polite. The Pole is still faithful to his ancient *thou*, but he adds courteously the word for Lord or Lady, saying, *Mash Pan*, "Thou Lord." The Italian, Spaniard, and Portuguese, all employ the most indirect way of addressing each other, substituting expressions like "Your Mercy," "Your Grace," and their representative pronouns for our *you*, actually saying to each other, "How is she to-day?" "I thank her." The Persian uses exceptionally our *you*, for generally all over the Orient the custom prevails of employing instead a mode of circumlocution which avoids all directness so repugnant to Oriental courtesy. Hence they prefer saying, "The gentleman says," or, "The son of my Lord shall be served." *They* is, like *she*, *it*, *thou*, and *their*, simply a part of the Anglo-Saxon demonstrative, used as a personal pronoun.

The possessive pronouns are in English, as in most known languages, nothing more than derivative formations of the personal pronouns, and it matters little whether they are, as some maintain, the genitives of the latter, or, as others believe, adjectives made from them by the addition of *en*. So much is certain, that their form and meaning were for some time of a most undecided character. Thus Wickliffe employs *oure* and *youre* not as possessive pronouns, but as genitives plural, and says *oure dreed*, the dread of us, and *youre feer*, the fear of you. What is more interesting for our day, is the gradual shortening which *mine* and *thine* have undergone in former ages, and are still undergoing. Originally they were probably the only forms used; afterwards, and for some generations, the full forms were preferred before vowels, and the shortened forms *my* and *thy* before consonants, in order to avoid the meeting of many consonants. Sir John Mandeville already has (59), " *Thin* hosen " and " *thi* schon," and (179), " *My* wif " and " *myn* husbond." Chaucer observes the rule, saying, —

> " Rise up *my* wif, *my* love, *my* lady fre," (10012),

and —

> " With *thyn* eighen Columbine," (10015).

In our Bible version we read accordingly (Psalms lv. 13): " But it was thou, a man *mine* equal, *my* guide, and *mine* acquaintance," and the same distinction is occasionally observed by modern writers. Thus we find Hamlet giving this advice, —

> " Give every man *thine* ear, but few *thy* voice."

Sir Walter Scott says, —

> " *Thine* ardent symphony sublime and high,"

and Byron has, —

> " Time writes no wrinkle on *thine* azure brow."

Generally, however, but little attention is given to the difference between the two forms ; on the contrary, even the shortened *my* is too long for modern haste, and must needs give way to *me*, simply. Fenimore Cooper observes on the difference between the old pronunciation, preserved in the States, and the more recent, that " *my* horse, *my* dog, the usual American mode, and *me* horse, *me* dog, the English counterpart, are equally wrong, the first by an affected egotism, the last from offensive arrogance." The wrong may exist, but the reasons are hardly stated with fairness. The English usage has at least this advantage, that it presents a means of emphasizing and dignifying the pronoun, of which the Americans are deprived by their uniform pronunciation. It is wasteful to say *my* servant when no other servant is spoken of, but there is advantage in the difference between " *my* Lord," addressed to the Creator, and the ordinary " my lord," given to peers, the orthodox pronunciation of which now is " me Lud."

Ours and *yours* are, among the illiterate, liable to even more violent ill-treatment, being changed into *ourn* and *yourn*, and yet apologists have been found for this vulgarism also, which they claim, like most vulgarisms, and especially Americanisms, to be but a well-preserved relic of former days. It cannot be denied that formerly *our own* and *your own* were often thus contracted, and it is not impossible that this may have given rise to the provincialism above mentioned. Master R. Laneham, keeper of the Council Chamber, and a traveled man, tells us of some person who presented a petition to Queen Elizabeth. at Kenilworth, in which he took even greater liberties, for after praying for her Majesty's perpetual felicity, he finishes with the humblest submission of *him* and *hizzen*. *His'n* and *her'n* may have had the same origin, being contracted from *his own* and *her own*, though the use of the dative plural in Old English, *hisum* and *herum*, might possibly have had the same effect. The old Bible version has " The kyngdom of hevenes is *herum*." They survive now only in affected style, as when Sam Slick says, " Drinking beer out of my pot and refusing *his'n*," or in old-fashioned songs like the Berkshire ditty, —

> " But t' other young maiden looked sly at me,
> And from her seat she ris'n —
> Let 's you and I go our own way,
> And we 'll let she go *shis'n*."

Its is one of the most recent words of the English language, and as such, a striking illustration of what may be called the life of an idiom. It was utterly unknown in the days of true Old English, because as soon as a thing was regarded as the possessor of another thing, it became to that extent personified, and the personal pronouns *his* and *her* were employed. Spenser has no *its* in his works; in fact, it was unknown in the days of Queen Elizabeth and King James. Mandeville shows his ignorance of such a word by saying, " Of that cytee bereth the contree *his* name,"

(256), and Chaucer has: "But loke that it (the whele,) have *his* spokes alle," (Canterbury Tales, 7838). Bacon says, " Learning has *his* infancy, when *it* is but beginning and almost childish ; then *his* youth when *it* is luxuriant and juvenile ; then *his* strength of years, when *it* is solid and reduced, and lastly *his* old age, when *it* waxeth dry and exhausted." Evidently *its* is wanting, and every time it is needed, supplied by *his*. Hence we find the same substitution repeatedly in the Bible: " The fig-tree putteth forth *her* green figs " (Sol. Song, ii. 13), and " the tree is known by *his* fruit " (Matt. xii. 33). In fact, this remarkable pronoun occurs in all but five times in our Bible version, which generally substitutes *his* or *of it*, as, " It (another beast) had three ribs in the mouth *of it* between the teeth *of it* " (Daniel vii. 5), or *thereof*, as, " Sufficient unto the day is the evil *thereof*." These remedies seem to have been early applied, for we find already in the very ancient " Auturs of Arther," (Camden Soc. 11–13,) what is probably the oldest instance of such a substitution : —

" For I will speke with the sprete,
And *of hit* woe wille I wete,
Gif that I may *hit* boles bete
And the body bare."

It was probably from the somewhat anomalous use of *it*, simply, instead of *of it*, that the modern *its* was derived. The earliest case of *it* being used as a possessive pronoun, occurs in the year 1548, in the Bible, where we find " The love and deuocion towardes God also hath *it* infancie and hath *it* commyng forward in growth of age." Sir Thomas More generally writes it *hit*, when he uses it thus as a possessive pronoun derived from *it*. Ben Jonson surprises us by writing " need will have *its* course," though the word itself is not even mentioned in his grammar. These early cases of *its* must, however, be viewed with great caution. Thus we are generally told that Shakespeare has it three or four times; in " Measure for Measure " (I. 2), we find " Heaven grant us *its* peace," and —

> "—— each following day
> Became the next day's master, till the last
> Made former wonders *its*,"

but the learned Mommsen discovered that these readings only occur in the later editions, which did not appear until 1623, twelve years after the publication of the Bible. Even Milton evidently preferred the substitutes, as in the lines, —

> "The fig-tree spreads *her* arms, and daughters grow about the mother-tree." — *Paradise Lost*, IX. 1100.

He has *its* but twice, (Paradise Lost, I. 254, and IV. 813,) and avoids it in many places, though in his day it was already popular. Shakespeare had, in his day, shown a repugnance to *him* and *her* for the neuter idea, by carefully avoiding the occasion for the use of the pronoun, and the idea itself probably did not exist in the mind of these authors. This shows beautifully the intimate connection between the mind of a people and their language, and the reciprocal action. For the use of *its* not merely changed the form of English, but actually modified the manner of thinking. Dean Trench has called attention to the fact that a careful sifting and thorough investigation of the mere words of a literary work would as certainly assign it its time in English literature, as the same process has done for ancient literature, when applied to the works of ancient writers. Thus Chatterton's poems, which pretended to have been written by a monk living in the eleventh century, could have been stamped as a forgery upon the ground of a single line: " Life and all *its* goods I scorn." Any well-read scholar would have known that the word *its* did not exist for several hundred years after the assumed date of the work.

It is a peculiarity of English that it has no reflexive pronoun, and that neither the Anglo Saxon nor the Norman French have ever fully supplied the want. The only substitute is found in the words *self* and *own*. The former is strangely connected with the possessive pronoun, and its etymology has given rise to many discussions among grammarians. Perhaps no stronger proof of the difficulty of the subject can be adduced, than the fact that even the great Jacob Grimm acknowledged the necessity of changing altogether opinions he had formerly held on the subject.

In Anglo-Saxon, *self* was coupled with the personal pronoun, and produced combinations like *ic self, thurh me selfne*, "thro' me self," *from me selfum*, and *min selfes bearn*, "my own child." This constant use, varied only in a few, probably ill-copied instances, proves clearly that *self* was not, as is frequently stated, a noun. Soon after the decline of the pure Saxon, however, *self* reappears combined with the possessive pronoun, and has, in Old English at least, become indeclinable. A few traces of the old declension show themselves occasionally in forms like *I myselven, he himselven*, and *ye yourselven*, but evidently without any difference in signification.

This constant combination led naturally to the result that *self* began to be looked upon as a noun, preceded by a possessive pronoun — an impression which was still further strengthened by the independent employment of the compound pronoun, as when Chaucer already says : " *This is to sayn, myself hath been the whippe.*" From that date *self* appears fully established as a noun, and is used even without a pronoun, as in the line of Moore's poem, —

"Too strong for Allah's *self* to burst,"

and hence come still more recent, inelegant phrases, as *my own self* and *your own dear self*.

Himself and *themselves* must originally have been objective cases, with the two words in apposition to each other. Hence the tendency to avoid such awkward and obscure forms, and to substitute for them *hisself* and *theirselves*, made in analogy with the other forms, but not admitted into classic English, and *hissel* and *theirselves* in the dialects of the North of England.

Pronouns enable us in another aspect to establish the claims of our English, the study of which is so sadly neglected for the benefit of Latin and Greek, to a full equality at least of etymological interest with the ancient languages. These, we are told, have a beautiful system of suggesting by the initials the nature of the pronoun; the demonstrative pronouns having —

In Greek a τ:	τό	the interrogative, now π:	
	τοῦτο,		
	τόσος,		πόσος,
	τοῖος,		ποῖος,
	τότε,		πότε,
	τῶς;		πῶς,
			ποῦ,
			πότερος,
			πόθεν,
In Latin a t:	talis,	the interrogative *qu*:	qualis,
	tantus,		quantus,
	tot,		quot,
	tam,		quam,
	&c.,		quomodo,
			quorsum.

But we ought, surely, not to forget that the Germanic languages have a similar system, in noways inferior, and based mainly upon their characteristic sound, the aspirate. This is represented in modern English, in spite of all changes and losses, by instances like the following : —

He, his, him,	The, (*German*) Der,	Who, (*German*) Wer.
Hit, here,	That, those, Dieser,	What, whose,
Here and its compounds,	There and its compounds,	Where and its comp. Wo.
(H)now,		(W)how,
Hence,	Thence,	Whence,
Hither,	Thither,	Whither,
&c.,	They, them, their,	Whom,
	This, these,	
	Thus, Da,	
	Though,	
	Then, Dann,	When, Wann.
		Whether, Weder.
		Why, Warum.
		Which, Welcher.

At the same time the ancient form of English in Anglo-

Saxon enables us to see the discreet economy with which the old pronoun has been made subservient to all the practical purposes of modern wants. Thus the Anglo-Saxon interrogative pronoun *hva* was declined in the following manner : —

	MASC.		NEUT.
Nom.	hva,		hvaet,
Gen.		hvaes,	
Dat.		hvam,	
Acc.	hvone,		hvaet,
Abl.		hvi,	

and from this complex scheme we obtain all our pronouns, thus : —

	MASC.		NEUT.
Nom.	who,		what,
Gen.		whose,	
Obj.	whom,		what,
Abl.		why, (adverb,)	

to which we only add *which*, from Anglo-Saxon *hveleik*, corresponding to *svaleik*, our *such*, and *whether*, from Anglo-Saxon *hwäder*, formerly used to express — *which of two*, but now employed only as a conjunction.

CHAPTER XIV.

" Take thy fingers."

THERE is no class of words of more interest for the history of nations than the numerals, for they afford us one of the most striking evidences of the unity of the race, divided as it now is into so many nations. Men to this day use everywhere the same way of counting. From the nation that leads civilization at the head of all Christendom, to the very dregs of humanity, the heathen cannibal, men have the same system of numerals. Even the forms differ so little, that we probably only need a better knowledge of the laws of sound and the history of words to find that they all belong to one and the same family. Hence they are even now looked upon as one of the safest criterions by which to judge of an original relationship between languages. Where they resemble each other in any two idioms, there, certainly, a close tie of common descent or common fate is soon discovered. They aid us as some casual expression which flits across the face of a long-forgotten friend, or the use of some peculiar but well-known phrase, reveals to us all of a sudden the companion of former days, or the son of a kinsman. Nations seem, for some important reason, to adhere with uncommon tenacity to the forms of their numerals, and to no class of words can the well-known words of Suetonius be more forcibly applied : " *Tu enim, Cæsar, civitatem dare potes hominibus, verbis non potes, inquit Capito.*" (De Illustr. Gr. XXIII.) For no misfor-

17

tune and no conquest has ever yet deprived a nation of its numerals, whatever may have been the fate of other parts of its language. Thus it is in our English. In spite of the Norman-French conquest, and in spite of the long rule of Norman sovereigns, not only have we safely kept all our Saxon numerals, but only two foreign forms have obtained admission to their number. The Anglo Saxon possessed no ordinal corresponding to its cardinal *two*, and used, instead of it, the word *other*, as is still done in the German *anderthalb*. Hence the Normans found it comparatively easy to introduce and to obtain ready admission for their word *second*. This comes from the Latin *sequor*, to follow, and retains always something of the meaning of its Roman ancestor, as when we propose to " *second* a question," and thus follow the first mover, or when we condemn the " *second* in a duel," because he followed his principal to the place of combat. Its application to time has another and very curious origin. The Romans, it is well known, facilitated the operation of counting by the use of little pebbles, *calcula*, from which we derive our own word, to *calculate*. One of these, a peculiarly small pebble, was. called *scrupulum*, and was used to denote what we also call a " minute " pebble, now a *minute*. When they proceeded to a subdivision they denoted one sixtieth of a minute by a *secundum scrupulum*, and thus we obtained, after the omission of the word *scrupulum*, the name of *second* for the same small space of time. The only other numeral of foreign origin in our language is *million*, from the Latin *mille*, with an augmentative syllable superadded.

This faithful and steady adherence to our numerals is perhaps partly to be ascribed to their small number, of which superficial observers have no conception. There is no nation on earth that counts beyond the ten fingers of the hands. They gave, and still give, the only mode of counting. A trace of this original manner survives in modern English : there is a custom preserved in technical language at least, although going out of use in ordinary conversation, to call the first ten numbers *digits*, from the Latin word for "finger." It was formerly universally so employed, and we read in Sir Thomas Brown's "Vulgar Errors:" "Not only the numbers 7 and 9, from considerations abstruse, have been extolled by most, but all or most other *digits* have been as mystically applauded." It is well known that certain nations of antiquity did not even go so far as ten, but were content with counting only the number of fingers of one hand. Thus, when Homer alludes to a shepherd who counts his sheep, he employs the word $\pi \acute{\epsilon} \mu \pi \epsilon \sigma \theta a\iota$, as if he were to say "he fived them," and in other authors we find in like manner, $\pi \epsilon \mu \pi \acute{a} \zeta \epsilon \iota \nu$ used to define counting up to five. Even now some tribes of Indians go no farther, and we are assured by modern travelers that there are savages whose numbers go only as far as 1, 2, and 3, at which point their language fails, and, instead of four, they employ a word which means at the same time "many" and "incalculable multitudes." Then the connection only can show in which of its different meanings it is to be taken.

Nations have, of course, numerals beyond the number of fingers, but after ten they are invariably compounds, thus showing that after all we possess genuine names of numbers only up to ten. Our own numerals afford, in this aspect, peculiar information as to the manner in which this remarkable class of words has generally been formed. Our *one* is a derivative of the Anglo-Saxon *ân*, so strikingly resembling the Greek *ἕν*, and the Latin *unus*, as to suggest at once their common descent from the Aryan stock. In German the radical *ein* serves to this day to designate unity, as well as the indefinite sense of the noun which it precedes. In English, however, at a very early period, the original *an* branched off into a full form to express the precise meaning of the numeral, and a shortened one to serve as an indefinite article. The former has now assumed the form of *one*, but retained, even in Old English, so much of the original, that our *any* was then written *ony*, and in the oldest MSS. had even its two genders. Thus we find, "And gif *oni* other *onie* cumen her ongenes," which we have to translate : "And if any man or any woman come against her." The shortened form is now *an*, which, however, in its turn, has undergone a farther reduction, and before consonants at least is always *a*. Our Bible version uses *an* indiscriminately before vowels and consonants, and even we respect an aspirate *h*, and speak of " *an* humble faith." Our *two* is derived from the Anglo-Saxon *tvâ*, which in like manner corresponds closely with the Greek δύο, and the Latin *duo*, whilst in German the prevailing tendency of changing the dental into a sibilant, has resulted in *zwei*. Of its modern forms but one is really important. The ancient *tvâ* had a dual, *twegen*. The dual, however, is one of those inflections which all languages drop as they become modernized, so that even the once so important and useful Greek dual does not appear in the New Testament, simply because it was no longer in use in common Greek. Thus, also, the dual, found so largely and so fully developed in Old Norse and Old German, has utterly disappeared as a grammatical form. A few dual words only have survived and serve now as evidences of former ages ; among them the form of *twain*. We still use it fully when we speak of " cleft in *twain*." Byron has it regularly in —

> " Ye seek it of the *twain* of least respect and interest,"

and Longfellow uses it in the same manner, saying, —

> " Let there be no further strife nor enmity
> Between us *twain*."

The true nature of the dual seems very early to have been forgotten by the people, or we would not meet so soon with the contracted form *twin*, and its absurd or at least most incorrect plural, *twins*. We shorten it still farther in *twilight* and from the compound *between* we derive a preposterous superlative *betwixt*. The former was once used with *a* instead of *be*, as in Chaucer's lines : —

> "Thy wife and thou mote hange atwynne,
> For that betwyt you shall be no synne." — *Miller's Tale.*

From the numeral *three*, recalling to us the τρία, and *tria* of the ancients, the Anglo-Saxons made an ordinal *thryd*, which we have changed, according to the prevailing tendency to transpose the *r*, into *third*. A curious descendant of the first form remains, however, in modern English. Certain districts were, it seems, of old divided into thirds, and these were called " third things," in the old sense of the word *thing*. Thus we find, in Magna Charta, a *thrithing* already spoken of, and the same term is repeated in Stat. 21, Henry III. c. 10, (1260,) and from it are probably derived the three *Ridings* of Yorkshire, the initial *th* having been lost at an early day. Our Saxon fathers formed words for the numerals up to nine, but there their power of invention seems to have abandoned them, for *ten* is not an original word. It comes from the Saxon verb *tynan*, to close, to shut in or up, expressive of the simple fact that when the calculation had gone on to the extent of the ten fingers, one after another having been turned in, both hands were found " closed " or " shut in." Nor is this use of the ancient word so entirely obsolete, that it could not be proved even from modern usage. There are very few forms, in the purely Saxon districts at least, of which a certain portion does not still bear the name of *tyning, e. g.,* the Middle Tyning or the Upper Tyning. The designation arose, like the more modern *close*, from the fact that these lands were carefully inclosed and cultivated, unlike the common, the not inclosed lands, which lay waste. From the same verb was derived the noun *tûn*, our *town ;* at first it meant nothing more than an inclosure, and as such we have already seen it was used in our Bible version, where Wickliffe substitutes it for the word *farm*. More recently still we have had recourse to the same root, when our new railway wants required the word *tunnel*, a diminutive of *tun*, and meaning an " inclosed way."

Before proceeding to the larger compound numerals, we insert here, for purposes of comparison, the first ten numerals in the kindred languages which form the family of our English :—

Eng.	Welsh.	A. Sax.	Old H. Ger.	Mod. Ger.	Gothic.
One, an, a,	Un,	An,	Ein,	Ein,	Ain,
Two,	Dau,	Tu, twa,	Zuene,	Zwei,	Tvai,
Three,	Tri, tair,	Thry,	Thri,	Drei,	Threis,
Four,	Pedwar,	Feower,	Fior,	Vier,	Fidwor,
Five,	Pump,	Fif,	Finf,	Fünf,	Fimf,
Six,	Chwech,	Seox,	Sehs,	Sechs,	Saihs,
Seven,	Saith,	Seofan,	Sipun,	Sieben,	Sibun,
Eight,	Wyth,	Eahta,	Ahto,	Acht,	Ahtau,
Nine,	Naw,	Nigon,	Niun,	Neun,	Niun,
Ten.	Deg.	Tyn, tig.	Zehan.	Zehn,	Taihun.

A similar correspondence is shown to exist throughout the whole Indo-European class of languages.

It is well known that our *eleven* is simply the *an lif*, one left, of our Saxon fathers, as this was really the case after both hands had been closed ; in the same manner *twelve* is the contracted form of *twâ lif*, two left, and these two numerals afford us in their simpler form an additional evidence of the duodecimal method of counting, which long prevailed among Scandinavian and Old German nations. Hence England has always had a small and a great hundred, — 100 and 120, — and the original ton contains yet 2400 lbs., in contrast with the modern or small ton of 2000 lbs. After *twelve* the numerals are simply compounds of *ten* and the lower numbers, until we arrive at *twenty*, which consists of the dual *twain*, and the old word *tig*, corresponding to the root in δέκα and *decem*, and meaning *ten*. Instead of twenty we still use frequently the old Celtic word *score* — one of the few true Celtic forms that have held their own in our language. It is a relic of the fondness the Celts had for counting by twenties, which survives in a very striking manner in the French substitute of *Quatre-Vingt*, four twenties, for eighty, *soixante-dix* for seventy, and all similar formations. Our Bible has "*fourscore* and ten ;"

Shakespeare uses, in "Measure for Measure," "*ninescore and seventeen pounds*," and Byron speaks of "six of my *fourscore* years." The frequent use of the verb to *score*, for counting, arises probably from the manner in which, in the days of Old England, archers called the distance of twenty yards a *score*, and thus *counted* up their relative merits. In *quarantine* the substitution of a Latin term for the Saxon *forty*, shows the danger we incur by using foreign words without adhering faithfully to their original meaning. In former days the time of trial for persons coming from regions where contagious diseases prevailed, was forty days; and this gave rise, in the Mediterranean, where this precaution against pestilence was most general, to the use of the word *quarantaine*. Now we have forgotten the true signification of *quaranta*, and speak ludicrously of a "quarantine of ten days." *Hundred* is a compound of *hund*, which meant either an exact number of hundred already, or merely served to designate a large, round sum; it is the same as the root in τριάκοντα and *centum*, as we may see at a glance by a comparison of the English *hundred* in our shires, with the *Canton* of the Swiss Confederacy. To this was added *red*, which is simply our *rod* or *reed*, an instrument universally used by the Anglo-Saxons to mark by notches cut in it the number of times they wished to remember. It is well known that this custom is by no means extinct, either in Scandinavian countries, or in the northern parts of the kingdom.

If we have, in common with all nations, made no progress in the formation of numerals, we have at least learnt to write them much better than our ancestors. The oldest inscriptions on the marble of Italy or the granite of Scandinavia, whether they contain weighty records of early races or mystic accounts of Northern gods, all unite in one common way of marking numbers simply by straight lines, such as could most easily be carved in stone or cut in wood. It was in Italy first that the custom of the Greeks to use their vowels for that purpose, obtained most largely, and as the Greek *v* is the Latin *V*, the Romans adopted this, the fifth vowel, as meaning five, retaining for the preceding numbers the ancient strokes, I, II, III, and IIII. Improving on this, they placed two Vs one over the other, $\underset{\wedge}{\vee}$, and contracting the figure in one, counted *X*, equal to ten. *C* as the initial letter of *centum*, became the sign for hundred, and as the ancient Roman alphabet was not written in round but in square lines, the lower half of the old-fashioned C resembled the later L sufficiently to let this letter stand for the half hundred, or fifty. M became, as the initial letter of *mille*, the sign for a thousand, and D, it is said, meant *dimidium*, or the half of thousand. These signs, however, long used for all purposes in England, had in their turn to give way to those which we now employ. These have been introduced through the Arabs, who themselves probably obtained them from the eastern part of India. They employed them in their admirable researches, mainly for the purposes of astrology, and afterwards for arithmetical problems. After they had conquered Spain, they introduced them, with the many branches of knowledge which Christian Europe owes to their faithful stewardship of the treasures of ancient lore, into the schools and universities of the Peninsula. There it was that Gerbert, studying Theology and the Black Art in the halls of Salamanca, became acquainted with them in the tenth century, and learnt to know their value. He afterwards rose rapidly in the Church, and when he bore at last the triple crown as Sylvester II., he introduced, with other fruits of his learning, the use of these Arabic signs throughout Christendom. They are found earliest in Astronomical Tables, then merchants discovered their great usefulness ; from 1300 we meet with them in inscriptions, but not before 1400 in manuscripts. How slowly they must have made their way into popular use may be judged from the fact that a hornbook, at least as old as 1570, and like all books of the kind, intended for the humbler classes, concludes with the Lord's Prayer and the Roman numerals, the Arabic numerals being omitted.

As one of the pronouns is used as definite article in English, and one of the numerals as indefinite article, it may not be amiss to add here a few remarks concerning the history and nature of that mysterious class of words, the articles. They belong so exclusively to modern languages, and throw so much light upon the transition of those derived from ancient idioms, that they have ever been a favorite topic with linguists, without being, on that account, any more satisfactorily explained than other subjects of philologic controversy. This only is universally admitted — that they have taken the place and perform, in part at least, the duty of the elaborate system of inflections in Greek and Latin. It is well known that the former possessed only a so-called definite article, ὁ, ἡ, τό, whilst of an indefinite article no other trace is found but the equivocal τίς, made enclitic. The Latin had really no article at all. Both these languages, however, had a very complete system of inflections for nouns, in their numerous declensions, most of which consisted in the addition of pronouns, by means of connecting vowels, to the end of the root. Thus ἀνήρ became ἀνδρός, and *homo* became *hominis*. In the Romance languages these varied terminations were lost at the time of the conquest of Rome and Roman colonies under the influence of causes identical with those which produced a similar loss of Anglo-Saxon inflections after the Norman conquest of England. The German tribes who made themselves masters of Gaul, Spain, and Italy, would not and could not learn these nice distinctions of sound, and curtly abandoned them. As soon, however, as new languages began to be formed out of the surviving Latin elements, and the German idioms that were mixed up with them, the necessity for such inflections became apparent once more, and was felt by all. Following, then, the example set already by later Roman authors, certain words suggestive of the same ideas formerly represented by declensions, &c., were chosen and used; but instead of being added at the end of words which had generally lost their original termination, and with it their vitality, these words were placed before the noun and hence called prepositions. All the Romance languages followed the same plan of choosing for this purpose the demonstrative pronoun *ille*, which gave the French *le* and *la*, the Italian *il, lo*, and *la*, and the Spanish *el, la, lo*, and the numeral *unus*, which gave a similar form to the daughters of Latin. The same causes led to precisely the same results in English, also. The Anglo-Saxon had, like the Latin, a large number of inflections for its nouns, which the Danish and the Norman conquerors alike rejected. As Old English arose, the old demonstrative pronoun *se, seo, thaet*, was chosen naturally to act as a definite article, having been used already in Anglo-Saxon very generally for that purpose. In Semi-Saxon it had lost almost all of its forms except *thaet*, the remaining cases being used but rarely, and the declension having become less distinct. It appeared, therefore, very early in Old English as *the*, of all genders, though with different case endings, and only in middle English became absolutely of all cases and genders. Thus we have obtained our article *the*. In like manner the Anglo-Saxon numeral *an* was employed with the meaning of an indefinite article branching off from the fuller form *one*, as has been shown above. The first instance of its use in this aspect occurs in " Layamon's Brut," but it does not seem to have come into general use until the middle of the thirteenth century. Before that time the indefinite article was generally expressed by the use of *sum*, our *some*, or, as in the ancient languages, by the omission of any designation.

The rare and judicious use of the article in English is one of the points in which its beautiful simplicity is best shown. In its proper omission, especially, whenever the sense of the noun is not limited or determined, lies an excellence of English even over Greek, where it is often used without giving additional weight or conferring a clearer meaning to the noun which it accompanies. This beauty becomes more striking yet, when we compare with it the use which the nearest relative of English, the German, makes of the article. Its almost insufferable repetition there mars often the most beautiful periods, encumbering them sadly, and thus depriving the language of the brief and impressive energy of her English sister. Few are aware under what curious disguises the article occasionally makes its appearances in English. There are large numbers of foreign words which presented themselves at the time of their introduction, accompanied by their article; the hospitable Englishman adopted them without inquiring what was their substance and what their shadow, and thus we have virtually nouns possessed of their own article, and yet preceded by the English article. In other words, again, we have imagined an initial *a* to be the article, and thus deprived them of part of their substance, in making them English. This has been, *e. g.*, the case with the Malay word *amuco,* designating the peculiar intoxication from rage and other sources for which the natives of those regions are remarkable ; we have fancied the word to consist of two parts, and although the phrase was at first correctly spelled "to run *amock,*" we now call it erroneously "to run a *muck.*" The same process takes place continually in other languages as well as in our own. The French have taken the Latin *hedera,* and called it, for years, *hierre,* as it is still written in Ronsard *l'hierre,* whilst since the days of that poet it has become *lierre,* and now takes an additional *le* before it. The same origin have *la luette, le loriot, le loutre,* and *la lonze,* whilst *l'en demain* has become *le lendemain,* and *Apulia* has degenerated into *la Pouille.*

In the majority of similar cases in English, we can plead our pardonable ignorance of foreign forms at the time that the latter were introduced into England. This is a suffi-

cient plea, for instance, for the double article we employ
with Arabic words, which contain already the Arabic article
al, as in *Algebra*, (al Geber,) *alcohol, almanac, alcali, elixir*,
(al Aksir,) *alchymy, alcove, admiral*, (from almirante,) *alem-
bic*, and *azimuth*. Even the Spanish, through which we have
obtained these Eastern terms, had already made a similar
mistake in many instances, and we only follow the example
it has set us, when we now speak of *a lily*, instead of the
Arabic *aleli*, from λειρίον, or of *a fan* from old *aban*, which
is still used in the diminutive form *abanico*. Our *saffron*
comes to us likewise from *azafran*, and *azure* from the Persian *lazur*, which we meet with again in a slightly altered
form in *lapis lazuli*. It is curious to observe how the Italian *arancia* has given us the correct *orange*, whilst the Spaniards have been misled by the indefinite article before it,
and now speak of *an orange* as of *una naranja*, repeating it
a second time. Our word *alligator* has a somewhat similar
origin. It comes originally from the Latin *lacerta*, a lizard,
in Spanish, *el lagarto ;* hence Sir Walter Raleigh writes of
a certain newly discovered land: " But for *lagartos* it ex-
ceeded." In Ben Jonson we find the contraction with the
article already established, as he calls the creature an
aligarta, and when English sailors landed in America and
saw there for the first time the crocodile of that Continent,
they called it very naturally a great lizard, an *alligator*.
We ought not to forget, finally, that the name of Spain
itself has undergone a change of the same kind before it
assumed its present English garb. It was first, of course,
Hispania, whence its name in the vernacular of *España*.
This, however, was constantly misspelt, until, finally, the
orthography, imitating the pronunciation, settled somewhat
into *Espayne*. Its frequent connection with the preposition
de, makes it appear in numerous MSS. first as *d'Espayne*,
and then as *de Spayne*, under the misapprehension that the
letter *e* belonged to the preposition, and thus it gradually
shaped itself into simple *Spain*.

The same plea of ignorance applies to mistakes made in French words only when their adoption can be traced to the days of great national trouble and profound ignorance. This is, however, generally the case; French was spoken only by the higher classes, and by them, even, without great correctness; the spelling was almost arbitrary, and we need not wonder, therefore, that the good people made free with these foreign terms, which for generations presented to them no very clear meaning. The indistinct pronunciation of English vowels contributed still farther to dim their perception, and hence almost any *a* or *e* at the beginning of a French word was liable to be mistaken for an English article. It is thus that *avant* gave us our *van*, *esprit* our *sprite*, and *esclandre* the double form of *scandal* and *slander*. The *enlumineur*, who brought his craft from France and adorned missals and romances with his quaint art, became in England famous as *a limner;* the *étincelle* dwindled into *a tinsel, étiquette* into *a ticket*, and *exemplaire, a sampler.* Among the curious plants brought back by the Crusaders from the Orient, was also the bulb that takes its name from Ascalon, and was naturalized in France as *échalote ;* we again took the *é* to be an *a*, and call it now *a shalot*, very much like the *échine* of beef and pork, which is now *a chine.* The skillful *escrimer* of the French was misunderstood in the same manner, and, long before we derived from it both *skirmish* and *scrimmage*, Laertes said to Hamlet's king, —

> " the *scrimers* of their nation
> He swore, had neither motion, guard nor eye,
> If you oppos'd them." — *Hamlet*, IV. 7.

The few cases in which we have added the French preposition *de* to our English word are easily understood, though the nature of the change is not always perceived at first sight. When Homer speaks of wandering κατ' ἀσφοδέλον λειμῶνα, we see it translated " thro' flowery meads of *aspodel;*" in the mean time, however, the *fleur d' affodille* had become fashionable, and we see the correct spelling changed into *daffodil*. Thus it happened with the name of Ypres, that busy town from which in the times of the Plantagenets table-cloths were brought to England which cost as much as whole coats of mail, and which became more famous still when the great Wolsey was made bishop of its see; the English ear became familiar with the word *d' Ypres*, and, unassisted by the eye, changed it soon after into the modern *diaper*. The common people to this day make free with the article, especially in words of foreign origin; *a num-berella* is heard often enough, and *an atomy*, substituted for a skeleton, has only recently given way to a better knowl-edge of the difference between the art itself and its object. If the cockney still persists in saying *a pottecary*, so he do not change it into *potcarrier*, he can plead the possible derivation not from ἀποθήκη, but from the Italian *bottega*, for which origin the name of *Pottinger* seems to speak.

Even the fuller form of the indefinite article *an*, has not escaped this tendency to absorption. In the "Comedy of Errors" (III. 2), there is a curious illustration of the manner in which this contraction took place. Ellen's name being demanded, the answer is, "*Nell*, Sir, but her name and three-quarters, that is, *an ell* and three-quarters." The same process has produced *Ned* from Edward, and *Nan*, or *Nanny*, from Ann. The oldest word of the kind is probably *nag*, which represents the Old Danish word *an ög*, for which in Old Saxon *ehu* (equus) was substituted. *Nale* was once very common for *an ale*, meaning an ale-house, and may be found in the "Friar's Tale" —

> "They were inly glad to fill his purse
> And maken him gret festes at the *nale*."

Nuncle, also, is frequent in Shakespeare, though it repre-sents, more probably, *mine* uncle. Thus in "King Lear," (I. 4), —

> "Mark it, *Nuncle*,
> Have more than thou showest,"

to which may be added the *good naunt* of " Beaumont and Fletcher" (I. 606). Mandeville calls our modern *eft* correctly enough *an ewte*, but both Chaucer and Shakespeare substitute for it *newt*, which was, no doubt, the common form in their day. The Old English phrase, *for than anes* (for then once) is now *for the nonce*. In a few other cases the word has lost an initial *n*, that being mistaken for a part of the article. The Anglo-Saxon *naugar* has thus changed into *an augur*, and the *naeddere*, which our forefathers probably derived from Latin *natrix*, is now *an adder*. The Germans have preserved the original word in their *natter*, as even in Derbyshire a *nedder* is still commonly used for a snake. Chaucer says still " Like to the *nadder*," but his contemporaries have already *eddere* instead.

CHAPTER XV.

LIVING WORDS.

"It will be proved to thy face that thou hast men about thee that usually talk of a *noun* and a *verb* and such abominable words as no Christian ear can endure to hear."—*Jack Cade's Charge against the Lord Say.*

IT is a quaint saying of that quaint and yet wise people, the Chinese, that verbs alone are living words; they call nouns dead words, and all other parts of speech but auxiliaries. They show here, as in almost every branch of science and letters, the acute and clear perception of truth, which, however, like a golden grain of corn, is by them safely stored away and there remains useless, while other nations have trustingly confided it to the bosom of their mother earth and thus reaped abundant and unceasing harvests. Western races, also, felt the same vitality in the verb, though less clearly and tangibly, and sought to give expression to it by the honorable name they bestowed upon this all-important part of speech. Thus it was to the ancient Greeks emphatically τό ῥῆμα, and when they referred to it in connection with its mental purpose in speech, they spoke of it as τά ἐμψυχότατα τοῦ λόγου, the one animating power of the sentence, its vital principle, without which a sentence can have no satisfactory meaning. In English we have adopted here also, as in other grammatical definitions, the Latin expression *verbum, the* word by eminence. But whilst we feel and thus vaguely express the superior importance of the verb, we have by no means yet agreed as to its precise nature. On the contrary, the apparently simple question, "What is the Verb?" has been, from of old, the subject "of the most ferocious controversies," as the witty philologist, Horne Tooke, expresses it. He has not himself escaped the temptation held out by that subtle part of speech, and much time and great violence is bestowed upon it in his admirable "Diversions." This only seems to be established beyond any controversy, that nouns and verbs are the two essential and indispensable parts of speech. We can do without all others, we cannot do without these two. The noun has, in point of time, the precedence, for we know that the first use made by man of his new power of language was to give names to the objects around him. These names were nouns. Then only, as he saw these objects move and act, as he perceived their form, their color, and other qualities, he began, secondly, to ascribe something to them, and his effort to give a name to this was the verb. Hence, in order to convey an idea, there must at least be given the name of a thing and an expression of our sentiments concerning it; these two suffice to make a sentence sufficient for the intercourse between man and man. But in proportion as what we think of an object is necessarily of far more interest and importance than its mere name, by so much is the verb also more important than the noun, and hence the original comparison of the noun to the body of man and of the verb to his soul.

Another effect of this peculiar relation between the two parts of speech is that the priority in time enjoyed, beyond any doubt, by the noun, has led to the opinion, entertained by many philologists, that it is the only really original part of speech, from which all others have been subsequently derived. It cannot be denied that, even in the best developed languages, the distinction between noun and verb is not yet absolute and at an end, as it is well known that in English, for instance, a large proportion of the verbs, about 4300 in all, are still, in outward appearance at least, simple nouns, and show their different meaning only by their

18

place in the sentence. It was the same in ancient languages, which we are so apt to consider as entirely different from our own. There, also, in numerous cases, the root of a verb was a noun; to this was added, generally by means of a connecting vowel, the oblique case of a pronoun, as in γραφ-ο-μεν (μέ) and *pet-i-mus* (nos). The root conveyed no idea of action or motion, neither of which was, or now is, inherent in the verb; the active power rested solely in the person or the agent; if we take this away, the Greek or Latin verb returns at once to the simple form of a noun. Thus it was in Anglo-Saxon also, but after a while, and especially under the influence of the Norman Conquest, the full force of the personal pronoun, so constantly added to the root, was no longer felt. It became necessary to give a new form to the verbal character of the root, but as in the noun, the inflection was no longer added at the end, but placed before it in the shape of pronoun and preposition. So in the verb, also, modern idioms place the pronoun before it and leave the words disconnected. Anglo-Saxon nouns now serve, therefore, as verbs without any change of form, and we use thus words like *love, hate, fear, dream, sleep,* and *book.* Norman-French nouns are not so indiscriminately fit for verbal use; still we have *motion, place, notice, minister, pain, place,* and *question* as nouns and as verbs. The tendency is to add to this class, and among more recent forms may be mentioned *station, post, provision,* and *preface.* Many occur now and then only to resume their allegiance. Milton says " to *syllable* men's names;" but of all authors Shakespeare uses the most unbounded liberty in this respect. He says, "This (calamity) *periods* his comfort;" "Come, *sermon* me no farther," and Portia, Cato's daughter, exclaims,—

> " Think you I am no stronger than my sex,
> Being so *fathered* and so *husbanded !* "

This power of turning almost any noun into a verb has been called the most kingly prerogative of the English language, and compared to the right of ennobling exercised by the Crown. For just because most English verbs of purely English descent are still in their simplest form, so as not to be distinguished from nouns, they bring up at once the full form and power of the object itself, from which the action is derived. The effect is still greater when the act, or the process itself, is to be suggested as a concreted thing or in a picture. This direct and undisguised descent gives our verbs, mainly, the peculiar vigor and liveliness for which they are distinguished, and which is not a little increased by their simplicity, as contrasted with the more ornate, but also less transparent, verbs of other languages. How powerful is the effect which the idea of man produces when we speak of "*manning* a vessel;" how strong and suggestive is our language when it expresses efforts to "*arm* a fortress" or to "*bridle* our passions."

There must, of course, be a limit to this abundant use of nouns as verbs in the very nature of their meaning; and the tendency of our time to increase the stock almost at random, can hardly be called an improvement of the language. Lovers of liberty, it is true, see in this promiscuous use of nouns and verbs but an effect of the general equalizing tendency of our age. Macaulay is occasionally bold in impressing new words, as when he says, "The *bark* of a shepherd's dog or the *bleat* of a lamb," where, heretofore, *barking* and *bleating* would have been used. New additions of the same class are, to *bag*, to *father*, to *air*, to *experience*, and to *bayonet*, and the most recent coinage now accepted is, perhaps, "to *progress*." By the side of these innovations, there appears no reason why we should not still speak of the "*childing* of a woman," or adopt Sylvester's substitute for *deifying*, in "some *godding* fortune, idol of ambition."

The free use made in English of proper names for verbal purposes is not original to our language, but was already well known in antiquity. Thus, when Demosthenes heard that King Philip of Macedon had bribed the oracle, in order to dispirit the Athenians, he used the word φιλιπ-πίζειν, when he meant to accuse the priestess of favoring Philip. In later days Antoninus (VI. 30) gave the warning μή ἀποκαισαρωθῇς, from the foreign name Cæsar. The Romans themselves were familiar with the process, and spoke of *Syllaturire*, when one meditated to act the part of Sylla, and of *Græcari*, when men played the Greek in fine living and free potations. With us the use, or rather the abuse, is so general as hardly to require any explanation. Few think of Virgil's Tantalus when they speak of *tantalizing*. Hamlet's " it *out-Herod's* Herod " is familiar to all, and so is " Noah's deluge *out-deluged*." The facetious Fuller, in his " Church History" (viii. 21), in speaking of Morgan, the sanguinary bishop of Queen Mary, says of him that he " out-*Bonnered* even Bonner himself," and in the time of William III. the writer of a pamphlet, which produced a great sensation, expressed his wonder that the people had not, when Tourville was riding victorious in the channel, *De Witted* the nonjuring prelates. In the same manner the " Tatler " says, " You look as if you were *Don Diego'd* to the tune of a thousand pounds." The Trojan Pandarus has left us the verb to *pander*, and we still say of a blustering, turbulent man that he *hectors*, or that he is a *hectoring* fellow.

Nor are modern authors less given to the formation of such verbs. Scott speaks in Waverley of a person who " *captain'd* and *Buttler'd* him." Southey mentions *sirring* and *madaming*, and even the polished style of the. author of " What Will He Do With It," condescends to a *de-Isaacised* Sir Isaac.

Among Americanisms of the kind we have heard more than is complimentary to the Republic of the process of *lynching*, said to be derived from an actually existing Judge Lynch. The origin of *levanting*, or escaping from troublesome creditors by a trip to the East, and of *japanning* certain articles, is clearly due to the Levant and to Japan. Modern additions to this class of verbs are, however, generally made after the manner of the Greek, by means of the syllable *-ize*, which generally indicates repetition, as in *civilizing, philosophizing*, and *hellenizing ;* the older *tantalize* is imitated by the more recent *galvanizing, mesmerizing*, and *macadamizing.*

A tolerably large class of verbs of this kind is made from the proper names not of men but of animals; they are very expressive, though often their constant use has made them so familiar to us that we hardly remember the association between their present meaning and the animal from which they are derived. But even where the suggestion is no longer so clearly marked, we are apt to feel instinctively the original idea, and thus these verbs lend no small force and beauty to our language. The ancients were not without this valuable class of words, and some of their formations have come down to us, as when Horace says already *similem ludere caprece*, and we still speak of children who *caper* about, conveying the idea that they are frolicsome like kids. To *ape* another is a very common expression, and the dog has furnished Shakespeare his —

"I have *dogged* him like a murderer."

To *rat* is, perhaps, rather technical, taken probably from the presumed sagacity of rats when they leave a falling house or a sinking ship ; but to *ferret* out a secret is only too common and belongs not, like ratting, to one sex only.

It is strange, and one of those mysteries of language which have so far defied all investigation, that the number of such verbs derived from quadrupeds should be so small, whilst birds and their habits have furnished many more. We speak of young people going out *a-larking*, when they are very apt to become *ravenously* hungry, and in their cups, at least, unhandsomely to *crow* over a fallen enemy, as the cock sings his chant of victory on his dung-heap. The fickleness of man's estimate of the other sex, or, perhaps, rather his just estimate of woman's high qualities in contrast with her foibles, is shown in the frequency with which he speaks of her as "a *duck* of a woman," and yet is still ready to *duck* a common scold in a village-pond. When we hear that a man has *quailed* in the face of danger, we are forcibly reminded of the words of an old song in "Relig. Antiquities," p. 69, "And thou shalt make him cowche as doth a *quaile*." The old form of the hawk's name has given rise to the use of the word *havoc* as a verb by itself, instead of the older form " to do havoc," which is sanctioned by both Spenser and Milton. The hawk must have been one of the most common birds in England from olden times, for we find that his habits, evidently familiar to all, have left many strong marks upon our language. Its untiring flight to and fro seems especially to have been watched with eager interest, and gave, probably, first its name to the wandering occupation of the petty dealer who, like the bird, went from house to house, buying then as he now sells, and *hawking* his goods all over the country. He became the *hawker*, whilst his female companion, or rival, was in Anglo-Saxon times a *hawkestere*, and survives even now in the modern *huckster*. Another allusion to the bird's restless flying about may be found in the game of which Halliwell says: " How much running to and fro, running forwards, running backwards, in the noble game of *hockey*." Its old name was *hawkey*. It ought to be mentioned, however, that others derive the verb *to hawk* from the German verb *hocken*, to offer for sale.

Even the smaller fry of animal life is not without its usefulness for our language. To *worm* one's way into the confidence of another, or to worm his secrets out, is a picturesque expression derived from the old usage of employing *worm* for all that creeps, and thus, also, for snake. The custom survives yet in the familiar word *blindworm*, and the disgust which is conveyed by the name of a *sneak*, or a sneaking fellow. We rise somewhat higher when we call a friend a *gad-about*, and *gadding* recalls to us the swift motions of a fly, suggesting thus most forcibly the ready flitting of a woman from house to house, not omitting, even, the little bite that is often left behind, and may prove more poisonous than we thought.

Besides nouns, few other parts of speech serve to form verbs. Now and then we meet with adjectives which are used as such, sometimes directly and without any change, as, to *idle*, to *warm*, and to *open*, at other times with the addition of a derivative syllable, as, to *whiten*, to *blacken*, to *brighten*, and to *lighten*.

Adverbs and mere particles, finally, occur occasionally used without any change, as verbs. This is especially the case in modern authors, among whom Dickens makes the freest use of this class of words. To them we owe expressions such as, to *over*, to *forward*, and to *even*, though already Shakespeare had (" Macbeth " III. 6), —

> " The cloudy messenger turns me his back
> And *hums*, as who should say, You'll rue the time
> That clogs me with this answer."

The number of verbs obtained by means of a change of form is much larger, and the process of thus making new verbs has been going on actively ever since the first existence of English, without being abandoned even in our day. The most popular change is simply the addition of *-en* to the root, nor are these letters merely accidental or arbitrarily chosen — nothing in language is accidental, as little as in nature. They are, on the contrary, the result of the three so-called primitive verbs which, in the very first stage of the existence of our language, were added to nouns in order thus to connect their own meaning with that of the root.

The simplest of the three was *an*, which seems to have had the vague, general meaning of adding, and often was doubled into *anan*. Its present participle *and* still survives in modern English, and when we say "father and

child" we still mean nothing more than "the father, adding the child." There was another form of this primitive word anciently in use, viz., *ge-anan*, which meant to
add and to produce ; this has given us our modern verb to
yean, though we limit its use to cattle and mainly to sheep,
and hence call a young lamb also a *yeanling*.

A fuller form is *gan*, which conveyed the general idea of
motion, as *an* did that of addition. It has given us directly
our word *go*, whilst the frequent double form, *gangan*, survives yet in a variety of forms. It gave life to the Scotch
term *to gang*, for our *to go*, and to a noun of our own,
when we speak of a *gang* of robbers, because they go together. Ben Jonson had, —

"And thence can see *gang* in and out my neat."

The diminutive *gangrel* is used, at least provincially, for
a vagabond, and the nautical term *gang*way has its name
from being the place through which people go to and from
a vessel.

Agan, finally, as it has a fuller form than *an* and *gan*,
also represents a higher idea, that of property. The latest
use made of the old verb may probably be found in the
famous proclamation of Henry III., made to the people of
Huntingdonshire in 1258, where this sentence occurs : "The
treowde thaet heo us *ogen*." Soon afterwards the word was
contracted, thanks to the soft pronunciation of the letter *g*,
until it assumed the present form of *own*. Our modern
English mixes up in sad confusion what we *own* and what
we *owe* to others : the idea of property (the German *eigen*)
prevails in both words, but the distinction between the two
parties has become effaced.

In Anglo-Saxon writings we find these three primitive
verbs appear still, from time to time, if not always in the
infinitive, at least in other tenses, but very soon the letter *g* lost its power, and *gan* and *agan* were reduced, in
composition, to *ian*, until, finally, all three endings were reduced to a uniform *an*. This continued to mark verbs until

the time of the Norman Conquest, as it still survives in German, where all verbs, without exception, terminate in *en*. The new masters, not accustomed to such a termination in their own tongue, from the beginning seem to have frequently disregarded it. This neglect was further increased by the fact that they were largely in the habit of giving a nasal sound to the combination *an*. It is well known that even the Romans already gave this, or a similar sound, to the letters *m* and *n* preceded by vowels, which led to the suppression of accusatives in *um, am, em,* &c., in Latin poets, whenever the metre required it. The effect was, no doubt, a similar one in regard to our Anglo-Saxon *an*, of the origin and meaning of which the Normans could not be expected to be aware. When the sound of the syllable had thus become indistinct, the whole was not at once dropped, but at first only the final consonant. Hence we find in Wickliffe verbs appearing quite frequently without the *n*, and then the diminution of the fuller *a* into the less distinct *e* followed almost as a matter of necessity. Hence we read, Luke i. 13, " Thi wif sceal *bere* to the a sone," and v. 16, " He schal *converte*." Chaucer ends almost all his verbs thus, and says, —

> " She wolde *wepe* if that she saw a mous,"

but yet he never fails to accentuate the final *e* and to count it as a syllable. Spenser has a few verbs in *en* remaining, as *e. g.* : —

> " That well may *semen* true."—*Fairy Queen*, VII. 7.

After his time, however, few cases occur, and soon even the final *e* was doomed to disappear. We need not wonder, therefore, that modern English has but a small number of verbs left in which the original termination has been preserved. Such are, to *learn*, which was at first *lear-an*, as is easily proved by the word *lore* for knowledge. To *mourn* and to *warn*, speak for themselves, but to *beckon* and to *reckon* are sad evidences of misspelling, both having originally terminated in *an*. At a later period it became the fashion to make new verbs, mostly from adjectives, by the addition of the former *en*. Thus arose our words to *soften*, to *strengthen*, to *weaken*, and to *quicken*, which do not show the old Anglo-Saxon form. This effort to introduce a new grammatical form was not, however, very successful, and we may judge of the difficulty of persuading the people to accept such innovations from the loss of certain verbs of this kind, that were really useful and desirable. Such is the verb to *worsen*, employed by Milton and by Southey, but now fallen into disuse.

About the middle of the thirteenth century all verbs had become so uniform as no longer to be distinguished from the nouns, as both classes of words were almost universally written with a final, but silent, *e*. It was then that the usage was established of prefixing the particle *to* to verbs, as *the* was placed before nouns. This was, of course, not an arbitrary choice. The particle *to* is the representative of the Old Gothic verb *tu-an*, from which we derive our verb to *do*, as the Germans have their *thun*. Prefixed to a word which, like *hate*, *love*, *fear*, and *sleep*, might be a noun as well as a verb, it indicated at once that it was to be taken in an active sense, and thus enabled the reader or the hearer immediately to avoid any misapprehension. It is the same process which we pursue now when we say I *do* know, in order to intensify or to emphasize the active meaning of a verb. Whenever a pronoun is added to the verb, it suffices to show the nature of the word, and thus the addition of *to* was and is necessary only in the infinitive, of which it is now considered an essential sign.

Another class of verbs, not very numerous but extremely interesting to the philologist, has been obtained by a process of derivation which belongs only to the most perfect languages, where the cumbersome mechanism of ruder idioms has been abandoned and a most delicate change, a mere hint, has the power to convey a change of meaning.

What can be more subtle, for instance, than the change of a final consonant merely from a sharp to a flat sound, with the addition of a silent *e*, to indicate the process of derivation? And yet by this slight modification we obtain from —

grass, *graze*,	price, *prize*,	wreath, *wreathe*,	half, *halve*,
glass, *glaze*,	breath, *breathe*,	cloth, *clothe*,	calf, *calve*,

and from *use* and *house*, without even that slight external evidence, by a mere change of sound, the verbs to *house* and to *use*.

The number of verbs derived from other and older verbs by a change of the root itself is much larger. This process is one of the most striking characteristics of all German idioms, and threefold. The change may affect the radical vowel only, and thus we obtain from —

bite, *bait*,	fall, *fell*,	rip, *rob*,	sweep, *swoop*.
bind, *bend*,	grind, *ground*,	rise, *raise* (rouse),	tint, *taint*,
breed, *brood*,	hang, *hinge*,	reel, *roll*,	tap, *tip* (top),
chip, *chop*,	lie, *lay* (lag),	sip, *sop* (sup),	temper, *tamper*,
creak, *croak*,	lose, *loose*,	stint, *stunt*,	wind, *wend*,
deal, *dole*,	pain, *pine*,	strike, *stroke*,	wreathe, *writhe*;
drip, *drop* (droop),	pick, *peck*,	sit, *set* (seat),	

or it may affect the radical consonant only, as in —

dip, *dive*,	gulp, (en)*gulph*,	twine, *twist*,
drive, *drift*,	lurk, *lurch*,	wake, *watch*,
hear (ear), *heark*(en)	rend, *rent*,	&c.

or it may affect vowel and consonant both, as in —

break, *breach*	draw, *drown*,	quail, *quell*,	wear, *worry*,
and *broach*,	drink, *drench*,	seave, *sift*,	wring, *wrench*,
dog, *dodge*,	lance, *launch*,	soil, *sully*,	&c.
drag, *dredge*,	poke, *poach*,	stink, *stench*,	

It is not quite so clearly to be ascertained, in the present state of our language, how verbs were originally obtained from other words by the addition of a letter at the beginning. Thus *c* was prefixed, and it gave us from —

log, *clog*,	ram, *cram*,	rumple, *crumple*.
lump, *clump*,	rib (rob), *crib*,	

Or *d* was changed by the addition of an aspirate into *th*, and drill became *trill* or *thrill*, and drive *thrive*. The letter *s*, when thus used, seems to correspond to the Latin *ex* in *exiguus*, the German *ur*, and the Gothic *us*. It is not limited to the formation of verbs only, for it gave us, also, the nouns *slime* from lime, and *stilt*, *spine*, and *strumpet* from tilt, pin, and trumpet. Among verbs we obtain from—

crawl, *scrawl*,	melt, *smelt*,	patter, *spatter*,	way, *sway*,
cold, *scold*,	mash, *smash*,	quash, *squash*,	wag, *swag*,
lash, *slash*,	nip, *snip*,	trample, *strample*,	wing, *swing*;

and with a slight modification of the root, from—

dip, *steep*,	leap, *slip*,	tap, *stab*,	whip, *sweep*,
lag, *slack*,	nose, *sneeze*,	weigh, *sway*,	wet, *sweat*.
heave, *shove*,			

The surviving influence of the Latin prefix *dis* has also occasionally left us the letter *s* before verbs, as in *stain* from *disteindre*, and in *scorch* from *discorticare*. By the force of analogy other verbs, also, have been made, which simply prefix *st* to ordinary words, and thus our language has been enriched with verbs like *stroll* from roll, *string* from ring, *strive* from rive, and *strip* from rip. The insertion of an *s* in the middle of the word has changed gap into *gasp*, and bake into *bask*, and at the same time slightly modified the original meaning.

Verbs, finally, have their diminutive terminations as well as nouns, though, unfortunately, the number is only small and not likely to be much extended, if we may judge from the few unsuccessful efforts made by some late writers. The addition of *er* changes chat into *chatter* and blind into *blunder*, flit into *flutter*, and blow into *bluster*. To *stut*, which Butler still mentions as one of the signs of melancholy, when he speaks of " *stutting* or tripping in speech," is now only used as *stutter*. The more fertile diminutive is *le*, which has given us,—

bab, *babble*.	crack, *crackle*,	drip, *dribble*,	gripe, *grapple*,
busy, *bustle*,	daub, *dabble*,	gab, *gabble*,	hurt, *hurtle*,

nip, *nibble*,	stiff, *stifle*,	tip, *tipple*,	wag, *waggle*,
prate, *prattle*,	stride, *straddle*,	top, *topple*,	wrest, *wrestle*.
rip, *ruffle*,	strike, *struggle*,	tramp, *trample*,	wring, *wrinkle*.
set, *settle*,	take, *tackle*,	wade, *waddle*,	
shove, *shuffle*,	throat, *throttle*,		

It will thus be seen that although our English cannot compare with her more fortunate sister on the Continent in the number and variety of verbs, it possesses, nevertheless, a keen perception yet of these delicate changes, by which the slightest modification of a single letter becomes the expression of a corresponding modification of meaning. Our Saxon fathers had another process by which they obtained new verbs from Saxon roots : it consisted in the use of two prefixes, *ge* and *on*, traces of which now survive only in a few cases under the form of *a*. The first of the two was a favorite and most distinguishing feature of the Anglo-Saxon verb, and its disappearance is one of the first, if not the very first, decided evidences of the change from Anglo-Saxon into English, even before the time of the Norman-French.

It was used not only as a mark of the participle past, for which purpose it is still employed in German verbs, but also as a verbal prefix before any verb and any part of a verb. Even the oldest authors, however, substitute a simple *y* for it, as in " Alesaundre," I. 1867 : —

> " The knyght is redy on justers
> Alle *yarmed* surthe well
> Bunny, and launce, and sweord of stele."

Even the " Brut of Layamon " has *idemed* for *gedemed*, *icome* for *gecome*, and *ispeken*, as the oldest of our songs has —

> " Sumer is *icumen* in,
> Lhude singe cuccu."

Chaucer occasionally reminds us of the old usage when he employs *ifalle, igo*, and *ifonden* for the participles fallen, gone, and found, and in 5599 he says, —

> " Thou hast *yhadde* five husbondes."

Spenser preserves some words with *y*, as he does many

antique words, not because they were in use in his day, but because they suited the peculiar character he wished to give to his verses. In like manner, Fairfax's "Tasso" abounds with words like *ibore*, *ibuilt*, and *ibrought*. Shakespeare uses now and then *yclad* and *yclept*, but probably only with a view to burlesque or grotesque effect. Thomson's "Castle of Indolence" has also a few such words, apparently in imitation of Spenser, and in Milton, even, *y* occurs at least three times. A curious evidence of the readiness with which we forget the original meaning of once familiar words is the use of *I wiss*, now nearly obsolete but once quite common, for *ywiss*, which corresponds to the German *gewisz*. Although this particle *ge* seems thus no longer to be used in our English, it is still preserved in part under various forms. Thus we meet, even now, occasionally with the antiquated terms of *yclad* and *yclept*, and often with happy effect. The latter term is now only used with reference to names, though originally it corresponded to all the meanings of the verb "to call," as in Matthew xx. 16, where the ancient version has "Manega synt *geclypoda*," for "Many be called." The modern *enough* retains in its first letter the marks of the Anglo-Saxon *genog* (German *genug*), which in Old English already was softened into *ynowh*. Few suspect the hidden manner in which this ancient *ge* still lurks in some compound words of our day, and yet we can easily trace the old "*hand ge weorc*," made by hand, in our hand*i*work, and we shall then understand the peculiar formation of other similar words, like hand*i*craft, hand*i*grip, hand*i*cap, and night*in*gale. We shall find, moreover, upon a somewhat more careful investigation of the matter, that it has not simply dropped out of the language, like a decayed member, but by a simple and very natural transition changed into *be*, under which form it is now frequently disguised. This is not a mere supposition, but can easily be proved by the fact that of the large number of modern verbs which begin with *be*, only about thirty or forty are found in Anglo-Saxon writers, while all the others may be traced to recent days, when they were made in imitation of others already existing. "The Paston' Letters," for instance, still have *headed* simply for *beheaded*, (vol. ii. letter 32,) and Chaucer says, "That appertaineth and *longeth* all onely to the judges" ("Tale of Melibœus"). It seems that anciently the particle *be*, by itself, had the power of giving an active meaning to verbs, and hence we obtained *bedim, beget, begird, benumb, bereave, beseech, begin, bespeak*, from Saxon words, and from French sources, *beguile, besot*, and *besiege*. *Bedew* and *bestrew, unbefriended* and *unbefitting*, are comparatively modern words ; others have gone out of fashion, as Shakespeare's *befortune, benetted*, and *beweep*, whilst *unbeknown* is now considered a vulgarism, although Chaucer says to *beknow*. Our modern *beloved* is evidently nothing else but the Anglo-Saxon participle *gelufod*, and in like manner *belong* was once *gelong*, and *believed* once *gelyfed*, for Gower uses frequently *leve* alone, and Chaucer, even, has the simple form quite often. There are even false forms of this kind existing, such as the contraction of *be* and *gone* into one word, *begone*. *Beware*, also, was originally not written in one word: the Bible said, "Of whom be thou *ware* also," (2 Tim. iv. 5,) and Pope says correctly, "Be ware of man," which Tennyson imitates in the line, —

"They were *ware* that all the decks were dense."

The prefix *ge* has lastly changed sometimes into a simple *a*, although it ought to be remembered that this same *a* is by some claimed as a remnant of the grammar of the Britons, and thus as a Celtic element of our English. We can, however, distinctly trace the change from *gebidan* to *abide*, and the like origin of *arise, awake, arouse*, and *abet*. Most of the forms now in use are participles, as the correctly formed, but now condemned, *afeared, adrift, ashamed, athirst*, etc. Occasionally the same letter represents the ancient prefix *on*. "The Knight's Tale" (1689) has "*On* húntyng ben they ridden," and the Bible of King James (Acts xiii. 36) has "fell *on* sleep," but already Bentley's "Dissertation on Phalaria" says, "Yet the same man here, in his great wisdom, would have a learned University make barbarisms *a* purpose," as *abed* and *aloft* mean "on the bed" and "on the loft." In a few cases the same prefix *a* can be traced back to its French origin. Thus *alarm* comes from *à l'arme*, *abase* from *à bas*, and *abandon* from the old *à ban donner*.

The number of English verbs obtained by genuine composition is, unfortunately, quite small, Latin substitutes having generally driven out the good old Saxon words. Our German sister is happier in this respect, and preserves to this day a host of simple, suggestive words of this class, which we once shared with her and now but imperfectly replace by foreign terms. Among the few classes of compounds which remain, those with *for* are peculiar, because they contain two different words, now often confounded. Some have their origin in the Saxon verb *faran*, to go, to travel, etc., whence our *farewell*, the wish and prayer for the *welfare* of our friends. *Fare* itself survives in the word for the price we give for traveling by land or sea, and names like Eel*fare*, a place near Chertsey, in the Thames, to which the young eels come up in spring. *Ferry*, as a passage by water, and *ford*, or *fared*, a passage on foot through the water, come from the same root. In compound verbs it assumes the form of *for* and suggests, like its German representative *ver*, always the idea of parting or destruction : hence our *forbid, forsake, forget*, and *forswear ; forgive, forlet*, and *forlorn*. The relation between the English and the German term is very clearly shown in " Robert of Gloucester," who always says *vergaf, vergon, vergyte*, and *verlore*, although " Piers Ploughman " already has " fier shale *for*brenne," (44).

The other class of these compounds derive their origin

from the word *before*, and hence *forego* means to precede, *forethink* to premeditate, and *foretell* and *forestall* have similar meanings. As the tendency to greater uniformity has already led to much confusion between these two words, and, *e. g.*, *forgo* and *forego* are hardly any longer distinguished, it is all the more important to remember, at least, historically the different origin of such words.

The large variety of verbs, and the almost unlimited freedom with which we can obtain them from other parts of speech, is out of all proportion to the use made of verbs. It seems as if all that our language nowadays desired was to have the verbal idea abundantly represented. It is no longer, as in ancient languages and in Anglo-Saxon, adapted by numerous inflections and changes to the various purposes for which it serves; a conjugation of the verb can hardly be said to exist; we have laid aside not only the passive and middle voice, the optative and other moods of Greek verbs, but we have abandoned also the many tenses of the Latin verb, which the Romance languages still retain, and after thus stripping the verb of all power to express time and mood, the tendency of our day is to free it more and more even of its connection with person.

The Anglo-Saxon verb had its usual complement of personal inflections, which, if they added little to the clearness and force of the language, certainly contributed much to the beauty and variety of its forms. Of these but few are left in our day. As far as a careful study of the language enables us to judge, the last remnant of the Saxon conjugation was the plural in *en*, which is still used in Lancashire, the North of England, York, and Derbyshire. Until the time of Henry VIII., it seems to have maintained itself in general use, although Chaucer already terminates his verbs both in *e* and in *en*. The fuller termination does not altogether disappear until the time of Spenser, for even Fuller uses it, though rarely; but when it at last was abandoned, there disappeared with it the last characteristic

19

of a grammar different from modern English. The gradual change is very perceptible in the Bible versions; Wickliffe still said: "And fluddes *camen* and wyndis *blewen*," while Tyndale has: "And fluddes *came*, and wyndes *blewe* and beet upon that house, and it fell, and great was the fall of it." The loss was not merely one of form, but also of sound, as Ben Jonson well remarks in his Grammar: "In former times, till about the reign of Henry VIII., they (the persons of the plural) were wont to be formed by adding *en*. But now (whatsoever is the cause), it hath quite growne out of use, and that other *e* so generally prevails, that I dare not presume to set this afoot againe. . . . . Albeit, to tell you my opinion, I am persuaded that the lack thereof, well considered, will be found a great blemish to our tongue." Poets, also, have reason to regret its loss, for it was an important aid to rhythm, as we may judge from many happy lines of Chaucer, like the following:—

> "And small fowles *maken* melodie
> That *slepen* al the night with open yhe."

The only personal inflections left us in our day are those of the second and third person singular. The termination *est*, limited of course to the rare use of the corresponding pronoun, is still of great force, and makes us regret the loss of a more general use. More rarely still do we meet with the *eth* of the third person, now almost exclusively employed in poetry, or when we speak with great emphasis on solemn subjects, and for sacred purposes. The loss of this syllable must have been very gradual and almost imperceptible, for in Sir Thomas More's works, as published in 1527 by order of Queen Mary, we find that *looketh*, *smileth*, &c., are still written, but evidently pronounced as one syllable, as we judge from the metre of his poems, in which he shows a very accurate and fastidious ear. On the other hand, it appears that the same *e* was as often elided in writing when it had evidently to be pronounced, for words printed thus: *whirlth*, *pluckth*, and *startlth* are clearly unpronounceable. The modern fashion of substituting *s* for the full syllable *eth* has not only led to greater uniformity, but also produced an increase of that letter which is already too frequent in English, and thus added to the hissing, which strikes the ear of foreigners with such unpleasant force.

The modifications of the verb which serve to designate the time of its action, have, in like manner, disappeared in English, until hardly more than two distinct forms have survived. The distinction of so-called tenses is, of course, a purely arbitrary arrangement, and nearly every nation has its own system. In one language the present is considered so fleeting that it is either still future or already past; in another, the past is subdivided into minute periods, and thus where one idiom is content with two or three tenses, another has a dozen. In fact, there is no reason why there might not be as many tenses as we choose to make subdivisions of time. Our English, however, goes here also farther than all other modern languages, disdaining to incumber the verb with numerous forms, and leaving it to the connection to suggest the precise time of its action. It has, properly speaking, but two tenses, the definite and the indefinite — all others suggestive of past or of future it expresses by what we call auxiliary verbs.

The indefinite tense, which our grammars persist in calling the present, is of course represented by the simple form of the verb itself, without any further change, and to *love* and I *love*, to *go* and I *go*, remain the same. The definite tense, however, which expresses the only time that can be spoken of with precision, the past, seems in Anglo-Saxon always to have been formed by genuine inflection. But although we are justified in presuming that in the first stage of our language all verbs were strong, we find that at the time of the earliest manuscripts the idiom was already so far modified as to have many weak verbs by their side. Since then, the number of the latter has steadily increased by the force of analogy, and the tendency to uniformity, and whilst in Old English strong verbs had still a large majority, they are now in so sad a minority as to be stigmatized by the name of irregular verbs.

The manner of inflection for the purpose of forming the past tense was, however, so varied as to produce now several classes of strong verbs. Purely strong verbs, which are almost all intransitive and radical, make it, in the first place, by merely changing the radical vowel, as in —

run, *ran;* sing, *sang;* spin, *span;* come, *came;* sink, *sank.*

The number of these is still quite considerable ; many, however, have been entirely lost, and still others survive only in certain localities. Thus *sew,* from *to sow,* is used by Gower in " De Confessione Amantis," V. fol. 936; *snew,* from *to snow,* by Holinshead, who, speaking of the tragedy of Dido, performed before Prince Alasco, says (1583): " It *snew* an artificial kind of snow ; " *crew,* from *to crow,* occurs in the Bible, when " the cock *crew* " to the grief of St. Peter, and *mought* from *I might,* now accounted a vulgarism, was correct in the days of Chaucer, and is so used by Fairfax. All these words, together with others like I *rep,* from *to reap,* and I *mew,* from *to mow,* are still in constant use in the North of England, and in Essex; and I *hove,* I *puck,* I *shuck,* I *squoze,* and I *clomb,* are frequently heard in Hereford and other inland counties. The last-mentioned preterit seems to have been yet in use in Milton's days, for he says : —

" So *clomb* the first great thief into God's fold,
So since, into his church lewd hirelings climb."
Paradise Lost.

How much fashion and the fanciful taste of poets must have had to do with these changes, may be judged from the fact that even the oldest authors used weak forms of strong verbs, which are not yet universally adopted in our day. In the " Morte d' Arthur " we find, —

" He *grow'd* in might and strength."

And in the " Franklin's Tale," —

> " Of fyshe and fleshe, and that so plenteouse,
> It *snewed* in his house of mete and drinke,
> Of all daintees that men could of thinke."

Other forms of the kind are even now in the process of changing; thus we seldom say *swoll,* but more frequently *swelled,* and not *hung,* but *hanged,* though the first named are certainly not incorrect.

A second class of strong verbs change with the radical vowel the final radical consonant also, as in —

bring, *brought,*	catch, *caught,*	buy, *bought,*
teach, *taught,*	seek, *sought,*	think, *thought.*

The reason of this additional change, so far from being irregular, is easily seen ; in all these verbs the final consonant *c, g,* or *k,* &c., comes in immediate contact with the harsh letter *t,* and then, as in all such cases throughout the language, always changes into *h.* Here, also, the gradual nature of the change from strong to weak verbs may be easily traced. *Catched* is not quite out of use yet, though generally superseded by *caught,* whilst Shakespeare's —

" He *raught* me his hand," (*Henry V.,* IV. 6,)

would be hardly understood now, and his *distraught,* (" Richard III.," III. 5, and *alias*), has been justly abandoned, because here a foreign word, the Latin *distraho,* was actually subjected to purely Saxon rules.

We have already above referred to the fact that the majority of strong verbs have become weak by the force of analogy ; there are, however, other reasons which have produced the same effect. Some, it seems, have changed their form slightly in order to indicate a corresponding change from the neuter to the active meaning, and in this transformation lost the power of making the past by inflection ; such are the verbs *drench,* from drink, *fell,* from fall, *set,* from sit, and others. A combination of strong verbs with other words seems to have produced a similar effect, for while *to do* and *to break* are strong, *to undo* and *to breakfast* are weak.

Weak verbs have, from of old, formed their past tense by the addition of *d*, which was originally nothing else than the past tense of the verb *to do*, — *did*. This has been clearly proved by a comparison of Anglo-Saxon with its near relative, the Gothic, where the full auxiliary *dedum*, &c., has been preserved. Hence *I loved* is the same as *I love did*, or as we still constantly say, *I did love*. If we ask the question which would naturally suggest itself to our mind, how *did* itself was formed, we find here also the explanation in kindred languages, and their rule to form strong verbs by reduplication. Now the final syllable in Anglo-Saxon *dide*, our *did*, is not a termination, but the verb itself, and the first syllable, *di*, is a re-duplication of the root, all preterits of old verbs being thus made in Anglo-Saxon, as well as in Greek and in Sanscrit.

This once being done, the preterite *did* was then added to other verbal roots in order to express that the action of the verb itself is *done* or finished, as we are still in the habit of saying, " I *do* say so," and as the illiterate of England and the blacks of America say, " I *done* do that." The additional *e* between the final *d* and the root of the verb is merely euphonic, used to preserve the sound of certain delicate consonants; hence the difference between *loved*, *longed*, and *loaded*, and *heard*, *said*, and *paid*. Since the days of Swift, who first complained of this change to Addison and thus brought the matter to public notice in the " Spectator," the " natural aversion to loquacity " of the English, as he calls it, has made this great change of suppressing the sound of the *e*. The " Spectator " mentions with regret, that the words drowned, walked, and arrived, are beginning to be pronounced *drown'd*, *walk'd*, *and arriv'd*, and that thus a tenth part of our words appear now as so many clusters of consonants. The spelling here also, soon followed the pronunciation of these words, and thus arose

the general tendency to contract all similar forms.   This
led, in the end, to a change of the final *d*, when placed after
two cousonants, into *t*, and hence our *learnt*, *rent*, and *bent*,
for learned, rented, and bended; or the *d* has entirely disappeared after another *d* or after *t*, as in *let*, *cut*, *set*, and
shred, *rid*, and *read*, changes which are, in truth, nothing
more than an orthographical convenience.

The so-called irregular verbs, finally, belong properly to
the same category to which irregular comparatives were
assigned; they are not really irregular, but prove, when
properly examined, to be parts of different verbs, united
only by that "*usus quem penes arbitrium est et jus et norma
loquendi*." Thus, *I went*, has nothing at all to do with the
verb *to go*, but belongs to the verb *to wend*, which was formerly in full use.   Chaucer says not only in his "Text of
Love" he *wendeth*, but even "It befell that he is *went*." In
the "Midsummer Night's Dream" we find "they shall
wend."   Milton has "thou *wentest*," (Paradise Lost, XII.
610,) and Lord Byron says, "Childe Harold *wends* through
many a pleasant place." Now its use is almost entirely
limited to the expression "to *wend* one's way," and grammarians call it irregular.

By the side of these few variations of form, by which in
one case the past time is distinguished from the present,
and in another case the second and third person are marked,
the verb possesses in our day but two additional forms: the
so-called participles, which Vossius quaintly calls mules,
because " they partake alike of the noun and the verb, as
the mule of the horse and the ass."

The present participle ended in Anglo-Saxon in *end*,
maintaining thus the analogy with the Greek ἔχοντες, and
the Latin hab*entis*.   This ancient termination is by no
means quite extinct yet in England; it is constantly heard
in Lincolnshire, Northumberland, and Scotland, and, in
fact, wherever traces may be found of Scandinavian settlements.   There words like *goand* and *strikand* are fre-

quently in use, reminding us of the *end*, which forms the regular German participle, (*gehend, streichend,*) and which is occasionally strengthened, as in the Scotch *farant*, its compound *auld-farant*, and the Shropshire word *farantly*. But it survives even in classic English ; the Saxon word *frean*, in German *freien*, meant to love, to hold dear, and has left us its participle in *friend*, anciently *freond*. So also the opposite sentiment expressed in the Saxon verb *fian*, to hate, has given us besides the other two derivatives, *foe* and *feud*, its participle *fiend*, as we read already in " Gower," V. : —

> " For he no more than he fende,
> Unto none other man is *fiende*,
> But all toward hymselfe alone.''

This termination *end* has been gradually transformed into our modern *ing*, and the change is probably due to two peculiar influences, which throw much light upon the gradual and often apparently arbitrary manner in which modern languages have acquired their present form. The Norman conquerors on one hand, were no doubt disposed to give to this syllable *end* the same sound which these letters had in their own tongue, and to pronounce it as they did their *grand, sang, en*, and other words. This led to a more and more nasal pronunciation, which easily passed into the corresponding *ing*, and from the spoken to the written word. On the other hand, our ancestors themselves contributed probably their share to the transformation. Every careful observer must have been struck with the frequent pronunciation of *ing* as *en* or *in* by the uneducated, a change which is almost the rule among the blacks in the Southern States. There, as among the common people everywhere, *seein is believin*. This tendency is further strengthened by the fact that many of these condemned vulgarisms are originally correct. If we hear a man say, " It was *owen* to my master," we ought to hesitate before blaming him for his bad English ; *owen* is just as correct as *owing*, for when we say " it is my own," we mean nothing more by it than " it is owen to me." Now, this confusion between *ing* and *en* or *end*, being once established and aided by the influence of Norman masters, the transition from the ancient *end* to the modern *ing* was easily though slowly accomplished, and we can trace the gradual encroachment of the new form distinctly from century to century. Nor ought we to overlook the lesser but not ineffective influence of the fact that the Anglo-Saxon already knew verbal substantives in *yng*, corresponding to those formed by the Germans in *ung*, so that very early indeed both terminations, *end* and *yng*, must have been found side by side, formed from the same verb. Thus our word *dwelling* was in Anglo-Saxon derived from *wunian*, to dwell, and made in *wuning*, (German, *Wohnung*), so that in " Prologue," I. 608, we read, —

> " His *wonyng* was ful fayr upon an heth."

The first regular participle of the kind occurs probably in " Layamon's Brut," though only once, in the word *waldinge*. Wickliffe uses still persistently the ancient form, and says, in Mark i. 7, " he prechyde *sayande*, a stalworther thane I schale come efter me, of whom I am not worthe down *fullande* or *knelande* to louse the thwonge of his chaucers (chaussure)." Chaucer, however, uses -*and* but rarely ; in return he puzzles his readers sorely by always accenting the more fashionable *ing*, as in —

> " *Seeking* for right, which I of thee entreat,"
> " *Damning* all wrong and tortuous injury,"

and —

> " *Riding* together both with equal pace,"

a peculiarity in which he is faithfully followed by his contemporaries and successors, even to Spenser's " Fairy Queen."

That the change must have obtained very early may be concluded from the fact that already in 1258, a genuine French word, barely naturalized, is found with the new termination, for in the translation of an edict of Henry III. from the Anglo-Norman for his Saxon subjects, the word *crouninge* appears.   As late as the sixteenth century, however, both the old and the new form still occur side by side; and it is not until the greater regularity of classic authors of that age settled our spelling permanently, that the modern form prevailed alone.   The few terminations in *end* which survive, have generally nothing to do with Saxon, but are more or less direct importations from the Latin.   Thus *legend* comes from *legendum*, although Horne Tooke sneeringly says, that it means more frequently *quod non legendum*.   *Reverend* entered through the church, and was at first given to all judges, as they were long by necessity clerks, though now to ministers only; *dividend* designated originally what ought to be divided, but now what actually is divided.   *Prebend, agenda,* and similar words, are to this day purely Latin terms.

The past participle can hardly be viewed as more than an adjective form of the past tense of the verb.   We need no other proof of this than the regular manner of its derivation from the latter.   In genuine strong verbs its form corresponds simply to that of the past tense.   We say I *bought,* and a *bought* horse; I *thought,* and a good *thought.* It is true that not unfrequently English verbs present so-called double forms, of which one serves for the past tense, and the other for the participle.   This does not, however, indicate a different origin of the participle.   The explanation is found in the fact that anciently these strong verbs changed the radical vowel from the singular of the past tense to the plural, using generally *a* in the former and *u* in the latter.   This difference of the two numbers was in accordance with a general law to which all Germanic languages are found subject.   Already in Old English, however, the custom of distinguishing singular and plural by any change of form ceased to be observed, and both became uniform, though not yet as much so as they now are.   For owing to the want of any absolute authority in matters of letters, and the utterly loose orthography of those days, the two forms in *a* and *u*, were, for a time, allowed to drift about loosely in the language. When, subsequently, a demand arose for law and order, not in society only, but even in language, the grammarians had nothing better to recommend than that one of those double forms was to be got rid of. But, in the mean time, the loose fragments had crystalized afresh into a fixed shape, simply in obedience to the common consent and usage of educated Englishmen, and now appear in relations which have nothing to do with their first position. Grammarians are still prone to call them irregular, thus relieving themselves of all responsibility for the change and its causes. Now, the forms in *a* are confined to the active past tense, and those in *u* all changed into participles. Hence we say, I *drank* and I was *drunk ;* we speak of money *sunk*, not *sank ;* of linen *spun*, not *span.* It is no longer considered good English to say I *sung* a song, but I *sang ;* yet nobody would say that a "song had been sang." This is one of the points concerning the history of a language on which grammarians have absolutely nothing to say, as they are purely historical. For there never has been a rule or a law to settle this ; yet the fact is tacitly admitted by all writers, and universally acquiesced in by educated persons. It shows, evidently, that there is a spiritual life in every living language, which makes itself finally manifest, and works through the minds of all speakers and writers as its own artist. As a necessary consequence of this explanation, we find that the process is still steadily going on, the distribution of the two forms being by no means finally settled. Thus we find even now good writers say with equal correctness, "the vessel *sank*," and "she *sunk ;*" and *swam* and *swum* were until lately used indiscriminately.

A further change has occasionally taken place in these strong past participles, when, as is very frequently the case, they have established themselves as regular adjectives. Thus *strong* is itself derived from to *string*, through the participle, as we see from Dryden's lines, —

> " By choice our longlived fathers earned their food,
>   Toil *strung* their nerves and purified their blood."

And in the " Lady of the Lake " we find a similar adjective, —

> " Of stature tall and slender frame,
>   But firmly *knit* was Malcolme Graeme."

The past participles of weak verbs are, in like manner, made from their past tenses by the addition of *d*, which has been explained above ; where the final *d* comes in contact with another hard consonant, there is at once a tendency perceptible gradually to contract the full form *ed* into *t*. This is not only the case with nouns derived from participles, as in *gift*, from what is *gived*, *feint* from *feigned*, and *joint* from *joined*, but even in simple verbal forms, as in *dealt*, *dreamt*, *burnt*, *meant*, *bent*, and *girt*. But here, also, the language is still in a state of transition, and lingers in it all the more readily because it obtains thus a greater variety of forms, which add to its beauty and harmony. Shakespeare uses *cast*, but, also, in " Henry V.," —

> " ——and newly mown
>   With *casted* slough and fresh celerity,"

and our Bible version says in verse 13 of 1 Kings viii : " I have surely *built* thee a house to dwell in," and in verse 27 of the same chapter, " how much less this house that I have *builded*." There are quite a number of verbs which even now hesitate between the fuller and the contracted form, as *lighted* and *lit*, *learned* and *learnt*, *decked* and *deckt*, *tossed* and *tosst*. In other verbs one of the hard consonants has been simply dropped, and thus we obtain the so-called irregular forms of participles, which agree with the infinitive, as *cast*, *hurt*, *cost*, and *put*.

A point much overlooked, and yet of great interest, is the strange power which our English possesses of making, by the mere force of analogy, past participles in *ed* from nouns, even where no verb of the kind is or ever was in existence — a power which may be traced back to the original force of this *d*, as derived from the verb to *do*. Thus we have *moneyed* and *landed* men; "a lily-*livered* knave" ("King Lear," II. 2), and *hunchbacked, cock-brained, cross-grained,* and *henpecked* husbands.

A smaller class of past participles is found in English, derived from verbs by the addition of that fertile source of adjectives, the termination *en*. Not unfrequently this form is found by the side of that in *ed*, as is the case in the two remarkable words, *head* and *heaven*, which are both derived from the Anglo-Saxon word *heah* (high), through the derivative verb *heave*, to put on high. The mode of derivation appears in remarkable clearness in a copy of the Bible of the time of Edward III., where we read: "And I saw an other strong aungel comynge down from *Heuene*, keuerid or clothid with a cloude, and the reynbow in his *Heuede*." (Apocal. x. 1). "Piers Ploughman" also has, "The *Hevedes* of holy churche and they holy were, Christe calleth hem salt."

Some of these participles have been but recently lost, for Milton still speaks of "a *foughten* field;" and older poets owed to them much beauty and variety, as in Spenser's lines, —

> "The barren ground was full of wicked weeds,
> Which she herself had *sowen* all about
> Now *growen* great of little seeds."

Where the full forms are preserved, they add much to the richness of modern verse, and Wordsworth makes the most of them, as in his "Wanderer:" —

> "—— his countenance meanwhile
> Was *hidden* from my view, and she remained
> Unrecognized, but *stricken* by the sight
> With slackened footsteps I advanced."

Frequently the full forms have been contracted after vowels, as in *drawn, known, born,* and *thrown*; in other cases the syllable is gradually disappearing. Thus we still have *stolen*, but *hidden* is slowly giving way to hid, like *bounden*, now used only with special meaning.

The strikingly small number of forms to which the English verb has thus been gradually reduced, would naturally render it very helpless, and lead to much obscurity and ambiguity, if the language, with its unfailing instinct, had not from the beginning seized upon a remedy. By its adroit use of the latter, it has not only supplied the apparent want, but actually added new strength to its verbs. The ancient languages, it is well known, expressed all the more common modes of action, existence, &c., by a number of varied inflections, and thus boasted of numerous tenses and moods. The Anglo-Saxon and English verb, on the contrary, contents itself strictly with its primary, legitimate duty, and with genuine simplicity claims to refer only to state or action. Hence its few forms. All other modifications of its meaning are expressed by the aid of other verbs, which thus become, in the true sense of the word, auxiliary verbs. By this, as already Camden said, our English has obtained a power, which the ancients, with all their variety of mood and inflection of tenses, could not attain. This is so characteristic of the peculiar mode of thought of the people, that these auxiliary verbs, like the personal pronouns, have ever remained purely Saxon, and neither suffered modification by the Conqueror, nor admitted a single Norman-French form to their number. The only trace to be found at all of French influence, is perhaps the use of the verb *to come*, with the present participle; " he comes running," " he came staggering," being probably an imitation of the French *il vint s'écriant*. There is less ground for supposing that the combination of the verb *to have* with the verb *to be*, in its compound tenses, was likewise due to French influence, though it is urged that the French alone uses the two verbs in such manner, the other Romance languages having different forms, and that the union of *to have* and *to be* is not met with in writers before the Norman Conquest.

The most frequent of these auxiliaries is also the one which has the most general meaning — the verb *to do*. We employ it continually for the sake of emphasis in the present, and place it once more before the past, because the original meaning of the final *d* has been lost. Hence we say "I *do* love," and "he *did* say so." Good English writers insist upon its use in questions, so that "did he come?" takes the place of "came he?" and in negative sentences, where we cannot well say "he came not," but substitute for it "he did not come."

The auxiliary verb *to be* is in English, as in all languages, one of the most interesting and yet one of the most difficult to explain. In no living language has it preserved its full, original form, but seems everywhere to have seized upon such parts of other verbs as could strengthen its meaning and add to its power. Already in the oldest Anglo-Saxon, in the form in which we first find it written, this verb shows by its great variety of forms, that it was even then no longer in a state of original purity and simplicity, or it would have been complete and regular throughout, as εἰμί was in Greek. It contained, instead, elements of at least five distinct substantive verbs, the primitive terms of which appear also in the other languages of the same family, as is the case with the Latin verb *esse*. This striking identity of our auxiliary with certain forms of ancient idioms, presents us another forcible proof of the intimate relationship existing between our English and the great family of idioms with which it claims kindred. On the other hand, it must not be overlooked that much of this apparent identity remains yet unexplained, and whilst the result cannot be denied, the connection has by no means been satisfactorily established in all cases.

The Anglo-Saxon *Ic eom*, our I *am*, bears upon its face evident proof of its identity with the Greek εἰμί, and the Latin *sum*. The second person *thu eart*, thou *art*, together with the plural form *are*, have, in like manner, been traced back to the Latin *eram* ; neither *art* nor *are*, however, can be called genuine Saxon, and with *wert* must be ascribed to

Scandinavian, probably Icelandic influence. The Anglo-Saxon forms *sy, seo,* and *sind,* preserved in the German *sein* and its derivatives, but entirely lost in modern English, corresponded, thirdly, with the Latin *sum* and *sunt.* I *was* and we *were,* belong, fourthly, to an ancient verb, *wesan,* Gothic *visan,* meaning originally to *grow,* which we have also unfortunately lost, whilst our German neighbors have preserved it not only as a verb, but in the form of some of their most suggestive nouns. Not less ought we to regret the loss of the many forms in which the verb *beon,* our to *be,* entered formerly into the conjugation of this auxiliary. Now we retain only the infinitive, and an occasional *beest,* as in " Paradise Lost," I. 84, —

> "If thou *beest* he — but O how fallen, how changed!"

Chaucer's frequent use of *ben* instead of *are,* as in the line —

> " That ye *ben* of my liffe and dethe the quene,"

has been rather violently imitated in Byron's " Don Juan," XIII. 26, —

> " Also there *bin* another pious reason."

We see, lastly, in the third person *is* a beautiful illustration of the gradual curtailment of certain forms, which by constant use lose more and more of their substance, even as small coins, in unceasing circulation, soon have their effigy and legend effaced. Its best-known ancestor is the Sanscrit *asti,* which reappears in the Zend *esti,* and the Greek ἐστί. The last vowel disappears alike in the Gothic *ist* and the Latin *est,* and their descendants on both sides reduce it finally to the present shortened form, thus: —

Gothic, *ist,*	Anglo-Saxon, *ys,*	Latin, *est,*	Spanish, *es,*
German, *ist,*	English, *is,*	French, *est,*	Italian, *è.*

The use of this verb as an auxiliary is as simple as it is familiar, but there are two ways in which it occurs which are more peculiar to English, and therefore deserve special mention. One is the idiomatic manner in which, by its aid,

English verbs express duration, or, as it is sometimes technically called, " a continued present." This is the purpose of expressions like *I am reading* and *I was saying*, known already to the Anglo-Saxon, and constituting one of those forms which give such remarkable precision for the expression of time to the English verb. " I am going to read," or " I was going to speak," present another of these peculiar forms by which we convey the idea of an immediate future, somewhat after the fashion of the French *je vais lire.*

The auxiliary *to have* is, on the contrary, a complete verb, and its apparent irregularities are nothing more than the result of gradual contraction, such as has taken place throughout all parts of speech under like circumstances. Thus Chaucer frequently uses the then prevailing form of the infinitive *to haven*, but occasionally prefers the shortened form *to han*. Other contractions were gradually introduced as we can trace them from one author to another, *e. g.*, —

Thou haefest, haefst, haest, hast.
He haefeth,   haefth, hath, has.
He haefde,   haefd, hadde, had.

Several of these auxiliary verbs have for so long served only to express certain fixed tenses or moods, that they are no longer full verbs, and now are used exclusively for one or the other meaning. They can, however, all be traced back to their once complete form. Such is our *I may*, derived from the Anglo-Saxon verb *magan* (German *mögen*), expressing the liberty of doing a thing. Anciently it was either *I may* or *I mow*, and had its regular past tense, *I mought*, which, although now considered vulgar and incorrect, was legitimately used by Chaucer, by Fairfax, and down to the end of the reign of Queen Elizabeth. Its ill-regulated orthography led, probably, most directly to its abandonment, especially as one way of spelling it produced no small confusion by the resemblance to

20

another auxiliary.　This was the form *mote*, as we find it in Spenser's " Fairy Queen," II. 9, 18 : —

> " She was faire as faire *mote* ever be,"

and in Fairfax's " Tasso," III. 13, —

> " Within the postern stood Argantes stout
> To rescue her, if ill *mote* her betide."

For there was another Anglo-Saxon verb, *motan*, which expressed the idea of necessity, now conveyed by our word *ought*.　Its past tense, it is said, which would have been *mot-ed* or *mot-t*, could, of course, not be pronounced, and was softened into *most*, the ancestor of our *must*, which now serves for past and present alike.　Its ancient use may be gathered from Gower's —

> " For as the fisse, if it be dry,
> *Mote*, in defaute of water, die,"

and from Chaucer's line, —

> " Men *mosten* given silver to pore freres."

Byron has left us in doubt as to the precise meaning which he gives to the word in, —

> " Whatever this grief *mote* be, which he could not control."

The apparently anomalous auxiliary *I ought* is a secondary derivation from the Saxon word *agan* (German *eigen*), our modern *to own*.　This divided, in the past tense, into *I owed* and *I ought*, with the meaning of owing something to duty or obligation.　An old political song has, —

> " All England *ahte* for to knowe,"

which shows us the manner of derivation, *g* always changing into *h* before *t*.

I will has not yet become quite obsolete as an independent verb.　Shakespeare says, —

> " He *wills* you in the name of God Almighty,"

and —

> " She *willed* me to leave my base vocation."

Its past tense, once *I wilede*, became early *I wolede* (German *wollte*), and this led to the modern contraction *I*

would, with silent *l.* Its meaning, so strikingly characteristic of the language, is the combination of futurity and
volition. Hence already in Wickliffe's translation we read,
"I *wolde* ye *schulden* sustaine a litil thing of my unwisdome."

I shall, on the contrary, from the Anglo-Saxon *scealan,*
(German *sollen,*) has a different origin and meaning. It
is the oldest English form of the future, and originally
meant *to owe,* for so even Chaucer uses it, saying, —

" For by the faithe I shall to God."

In Scripture *shall* is also a common form of the future,
where ordinary language, in speaking of earthly things,
would prefer *will.* When applied to God, it conveys, of
course, the acknowledgment that with Him the idea of
constraint is naturally excluded; hence, "Thou *shalt* endure, and thy years *shall* not change," or "The righteous
shall hold on his way and he that hath clean hands *shall*
wax stronger and stronger." They have been well called
regular futures, uninfluenced in form by human fears, or
courtesies, or doubts. Elsewhere, however, *shall* suggests
rather futurity, as dependent on duty or necessity, and
hence already in Wickliffe, "Sothely the unwisdome of
them *schal* be knowen to alle men." This double future
of the English, by means of two different verbs, is one of
the greatest beauties of the language. Used with equal
variety and precision, its thoroughly idiomatic employment
has been gradually worked up to such nicety of distinction
and power of expression, that it can now be acquired only
by instinct, and is a sore puzzle, if not an insuperable difficulty, to all foreigners. It must be admitted, that there is
no absolute rule given by any grammarian that will apply
to all cases, without leaving room for doubt. Archdeacon
Hare explains the law of the future, after Jacob Grimm,
upon ethical grounds, saying that "when speaking in the
first person we speak submissively, when speaking of
another we speak courteously." This is true as far as it

goes, but it does not cover all the ground. For *I shall
can*, by accent or merely by the connection, be as presumptuous as *I will*, and *you shall have it* is fully as courteous as *you will*. As the variety of meaning to be
expressed by the two verbs is almost infinite, there is no
sure guide but that instinct which is given to all who learn
a language with their mother's milk, or who acquire it so
successfully as to master its spirit as well as its form.

The auxiliary *I can*, simple in its meaning, presents to
the careful inquirer a curious example of the power of
analogy. Although a regular verb, it was already, in the
days of Chaucer, as frequently written with an *o* as
with an *a*, and *I con* and *I conde* (German *konnte*), are
met with as often as *I can*. In its use as an auxiliary,
I conde occurred continually by the side of *I would* and *I
should*, and by the mere force of analogy it also took an
inorganic *l*, which was never pronounced, as was the case in
the other two verbs. Then the letter *n*, unpronounceable
where it stood, was dropped, and thus *I conde* became *I
could*. The transformation was no doubt aided and accelerated by a desire to distinguish it from the similar *to ken*,
and its past tense, *I kennede*, (German *kannte*,) which still
survives in "not to my *ken*," the Scotch *canny*, and our
cunning.

A severe loss to our English is the giving up of *to weorthan*, once a full, regular verb, expressive of what is to be
in the future, and so eminently useful in German as *werden*. In our day it survives but here and there, in isolated expressions, as when we speak of the Parcæ, spinning
the Future, as "*weird* sisters." Besides, we use the Old
English "way *worth* ye" in emphatic expressions, as in
Chaucer's imprecation : —

> " Wo *worthe* the fayre genie virtutesse,
> Wo *worthe* that herbe also that doth no bote,
> Wo *worthe* that is ruthlesse,
> Wo *worthe* that wight trede eche under fote."
> *Troylus*, III.

Walter Scott follows it in his lines, —

> " Wo *worth* the chase — wo *worth* the day
> That costs thy life, my gallant gray."

And even in our Bible version occurs, " Thus saith the Lord God : Howl ye, Wo *worth* the day !" (Ezekiel xxx. 2).

Another class of verbs rapidly going out of use, and now surviving only in a few peculiar expressions, are the so-called impersonal verbs. The Anglo-Saxon, especially in its older form, seems to have employed the third person of verbs with the pronoun in the dative, and occasionally in the accusative, very frequently, and it is not unlikely that this was done in imitation of the Latin usage. As the Saxon gradually emancipated itself from the influence of Church-Latin, these expressions became rarer, and were soon limited almost exclusively to verbs like *to think, to seem*, etc. At all events, these are the only class now used with the pronoun in this manner. "The Romaunt of the Rose" (I. 1231), has, "*Her thought* it all a vilaine ;" and Gower says, —

> " With such gladness I daunce and skip,
> *Me thinketh* I touche not the floor."

Our Bible version has frequent instances, as, *e. g.,* 2 Samuel xviii. 27, "*Me thinketh* the running of the foremost is like the running of Ahimaaz." In " Paradise Lost " (I. 264), we find, —

> " *Him thought,* he by the brook of Cherith stood."

And the reading of " Richard III." (III. 1), now altered to *it seems*, was formerly, —

> " *Prince.* — Where shall we sojourn till our coronation ?
> " *Gloucester.* — Where *it thinks* best unto your royal selfe."

Even Pope does not disdain to use it in the line, —

> " One came, *methought,* and whispered in my ear."

"*Me listeth* " is of still rarer occurrence, and now used only in imitation of older authors, as of Ro. Brunne's, —

> " To the holy land *him list ;* "

and of Surrey's " Virgil," —

> " To whatsoever land,
> By sliding seas, *me listed* them to lede."

The past tense was formerly *lust* or *lest*, and hence is derived the kindred verb *to lust*. Modern authors, when they use such expressions at all, now generally substitute *me seems*, as in " Richard III." (III. 2), —

> "*Me seemeth* good that, with some little traine,
> Forthwith from Ludlow the young prince be fetched
> Hither to London, to be crowned our king."

Chaucer has, —

> " And al that *likith me*, I dar wel sayn
> It *likith the*."

In the dialect peculiar to the seventeenth century we meet frequently with the phrase " it likes me well," instead of our modern " I like it," and hence the repeated occurrence in Shakespeare of " it *dislikes me*," (" Hamlet," V. 2 ; " Othello," II. 3), and in " King Lear," " His countenance *likes me* not."

This peculiar use of so-called impersonal verbs must, however, be well distinguished from the mere expletive use of the pronoun, often called " Dativus Ethicus," and not as Gould Brown has it, " a faulty relic of our old Saxon dative case." It is, on the contrary, a legitimate use made of the same pronoun in all modern languages, giving great force and even occasional elegance to certain expressions, which, we fear, is unnecessarily neglected by modern writers. Shakespeare knew well how to use it with effect, as when he says, —

> " She leans *me* out of her mistress' chamber window,
> And bids me thousand times good night,"

and in another place, —

> " He presently, as greatness knows itself,
> Steps *me* a little higher than his son,
> Made to my father while his blood was poor,"

and even the " Spectator " still says, " A Jew eat *me* up half a ham of bacon."

These expletive pronouns must, of course, be read unemphatic and without accent, or they lead to sad misunderstanding, as in the well-known instance from the Bible, "And he said, Saddle *me* the ass, and they saddled *him*."

This use of the pronoun occurs, also, in the cases where *it* is employed merely as an expletive, without reference to a particular thing, as in Milton's lines, —

> " Not lording *it* over God's heritage,"

and —

> " Come and trip *it* as you go,"

and in Shakespeare, —

> " I 'll queen *it* no inch farther," (*Winter's Tale*, IV. 3.)

and even —

> " I come to wive *it*." (*Taming the Shrew*, I. 2).

CHAPTER XVI.

ADVERBS.

" Omnis pars orationis migrat in adverbum."

In the society of every country we meet, occasionally, with adventurers of unknown origin, whose place is as uncertain as their claims are vague, and who yet, because of some useful quality, or on account of the respect paid to established usage, are tolerated and entertained. In like manner, we find that every language also has its adventurers, words of more or less obscure descent, belonging to no one of the regularly defined classes of nouns or verbs, subject to no laws and rules, and yet not only incorporated in the idiom but always of undeniable importance. This exceptional, and generally ill-treated class of words, we call, after the fashion of ancient grammarians, adverbs. For already the old Latin writers, whenever a word was found to be established in use which differed from its ordinary manner of signifying, thrust it aside into the class of adverbs. Horne Tooke, with his usual bluntness, went still further, and called them " the common sink and repository of all heterogeneous and unknown corruptions." This view was long considered so satisfactory and, we apprehend, especially so convenient, that but little attention was given to these pariahs, and they were allowed to hide in dark corners and to lose daily more of their original substance and appearance. When, at last, the attention of learned men was drawn to these unfortunate words, they were made the sport of every scribbler, and especially of —

> " Those learned philologists who chase
> A panting syllable through time and space,
> Start it at home and hunt it, in the dark,
> To Gaul — to Greece — and into Noah's ark."

Even the more exhausting research and the more cautious investigations of modern linguists have but imperfectly succeeded in restoring order to this lumber-room of our language. All we know with certainty is, that in form the adverbs are, almost without exception, abbreviations and often corruptions of other parts of speech, and that in meaning they denote qualities which do not belong to objects (nouns), but rather to actions, etc. (verbs). Hence their one unchanging peculiarity, common to all, that they cannot be joined to a noun, but only to verbs, and, through them, to adjectives and other adverbs, as when we say, "The orator spoke *fluently* but not well," or, "She was *exceedingly* fair," and "He looks *uncommonly* badly." As it cannot stand alone, but must needs be accompanied by a verb, it received in ancient Greece its name of ἐπίρρημα, and in Latin was called an *ad*verb.

Our English adverbs, also, as far as we have been able to trace them to their first origin, are but remnants and degenerate forms of other parts of speech, and owe their descent, without exception, to other classes of words.

Nouns furnish us numerous adverbs, generally in the form of the genitive in *s*, which early became so characteristic a mark of the adverbial use of a noun that, although originally belonging to masculines only, it was soon added to feminine nouns also. When we say, "It must *needs* be," we employ the genitive of the Anglo-Saxon noun *need*, originally *neades*. The noun *way* has thus furnished us with quite a number of adverbs, in which, however, the word *wise* is occasionally mistaken for *ways*. Thus the familiar *longways* is, strictly speaking, derived and often actually written *longwise*, as derived from the old *wise* for *guise*, used, *e. g.*, in our Bible version: "The birth of

Jesus Christ was on this *wise*." *Always* and *noways* are, however, legitimate descendants of *way*; so, also, *straight-ways, sideways, lengthways, endways*, the rarer "*anyways* afflicted" in our "Common Prayer," and the "come a little nearer this*ways*" of Shakespeare, ("Merry Wives," II. 2). "Day" has furnished us the modern *nowadays*, formerly written as in "Douglas,"—

> " But certainly, the dasit blude *now on dayes*
> Waxis dolf and dull throw myne unweildy age."

"While" has given us *whiles*, shown in its old meaning in Shakespeare's "Much Ado,"—

> " She died, my lord, but *whiles* her slander liv'd,"

and now not unfrequently augmented, by mere force of analogy, into *whilst*. *Amidships* and *athwartships* are well-known forms of this class, but *perhaps* is less familiar as to its derivation, as we have lost the old noun *hap*, or *happe*, used thus in Gower, —

> " The *happes* ouer mannes hede,
> Ben honged with a tender threde."

Scotch dialects abound in similar formations, rarely heard south of the Tweed, as *landgates, haufgates* (halfway), *gee-ways* (bias), *nextways*, and *landways*. In "Hudibras" we meet with the quaint word *anothergates*.

The dative of nouns has furnished but few adverbs now in use. Generally it is the dative plural, which thus sur-vives from the early days of the Anglo-Saxon in the *whilom* from *while*, *seldom* from *seld*, still used thus by Shakespeare, and *piecemeal*, which has now lost its termination but was formerly *piecemealum*. Rarely do we meet with the da-tive singular, and then always with the feminine, as in *ever*, from Anglo-Saxon *efe*, anciently written *aefere*, and its negative form *never*. *Athwart, then*, and *when*, are looked upon by many as accusatives, and *why, how*, and *thus*, as ablatives.

A much more numerous class of adverbs has been

derived from nouns by means of additional prepositions, which have not unfrequently been incorporated with the adverb in our day. *In* thus forms words like *indeed, in fact, in truth; to* makes *to-day, to-night, to-morrow; at* furnishes *at length, at times, at will; by*, now but rarely used in its full form, as in *by rights*, is generally shortened into *be*, as in *betimes, besides*, and the rarer —

" *Belike* they had some notice of the people." — *Julius Cæsar*, II. 2.

In like manner have been derived *of course, forsooth, up-stairs*, and even the French *per* had to furnish *peradven-ture*, and —

" Gentles, *perchance*, ye wonder at this show."
Midsummer Night's Dream, V. 1.

In Old English the preposition *on* seems to have been of all the most generally used, but its very frequency has led to its almost constant abbreviation in *a* or *o*. Thus, what was in older authors *on righte, on gemang, on baec, on veg*, and *on gegen*, is now *aright, among, aback, away*, and *again*, and in accordance with these forms new ones have been made, like *abed, aboard, abreast*, and *aloft*. Our modern *o'clock* is an instance of the change of *on* into simple *o*, which was formerly more frequent, as we may see from the line in " Julius Cæsar," —

" Such as sleep *o'nights*."

It seems that in the older stages of the language the nice difference of meaning which now exists between *on* and *in* became less distinct, and people using the one for the other, they were all represented by *on, un, an*, or *in*, and in composition by the shorter forms of simple *a* or *o*. The former, especially, whatever may have been its first origin and meaning, was already in Anglo-Saxon used with apparent caprice, being now added and now omitted. As far as we can judge in a matter so entirely dependent on the taste or the fashion of the time, it seems to have been mainly used to add expressiveness to all words of an emo-

tional character, like *awake, ajoy*, etc. Hence its frequent
and powerful use in Shakespeare, as, —

> " For Cassius is *aweary* of the world." — *Julius Cæsar.*
> " I 'gin to be *aweary* of the sun." — *Macbeth.*
> " Tom 's *acold.*" — *King Lear.*

The same explanation applies, probably, to the fuller form
an, (so often met with in our Bible version, as in the words,
" When I was *an* hungered,") before vowels and the letter
h. That even now the use of this adverbial prefix depends
more on caprice than on any rule, appears from the fact
that many words which formerly had it, are now used without it, whilst others have assumed it only in modern times.

Adjectives have furnished us with adverbs by similar
changes. In some cases it is here also the genitive in *s*,
which is employed for the purpose. Hence, *e. g.*, our *else*,
formerly *elles*, which curiously coincides with the Greek
ἀλλῶς and the Latin *alias*. In Ritson's " Ballads " we
find, —

> " And *elles* I swere withouten fayle."

Chaucer has —

> "*Te Deum* was one songe and nothyng *elles*," (*Sumptner's Tale*, 43.)

and in the " Reve's Tale " (16), —

> ' Or *els* he is a fool, as clerkes sayn,"

showing the gradual process of abbreviation. *Eftsoons*,
which still occurs in Shakespeare, is now entirely out of
use, but *unawares* and all the compounds with " ward," as
upwards, homewards, backwards, towards, and *afterwards*,
were adverbs already in Anglo-Saxon, and are not, as Johnson says, " less correct forms."

Other adjectives give us adverbs by adding the comparative form *-er*, a process which is used in all languages for
the purpose of making adverbs of locality. The Greek
had its πρότερος, ἔντερον, and ἐξώτερος, from πρό, ἔν, and
ἔξω; the Latin its *prior* from *pro*, *inter* from *in*, *exterior*
and *exterus* from *ex*, *subter*, *præter*, *posterus*, and *obiter*.
The corresponding forms in our English are *inner*, *upper*,
outer or *utter*, *yonder*, and many others.

It is another peculiarity of our idiom that many adjectives are used as adverbs without any change of form. Generally we now obtain adverbs from adjectives by the ordinary method of adding *-ly* to the latter, but many of these show a mysterious reluctance to take this termination. In cases like *illy* and *stilly*, the objection might be explained by the unpleasant accumulation of *l;* in most instances, however, it is simply felt but cannot be explained, though not unfrequently it is overruled by individual taste or preference. We speak thus of selling *cheap* and *dear*, although we may pay *dearly;* we say to play *fair*, to fall *flat*, to labor *hard*, to write *close*, to come *late*, to wait *long*, to speak *loud* or *low*, to run *quick*, and to stop *short*. We go even further than that, and say *full* well, *pretty* good, and *wide* open; though Hume's "the people are *miserable* poor," and the " Spectator's " " How *unworthy* you treated mankind," would not now be considered correct. Shakespeare's " *indifferent* well," and Butler's " *wonderful* silly," would no longer be tolerated. With all this diversity of taste there is no rule limiting the adverbial use of these adjectives. The only point which they have in common is that they are all original Anglo-Saxon adjectives, not one of French origin being thus used unchanged. It may be added that, in modern style, the adjective is considered as giving greater force than the derivative adverb. Thus we find in Gray, —

> " *Full* many a gem of purest ray serene,"

and we read —

> " Drink *deep* or taste not the Pierian spring,"

in Pope, and —

> " Science by thee flows *soft*, in social ease,
> And virtue, losing rigor, loves to please,"

in Savage, and in Milton —

> " As when the sun, *new* risen,
> Looks through the misty, horizontal air
> Shorn of his beams."

There can be no doubt that this constant use of adjectives as adverbs, without any apparent change of form, had its origin in the fact that in Anglo-Saxon and in Old English adverbs were very commonly made from adjectives by the simple addition of an *e*. It matters not whether this letter was the old ablative ending, as some maintain, or had already then lost its primary power, and merely served to distinguish adverbs. This only is certain — that the adverbial *e* shared the fate of almost all final *e*'s, and was quietly dropped in the course of time, so as to reduce adjective and adverb alike to the same form.

Some of these adverbs we can clearly trace through Old English writings, *e. g.*, we say "The thing is *clean* gone," from the old adverb *clæne* which meant entirely. In like manner the Anglo-Saxon adverbs *hearde*, *hlydde*, *rihte*, and *wide*, have given us our expressions, "he rode *hard*," "she spoke *loud*," "it was done *right* well," and "the door is *wide* open." An additional evidence of this explanation is found in the ample use which poets make of such simple adverbs, from the preference they naturally give to antique forms, while in prose the fuller and more modern form in *-ly* is more common.

The fact is, however, that in this and similar matters the established usage has, in English, a force far greater than any law or rule. It constitutes the idiom, in the true sense of that word. There is no explanation needed for what is sanctioned by usage, for to alter it would involve the necessity of altering the mode of thought — the whole mind of the nation. We cannot change, by any force of reasoning, the smallest rule in English. There is, for instance, no apparent reason why the two words *very* and *much* should not be used in the same manner, or exchanged the one for the other, and yet it cannot be done. We may say "I am very happy to see you," but not "I am much happy." On the other hand we may say, "I am much misunderstood" (or mistaken), but not "I am very mistaken." Max Müller, noticing a change in this rule which is taking place in this country, where " I am very pleased," and like.expressions, are beginning to prevail, ascribes it to an inner necessity, a development of the language. It would seem, however, as if it were rather the change in the way of thinking which distinguishes the Englishman from the American. The tendency with the former is to worship wealth and to revel in *rich* colors, *rich* stories, and *rich* exposures ; the latter is, as yet, more struck with power, and hence dwells upon a *strong* likeness, a *powerful* speech, and an *almighty* dollar. - Thus he comes to prefer *very*, as suggestive of vigor, to *much*, as expressive of abundance and wealth.

Numerals produce adverbs like adjectives, through the genitive form, and give us thus *once* instead of *ones*, which, although not found in Anglo-Saxon, was probably common in early dialects, as it occurs so frequently in old authors. Chaucer says in the " Knight's Tale," —

> " Ye wote your selfe, she may not wedde two at *ones*."

and in the " Nonne's Priest," —

> " And first I shrew myself, both blode'and bones,
> If thou begyle me ofter than *ones*."

The frequent use of this word *ones* with a demonstrative *than* before it, has led to the contraction of the two words into one, after the same manner in which *nadder* has come from *an adder*, and *newt* from *an eft*. Thus in Madden's " Glossary to Gawan," we still find the forms separate, " for *than ones*," but afterwards they were contracted, and produced our English word *nonce*, now commonly used only in the phrase, " for the *nonce*."

Twice and *thrice* are formed in the same way, as we may see again in Chaucer, —

> " That had been *twies* hot and *twies* cold,"

and —

> " He hadde foughten in listes *thries*."

These words are but so many additional proofs of the general tendency of English to shorten, and in the process, also, to harden *ies* into *ice*, which has already been remarked upon in the formation of the plural, where *mies* became *mice*, dies, *dice*, and pennies, *pence*. But what is more remarkable still, is the analogous formation of adverbs from the genitive of personal pronouns, a derivation so little apparent in the modern form of the adverbs as to be continually overlooked. The Anglo-Saxon *hen*, still used in Lincolnshire, made formerly its genitive in *hennes*; this Chaucer shortens in "*Hens* over a mile," and now we write it *hence*. "Piers Ploughman" (19) speaks of "Ere she *thennes* yede," which gave us our *thence*; and *whence* is formed in like manner. Following, however, the example of adjectives, the pronouns also make adverbs in three ways: the genitive masculine in *es*, now shortened into *ce* with silent *e*, the genitive feminine in *er*, and the comparative termination, thus furnishing us with three classes of adverbs, corresponding to the above-mentioned three classes of pronouns : —

here,	there,	where,
hence,	thence,	whence,
hither,	thither,	whither,
	then } (*A. S.* thenne),	when,
	than }	why,
	thus	
	though (*German* doch),	(w)how.

Verbs furnish but few adverbs, and only such as are either simple forms of the verb itself, or gradually becoming obsolete. Such are our familiar *may be*, for perhaps, and " *Mayhap* you will do more " (Tom Jones, III. 28). The once very popular *to wit* is now hardly used, except in public or legal documents, and so are *albeit* and *howbeit*. *Notwithstanding* is of all verbal adverbs, in spite of its awkward length, the most generally used in our day.

A class of adverbs marked by striking peculiarities in all languages, and not least so in our English, contains the words used for negation and affirmation. One of the characteristic features is, that almost all languages possessed originally two forms for both, like the Greek οὐ and μή, of which one has gradually disappeared. Our French neighbors distinguish to this day carefully between their *si* and *oui*, and so do the Swedes, but most of the European idioms now employ but one. Our Saxon fathers also had two negative and two affirmative forms, which have not yet altogether disappeared from modern English. The former were *na*, which has given as our *no* and *neither*, and *ne*, our *not*. The difference, according to our usage, however, is not the same as of old; now we employ *no* to express a negative of things, and not of actions, as when we say, " He has *no* money," being in reality used as an adjective, and not as an adverb. But in the phrase " He has *not* money enough," we use the verb negatively, and therefore employ a genuine adverb. Old English authors frequently substituted *naye* for *not*, a word the origin of which is by no means satisfactorily explained. Those who consider *aye* to be derived from the French *aye* and *ayez*, go so far as to presuppose already a French *n'aye*, which might have crept into our English with other Norman French importations. Others trace our *aye* simply back to the *aye*, explained before, which we use for *always*, and these see in *naye* merely a contraction of the Anglo-Saxon *ne* with it, as if meaning *not always*. It is, however, certain that the word was at an early period already spelt *n'aye*. All the older writers are very careful in observing the distinction between these two negatives, using *no* in reply to negative, and *nay* in reply to affirmative questions, in precisely the same manner in which the French *oui* and *si* are employed. Sir Thomas More in his " Confutation of Tyndale " (448) explains the use very explicitly, thus : " If a manne should aske Tindale hymselfe : Is an heretike mete to translate Holy Scripture into English? To this question, if he will answer trewe, he must aunswere Nay and not No. But and if the question

21

be asked hym thus lo : Is not an heretique mete, &c. To this question, if he will aunswer true English, he must aunswer No and not Nay." A small matter, one might imagine, to reproach Tyndale with in a work of such vast importance, but showing the great weight given to the use of these negatives in the days of yore.

Our *not* is more easily traced back to its first descent. It is a compound, consisting of the negative *ne*, and the old word *viht* or *wiht*. The latter meant originally any thing that really exists, a creature, and is the same, in form, as our modern *wight*, which we, however, only use for a man. But the Anglo-Saxon *viht* was also the same as *whit*, and when we now say " not a *whit*," or, as in Shakespeare's " Julius Cæsar," —

"Our youth and wildness shall *no whit* appear,"

we use it exactly in the old sense of not any thing, not at all.   From such a very general meaning, suggesting any created being in the vaguest sense, it seems to have come to signify, after a time, an elf or other uncanny being.   In this sense it occurs in the " Miller's Tale," —

"I crouch thee from elves and from *wights.*"

The next step, no doubt, was to lose sight of the feature of life in these beings, and *wight* was employed to express any thing, somewhat after the manner in which the French *rien* is derived from the Latin *rem*.   The word, by itself, is unfortunately going out of use, and our English is thus deprived of a term of original, simple force, the loss of which is much to be regretted.   We generally substitute for it nowadays the Latin *persona*, a *person*, which originally meant in English not a man but a mask, and is still used so on play-bills. Quite recently a still worse expression has intruded itself into good society in the word *individual*, which suggests no clear idea to the mass of the people, and when used to designate biblical characters, or the Saviour himself, as is frequently the case in our churches, sounds almost irreverent. It is a pity that so few of us remember and follow the excellent advice given by the author of " Guesses at Truth : " " When you doubt between two words, choose the plainest, the commonest, the most idiomatic. Eschew fine words as you would rouge, love simple ones as you would native roses on your cheek!" Measured by such a standard, how absurd appears the *individual* by the side of the poor *wight!*

It was in this very general meaning of *any thing*, probably, that the negative *ne* was first added to *viht*, and thus produced by the side of the still surviving *aught* the compound form *naught*, which was finally shortened into *not*. Chaucer retains the original word, *e. g.*, in " There is no *wight* that hath soverein bounte save God alone." Soon after the more recent form appears very generally, and is still occasionally used, mainly in poetical language. Thus T. H. Bailey says : —

> " But should *aught* impious or impure
> Take friendship's name, reject and shun it."

Longfellow has, —

> " *Naught* else have we to give,"

as already our Bible version used it (Proverbs xx. 14), " It is *naught*, it is naught, saith the buyer : but when he is gone his way, then he boasteth." In Milton's " Paradise Lost " the word is rather a favorite, as *e. g.*,—

> " Nor *aught* avails him now
> To have built in heaven high towers."

It is probably little more than a caprice of the idiom, that our modern English requires the aid of the auxiliary *to do*, with negative verbs. Older writers knew of no such rule; Shakespeare says simply " she *not* denies it," and Dryden has, " I *not* offend." Now, however, *not* is admissible by itself only after the verb, and then only in very emphatic expressions, as when we say " I will *not*," or " I went *not*."

The Anglo-Saxon had, as the Romance languages now

have, a so-called double negative, using this *not* in conjunction with other negative adverbs. This is no longer admissible, though occasionally occurring. Chaucer follows the old usage in —

> "He *never* yet *no* vilainee *ne* sayde."

In Dayton's "Nymphidia" we find, —

> "She mounts her chariot in a trice,
> *Nor* would she stay for *no* advice,
> Until her maids who were so nice
> To wait on her were fitted."

Shakespeare makes frequent use of this peculiar kind of "strong language." In "Richard II." he says:" —

> "I *never* was *nor never* will be false,"

in "Measure for Measure," —

> "Harp *not* on that *nor* do *not* banish reason
> For incredulity; "

and in "Romeo and Juliet" (IV. 11) we read of —

> "a sudden day of joy
> That thou expectedst not, *nor* I looked *not* for."

The English possessed of old the same power which produced so remarkable results in the ancient languages, of uniting the negative (*ne*) with those words to which it applied most directly. This was of constant occurrence when the latter commenced either with *h* or with *w* — letters of such faint sound and fleeting import that they were easily lost under the sterner influence of the negative. Following thus the example of the Latin in *nemo*, from *ne-homo*, the Anglo-Saxon had *naebbe*, from *ne-haebbe ;* as *nullus* arose from *ne-ullus*, so did *nys* from *ne-is ;* and as *nolo* from *ne-volo*, so *naes* from *ne-waes*. Our German cousin also has, by the same process, *Niemand* and *Jemand, Nein* and *Ein, Nirgends* and *Irgends, Niemals* and *Jemals*. Older authors still present us occasionally with the contraction of *ne* and *willan*, as in Wickliffe's translation (Judges xviii. 9), —

> "*Wyle* ye be negligent, *nil* ye cecse,"

and Sylvester says, as late as the end of the seventeenth century, —

"Who *nill* be subjects shall be slaves in fine."

Chaucer had a long list of similar forms, which, to the injury of the language, have since been lost, as *nis, nam, niste,* and *nadde.* Our modern English retains a few, as *naught* and *never, none* and *neither ;* others, now out of use, might, we think, be profitably and easily recovered, as the process of thus prefixing *ne* is by no means repugnant to the language, and the meaning of the negative has not been dimmed by long oblivion as that of other similar particles. A few expressions of this class are often instinctively used, the speaker having no very clear idea of the origin, nor perhaps of the precise meaning of the words themselves Thus *willy-nilly* is simply the old *will he nill he,* after the manner of the Latin *nolens-volens,* and survives at least as a familiar phrase. The great Wesley once tried to revive its original form and force, and said : " Man *wills* something because it is pleasing to nature, and he *nills* something because it is contrary to nature," but for some reason or other he found no imitators. Our *hob-nob,* also, suggests but to the few learned in ancient lore, its derivation from *haeb naeb,* used from of old convivially, when asking a person whether he will have or not have a glass of wine. Hence its present use as a verb, though Shakespeare seems to have been accustomed to the word in a larger meaning, for he translates it as it were in these lines, ("Twelfth Night," III. 4,) "And his incensement at this moment is so implacable that satisfaction can be now but by pangs of death and sepulchre ; *hob-nob* is his word, give 't or take 't."

Modern English seems to have a tendency of contracting words with the negative at the end, rather than at the beginning. Hence our familiar *I wo'nt* and *I do'nt.* These forms are probably of comparatively recent date, for in the days of the " Spectator," they were apparently not approved of, and we read in No. 135, of this contraction, that " it has

very much untuned our language, and clogged it with consonants." In our day, however, the moderate use of these
forms is, we believe, universally admitted, and even preferred in simple and unaffected language. They are, of
course, legitimately excluded from solemn addresses, and
the license must even in lighter trifling not go quite as far
as Sam Slick's "I *sha'nt* say I *ha'nt*," or "if it *wa'nt*." The
affirmative presents to us much less variety of form and
meaning. There used to be, as with the negative, so here
also two distinct forms, *Aye* and *Yes ;* the former now antiquated, and the latter alone surviving. *Aye* seems to have
been originally the same as that *aye*, which meant *ever*, and
hence the familiar expression, "forever and for *aye*." It is
probable, however, that it was pronounced differently from
the beginning, for as far back as the days of Shakespeare,
we find it continually spelt a simple *i*, as in " Hamlet," III.
1 : —

> " To sleep, perchance to dream, *I*, there 's the rub,"

and hence, also, Romeo's unpardonable pun, —

> " Hath Romeo slain himself? say thou but *I*
> And that bare vowel I shall poison more
> Than the death-darting *eye* of a cockatrice."

Yes is probably a contraction of the ancient affirmative *yea*
with *se* or *sy*, the old subjunctive of the verb *to be*, so that
it meant originally *so be it*. Our oldest authors continually
use *gea* (now *yea*) as a simple affirmative, as in Chaucer's
" By *gea* and *nay*," and Shakespeare, (" Merry Wives," IV.
2, and elsewhere,) " By *yea* and *nay*." But the use of these
important words was strictly limited by the nature of the
question to which they furnished a reply. *Yea* and *nay*
answered affirmative, *yes* and *no* answered negative questions, as is still the case in Icelandic and in Swedish, where
the same difference applies to *ja* and *jo*. The rule was observed by Chaucer. and faithfully down to the middle of the
sixteenth century ; since then *yea* and *nay* have been assigned to the sacred dialect exclusively. Even, there, how-

ever, it was not always regarded, or Sir Thomas More would not have found occasion to blame Tyndale so sharply for his neglect, and in our modern version it is not at all observed, for we find (Matth. xvii. 24, 25), " Doth *not* your master pay tribute?   He saith, *Yes!* "

CHAPTER XVII.

PARTICLES.

" Bolts, pins, and hinges of the structure of language." — *Jamieson*.

THERE remains, lastly, of all the words that make up the proud fabric of our English, a little people of small particles, insignificant in appearance, and at first sight of but small importance. But like the long unseen infusoria of our globe, which Ehrenberg at last proved to have raised lofty mountains and to bear on their accumulated remains vast cities, so these despised words, long considered as little better than mere rubbish, have of late risen in the estimation of men and obtained admittance to the honored family of words. Once called contemptuously " particles," as if they were mere fractions of larger words, and even by Plutarch designated as " little fragments of words, used in haste and for dispatch, instead of the whole words," those, at least, which we know as prepositions have now established their claim to be considered as genuine adverbs. The use we make of them in modern English goes far to prove the justice of this demand, for we employ them continually without other nouns, simply with the verb, as when we say " I will call *in*," " she came *to*," " he goes *by*," and " it is *over*." Their importance rises in proportion as a nation begins to think more acutely and to express its thought more accurately. An uncultivated idiom can do without them, a refined idiom even can express a common truth in short axioms and direct assertions without their aid. But as soon as the maturer mind begins to connect thought and thought; as soon as it wishes to modify what is not absolute; to reason, in fine, logically, and to follow the metaphysician, these particles become not only important but indispensable. On their proper use depends the train of thought and the course of reasoning. Without them we can never obtain that perspicuity which is the first and greatest beauty of style, and without which the progress of the mind in continued discourses can never be clearly shown. Hence it is that the Attic writers all, and especially Plato, abound in conjunctions, to the distress of the unlearned and the intense delight of the thinker.

Another field in which these particles have, of late, acquired unexpected importance is that of Comparative Philology. They owe this mainly to Jamieson and to Horne Tooke, whose prodigious labor and unsurpassed ingenuity, though by no means always successful, deserve great credit. We look to these fragments now as a seldom failing proof of the living affinity between two languages, because they possess certain qualities which are not found in other parts of speech. They are generally of high antiquity, most of them, even in the ancient languages, — having taken their established form and meaning in ages prior to history. At the same time, they have been more permanent than other terms, as they are the fruit of the mode of thinking peculiar to a whole nation, determining the meaning not only of numerous compound words, but of almost every phrase. Finally, they derive no small importance from the fact that they are, of all words, least likely to be introduced into other languages, because, from the various and nice shades of signification which they assume, they are far more unintelligible to foreigners than the names of objects or actions. They, not unfrequently, more resemble arbitrary sounds, endowed with a conventional meaning, attached to them by long habit, than real words. This very peculiarity, however, has also exposed them to great corruption, as foreigners were little willing, and often as little

able, to catch the fleeting sound of apparently insignificant
words, which, moreover, did not seem to affect the meaning of the sentence very seriously. Hence they have suffered more than any other part of speech from phonetic
corruption, and it is, in most cases, extremely difficult to
trace them back to their original form and nature. It is
in this department, especially, that Horne Tooke has shown
the true merit of his prodigious labor and unsurpassed
ingenuity, though even he has by no means been always
successful.

Prepositions are like all so-called particles, not mere
fragments of other words, casually broken of and aimlessly
floating about among the mass of other well-classed words,
but they also were, once upon a time, the names of real
objects. After a while they were employed to give merely
a certain coloring, a slightly different shade of meaning, to
other terms, as we even now speak of *blood*-thirsty, *lily*-
livered, or *stone*-deaf men, without intending seriously to
refer to blood, lilies, or stones. Having been found eminently useful for the purpose, they were continually used in
the same connection and finally ceased to have an existence
of their own. They were shortened, as being the inferior
word belonging to a more important one, and finally lost
their resemblance to the parent so completely as entirely to
disguise their first origin. Very few, therefore, can now be
traced back to their original, full form.

Much has been done in this direction, especially upon
the basis of Horne Tooke's ingenious and plausible conject-
ures. The more the subject is investigated, the more
clearly it is shown that these so-called particles were once
upon a time independent words. A new proof of this has
been deduced from the fact that the majority of these
words serve for a variety of purposes.

Modern conjunctions, for instance, were in Old English
prepositions, and on that account followed by " that," as in
" *Before* that certain came from James, he did eat with

the Gentiles" (Gal. ii. 12); "*After* that I was turned, I repented" (Jer. xxxi. 19); and "*Sith* that I have told you," in Chaucer. Others have to do duty in several departments. *After* is an adjective when we speak of "the *after*-part of a ship," an adverb when we say, that "some are they who come *after*," a preposition in the words "*after* a while," and a conjunction in "I will call again *after* you return."

Whilst this confirms the opinion that all such particles were originally nouns or verbs, it must be admitted that the constant use of this class of words has so completely effaced their date and original character, that it is now extremely difficult to explain them satisfactorily. Still, something may be done, as in the case of *through*, which, with a frequent transposition of the letter *r*, was anciently written *thurh*, and is the same word as the noun *door*. Its German representative is *durch*, resembling more our expanded form *thorough*, which we continue to use by itself and in words like *thoroughfare*. In old MSS. it is simply *thurh*, as in —

"*Thurh* the means of mercie."

But already in Chaucer we find an odd lengthened form, —

"Ydlenesse is the *thoruke* of all wycked and vilaine thoughtes."

Our modern *with* is nothing but the root, or the imperative form, of the ancient verb *withan*, which meant "to join." This has given us, in like manner, the corresponding noun, so that we speak of a tough *withe*, to cut *withes*, and to fasten a boat with *withes*. Other prepositions are of such antiquity that all efforts to furnish them with a pedigree have proved useless, especially as we find them to have appeared, as much shortened forms, in the ancient languages. Thus our *in* is the Greek ἐν, we recognize ἀνά in *on*, ἀπό in *of* and its derivative *after*, *ad* in *at*, ἐπί in *by*, περί or παρά in *for*, with its second form of *fore*, and ὑπέρ in *over*.

Some of these words have become obsolete by that mysterious force operating in language, which defies all outward control and makes itself felt only in its final effects. Thus the Greek μετά, which has its genuine representative in the German *mit*, was once known to Old English also as *mid*, and used as a preposition as late as the year 1530, when it occurs in a Kentish MS. Since that time, however, it has gradually disappeared as such, and now serves only to make useful compounds, as *mid*wife, *mid*shipman, and others. A like fate seems to have befallen the old *ymb*, in German *um*, and representing the Greek ἀμφί. The early Bible version still uses it, saying, —

" Mycel menige *ymb* hime saet."—*Mark* iii. 32.

But in modern English it has been entirely superseded by *about*. The Anglo-Saxon *sithe* (in German, *seit*), has undergone a remarkable change. It was anciently used as a noun, meaning *time*, and from this an adverb was formed by the use of the genitive case, as *sithanes*. This was shortened in Old English into *sithens*, and has since suffered still further contraction into the present *since*.

Other prepositions again consist of two or more elements, which combined have a peculiar meaning of their own. Such are *up-on*, *be-fore*, *about* from on-be-out, and *above* from on-be-upon. This process of joining two together is still going on, and we use thus *out of* yet separately, though they are united in meaning. A few only are formed from nouns, either by composition, as in *despite* and *across*, or by mere juxtaposition, as *in behalf* and *by means of*. There is, lastly, a small number of foreign words even, which are thus employed. We read of the hero of a romance that he sailed " *via* the little island of St. Thomas ; " the " Spectator " says, " *in lieu* of what he had parted with ; " Byron, in his " Don Juan," VIII. 42, uses "*Malgré* all which people say of glory," and in " Love's Labor 's Lost," V. 2, we even meet with the unpardonable, "*Sans* crack or flaw ; *sans sans*, I pray you." ·

As these prepositions were words added to nouns, mostly for the purpose of expressing their more delicate relations to each other, which the mutilated substantives, for want of a declension, could no longer suggest, and which position alone might leave doubtful, so conjunctions were employed to convey the relation which sentences and parts of sentences bear to each other. The English is, on the whole, remarkably poor in this class of words; at least, much poorer than the Greek and the German, which abound in such helps to thought. Nevertheless, here also the Saxon element has held its own and admitted but very few Norman adventurers; among the intruders we have *because, except, save, concerning,* and a few others. Those which are of native growth can generally be traced back to the original word of another class from which they are derived. Thus our *and* has already been mentioned as being nothing less than the present participle of an ancient verb, *anan,* to add; though some etymologists prefer deriving it from the past participle of the same verb, *anad,* which would naturally, by constant use, contract into *and.* The now obsolete *an,* which has of late been entirely superseded by *if,* may be traced back to the same root; it conveyed the idea of giving or granting, so that "an it please you" was originally the same as "granted it please you."

Our *or* is, in like manner, a contracted form, and derived from the adjective *other,* which in ancient writers is found almost exclusively used for *or.* *Till* is a more complicated form. It is derived from the two words *to hvil,* which latter is now represented by *while,* and thus means in effect, "to the while," or, "to the time." Hence it is in modern English generally limited to expressions of time, whilst in old authors it is mixed up with the idea of space. Thus Chaucer has, —

> " Now are we driven *til* hething and *til* scorne," (4108,)

whilst Shakespeare says correctly, —

> " Never *till* to-night, never *till* now,
> Did I go thro' a tempest dropping fire."—*Julius Cæsar,* I. 3.

The ungraceful compound *until* represents "on to the time."

But is, in like manner and in spite of its simple appearance, a compound of two words, being formed, after the manner of *beyond, beneath, before,* and *behind,* of *be* and *ut,* the modern *out.* The old *be* had manifold duties to perform, but in these words, as in *between,* literally *inter binos,* it simply conveys the idea of locality, as our modern *by,* and thus *be-ut, but,* corresponds exactly to the Greek παρεκτός. That this derivation of *but* from *be-out* is not a mere fancy of etymologists appears from the fact that the word is provincially still used in its original meaning. In many localities *but o' house* means the outer part of the house, or the outer room, and *ben o' house* (by-in) is the inner or more retired part of the house. Cottagers often desire their landlords to build them a *but* and a *ben.*

It is curious to observe the varied methods by which the purpose of discriminating between several has been accomplished in different languages. The office of the English *but* is simply to state what is out, or outside, of that which has been mentioned,— a distinction which is made with more or less precision, according to circumstances. The Greek accomplished this by speaking of other things, ἀλλά ; the German *sunders* one from another, and employs *sondern,* whilst the Romance languages use the idea of preference, by means of *magis,* which gives them *mais, mas,* and *ma,* somewhat after the fashion of our English *rather.*

The short *as* conceals, also, two component parts, its Anglo-Saxon form having been *eal svá,* meaning " all so " or " quite so," which survives in our adverb *also.* In the twelfth century it had already shrunk into *als,* a form which still continues in German, and since that time it has still further lost of its substance so as to be reduced to *as.* *Lest* consists of *leas* and *the* in the meaning of " less that," but it read already in 1250 *leste* (R. A., I. 69). The latter part, *thaet,* is nothing more than the pronoun of the same

form, and was already so explained by the famous but
little appreciated " Grammaire des Messieurs de Port
Royal," who learnedly pointed out the analogy with the
Latin *quod.*

If has long since been known to be the imperative of
the Saxon verb *gifan*, " to give," and shows with perfect
certainty the gradual process of corruption it has undergone. The connection with the verb " to give " is as evident in meaning as in form. If we say, " I will come if I
can," we mean literally " Give (or given) that I can, I
will come." It was long written with the initial *g*, as in —

" My largesse
Has lotted her to be your brother's mistresse,
Gif she can be reclaimed, *gif* not, his prey."
Sad Shepherd, II. 1.

By the side of this probable imperative form the participle
is not wanting. We find in " Lodge's Illustrations " how
the Queen wrote to Sir W. Cecil in one place, —

" *Yeaven* under our signet,"

and in another, —

" *Yeven* under seale of our order,"

showing the fragile nature of the initial *g* and its natural transition from a hard to a soft sound, until it finally disappears
altogether. Chaucer writes it in a curious variety of ways,
now *gif* and now *if*, then *yeve* or *yef*, and even *yf*. The
initial held its own, however, as late as 1500, and in Lincolnshire it may be heard to this day. The Scotch are
partial to *gin*, a contracted form of *given*, just as they love
to shorten — they would call it to soften — *give* into *gie*.

The general tendency of the English to dispense with all
parts of the language that are not essential and indispensable to the conveyance of thought from man to man, however
ornamental they may be deemed by some, has led to the
neglect of a large number of conjunctions formerly in use.
This process was accelerated by the sad abuse into which the
the writers of the thirteenth century fell, and especially Man-

deville. In looking over their pages we are at once struck by the prolific family of " all be it " and " how be it," the " for as much " and the " in as much," together with what Shaftesbury, in his " Miscellanies," calls " the gouty joints . . . . of whereuntos and wherebys, thereofs, therewiths, etc., and the perpetual drawl of those huge monsters of particles, peradventure, notwithstanding, etc." How soon and how completely this fashion changed may be judged from the fact that Hume objected to Robertson's use of the word *wherewith*. " I should as soon take back," he says, " whereupon, whereunto, and wherewithal. I think the only tolerable, decent gentleman of the family is *wherein*, and I should not choose to be often seen in his company." Campbell also speaks of what he facetiously calls the " luggage of particles," but it is extremely difficult to draw the line with accuracy. Much of it, no doubt, is cumbersome, and yet we soon find that without it we cannot well do. Thus the judicious use of these conjunctions has become one of the most characteristic features of good writers in our day, while their abundance in older authors gives to their writings a quaint and old-fashioned, but by no means unattractive, flavor.

If the English is poorer in conjunctive particles than either the Greek or the German, it abounds, by way of strange compensation, in interjections, for which there is no equivalent, at least in the refined form of other languages. This is all the more surprising, as generally only southern nations, of excitable temper and vehement utterance, are considered fond of this class of words, whilst the staid, sober Englishman would not seem given to like indulgence.

. The tendency to energetic brevity, which characterizes our language, has, no doubt, led to the frequent use of not only genuine interjections, but also of numerous spurious ones, which are, in fact, abbreviated sentences, oaths and exclamations, like the Latin *eccere* (per aedem Cereris), *Mehercle* (ita me Hercules), *medius filius* (me Dius filius), and

the English *strange! hark! adieu! welcome!* They roused
Horne Tooke's indignation, and he complains that "the
brutish, inarticulate interjection, which has nothing to do
with speech, and is only the miserable refuge of the speech-
less, has been permitted, because beautiful and gaudy, (sic),
to usurp a place among words." He strengthens his case
by adding with some force, "And where will you look for
the interjection? Will you find it among laws, or in books
of civil institutions, in history, or in any treatise of useful
arts or sciences? No; you must seek for it in rhetoric and
poetry, in novels, plays, and romances!"

What would his indignation have been if he could have
foreseen the day on which men like the learned author of
" Chapters on Language," and others, would stand up for
this despised class of words, and in the face of high authorities like Max Müller, insist upon it, that they, like the imitation of natural sounds, are "a stepping-stone to true language, both by suggesting the idea of articulate speech, and
by supplying a large number, if not the entire number of
actual roots." He would have been distressed in honest
grief, to find that many look upon them as the very fountain
from which all other words have come down. Although
this view is now no longer entertained as generally, nor
with the same zeal as it was a generation ago, the argument still exists, that interjections have occasionally led to
the formation of certain classes of words, as *Ah !* which no
doubt has produced the whole series of Aryan terms: $\mathring{a}\chi o \varsigma$,
achen, ache, anguish, angustus, and the word *agony* itself.
Nor can it be denied that, as Max Müller himself admits,
interjections might, in case of necessity, suffice to form
some kind of language. This means, of course, no more
than that they would form part of the raw material, exactly
as we now trace all classes of words more or less clearly
back to some first root. As the latter is often forgotten, if
not altogether extinct, so it has frequently happened with
interjections ; they were —

22

> " the ladder
> Whereto the climber upward turns his face,
> But when he once attains the utmost round,
> He then unto the ladder turns his back,
> Looks in the clouds, scorning the base degrees
> By which he did ascend."

Even thus, forgotten and forlorn in their apparent solitude, they are useful members of language : a long speech often does not convey as much as one short interjection, and how much can be done by them, when aided by gestures and an active play of the features, was proved by the last king of Naples, who once entertained his inflammable subjects from his balcony by a speech consisting of nothing but gestures and a few interjections, and succeeded in sending them away contented. There is no doubt, that the best of his speeches would have failed in producing the same happy result. This use of interjections is, of course, possible only where nervous sympathy is still active, and nervous organization both delicate and sensitive — among children, savages, and nations that resemble them in their temperament. To such a people refer the words, " He winketh with his eyes, he speaketh with his feet, he teacheth with his fingers." (Proverbs vi. 13.)   The voices of nature are therefore many, though Dr. King maintains that —

> "Nature in many tones complains,
> Has many sounds to tell her pains,
> But for her joys has only three,
> And these but small ones: Ha! ha! he!"

Fortunately man has more, and as many of them have passed unaltered into the domain of finished language, they have there their own province, and by no means ignoble purpose. They are indispensable for the full expression of feeling and passion, and when we remember that the tender sentiments and passionate emotions of man have at least as much to do with his happiness as logic and abstract thought, we shall see at once the important part interjections play in the drama of life. Mr. Marsh mentions very happily that Whitfield's "Ah! of pity for the repentant sinner, and his Oh! of encouragement and persuasion for the almost converted listener, formed one of the great excellencies of his oratory," and we can easily recall the singular charm which some of the loftiest and loveliest passages of our poets owe to such words. We will mention only Wordsworth's touching lines, —

> " She lived unknown, and few could know
>   When Lucy ceased to be,
>   But she is in her grave, and *oh !*
>   The difference to me ! "

Some of these interjections are not even aspiring to the dignity of words, but remain what Heyse in his great work on the " Science of Language " calls happily vocal gestures, utterances which are not only apt to be connected with certain gestures, but also capable of being represented by them. Such are *st! hush! pish! pshaw! pooh!* and other expressions of contempt or aversion. It is this class, no doubt, which first suggested the term interjections, as representing a class of sounds, so to say, thrown in with the sentence and yet capable of expressing some emotion, even when no verb was added.

They must, by their very nature, necessarily be brief, else they cannot be energetic. Hence they assume, in all languages, a contracted or curtailed form. Thus in the Roman *Eccere,* for *Per aedem Cereris, Mehercle* for *Ita me Hercules juvet.* Thus in the French *Morbleu* for *Par la mort de Dieu,* and in our *Zooks* for *By God's looks.* These, however, can hardly be called genuine interjections, as they are rather abbreviated sentences, of which but one word, or at best fragments of two words, survive for practical use. Such was even the single letter O, for the Greek *οὐ* (not), with which the poet Philoxenus is said to have replied to the tyrant Dionysius, who had invited him to his court at Syracuse.

The most ancient interjection in English is probably the

Anglo-Saxon *vala*, literally, *woe-lo!*   The latter part is familiar enough; it is one of the almost instinctive ejaculations, for which no explanation is needed.   But the two together have suffered sadly in the course of their subsequent history.   Chaucer already expands the exclamation into his habitual *wella-way!*   Shakespeare employs it, no doubt, as it was used by his contemporaries, and calls it, with one of those perversions which the common people affect so much, and of which we have seen numerous illustrations in another chapter, *welladay!*   The same change took place in two other words of the same class.   One is the French *hélas*, itself but a spurious interjection, derived from the Provençal troubadours, who were fond of sighing, *Ai lasso!* literally, "Ah me weary!"   It became our English *alas!* though it is noteworthy that it is hardly ever used by the common people, to whom no doubt, there was always something foreign about the word, and hence it comes not naturally, just as they consistently substitute *fall* or *harvest* for the foreign and unintelligible *autumn*.   But even the better knowledge of those who used *alas!* did not preserve it from a speedy change into *alack!* as if the hard consonant at the end gave it both greater force and a more English air, and from this was subsequently derived the still fuller *alackaday!* which, in its turn, gave us the familiar *lackadaisical*.   The same happened to the simple exclamation *hey*, which was by force of analogy connected with the same word, and became *heyday*.   It may be added that the original *vala* still survives in the mournful complaint of the men of Ayrshire, who exclaim: *Wallywae!* whilst in Scotland we hear the well-known song, —

"O *waly waly* up the banks."

The contemptuous *fie* is a regular form of the Anglo-Saxon verb *fian*, to hate, from which we have also derived, in the form of its present participle, *fiand*, the modern *fiend*, the man who hates us.   Its meaning is now limited to the one great fiend of the human race, whilst for other purposes the

French *enemy* has taken its place. It ought not to be over-looked, however, that even aside from this very apparent and indisputable derivation, there seems to be an inherent expression in this combination of letters ; at least, the correspondence is singular between the French *fi*, the German *pfui*, the Greek φεῦ, and the Latin *phy*, as quoted in Terence. There occur occasionally, in English authors of all ages, similar interjections, like *foh* and *faugh*, which are, in all probability, but the same word in slightly altered forms. Thus Shakespeare's Othello says, —

" Foh, one may smell to such a will most rank."

A class of great importance, however objectionable on account of the want of respect and reverence which their use necessarily implies, are those interjections which contain an appeal to God or sacred personages. In almost all cases an effort has been made, for decency's sake, to disguise the original word, however transparent the veil may generally be by which it is hidden. An old author ascribed this desire to conceal to a wish that " the good God would not recognize Himself when thus disguised." The Normans were great swearers, and their most usual oath was " By God ! " so that, as in modern times, an Englishman on the Continent was often designated but too truly as a *Goddam ;* the Normans also were called by the people of England *Bygods*, and hence, in all probability, our word *bigot.* It is certain that in olden times *Norman* and *Bigot* were synonymous; the latter word, for a long time, only meant superstitious, and its present meaning is of comparatively recent date. Even the later kings were still fond of such interjections, and —

" hay, hay, the white swan
By God's soul, I am thy man ! "

was the motto of King Edward III., whilst one of Chaucer's men swears, —

" I make a vow by Goddes digne bones."

Thus it came about that the corresponding French form, *Par Dieu*, also soon became well-known all over England. It was naturalized as *Pardee*, but often sadly ill-treated, as in Spenser, —

"*Perdy*, said Britomart, thi choice is hard." — *Fairy Queen*, III. 127.

The same oath — we hope not its constant use — gave the proper names of *Pardee*, *Pardoe*, and similar ones, as *Parsall* represents the kindred *Par Ciel*.

From the abuse of the name of God, to that of his parts and qualities, there was, of course, but a step, and older writers are soon found to abound in odd combinations. The sovereigns themselves set a bad example, Queen Elizabeth having a fancy for *God's death*, and Charles for the shortened *odd's death*. This thin disguise became a great favorite with the people, and gave rise to numerous *odd's blood*, *odd's life*, *odd's heart*, and even —

" *Odslifelings* here he is!" — *Twelfth Night*, V. 1.

and the profanely vulgar *odd's bobs*, *odd's pittikins*, *odd's hounds* (probably in reality God's wounds) ; in Smollett even *odd's muggers*.

A still more violent shortening reduced the holy name to a single *s*, as in —

"'S blood, I 'll not bear my own flesh so far
Again for all the coin in thy father's exchequer."
Henry IV., Part II., II. 2.

and in the contemporaneous *'s death*, familiar to all readers. The combination already mentioned of *God's wounds*, having reference to the much revered five wounds of the Saviour, and used fully in —

"Ah, *by God's wounds*, quoth he, and swore so loud
That all amazed the priest let fall his book."
Petrucchio and Catherine.

was subsequently contracted into *zounds*, *zoons*, and *oons*, as the now poetical sound of *wounds* (like sounds), changed into the present pronunciation.

Another series of transformations is that from *God* into *Gad*, and thence into *egad, ecod, gadso, gog,* and finally *cock!* The frequent affirmation of the Bible, " May God do so and so to me," was no doubt in the mind of those who used *God-so* and then *Gad-so,* though Horne Tooke wishes to refer the expression to an Italian word, *cazzo,* which was introduced into England in the time of James I. From *cock* are again derived numerous modifications, the oldest of which probably occurs in —

" They sware all by *cokkes bone,*" — *Huntyng of the Hare,* I. 117,

and to which may be added *cockes wounds, cockes passions,* and *cockes mother,* so frequent in Chaucer's and in Shakespeare's writings. Hence, also, the almost unintelligible *By cocke and pie,* once the most solemn oath that could be taken, and considered equal in weight and awe to the formidable " By God and his holy word." *Cocke,* as has been mentioned, usurped the name of God, and *Pie* was the familiar name of the table in old Roman missals, by means of which, as by our Golden Number, the service of the day could be found. Grandison uses *od's my life,* and thereafter the word expanded still further into *Gadzooks,* used by Dickens.

Another combination again was *God's body,* which led to *God's bodikin* and *od's bodikin.* Shakespeare says, —

" *Odsbody,* the turkeys in my pannier are quite starved."
Henry IV., Part I., II. 1.

and —

" *Bodikins,* Master Page, though I now be old and of peace, if I see a swords out my finger itches to be one." — *Merry Wives of Windsor.*

In provincial dialects, finally, we meet with still other disguises, like *begor* and *begosh* which occur in Dorsetshire, and *begorra* in Ireland.

The name of *Jesus* is more rarely abused thus. We meet only among the most vulgar with its corruption, *jingo* and *jinkins* or *jinkers.* The only important form is the ancient *'s fax,* meaning originally *Christ's fax* or hair, the *per capillum Christi* of the church, an oath that was specially forbidden by a separate canon. The *fax* in it is the Anglo-Saxon word which has, among others, given us the two names of *Fairfax*, the fair-haired, and *Halifax*, the holy hair.

The Virgin *Mary* appears first as *Ay Mary*, which, like similar words, was soon shortened into *I Marry*, or *Marry!* simply. In Chaucer, men's most modest oath seems to be an undisguised *Mary*. Shakespeare has —

> " *Marry*, none so rank
> As may dishonor him."— *Hamlet*, II. 3.

and Johnson seems to speak of it as still in common use in his day. A less direct form of the same oath was the favorite *By our Lady !* often treated curtly as *Birlady !* and subsequently much used in the diminutive form as *By Leakins, Our Lakin.* Thus we find, —

> " *By'r lakin* a parlous fear."
> *Midsummer Night's Dream*, III. 1.

and —

> " *Birlady*, Sir, ye have rid hard, that ye have."
> *Beaumont and Fletcher.*

Of heathen oaths, so common in Italian, we have probably but one really naturalized in our midst ; that is the vulgar *O Jeminy !* originally *O Gemini*, an appeal to Castor and Pollux.

CHAPTER XVIII.

"Verba volant, nec non litteræ."

AMONG the apparently arbitrary changes which take place in all languages, there is none more curious, and, at the same time less carefully noted, than the fate of certain letters, which are either entirely omitted for no ostensible reason or so frequently transposed from one part of the word to another, as to make us suspect an inherent tendency in all nations to treat them as what grammarians call liquids, and let them flow to their level. As our English, also, has a few traces of this mysterious power in language, it may not be amiss to mention here one or two of the more important illustrations.

The liquid *r* is of all the letters of the alphabet the one that most frequently changes its place. Already in Greek it would thus transform κάρτος into κράτος, and καρδία into the Ionic κραδία; in Latin, the sea-monster *pristis* became *pistris*, and verbs like *cerno* made forms like *cretum*. Hence also, in French, the *r* is transferred in the change from the Latin: *vervex* becomes *brebis*, although *berger* retains the true form, and *formagium* reappears as *fromage*. It may be through such French manipulation that certain English words, derived from the Latin, present us their *r* in new places. Thus *turba*, through a secondary word, *turbular*, became the French *troubler*, and is now our *trouble*, as *thesaurus*, through the French *trésor*, is our *treasure*. Others cannot be traced beyond their French ancestor, and have changed in the transition from Normandy to England, as *grenier* into *garner, proposer* into *purpose,* and *bordel* — if that be not an Anglo-Saxon word — into *brothel.* The Italian, also, has furnished us a few such words, in which the transposition of the *r* is clearly traceable. The Greek φρενέτικος became Italian *farnetico,* and now reappears in our midst as *frantic;* a ship of the town of Ragusa, once a very important port with considerable commerce, was called an *Argosy;* the *kermes,* which already in Italian is called *chermosino* or *cremisino,* gives us the two words *crimson* and *carmine,* and the ancient Κιμμερία has become famous again as *Crimea.*

Proper names, even, had not escaped the vagaries of this strange letter. Our Anglo-Saxon fathers formed one of Eal (all) and Bright, which we have changed into *Albert,* whilst the Germans retain *Albrecht; Frobisher* is but a furbisher of arms in olden times; *Brougham,* the man from the home-burg or borough; *Winthrop* and *Crackenthrop* contain the old word *thorp,* and the town of *Dunbarton* was originally the town near the Briton's down.

Our own English words abound in examples of this transposition, and often form numerous varieties by a simple transfer of *r,* occasionally accompanied by a corresponding modification of the radical vowel. The one root *bear,* in Anglo-Saxon *beran,* thus gives us directly *bairn* or *born,* as in —

> " for man's love of heuen,
> That *bare* the blissful *barne,* that brought us on the rode,"
> *Piers Ploughman;*

and, developing still farther, *birth,* then *bier,* then *berry, barley, beer,* and even *burden.* Transposing now the *r* to join the initial, the same root produces *bred, breed, brat, brood, brother,* and *bride,* ever retaining the under-current of the meaning to *bear,* however variously modified to designate its various relations and results. A similarly fruitful root, in which *r* plays a prominent part, is our verb *to burn,* from the Anglo-Saxon *brennan.* Wickliffe has still, " The chaffis

he schal *breune* a fier unquenchable" (Luke iii. 17), and
" Forsothe it is better for to be weddid than for to be *brent* "
(Corinth. vii. 9). Even Sir Thomas More says, —

> " But would to God these hatefull workes all
> Were in fyre *brent* to powder small."

The Germans have here also retained the original form,
and use to this day *brennen*, and so we form almost all the
derivatives of the root, except *burnish*, which we get from
the French *brunir*. Thus we speak of a *brand* snatched
from the fire, and of a *brant fox*, when his hair looks burnt,
whence Longfellow sings, —

> " I have given you *brant* and beaver."

From the same word comes our *brandy*, which was at first
brand-wine, distilled by fire, as the Germans still call it
Branntwein ; bran, also, retains the meaning, suggesting the
brown, husky part of ground wheat, and that which is *bran
new, i. e.*, newly come out of the fire, and still shining.
Brown is the burnt color, as *bronze* is designated in the
same way.

Board and *broad* are thus one and the same word, both at
first written alike, *brede*, and hence the Old-English Bible
version speaks of —

> " Nayled on a *brede* of tre,"

whilst the Germans retain even now the *r* in the first place
in both words, *Brett* and *breit*, and we return to the older
form in *breadth*, instead of saying *broadth*. The *boar* makes
an adjective, anciently *boaren*, but now *brawn*. A *cart* and
a *crate* are again the same word, and so are *gross* and *coarse*.
Our *cress* (nastúrtium) was, in its Anglo-Saxon form, *cerse*
or *caerse*, and hence, at a very early period, the absurd mistake in the popular phrase, " I do not care a *curse*," which
was meant at first to express, " I do not care a (water)
cress." Even Chaucer says, —

> " Of paramours ne raught he not a *kers*." — *Miller's Tale*,

a form from which the transition to *curse* appears very short and natural. Very much the same process has gone on in *grass*, which was originally *gars*, from which our *gorse*, and, perhaps, also, our *grouse*. Douglas has, —

"The greene *gers* bedewit was and wet," — V. 138,

and the people of Yorkshire say to this day *gerse* for *grass*.

It has already been mentioned that the so-called vulgarism *afeard*, is so only as far as fashion is allowed to control a language, for the word is correctly formed from the verb *to fear*, and it is only this tendency to transpose the *r*, which has produced words like *afraid* and *fright*.

It need hardly be stated that there is no difference between *firth* and *frith*, nor between *frame* and *form*. The modern word *horse* is an example of violent change; it was anciently *hros*, remains so in German as *Ross*, and survives, even in English, in the *walrus*, the *whale-horse* or *sea-horse* of our ancestors. The Anglo-Saxon verb *scearan* has retained its *r* in its first place in most derivatives — in *share* and *shears*, and *sheers*, in *shire*, *shore*, *shorn* and *short*, in *shirt* and *skirt*, in *sheer* and *sharp*, but not in *shred*, which exists by the side of *pot-sherd*, the contracted form of *sheared*. It has been shown already how *thur*, the German *Thür*, and our *thorough*, is the same with *door*. *Thrill* is derived from the Anglo-Saxon *thyrlian*, probably connected with *thur* and *thyr*, of which it looks like a diminutive form, and hence "The prayer of hym that loveth hym in his prayer *thyrleth* the clowdes," and more curiously our modern word *nostril*, as we learn from Spenser, —

"Flames of fyre he threw forth from his large *nosethrills*."
Fairy Queen, I. 11, 22.

Work has transposed the *r* in *wright* and *wrought*, but retained it in its place in *irksome*, anciently *wyrksome*.

Occasionally this same letter *r* is capriciously inserted where it is not due, or left out where it ought to make its appearance. Thus the Anglo-Saxon word *guma*, a man, has, for some now unknown reason, been endowed with an *r*, and for the correct form *bride-guma*, the man of the bride, we now say *bridegroom*, and speak even of a *groom* without such support. The French *piquer* has become with us *to prick;* and the Tatars of Asia, with a faint disposition perhaps to trace them back to Tartarus, from whence their wild hordes invading Europe in the fourteenth century were said to come, have been changed into *Tartars,* so that Spenser already uses *Tartary* for hell.

The Anglo-Saxon *sprecan,* on the contrary, has lost its *r,* and become to *speak,* although the Germans still say *sprechen;* *preon* is now simply *pin,* and *spreckle,* which is not unfrequently heard in Scotland, plain *speckle.* The Latin *fringilla,* is our *finch,* and *temperare,* in French *tremper,* our *temper.*

The word *ort,* which in Anglo-Saxon stood for the later *wort* (German *Wurzel*), has lost its *r* in *ort-yard,* our *orchard,* and transferred it to the beginning of the word in its modern form *root.* *Lychwort,* the herb pellitory, as Halliwell calls it, presents us the old form fully, whilst we see it most successfully disguised in the expression, " Odds and ends," which comes from the once usual " *ords* and *ends.*"

Other letters are not so regularly, but still occasionally liable to be transferred from one place to another. Thus there is good reason to believe that *flock* and *folk* are originally one and the same word. The French *ingot,* with the article *an* before it, soon became *niggot,* as it is spelt in North's " Plutarch ; " and in our day it has unexpectedly reappeared as *nugget.* *S* and *k* interchange not unfrequently, and the much blamed vulgarism of substituting to *axe* for to *ask,* finds more than one justification in older authors. The fact is, the verb was originally *acsian,* and hence Wickliffe is not so far wrong when he says, "*Axe* ye and yhe schulen take ; " nor Chaucer in his constant use of " *to axe* " and " an *axing.*" Hence, also, the close connection between a *tax* and a *task,* so that Hotspur can say " has *tasked* the whole state," when he means *taxed.*

ETYMOLOGY.